"**Y**ou're a tough one, Daniela Chiaramonte. God knows you'll make one hell of a queen."

"What are you talking about?" she rasped, her face searing red.

"Did I forget to mention? You are going to marry me. That is your sentence. . . ."

"Are you out of your mind?" she nearly shouted.

He smiled—charmingly.

"I will not marry you! No! *No!*" she said again.

"Of course you will, my dear. Come, Daniela—here I am, down on bended knee for you. I lay my kingdom at your feet." His tone was jaunty, his eyes twinkling.

"Don't you dare try to charm me, Rafael di Fiore!" Wretched with nausea and fury and disbelief, she glared at him, her hair hanging lankly in her face. She could not believe a woman could look such a wreck and receive a marriage proposal from the catch of the century. "First you shoot me! Then you have me dragged to you so you can seduce me! What kind of perverse game are you playing with me now?"

By Gaelen Foley
Published by The Ballantine Publishing Group:

THE PIRATE PRINCE
PRINCESS
PRINCE CHARMING

PRINCE CHARMING

Gaelen Foley

IVY BOOKS • NEW YORK

An Ivy Book
Published by The Ballantine Publishing Group
Copyright © 2000 by Gaelen Foley

Ivy Book and colophon are a trademark of Random House, Inc.

www.randomhouse.com/BB/

Library of Congress Catalog Card Number: 99-91741

ISBN 0-449-00635-2

Manufactured in the United States of America

First Edition: February 2000

10 9 8 7 6 5 4 3 2 1

For Eero—

With a huge hug across the miles.

My crown is in my heart, not on my head.

—SHAKESPEARE

❧ CHAPTER ❧
ONE

Ascencion, 1816

The greatest lover of all time was at it again, smoothly seducing the artless country girl Zerlina, as Mozart's famed duet *"La ci darem la mano"* filled the sumptuous theater with a graceful spire of twining voices, tenor and soprano making love to each other in exquisite song.

No one was paying attention. The wink of opera glasses and the rustling whispers betrayed that the glittering audience's fascination was fixed, not on the stage, but on the first and finest theater box on the mezzanine, stage right, perched over the orchestra. Cloyingly sculpted with cupids and urns and draped plasterwork ribbons, the box was permanently reserved for royalty.

He sat at the carved marble rail, half in shadow, unmoving, his suntanned face expressionless. Light from the stage gleamed on the signet ring on his finger, played over the patrician angles of his face, and gilded his long dark-gold hair, which was swept back in a queue.

The audience watched with bated breath as he moved for the first time since the performance had begun. Slowly he reached into the pocket of his extravagant waistcoat, took a peppermint from a flat metal tin, and placed it in his mouth.

1

Ladies watched him suck the candy and blushed, fluttering their fans.

I am so bored, he thought, his eyes glazing over. *So, so very bored.*

The favored members of his entourage sat around him in the theater box, sullen, gilded young lords, gorgeously dressed. Behind their air of studied idleness, they had hard, hooded eyes, weapons concealed beneath their coats. With a few, the scent of opium smoke clung to their rich clothes. Some in his little flock went further than others, but everything was allowed.

"Your Highness?" came a whisper from his right.

Never taking his dull, heavy gaze off his beautiful mistress on the stage, Crown Prince Raffaele Giancarlo Ettore di Fiore flicked one jeweled hand, brushing off the proffered flask. He was in no humor for liquor, brooding in a cynical mood that Dante had had it all wrong.

The Inferno, with all its fire and brimstone, could not be worse than this echoless realm of Limbo where he was suspended in eternal waiting.

Being born the son of a great man was a hard thing; yet somehow Rafe had managed to get himself sired by one who was not only great but also evidently immortal. He did not by any means wish his father's demise, but in light of the fact that he would turn thirty tomorrow, he was besieged by a general sense of doom.

Time was flying past and he was getting nowhere. Had any aspect of his life changed significantly since he was, oh, eighteen? he wondered as the robust song from *Don Giovanni* faded into the background of his awareness. He still had the same friends, played the same games, still languished in pointless luxury, a prisoner of his rank.

Unable to make a move in control of his own destiny, he was merely his father's puppet, nothing more. Every matter of consequence concerning his existence must first be debated over, voted on, and approved by the court, the newspapers, and the whole damned senate, and Lord, he was tired of it. He felt more like a prisoner than a prince, not a man but an overgrown adolescent.

He had given up arguing with Father to assign him some meaningful task worthy of his ability and education. It was futile. The old tyrant refused to part with an ounce of his power.

Ah, what was the point of caring? He fancied he might as well sleep the years away in a glass coffin behind some enchanted wall of thorns. They could wake him when it was time for his life to begin.

After an eternity or so, Don Giovanni was dragged off to Hell and the opera was finally done. He and his followers left the theater box while the audience was still applauding.

He stared straight ahead as they strode in a pack down the marbled hall, pretending that he did not see the people lined up, beaming eager smiles at him, all the nice people who wanted a bite of him, like the stout, vaguely familiar matron who attempted to stop him presently.

"Your Highness," she gushed, curtsying with her nose almost to the floor, "how marvelous to see you this evening! My dear husband and myself and our three lovely girls would be so honored if you would come to our soiree—"

"My regrets, madam, thank you and goodnight," he muttered harshly as he kept walking. *God, save me from hopeful mothers-in-law.*

One of the dread journalists pushed his way to the fore. "Your Highness, did you really win fifty thousand lire in a wager last week and did your phaeton really break an axle in the race?"

"Get him out of here," he muttered to his boyhood friend Adriano di Tadzio.

Then Lord Someone-or-other stepped partly into his path with a dignified bow. "Your Highness, what a smashing performance by Miss Sinclair! Beg pardon, I have some people here who would love to meet you—"

He growled and moved past the bald man, then he and his entourage did not stop until they reached the backstage regions of the large, elegant theater.

With a slow swagger, chin high, Rafe stepped inside the actresses' dressing room and instantly began to feel better, the tension easing marginally from him. There were scantily clad women everywhere and that was a sight to lift any man's spirits, however jaded. *Women.* The warm, sweet smell of their flesh made him breathe easier. With a rather cool half-smile he glanced around slowly, surveying the selection.

"Look! He's here!"

A shrill chorus of feminine screams of delight filled the drafty, candlelit dressing room. They raced at him from every quarter.

"Raaaaafe!"

A pack of screaming, squealing girls swamped him. All talking at once, they pulled him down into a chair, three of the actresses sitting on his lap, giggling and stroking his chest, and two draped around his neck, covering his face in kisses.

"Ah," he sighed, smiling slightly for the first time that night as he leaned back lazily in the chair, closing his eyes and drowning pleasantly under the soft, scented, writhing mass of lovely limbs and unbound breasts and lace flounces and careful curls. "I love the theater."

He heard them giggling, felt them rummaging in his coat and waistcoat like pickpocket children searching for treats. Ah, well. He supposed he had spoiled them, rolling them a handful of jewels last time he'd been here, foxed as Pharaoh.

Soft lips alighted on his mouth, caressing lightly. After a judicious moment, he began kissing back, willing ennui away. Touching wherever he pleased, he sampled their kisses one by one, but the fun ended when Chloe arrived.

Rafe watched the English diva strutting toward him in her clinging silvery gown.

She had a perfect body and a gleaming smile, his latest toy. They had been lovers for four months now, a record for Rafe. He did not quite know how to tell her that he had begun losing interest. He was rather hoping she would figure it out for herself.

Chloe huffed to see her sister thespians all over her royal protector. She slid her feather boa off her creamy shoulders and pushed her way into their midst, catching Rafe around the neck with it. He glanced up with an unrepentant half-smile. Chloe gave him a disapproving look, but didn't dare reproach him.

Instead, she fluffed the feather boa on him. "Darling, how avant-garde."

"Ooo, it looks so pretty on him!" one of the girls exclaimed, fixing the pink feather boa over his shoulder like a scarf.

"Everything does," another sighed.

He stared dully at the chit, wondering if he had ever been that young and easily impressed.

"Look at this, Prince Rafie!" a buxom brunette said eagerly, climbing off his lap. Daringly, she lifted the hem of her chemise and bared the left cheek of her pretty, rounded bottom for him.

He lifted his eyebrows, admiring the *R* tattooed there. He traced the monogrammed letter with his fingertip lightly over the curve of tender flesh. "How sweet of you, my pet. What was your name again?"

"Begone, you little tramps, or I'll speak to the house

manager and you'll all be out of a job!" Chloe snapped, shooing them off.

Rafe chuckled at his mistress's pique, saying nothing as the girls sadly drifted away, curls drooping. He smiled to himself, watching his friends intercept them, flirting, billfolds at the ready.

"Lovely, lovely little tarts." He glanced up at the haughty blond with a wicked gleam in his eyes. "And then there's you, madam witch."

She leaned over him, grasped both ends of the feather boa, and tugged. "That's right," she whispered, holding him in a sultry stare, "and you, my devil, are coming with me. I must punish you for sleeping through my aria. Don't think I didn't see you."

"I was awake . . . but you can punish me as you see fit," he murmured softly as he stood, towering over her. As she laughed and led him by the gaudy feather boa, Chloe's hungry gaze teased him with pleasures yet to come. He pretended not to notice the sheer worship in her eyes, looking away to nod at his companions. "See you around two at the club," he said, holding the door for Chloe, who slid the feather boa off his shoulders.

"Ciao," said Adriano with a toss of his black forelock.

"Enjoy," Niccolo drawled with a smirk.

Just then, Rafe heard someone calling him.

"Your Highness! Your Highness! Sir!"

Halfway out the door, he turned around and saw a courier in royal livery bustling through the dressing room. Instantly every muscle in his body tensed with checked hostility.

A message from the king.

As the courier hurried toward him, Rafe drew a deep breath and let it out slowly, for he was not a man who lost his temper. His father was the blustery hothead in the family; he prided himself on remaining coolly graceful at all times. He lifted both brows expectantly as the courier bowed.

"How *does* my good father this night?" he asked, his tone soft but edged with the barest hint of irony.

The courier bowed apologetically. "His Majesty summons you, Your Highness."

Rafe stared at him for a long moment, his slight, urbane smile pasted in place, his marble-green eyes snapping with anger. "Tell him I will call on him tomorrow around noon. After I have had my breakfast."

"Pardon, Your Highness," the man said with a gulp, bowing again, "the king insists you come anon."

"Is it an emergency?"

"I know not, sir," the man stammered. "His Majesty sent the carriage—"

"I have my own carriage," Rafe said pleasantly through gritted teeth, realizing that Father must have sent the gaudy state coach because, hang it all, he had probably heard about his drunken race, roaring across the countryside in the dead of night last Wednesday.

No doubt the reason for the summons was that his father wished to scald his ears again as usual with another recounting of his many failings as a future king, how the responsibility was going to crush him because he was just a dreamer, and how the courtiers were going to eat him alive, et cetera, et cetera.

He was really in no mood to hear it.

Meanwhile, his friends, his mistress, and his charming young devotees were all watching the exchange with worried looks, as though they expected him to explode any day now, any moment.

He saw he had a choice—the same choice as always. Either he could make a scene like a churl and stand on his pride, or, as usual, swallow the humiliation of having to jump whenever his father snapped his fingers and exit like the prince he was down to his fingertips.

His voice was velvet, his slight, cold smile angelic. "I will be pleased to attend His Majesty at once, but rest assured, I will take my own carriage."

The courier bobbed as though he might collapse with relief. "As Your Highness wishes." He backed away from Rafe, still bowing.

Rafe turned to his mistress, lifted her hand and kissed it in taut gallantry, his angry thoughts a million miles away. "Apologies, my sugar-sweet."

"It's all right, darling," she soothed, caressing his arm, then looked meaningfully into his eyes. "As long as I can still give you your birthday present tomorrow."

"I cannot wait to see what it is," he murmured with a knowing half-smile.

Then he walked out alone, still shaking his head to himself at the thought of his father's high handedness, though the same routine ought to come as no surprise by now.

Outside, the ornate gilded state coach which the king had insultingly sent to collect him was just pulling away. Waiting for him in front of the theater crouched the smart, new, exceedingly expensive landau with mahogany panels and elliptical springs that had been lent to him, gratis, by the city's finest carriage-maker, who was fixing his phaeton's broken axle.

The generous gesture had been a prudent move on the wheelwright's part, Rafe thought cynically, for now that model of equipage was selling like mad. Strange how the world at large disparaged him for his wild ways, yet their slavish mimicry of his every passing whim had made him the kingdom's arbiter of fashion. He could not boast of a stainless conscience, but at least he had excellent taste.

The street was crowded in front of the lavish theater, people still thronging the area since the opera had just let out. Vendors were selling them flavored ices. Since the grand opera hall in Belfort was being renovated, the ton had flocked to this smaller theater in the quaint coastal town a few miles down the hill. The cafés along the beach had become all the rage.

Walking out to his waiting coach, Rafe breathed the flowery, salt-laden air of his homeland and paused to stare up the hill at the great crooked bulk of the Italian island where his family had ruled for seven hundred years.

Under the moon, the port town before him was narrow and long, hugging the steep terraced hillside. The lampposts, frugally spaced along the quay to his right, cast a dim glow upon stout palm trees blowing in the night wind. He turned, the breeze caressing his clean-shaved cheeks as he stared at the lush purple mounds of oleander waving amid the dark boulders that abutted the beach.

He looked at the row of narrow shops with painted hanging signs. On the upper stories, small wrought-iron balconies overlooked the harbor and the rocky strand. Every doorway slumbered under thick cascades of white jasmine, whose sweet perfume softened the stink from the fish markets farther down the docks.

Ascencion, he whispered in his mind, as if savoring a lover's name. Fairer even than the isle of Capri, *she* was his sacred heritage. For Ascencion, he would endure his cage and take whatever humiliations his father dealt him. Somehow, he would hold on, though he knew he was dying on the vine. The one thing that kept despair at bay was the promise that one day he would truly rule this peerless gem of the Mediterranean. The one desire he had not yet fulfilled was his longing to be a good king.

Everyone thought he would be a disaster, he knew. He would show them. One day.

Sighing, he stepped up into the coach. A groom briskly

shut the door. He rapped boredly on the inside and his unmarked vehicle slid into motion, passing quickly through
the little port town to turn onto the King's Road, which
wound up the hillside to the great capital, Belfort.

He suddenly remembered he'd forgotten to let the royal
bodyguards know he was leaving. *Ah well, they'll figure it
out and catch up soon enough.* He didn't need them anyway.
Being trailed constantly by six hulking thugs in uniform
was just one more reminder that until he came to power,
he was naught but a coddled, glorified prisoner.

In the dark cab of the coach, he rested his elbow on the
edge of the window and leaned his cheek on his hand. He
stared out pensively at the landscape. Silver and indigo in
the moonlight, his kingdom rolled out along the road, like
his life passing him by.

Devil take birthdays, he thought. When he was king, he
would outlaw them.

The King's Road was a blue ribbon in the moonlight.
They watched in tense silence from the woods, wondering
if their night's vigil was done. A short while ago, they had
watched the gilded royal state coach pass. Now a sleek vehicle of gleaming black and mahogany was barreling up
the road, pulled by a team of four galloping matched bays.

"Looks promising," Mateo whispered, even as his
youngest brother signaled the owl's hoot from the distance, calling them to alert.

The Masked Rider nodded and gestured the others into
position.

Stealthily, they maneuvered their horses among the
trees, assuming their posts on the high embankments over
the road. They waited. . . .

The coach hit a rut in the road and bounced violently on
its newfangled springs. Rafe winced in annoyance and

drew breath to shout an imperious rebuke at the driver to have a care—he didn't want to have to buy the damned thing—when suddenly he heard shouts outside.

A horse whinnied frantically and the coach began to slow. A gunshot ripped through the night.

His eyes narrowed in the gloom. Instantly alert, he crept forward and stole a glance from behind the window's shade and stared, feeling a rush in his thrill-seeker's soul.

Well, I'll be damned. The Masked Rider. His expression broke into an extremely devilish grin. *At last we meet.*

He saw he was considerably outnumbered, but according to the reports, none of the famed highwayman's robberies had been accompanied by bloodshed, so he was more intrigued than alarmed. Nevertheless, his own safety was a national priority. Leaning down, he opened the compartment beneath the opposite seat, reached into the little storage space, and smoothly took out the pair of pistols that he kept there, ready and loaded. Tucking one into his waistcoat, he cocked the other and thought with a narrow smile, *Impudent little bastard, you're in for a surprise.*

He had been following the bold lad's career with some interest, as tales of the so-called Masked Rider appeared side by side in the same gazettes that recounted his own wicked deeds. He had laughed every time the young highwayman robbed yet another of his friends—though they hadn't found it amusing.

Not even his father's authorities could catch the Masked Rider and his gang. The common folk of Ascencion adored the young highwayman, whose identity remained a mystery, and who, it seemed, truly robbed from the rich and gave to the poor.

Rafe rather thought the kid had style. Still, it would not do to have this mysterious Robin Hood out there somewhere bragging about robbing *him,* making a mock of his name. He had problems enough with the public's disapproval of his occasional, admittedly wild excesses. His people merely didn't know that a bit of hell-raising was merely his one solution to avoid going mad.

Well aware that his half-dozen Royal Guardsmen would not be far behind, a narrow, crafty smile curved his lips. He raised his gun and laid hold of the door latch, gathering himself for his counterattack.

Meanwhile, out on the road, the Masked Rider was shouting at the coachman, "Halt! Halt!"

Astride a leggy gelding whose true color was obscured by the cinders rubbed into its coat, the Masked Rider urged the horse alongside the galloping team and reached out a black-gauntleted hand for the leader's traces. The coachman was waving a pistol, but the Masked Rider ignored him—such men never used their weapons. The thought was barely finished when the moving coach's door swung open and a large male figure leaned out from the inside, firing a pistol into the air.

"Stand down!" a commanding voice bellowed.

The Masked Rider ignored the warning shot, riding low over the horse's neck, trying again unsteadily to grab the leather strap—

A thunderous crack rent the air with a flash of orange.

The Masked Rider gasped out a cry and was jolted forward over the horse's neck.

"Dan!" Mateo shouted, aghast.

The gelding veered away from the coach's team with a scream, rearing at the smell of the blood spattered on his sooty coat.

"Turn back! Turn back!" Alvi shouted at the others.

"Don't you dare turn back! Never mind me! Get the loot!" the Masked Rider roared back at him in boyish tones, fighting the horse.

Then the gelding bolted.

"Stop, whoa! You miserable nag!" A stream of oaths she had never learned in convent school followed from Lady Daniela Chiaramonte's lips as her horse careened through the brake.

All the while her shoulder and arm burned as though they were on fire. *He shot me!* she thought, her astonishment equal to her pain. She couldn't believe it. Certainly in all her adventures she had never been shot before.

She felt hot blood streaming down her right arm as her panicked horse crashed up over the wooded embankment. Heart pounding, she brought the animal under control, reeling him around in small circles.

When at last the horse stood heaving for breath, she suppressed the angry urge to punch the animal for his skittishness, and peered down anxiously at her wounded right arm. It was bleeding and it hurt like hell. She felt lightheaded at the horrid sight of her own torn flesh, but when she carefully probed her bleeding arm with her fingers, she concluded in relief that it was only a flesh wound.

"That blackguard shot me," she panted in lingering amazement. Then her gaze zipped back to the road, and she saw that the Gabbiano brothers—her men, such as they were—had brought the coach to a standstill and extinguished the carriage lantern, working by moonlight.

The driver was sprawled on his arse on the ground, Alvi holding him at sword point. She scowled indignantly at the coachman's pitiful display, babbling for mercy. Did the man think them common cutthroats? Everyone knew the Masked Rider and company never killed anybody. Occasionally they left some popinjay in an embarrassing predicament, naked and tied to a tree, perhaps, but they never drew blood.

Better get down there before we have a change of policy, she thought as she saw Mateo and Rocco, still astride their mounts, holding the big lean passenger at bay with their swords before the open coach door. Even from a distance, their prisoner looked more than able to fend for himself.

Fortunately, her men had disarmed him, she saw. His hands were up and his two pistols lay in the dusty road. Her gang would not attack an unarmed man; still, Mateo was a hothead likely to start a brawl at any insult, while the giant Rocco didn't know his own strength. Both were as protective of her as if she were their own sister. She didn't want anyone getting hurt.

Dani passed her forearm over her brow, then adjusted the hoodlike black mask over her face and hair to make sure her identity was still neatly concealed after her horse's mad dash. Satisfied, she urged her horse aboutface and back down onto the road, highly curious to see which of the idle citified peacocks she had snared this time and what it would profit her.

Hopefully enough to pay the crippling new taxes on her estate and to feed her people in spite of the drought.

She drew her light, quick rapier as she guided her horse toward the tense trio of men. Mateo and Rocco parted to admit her between them.

"You all right?" Mateo, her oldest childhood friend, muttered to her.

She shook off her momentary awe at the sight of her tall, powerfully built captive and seized upon her bravado, forcing herself forward in a show of fearlessness, though her heart beat rapidly. "I'm just . . . dandy," she drawled, urging her horse closer. She stopped when the tip of her rapier floated gracefully under her captive's square jaw, which was clenched. "Well, what have we here?" she mused aloud, using the tip of her sword to force him to lift his chin.

It was too dark to see much, but the silvery moonlight picked out gilded threads in his hair, which appeared to be of a tawny gold shade, quite long, but pulled back in a queue off his broad, straight forehead. He had an imperious nose and a hard, angry mouth. Head high, his narrowed eyes glittered, fixed on her. It was too dark to make out their color.

"You shot me," she said in reproach, leaning toward him from the saddle. She knew she mustn't let him see her fear. "Lucky for you, you merely grazed my arm."

"If I had wanted you dead, then dead you would be," he said in a soft, murderous purr that fell like silk on her skin.

"Ha! Some excuse! You are a poor marksman," she taunted him. "It doesn't even hurt."

"And you, boy, are a poor liar."

Dani sat up straight again in the saddle, considering him. A worthy opponent, she had to admit. As her gaze traveled over the length of his warriorlike physique, her simple feminine admiration mingled with a growing sense of inner warning. Her captive was over six feet tall and appeared to be built of pure muscle, so why wasn't he putting up more of a fight? True, his weapons lay beyond his reach, but there was a gleam of treachery in his eyes that made her wonder what he had up his sleeve.

She wondered which one he was, exactly, of the useless Prince Rafe the Rake's self-indulgent flunkies. She certainly would have remembered seeing him before. Her better sense whispered to clear out immediately, but she needed the money and was frankly too intrigued to abort the robbery, which was moving along efficiently.

Mateo had relieved his brother at the task of holding the coachman at sword point. The prisoner's gaze, hard and brilliant as a diamond, followed Alvi as the wiry youth hopped into the coach with an empty sack. While her prisoner watched Alvi pass, Dani eyed him in mingled attraction and scorn.

Oh, she despised his type, haughty and carelessly

elegant in his formal evening wear, down to his creamy white breeches and shiny black shoes. His smartly cut, dark green tailcoat alone probably cost as much as her past six months' taxes. She glanced at his no doubt excellently manicured hands, which he lowered slowly to his sides, as though he had decided she was not much of a threat.

"Your ring," she ordered. "Hand it over."

His large and capable fist clenched beside his hip. "No," he growled.

"Why not? Is it your wedding ring?" she asked sarcastically.

The way his eyes narrowed on her in the dark, she thought he would have happily torn her beating heart out of her body if he got the chance.

"You will regret your audacity, boy," he said, his voice soft and deep and dangerous. It rang with an air of command. "You have no idea with whom you are dealing."

Oh, he was not taking his humbling well. Smiling at his ire behind her mask, Dani laid her rapier gently on his cheek. "Shut up, peacock."

"Your youth will not save you from the hangman."

"They'll have to catch me first."

"Fine boasts. Your father ought to thrash your hide."

"My father is dead."

"Then I will thrash you for him one day. That's a promise."

In reply, she traced her rapier ever-so-tenderly under his chin, forcing him to tilt his proud head higher or feel the prick of her sword point. His lordship clenched his handsome jaw. "You don't seem to understand your position," she said sweetly.

Holding her gaze, he smiled chillingly. "I will have you drawn and quartered," he answered in a pleasant tone.

Under her mask, Dani blanched in spite of herself. He

was trying to shake her up! "I want your shiny ring, milord. Hand it over!"

"You will have to kill me for it, boy," the prisoner said with the white, defiant gleam of a smile.

Was he mad? Standing there in blue moonlight and black shadow, he was huge, powerful, and not lifting a finger to stop them. Maybe he didn't know how to fight, she suggested anxiously to herself. These rich fellows never dirtied their hands. But one summary glance over the lean, classically proportioned length of him made her scoff at her own suggestion.

Something was definitely wrong.

"Not losing your courage, are you, boy?" he taunted softly.

"Be quiet!" she ordered, faltering and feeling herself inexplicably losing control of the situation somehow to her vexing prisoner. Absurd! Posturing males would never intimidate her.

Rocco, her tame giant, looked over at her in worry.

"Get the ponies loaded," she ordered him in a suddenly testy mood, scowling under her mask. Obviously, her prisoner had somehow called her bluff and sensed she wasn't going to kill him, though God knew he vastly deserved it. Her arm hurt like the blazes. She ducked her head to peer into the coach, wishing Alvi would hurry up. "How's it going in there?"

"He's rich!" Alvi hollered, tossing out one full sack. "Filthy rich! Give me another sack!"

As Mateo hurried to fetch another sack from his horse's saddlebag, Dani saw the prisoner cast an almost imperceptible glance down the road.

"Expecting someone?" she demanded.

Slowly, he shook his head, and she found herself gazing at his enticing mouth, where a half-smile of pure deviltry tugged.

Suddenly a high-pitched voice pealed through the night from some distance down the road. *"Run!"* The littlest of the Gabbiano brothers, Gianni, age ten, was running toward them, arms churning. "Soldiers! They're coming! Run!"

With a gasp, Dani stared at her prisoner. He smirked coolly at her, pleased with himself.

"You bastard," she hissed. "You were stalling us here!"

"Move out, move out!" Mateo was yelling at the others.

Gianni kept shouting. "Go! They'll be here any second!"

Dani's gaze snapped down the road again. She knew her horse was the fastest. Every womanly instinct in her blood screamed for her to go scoop the little boy up into the saddle with her before the soldiers were upon them. The child had no place here—it was her fault. A dozen times they had forbidden Gianni from following them, but he never listened, until finally she had given in and assigned him the relatively safe job of signaler.

"The hell with you, peacock," she muttered, abandoning her prisoner. She tugged on her gelding's reins, reeling the horse away, while Rocco lumbered up onto his slow draft horse. Alvi and Mateo each took one of the coin-laden bags and swung up onto their ponies' backs.

The little boy was running desperately toward them. But as she turned, out of the corner of her eye she saw the big man dive for his second pistol in the dust and roll on his shoulder, taking aim at Mateo.

"Mateo!" She reeled her horse around, lurching him straight at the prisoner. The gun went off, shooting skyward.

The prisoner leaped up onto his feet with astonishing agility for a man his size. Then he seized her, trying to pull her bodily off her horse. She punched and kicked at him. Mateo drove his pony toward them to help her.

She shot him a fiery glare. "I can take care of myself! Get your brother!"

Mateo hesitated.

The thunder of the soldiers' approach was growing louder.

"Go!" she roared as she kicked the prisoner in his broad chest. The big man fell back a step, holding his ribs protectively with a curse.

Seeing this, Mateo whirled his pony to go fetch the little boy.

His lordship charged her again the moment Mateo galloped away.

As she and the prisoner grappled in the road, her horse reared with a frightened whinny. She clung to the reins, fighting to keep her balance, but she felt herself being slowly overpowered by the man's sheer physical strength.

Suddenly he pulled her down out of the saddle. Freed of its rider, her thankless gelding bolted at once.

She let out a wordless cry of fury and found herself standing in the road, clutched in her erstwhile prisoner's grasp. He towered over her. His eyes were like lanterns and he was grasping her hard by her arms, and he was ever so much taller now than when she'd been on horseback. Strands of his hair had fallen free from the queue; he looked ferocious and huge, barbaric in his elegant clothes.

"You little shit," he snarled in her face.

"Let me go!" She fought him. He gripped her harder, and she shouted in pain when he jerked her hurt arm. "Ow! Damn it!"

He gave her a shake. "You're caught! You understand?"

She hauled back and punched him across the face with all her strength, tore out of his arms, and fled up the embankment. He was but two steps behind her.

Her heart beating wildly, she scrambled up through the dust and slippery dried leaves. With a frantic glance down the road, she saw Mateo lift Gianni into the saddle with him and crest the far embankment, riding hard toward home.

Her relief was short-lived, however, for then the prisoner tackled her at the top of the embankment, hooking rock-hard arms around her hips.

He smashed her under him as they fell to the ground, snaking his forearm around her throat.

I hate men, she thought, closing her eyes in distress.

"Hold still," he growled, panting hard, his body like heated iron around her.

Dani rested for half a second, then did the opposite, kicking and squirming, thrashing and punching and scrabbling with her leather-gauntleted fingers in the dust.

"Let me go!"

"Stop squirming! You're caught, damn it! Give in!"

Dodging the boy's blows, Rafe held the slim body pinned beneath his own, glad that wrestling was one of the chief sports at which he had excelled as a youth. He never would have thought it would come in handy. The boy bucked and thrashed, fighting him furiously.

"Yield," he ordered through gritted teeth,

"Go to hell!" The pitch of the young voice climbed higher, shrill with fright.

Panting with exertion, he drove his full muscular weight more firmly down to still the little hellion's writhing. "Hold still!" He jerked a look over his shoulder toward the road and his approaching men. "Over here!"

At his movement, the bloodthirsty little bandit somehow flopped over onto his back, still trapped by Rafe's arms.

"I told you you would hang," he growled.

"No, you said I would be drawn and quartered—"

Rafe caught a flying fist in his hand. "Be still, for God's sake!"

Suddenly the boy froze and drew in his breath, staring at his signet ring.

"You . . . !" the boy croaked in a hoarse gasp.

Scowling toward his men, Rafe glanced down and narrowed his eyes in satisfaction. "Aha, brat. Finally catching on, are you?"

The light-colored eyes behind the mask never blinked, staring at him, looking horror-stricken.

Rafe's laugh was throaty and smug, then he stopped abruptly. *What the devil?* He furrowed his brow as he caught a whiff of a scent his instincts knew, but recognition danced just beyond his mind's reach.

"What is your name, you miserable urchin?" he demanded in regal hauteur, laying hold of the boy's black, hoodlike mask.

Suddenly the little bandit moved like a flash of lightning. Rafe supposed he should have seen it coming. The dusty, bleeding little hellion kneed him hard in the groin, a direct hit to the royal jewels. He gasped for breath in a momentary state of pure helplessness. The boy pushed against his shoulder, rolling him off onto his side, then scrambled clear of his feebly grasping hand.

Through blinding agony, Rafe summoned the full, furious power of a kingly roar: *"After them!"* he bellowed, as the boy tore off into the woods.

⚜ CHAPTER ⚜
TWO

Dani didn't stop running even when she heard his deep roar echo through the woods behind her. She ran for her life down the little deer path, tearing through the sharp net of briars and branches that tried to catch her, leaping fallen logs, her heart racing in terror. The thunder of hoofbeats filled her ears from the soldiers on the road. She could see them through the trees.

The shortcut, she thought, and raced deeper into the woods while the soldiers chased in the direction Mateo and the others had gone.

She found her horse grazing in a cornfield halfway home. Heart pounding with terror and dread, hands shaking, she swung up onto the gelding and rode at a hard gallop all the way to the rusted gates and up the dusty, overgrown drive lined with tall, columnar poplars.

Behind the stable, she had the half-bucket of water waiting to splash the soot off her horse's coat. Still no sign of Mateo and the others. *Please, God. I know they're not much, but they're all I've got.* The Gabbianos had been like brothers to her since she was a knobby-kneed, nine-year-old tomboy and none of the other little girls wanted to play with her.

She put her horse away, hot but clean, and ran into the house. Maria came hurrying to her.

"Get the hiding place ready—the boys will be right be-

hind me!" Dani ordered. The hiding place was a false wall
built into the corner of the wine cellar beneath the ancient
villa. "Oh, and fix something to eat," she added. "We'll
soon have company."

Experience had taught her that the soldiers would believe whatever she told them if she played the demure
young gentlewoman and put food in their bellies and wine
in their cups. The fact had saved her hide several times in
the past, though her cupboards held precious little to
spare.

As she turned, pounding up the stairs toward her room
to make the necessary transformation from outlaw back to
genteel-poor lady of the manor, Maria gasped behind her.

"My lady! You are hurt!"

"Never mind that! We have no time!" Dani hurried
down the narrow corridor to her room. At once she closed
the curtains against the night air, then pulled off the sti-
fling black mask.

A cascade of wavy chestnut hair tumbled down to her
shoulders. With trembling hands, she stripped off her shirt
and used more of the carefully rationed water to wash her
wound. Thankfully, she saw it was no longer bleeding. The
sight of her gunshot wound frightened her, but not as
much as the terrible realization of who she'd robbed—who
she'd *seen*!—as well as the knowledge of what would
happen to her men if she allowed Prince Rafael's soldiers
to find them.

With that thought, she stripped off her trousers and
wiped the dust quickly from her skin, relishing the cool
wet cloth after her ordeal. She pulled back on a chemise, a
simple dreary-beige work dress of linsey-woolsey, and
worn kid slippers, then tied her hair up in a hasty knot, her
hands shaking. She hurried back downstairs and put on an
apron, smoothing it as she met Maria in the hall.

"Are they here yet?"

Maria shook her head grimly.

They can't have gotten caught. "They'll be here any minute now. I'm sure they will. I'm going to check on Grandfather."

Willing calm, Dani folded her hands demurely over her stomach, though her heart was still pounding in fright for her friends. She drew a deep breath and walked to her grandfather's bedroom. He was sleeping and Maria had left the taper burning because if Grandfather awoke in the dark, he was wont to start screaming with night terrors. He, the great Duke of Chiaramonte, who had once stood unflinchingly at the head of an army, now needed the care of a small child.

As she stood in the doorway, her gaze skimmed his aristocratic profile, the jut of a pointy nose, a most distinguished mustache, a lofty, wrinkled forehead. She closed the door quietly, went over, and knelt down by his bed, taking his gnarled hand between both of hers. She laid her head on his hand, trying to stay brave, but her arm hurt so badly and she had the most awful feeling about this night.

Prince Rafael . . .

Splendid, fallen angel. The king and queen had produced in their son a golden god with impeccable good grace, a smile as sweet as the summer sky—and a heart full of vice and perfidy. Prince Rafe the Rake was a known seducer: flamboyant, silver-tongued, devil-may-care.

Having singled out the useless lords of his entourage as her prey, Dani knew all about the royal scoundrel and his friends.

He drank, the gazettes said, referring to him merely as *R.* He gambled. He squandered fortunes on beautiful but useless things, like the paintings and the priceless objets d'art he collected and the jewel box of a pleasure palace that he had built himself on the edge of the city. He dueled. He swore. He flirted with virgins and old maids alike, so ludicrously charming to all women equally that it was clear he wanted none to take him very seriously. He laughed too loud and played practical jokes; he sailed that blasted yacht of his around the islands morning and noon, whooping and bare-chested under the sun like a savage. He frequented houses of ill repute and merrily tormented the night watchman as he went staggering home with his friends in the wee hours of morning.

Yet for all his faults, there was not a female in the kingdom who had not dreamed of what it might be like to be his princess for a day. Even Dani had lain awake wide-eyed in her bed for several nights, pondering her questions about him following the single occasion on which she had glimpsed the man himself, when she had ventured into the city with Maria to buy the winter's grain. What was he like? she had wondered. What was he *really* like? What made him so mad? Behind his wall of guards, he had been coming out of a posh boutique with a stunning blond on his arm, who dripped with diamonds. The prince's head was lowered as he listened attentively to what she was saying and he had laughed softly at her words.

Scraping their half-pennies together, Dani and Maria had been standing right there on the sidewalk, nearly close enough to touch their exquisite clothes as the celestial pair passed and disappeared into the coach that waited in the middle of the street, blocking traffic.

She winced at the memory of her own girlish awe and her certainty that she had just fallen in love at first sight with him. It was easier now to remember that the man cared for nothing but himself and his pleasures. The present throbbing of her arm where he had shot her was enough to dispel any leftover fantasies. In this world of unreliable men, a wise woman dared depend only on herself.

A shout from outside suddenly broke into her thoughts. *Finally! Thank God they're all right.* Dani swept away from her grandfather's bedside and dashed to the window, but then her blood ran cold.

She stared down at the dusty lawn, gripping the window frame. Mateo, Alvi, Rocco, and little Gianni had made it onto her property, but even now, before her eyes, a thundering pack of soldiers closed in on them, surrounded them, and pulled them down out of their saddles, brawling on her lawn.

One soldier brought the butt of his pistol down on the back of Alvi's head. Another knocked little Gianni to the ground, and she knew the fire-eater Mateo would fight them with all he had and likely get himself killed.

She whirled away from the window and ran for the door. Brushing past Maria, she tore down the steps. Enraged and reckless, she threw open the door and burst out into the night, but when she saw them, in her heart of hearts she knew already it was too late.

Mateo and the others were already being placed under arrest by the prince's soldiers. Even the child was being seized.

She saw red. Descended from a line as proud and old and nearly as royal as the prince's own, she stood clenching and unclenching her fists for a second, feeling the blood of dukes and generals surging in her veins.

Then she charged forth with a battle cry. *"Let them go!"*

Bested!—by a mere slip of a lad, he thought. He was surely going to wring someone's neck. "Little cutthroat savage little hellion," Rafe was muttering in fury as he staggered to his feet a moment or two later. "A cheap and ungentlemanly shot! I'll get you, vile little wretch!"

Nobody made a fool of Rafael di Fiore and got away with it. He swatted bits of twigs and dried leaves off his clothes, noticed in disgust the dirt patches on the knees of his white breeches, then scuffled lightly down the embankment, the bone-dry earth crumbling softly under his no-longer-shiny shoes.

"Your Highness, are you all right?" cried the two guards who had stayed behind to assist him.

"I'm just perfect," he spat, ignoring the fact that he had indeed lost his lordly temper. He stomped past them to the large white stallion from which one of the soldiers had dismounted. "I want them caught! Do you understand?" he said in crisp fury. "I want them jailed by morning and I don't care if I have to do it myself! You!" he ordered the first man. "I'm taking your animal. Help the driver and follow us with the coach. That way." He pointed up the road.

"Y-yes, Your Highness," the man stammered while the other swung up onto his mount and galloped off with Rafe to join the chase.

"Let them go, I say!" Dani shouted, choking in the dust the soldiers' horses had kicked up. "Get off my land!" She was nearly trampled by the stamping, rearing horses on her lawn as she pushed into the soldiers' midst.

One of the soldiers captured her around the waist before she could reach her friends. "Not so fast, little lady!"

"What is the meaning of this?" she demanded, shoving him off.

"Stay back, ma'am! These are dangerous men!"

"Don't be absurd! This is the village blacksmith and these are his brothers. Obviously, you've made a mistake!"

"No mistake, ma'am. They're highwaymen, and we caught 'em red-handed."

"That's impossible!" she scoffed.

A gray-eyed man approached her, frowning. By the insignia on his coat, she saw he was their captain from the Royal Guard—the toughest soldiers in the kingdom.

God help us, she thought.

"Do you know any reason they'd be riding here to your house, ma'am?" he asked suspiciously.

"We have a shortcut through her field!" Mateo snarled at him.

The captain glanced at him skeptically, then looked at her again. "And who might you be, miss?"

She lifted her chin. "I am Lady Daniela Chiaramonte, granddaughter to the Duke of Chiaramonte, and you are trespassing on our land!"

Some of the soldiers exchanged awed glances at the name, she noticed proudly.

"Go inside and stay out of this, milady," Mateo warned her through gritted teeth.

"He's right, ma'am. You'd best go back inside," the gray-eyed captain said warily. "These are dangerous criminals, and I'm under orders from Prince Rafael himself to place these men under arrest."

"But surely not the boy as well!" she cried in distress, pointing at Gianni. She looked at the child and saw his chin trembling as he watched them arguing. He moved closer to Mateo's side.

The man glanced at the child, weighing the decision as Maria came down from the front door carrying a lantern. The small, stout housekeeper held up the lantern and faced the big men with a pugnacious look, slipping her arm around Dani's waist in a seemingly comforting gesture, but one which Dani knew was intended to hold her back.

The captain bowed to her. "Ma'am."

"What is going on here?" Maria demanded as Mateo, Rocco, and Alvi were manacled. "We don't want any trouble with you!"

Just then, a shout sounded from down the drive by the rusty gates. Dani looked over and saw that two more riders were joining them. Her stomach plummeted all the way down to her feet when she saw the broad-shouldered rider charging up the drive astride the huge white horse.

She held her ground for the simple reason that she could not move a muscle.

"Santa Maria," the old woman breathed. "Is that who I think it is?"

Prince Rafael eased his mount from a gallop to a vigorous canter, bouncing the horse to a masterful halt in a cloud of dust between the group of men and the two women. He ignored her and Maria. His forceful gaze swept the group of men, probably counting them, then he scanned the tree line, the reins taut in his low, still hands. Without any visible signal, he urged the blowing animal into an edgy walk. He angled his chin downward, staring at the Gabbiano brothers as he walked his horse down the line of them.

"Where is he?" he asked in an icy tone.

Dani closed her eyes, knowing from the marrow of her bones that he was the sort of man who would not stop until he got what he wanted.

"I'm waiting," he said in an ominously gentle tone.

Still the boys refused to answer. Dani's eyes flicked open. *She* was the one he wanted. She knew they would never reveal her identity, no matter what the cost to themselves. Conscience and loyalty to her friends clamored for her to step forward and try to save them by taking the blame she deserved. But she somehow fought the need for this moment's justice, knowing that if she landed herself in jail alongside them, they would lose their only hope of rescue.

And rescue them she would, she thought in determination. She had gotten them into this and she would bloody well get them out of it, too.

"Where is he?" the prince suddenly bellowed without warning, startling even his horse, but the white stallion's

low rearing did not so much as jar his smooth mastery of the animal.

"Gone," Mateo ground out.

Dani glanced down to the gates of her home as the prince's carriage turned presently onto her drive. It came clattering up as His Highness continued badgering Mateo.

"Gone where?" asked Prince Rafael from high astride his horse.

"How should I know?" Mateo snarled.

He raised his riding crop in warning at Mateo's insolent tone, but he didn't hit him, lowering his hand, his expression grim. Instead, he looked at his men, a glaring light in his eyes, his chiseled face cold with authority. "You two: Put these creatures in the carriage and take them to Belfort Gaol."

"This one, too, Your Highness?" the captain asked, dangling Gianni by his arm.

"All of them," he said crisply. "There is one more of their gang still at large. The leader. A boy of about eighteen. He is on foot, with a gunshot wound to his right upper arm. He is no doubt still hiding in the woods, where I'm sure you will find my gold as well, since these brigands had the wits at least not to get caught with it on their persons. And by the way, gentlemen," he said to his men, "if any of you steal from me when you find my gold, you will suffer the same punishment as these thieves. Go."

The men glanced at each other uncertainly.

"Go, damn it, before he gets away!"

Dani and Maria jumped at his roar, holding on to each other. Dani was trembling. Maria glanced quickly at her in fright, for she had seen her wounded arm. Maria, of course, knew of her illegal activities.

"My lady, please tell my mother what has happened," Mateo called tensely to her while his brothers were herded into the very carriage they had robbed. His dark, expressive eyes were full of fury. It was strange to hear him use her title for the benefit of the men present.

"Don't worry," she answered, playing her role as lady of the manor, and wincing as they shoved him into the carriage with his brothers. "This has all been a misunderstanding which I am sure will be remedied by morning!"

"Who are you?" the prince suddenly demanded, discovering her for the first time. Arrogant as Lucifer, he stared down his patrician nose at Dani from astride his towering steed.

Maria's arm tightened around her waist, as if trying to squeeze a civil answer out of her rather than the stinging retort on the tip of her tongue, but his high-and-mighty manner was quite offensive. Nor did it escape her that their positions were most woefully switched from a short while ago. She lifted her chin. "I am the lady of this house and I might ask the same of you, since you are trespassing on my property."

"You don't know who I am?" he said in apparent astonishment.

"We've met?"

His eyes narrowed. He looked her over as though she were an insect. His haughty stare climbed from her threadbare slippers, to her stained apron, up to her defiant face.

She wanted to laugh at his arrogance. Instead, she crossed her arms over her chest and lifted both brows, regarding him in cool surprise, but inwardly her heart was pounding with anger and fright. It was all she could do not to shrink back from his outrageously rude scrutiny.

So he was used to ladies in silk and satin, ladies who would never dream of speaking crossly to their golden god. Perhaps she was in rags, but she knew a scoundrel when she saw one. They didn't call him Rafe the Rake for nothing.

He frowned at her, looking irritated, then his gaze

moved to the entrance of the sprawling but dilapidated
villa behind her, with its tangle of overgrown white jasmine dripping from the red-tiled roof. Above the doorway,
her family's coat of arms was depicted. He narrowed his
eyes, staring at it.

"Whom do I have the pleasure of addressing?" he asked
warily as he rested his riding crop over the horse's neck.

For a second, she hesitated to tell him her name because
of her crimes.

He scowled impatiently. "Are any of the family at home?"

She went pale, staring up at him. For a moment she
wanted to die. This beautiful god of a man thought she was
a servant.

Suddenly the door banged from the porch behind them.

The prince glanced toward the villa again. Dani turned.
Maria uttered to the saints and Dani's heart sank to see
Grandfather shuffling out in his nightdress and cap, holding
the candle. He was wearing only one bed slipper.

"I'll go to him, my lady," the old woman murmured,
leaving Dani there glaring up at Prince Rafael, daring
the infamous, selfish, oh-so-fashionable rake with her
challenging stare to say one word of mockery about her
grandfather.

Instead, the prince merely studied the testy, senile old
duke curiously.

Then Dani froze as her grandfather's raspy voice floated
out across the lawn.

"Alphonse? Dear Lord, my king, is it you?" Grandfather
cried.

Dani saw an ineffable expression flit over the prince's
fine features. She glanced warily at him then turned and
gasped to see Grandfather running unsteadily toward them.
The lit candle he'd brought fell out of his hand onto the dry
grass, which started to burn. Maria shouted and quickly
put out the fire while Dani turned and tried to catch Grand-

father. Prince Rafael dismounted with quick, neat grace, just in time to intercept the old man as he burst past her.

"Easy, there, old fellow," the prince said softly.

Dani stared at the pair, wanting the earth to swallow her as Grandfather grasped Prince Rafael by the shoulders with tears in his eyes. "Alphonse! You! You look precisely the same, the same, my dear friend! You never changed! How did you stay so young? Oh, but that is the royal blood for you," he said in heartfelt warmth, his bony fingers digging into the prince's powerful arms. "Come and have a drink and we'll talk of the old days at school when we were boys . . . oh, such days!"

"Grandfather, you are mistaken," Dani chided, agonizing privately for her grandfather's dignity. She laid her hand on his thin arm. "This is Prince Rafael, King Alphonse's grandson. Come back inside now. You'll catch a chill—"

"It's all right," Prince Rafael murmured to her, meeting the ancient knight's frantic, joyful, searching stare with a calm, steadying gaze. "King Alphonse was my grandfather, sir, but are you not Colonel Lord Bartolomeo Chiaramonte, his great friend?"

As quickly as the recognition of his mistake had sent a crestfallen stoop into the old man's shoulders, his bleary eyes brightened with a renewed spark of hope at the prince's question, as if he thought, *Yes, I am not forgotten. I matter still!*

He was nodding, the end of his nightcap dancing. "I attended Santa Fosca with that great man and, oh, we were merry then," he said in a choked voice.

Moving with tender gravity, Prince Rafael put his arm around Grandfather's frail shoulders and gently turned him around to face the villa. "Perhaps you will tell me of my grandfather as I walk you back to the house, Your Grace. I never knew him. . . ."

Dani stared, an inexplicable lump rising in her throat as Grandfather went obediently with him.

It was the last thing in the world she had expected, but she knew then as surely as she stood there that Rafael di Fiore was indeed a prince.

As he listened attentively to her grandfather's enthusiastic ramblings, he sent her the slimmest glance over the old man's head, with an arrogant, scoundrelly half-smile that seemed to say, *I thought you didn't know who I am.*

She narrowed her eyes, then followed at a safe distance.

He stayed for nearly an hour.

The whole time, Dani could not bring herself to go into the threadbare salon where he sat with Grandfather, golden, magnificent, larger than life, like a visiting archangel.

As she had failed to recognize his true identity out on the dark road, likewise, when he had stepped into the lit foyer, she saw she had woefully underestimated just how good-looking Prince Rafael di Fiore was.

With an annoying chivalry which must have been injected into him in the womb, he had waited for her to come safely inside, even holding the door for her before he would follow Grandfather down the hall to the sitting room. She didn't need any male's protection—but she had thanked him anyway, blushing, to her mortification.

She had brushed by him with a wary glance up at his face. That was when she had seen that, just like the papers said, he truly did have sweeping, gold-tipped lashes veiling his deep-set eyes. His eyes were subtle and cool, dark green dappled with fractured chips of gold, like sunlight flung into a shadowy pine forest.

Light from the modest chandelier had haloed his thick, golden mane, and when she looked up, his chiseled face was so far beyond handsome that she had to catch her breath. With a classical perfection beyond wishes, beyond dreams, his face was incandescent with the fierce, burning beauty of an archangel fallen to earth—a prince of angels, not a mortal man at all.

With his chin slightly lowered, his expression had been intense but coolly serene, with smoky, sensuous interest in the depths of his gaze as he watched her pass.

She had felt bewilderingly delicate, feminine, and small next to him; had been jolted by the sudden consciousness of her own naïveté beside the high sheen of his hard, worldly polish. He smelled of brandy and dust from the road mingled with the faint, pleasing note of some clean, dashing, no doubt expensive cologne. And she had felt the heat radiating from his hard, athletic body.

He had said not a word, but had locked the door behind her, then had gone after Grandfather, marching down the hall with a swift, lordly stride that seemed to claim for his own every inch of the ground beneath his feet. He moved with the self-assurance of a master swordsman.

To her annoyance, her heart had not stopped pounding since.

His dynamic presence seemed to fill the house, luring her like a siren's call and making her impossibly nervous. She couldn't even clear her mind to begin thinking up a plan of how she was going to rescue her friends from jail. She only knew it would require a trip into the great, noisy city—a daunting proposition. Instead, she put her strategy-making off for later and went to spy on Grandfather and Prince Rafael.

Listening outside the salon door, she heard him let out a robust laugh at the old man's stories of schoolboy antics. Apparently King Alphonse had been as thorough a rogue in his youth as his notorious grandson. He was incredibly patient with Grandfather's meandering tales, she thought, cocking her head as she eavesdropped. She never would have believed so famous a rake could have a kind heart. She felt almost guilty for robbing him.

When Maria came bustling past her to bring the men wine, Dani dove behind the corner of the wall so she would not be seen when the housekeeper opened the salon door. Fortunately, the woman had also managed to bundle Grandfather into his dressing gown so he looked slightly less ridiculous.

"My lady, you are being rude. It is the *crown prince*," Maria hissed, frowning at her.

"I don't care if he's Saint Peter, I'm not going near him!" she whispered, frantically beckoning the old servant in alone. Maria cast a long-suffering glance heavenward, pushed the door open with her meaty hip, and went in.

Dani sank against the wall, her pulse racing, her wounded arm throbbing. She told herself the reason she stayed away was for fear that he might begin to suspect the truth, but even as she clung to this excuse, she knew it was a lie. The fact was, he was gorgeous and fascinating and she was poor and unsophisticated and desperately shy. She knew he only sat with her grandfather out of compassion, but her pride could not bear it if he turned his pity next on her.

Eventually, however, she could not stand her curiosity any longer. Sidling into the room yet hanging back like a cautious but hungry alley cat, she ventured into the salon, her feelings in a tumult of guilt, worry, excitement, and animosity.

"And here is my granddaughter, Your Highness," the duke said with a wreath of smiles. "Daniela."

Prince Rafael rose and smoothly bowed to her. "My lady."

Feeling instantly put on the spot, she managed to curtsy. "Your Highness. Please, do sit."

As he nodded politely, swept back the tails of his coat, and sat, crossing his legs in a pose of cool, masculine elegance, she had to shake herself out of a stare. Silently, she went over to the slipper chair and lowered herself into it, her heart beating rapidly.

Grandfather looked from her to Prince Rafael with a twinkle in his rheumy eyes. "What do you think of her, Rafe?"

"Grandfather!" Dani gasped.

The prince blinked. His startled look vanished. "Well, I don't know anything about her, I'm afraid."

"Then I shall tell you a few things about my Daniela, since she is too shy to tell you herself."

"Grandfather!" Surely she was going to fall out of the chair and expire on the spot of mortification.

The prince's eyes danced in the candlelight as he regarded her in mischievous amusement.

If only he were a little less beautiful, perhaps she might be a little less agonized.

"Do go on," he said.

"Daniela has been looking after me since she was nine years old, after the nuns tossed her out of the fourth school we had sent her to."

"It was only the third, Grandfather. I'm sure His Highness is not interested in this!"

"No, please. I'm all ears," he said, plainly amused at her discomfort.

"Daniela received an education more befitting a lad, you see. That is why she isn't tedious to be around, like so many of her sex. When other little ladies were learning how to do needlepoint, she was learning how to mix gunpowder. I taught her myself," he added proudly.

"After Grandfather retired from the artillery, he took up making the fireworks displays for some of the local festivals," she hastily explained to the prince before he began to suspect anything involving gunpowder.

"Why, my Daniela could ride her pony standing astride its back when she was barely ten!" Grandfather went on.

"Astonishing," the prince exclaimed lightly.

Dani dropped her head, her cheeks flaming.

"I'm not embarrassing you, am I, my dear?" Grandfather asked, lifting his bushy white eyebrows. "Dear me, perhaps I've said enough."

"I should think so," she said, shooting Grandfather a scolding look.

He gave her a wide smile of childlike innocence.

Then she realized the prince was staring at her with an odd, musing expression, his hand idly obscuring his mouth, his elbow resting on the chair arm. Her heart skipped a beat at the smoky sensuality in his eyes. She looked away, blushing anew.

"Well," the god said suddenly, "I really should be on my way. My father is expecting me."

Dani let out a slow exhale of relief as His Highness rose and leaned down to shake hands in farewell with His Grace.

She stood and walked on wobbly legs over to the door, where she waited to see their honored guest out like a proper hostess.

God knew she wished the man would leave.

Rafe was contemplating seduction.

He was not quite sure what to make of old Chiaramonte's granddaughter, but it would have been of great help if someone could tell him why Lady Daniela seemed determined to treat him as though she were too good for him. It would also have been helpful if someone could tell him why he found her aloof disinterest so potent a lure.

From the moment the defiant minx had tossed her chin at him, sassing him as though he were beneath contempt, she had caught his attention. One did not make a mistress out of a duke's virginal granddaughter, ah, but rules were made to be broken.

Tomorrow was his birthday and she was a present he had decided to give to himself—and why the devil not? She was obviously in difficult financial straits. Perhaps with a few soft words and the right persuasion, he could entice her into an arrangement that would please them both.

The only challenge was that the girl would barely even meet his gaze, let alone speak to him. He had the feeling his reputation had preceded him, and oddly enough, her silent judgment of him stung. Odd indeed, when he could laugh off the prime minister's tirades against his wanting character without a care.

He followed her down the hall at a leisurely stroll, weighing words to lead this wholesome country girl off the virtuous path and into his den of iniquity.

He did not expect an easy conquest—a fact which delighted him. Lady Daniela, he had swiftly concluded after her display of nerve outside, was one of the thankfully rare breed of intelligent and unsinkably poised females who had the power to make a man feel like a bumbling ass with a mere, slightly baffled look. She was unconventional, willful, and fresh, and a redhead, to boot, and in his experience, redheads were pure trouble.

Unfortunately, he craved trouble.

Clearly, to his amusement, she was not impressed with him. Yet looking around him, he could not fail to note the condition of their villa, their sorry lack of servants, the old man's frail health, the lovely girl's poor clothes when her skin, tender as flowers, ought to be swathed in silk, as befitted the heiress to so noble a name. Plans of getting her into bed aside, he ached to do something for these people.

There was the possibility of marrying her off to one of his titled, well-heeled friends, but that could come later, after he had had his fill of her. At the moment, he couldn't bear the thought of her in anyone else's arms but his.

Lady Daniela was stiff and silent as they walked to the villa's front door. Her small, work-reddened hands were folded demurely over her middle. It was a crime, the condition of those poor little hands, he thought. He would give her a battalion of servants so she need never lift a finger again.

Gunpowder, eh? he thought in amusement. She was like a little keg of it herself.

He was highly curious about her equestrian gymnastics and could not help wondering, with his dirty mind, if her agile skills could be carried over into other arenas where he, in turn, could boast a certain expertise. He tried to gauge what she might be thinking, but her lowered cinnamon lashes veiled her eyes.

He didn't really know why he wanted her. A whim, perhaps. A passing fancy, the simple, selfish impulse of a seasoned rake. Chloe was ten times more beautiful, talented, sophisticated—a courtesan at the height of her powers. But then, he had Chloe wrapped around his finger, and where was the fun in that?

She must be very young, he mused, eyeing the prey furtively askance. She had the look of a developing child, with a round head perched atop a willowy body. She was a pleasing height, the top of her head a couple of inches below his shoulder.

The more he looked at her, the more intrigued he became. She had wide, prominent cheekbones angling down to a small, delicate mouth like a rosebud, and a firm, saucy little chin that he longed to pinch, just to see if he could make that young, serious face break into a smile. Her nose was small and pert, and he wished she would at least glance at him so he might learn the color of her eyes.

Because she had chosen the farthest seat away from him

in their dim salon, he had only been able to make out the blazing expression of those large, intelligent eyes, full of fiery will and inborn command . . . full, too, of an innocent poignancy that made his chest tighten oddly.

Ah, she would give him a run for his money. It would be heaven to feel such a wild, untouched creature soften and yield beneath him. Tame her. She was a tough one, all right, he thought as they stepped outside into the starry black night. Somehow he knew she was the one holding this desperate household together. An awfully young girl for such a job, he thought, saddened and yet admiring her all the more for it.

"Thank you for your kindness to my grandfather," Daniela Chiaramonte said quietly.

He turned and looked at her—a young girl out here in the middle of nowhere with no one to protect her and a criminal on the loose. God knew if the family even had enough to eat, for she was too damned thin.

Suddenly his mind was made up. He would seduce her and be damned. At least as his mistress she would be protected and well fed.

"It is my birthday tomorrow," he said abruptly, tapping his riding crop lightly against his knee.

She gave him a startled look. "Oh! Many happy returns, Your Highness."

"No, no," he said impatiently, "you see—that is—my friends are giving a ball at my palazzo for the occasion. I wish you to come."

She looked up quickly. "Me?'"

But Rafe neglected to answer, staring at her eyes as they caught the light from the lantern that the old housekeeper had left on the hook by the door.

Aquamarine.

Of course. He found himself gazing into wide, wary,

very innocent eyes the most extraordinary shade of pristine aqua-blue, like the secret coves where he used to swim as a youth, where he used to fall asleep on the flat rock with the sun on his skin and the waterfall music lulling his ears, escaping now and then the crushing pressure of his destiny and the hopeless quest of ever pleasing his sire.

Staring into those crystalline eyes, their expression honeysweet, his mood suddenly soared for the first time in thinking of his birthday.

It meant he would see her again.

"Yes, you must come," he said with a determined smile. "Don't worry over the practicalities. I shall send a carriage for you. You will be my guest of honor."

"What?"

He searched for a delicate way to explain how he wanted to help her, then decided she was too green to take a hint. Best to lead her along slowly and make his wishes clear bit by bit. He favored her with one of his most winning smiles. "I would very much like to get to know you better, Lady Daniela," he said. "Do you dance?"

"No."

"No," he echoed. Well, she hadn't swooned at the request for a dance. Damn.

Pursing his mouth in thought, he stared at her consideringly. He longed to touch her, perhaps a light caress along her cheek, but thought better of it. "Do you like music?"

"Some."

"What of pleasure gardens? Do you like those?"

She was furrowing her brow and staring at him in baffled suspicion, shaking her head slightly. "I haven't seen any."

He leaned toward her and lowered his voice to a wicked whisper. "What about sweets?" He slid a small flat tin out of his pocket and opened it, setting two peppermints on his palm. "I have a sweet tooth myself." He lifted his hand and waited for her to take one of the mints. "It is my only vice."

"Is that so?" she asked skeptically, as she looked up from the candies to his face, hesitating to indulge.

He laughed. "Come, have one. They're not poison." He watched her take one of the striped peppermints and place it warily in her mouth. "You, Lady Daniela," he said, "are coming to my birthday party and together we shall indulge shamelessly in chocolate truffles, champagne ices, and delicious little quivering pink cakes called Breasts of Venus, which my chef makes"—He kissed his fingertips— *"alla perfezione."*

"Thank you," she said, the mint puffing her cheek, "but I really can't possibly—"

"Don't talk with your mouth full," he chided, neatly cutting off her protest. "What if I were to insist?"

The innocent confusion in her eyes intensified. She looked overwhelmed. She stared at him with an earnest expression, diligently sucking the mint.

To his amusement, she obeyed his injunction, not attempting to speak again until she was finished eating it.

God, he wanted her. The shivery, wild thrill of pursuit cascaded through his body.

"Your invitation is very kind and I know you are probably only saying all this because you feel sorry for me in this ramshackle place with no one but a dear, mad old colonel for company"—Daniela glanced over her shoulder at her house—"but I assure you, Prince Rafael, I cannot possibly attend your party." She hesitated. "If you truly wish to do me a good turn, see that the child, Gianni, does not spend the night in jail."

He tilted his head with a cajoling little half-smile that had worked on females since he was a tot in the cradle. "If I do that for you, will you come to the ball?"

"Truthfully, I don't see how I could—"

"Hush. It's settled, then." He gave her his most dazzling

smile. "I will send a carriage for you at six tomorrow evening. That will give you plenty of time to dress. A lady friend of mine will lend you a brilliant gown and I daresay I can get my hands on a necklace of fire opals that would superbly set off your complexion. Trust me, I have an eye for these things. Until tomorrow night, my lady," he said, lifting her hand from her side and kissing her knuckles lightly as he sent her an intimate look. Then he released her and turned away. With a cool smile of victory, he jogged lightly down the few front stairs and strode toward the grazing white horse, whistling *"La ci darem la mano."*

"Sir, I said no."

He paused, then turned, a little surprised, but pleased by her maidenly resistance. One didn't want too easy a conquest. He rested his riding crop jauntily on his shoulder. "Lady Daniela, surely you are not averse to having a little fun in life?"

Her arms were folded tightly over her chest and she lifted her chin. "With all due respect, Your Highness, my friends have just been arrested. It isn't a good time."

"You should not be consorting with criminals in the first place, my dear," he said with condescending patience, then smiled. "Our bargain is sealed. I will remove the child from the jail and see that he's placed in safer quarters, and in return, you will dance with me tomorrow night—and you will try one of my chef's pink cakes. I insist on it."

She placed her hands on her waist, her brow knitted, her tone growing belligerent. "I said I will not come, sir. Are you deaf?"

Deciding that he adored the fight in her, he cupped his ear. "Pardon?"

"How can Your Highness ask me to be so selfish as to think of idle entertainments when my friends may be sentenced to hang tomorrow?"

Two realizations suddenly pierced Rafe's brain, soaked

as it was with music and *amore*. One, she still hadn't taken the slightest hint about the true nature of his invitation; and two, her answer was no anyway because, it presently dawned on him, she was in love with that fiery young hothead he had just arrested.

Flat, unequivocal no.

The realization acted as a bucket of ice water dousing the gathering heat of his enthusiasm. He could scarcely believe it.

"Well, this is rich," he said, staring at her, one fist cocked on his hip.

He recalled that the eldest of the rebellious young highwaymen whom he had sent to jail over an hour ago had been a tall, strapping farm boy of perhaps four and twenty, whose name the men had logged as Mateo Gabbiano. Clad in sturdy work clothes with a brown vest and a red bandanna knotted around his neck, Mateo Gabbiano had been the handsome sort of rustic youth, with curly dark hair and the kind of big brown eyes that melted tenderhearted women.

Aha. Now Lady Daniela's indifference to him from the start made sense.

Having been worshiped and adored by women from the day he was born, Rafe had had too little experience with rejection to take it well.

His opinion of her plunged.

A scowl settled over his face. How could the foolish wench give her heart and perhaps her favors to a skulking criminal? he thought with an inward, aristocratic snort of disdain. Maybe she was lonely in this isolated place, but had the woman no feeling for her rank? How the devil could she choose that peasant over . . . him?

"Well, my lady," he said with cold hauteur, "I'll see what I can do for the boy. Fare you well."

He pivoted and stalked down the few front steps of the

villa, marching stiffly toward the white horse. His better sense pointed out that the highwaymen had made a dash for her property, and she might well be mixed up in their crimes. But if she was involved, he did not want to know it.

A few steps away, Rafe stopped and abruptly turned.

She was still standing there, her slim body silhouetted in the light from the lantern.

"Why did you pretend not to know who I am?" he demanded.

"To lower you a peg," she replied. "Why did you spend an hour with a senile old man when you were so determined to catch an outlaw?"

"Because, my lady," he said crisply, "there are times when an act of kindness outweighs one of justice."

She was silent for a moment, holding his gaze. "I am obliged that you wanted to help me," she called. "But instead, I shall help you."

"Help me?" he replied in worldly sarcasm. "I doubt that."

"Look into the books of this county's tax collector, Your Highness, and you may find the real criminal at large."

He narrowed his eyes. "What are you implying, madam?"

"You'll see."

He tapped his riding crop across his palm. "Graft does not flourish under my father's rule. Not so much as a bee drinks from the wrong flower without the say-so of King Lazar di Fiore."

"Tell that to Count Bulbati."

"Who is that?"

"The man who raises my taxes each time I refuse to marry him."

His attention came to a point like a saber. He made a mental note to look into it, then pushed the accusation of embezzlement aside, concentrating on her. "Why do you refuse him? Wouldn't a prudent marriage relieve your situation here?"

"Perhaps. But firstly, Count Bulbati is a corrupt and greedy swine, and secondly, I shall never marry. Not anyone. Ever."

"Why, for heaven's sake?" he demanded in shock, as though he had not said those very words countless times himself.

She lifted her chin, starlight on her hair. "Because I'm free." She gestured toward the villa. "Our house may need repair, but at least it's my house, and all these lands . . ." With a sweep of her hand, she showed him the landscape. "Though they thirst with drought and the crops are low, they are *my* lands. All of it is entailed on me until my death. How many women can count themselves so fortunate?"

He glanced around, mystified that she felt lucky or grateful when he doubted she'd had enough to eat in days or maybe longer. "Looks like nothing but a lot of work and headaches to me."

"I need answer to no one but myself," she replied. "Why should I become the legal property of a person who is no better than me, and in all likelihood my inferior in most respects?" Her thin shoulders lifted in a shrug. "I don't expect you or anyone to understand. It is merely the choice I have made."

"The choice you've made," he echoed, feeling disoriented merely talking to the chit. He could not fathom where she had come by her sturdy little opinions, but she certainly seemed in control of her life, which was more than he could say for himself.

The thought irked him.

Hearing riders approaching, he looked over and saw his men coming toward him from the woods. He saw that they had his gold but no Masked Rider. He sent a scowling look over his shoulder at Daniela Chiaramonte, standing there on the step with her hands folded demurely over her too-skinny waist.

He had thought to leave two soldiers posted at the villa to protect her and her family, but he abandoned the idea, for he doubted that the Masked Rider posed any kind of threat to her, considering that the outlaw's right-hand man was apparently her beau.

The thought made his mood fouler. "If you are quite through instructing me, Lady Daniela, the king awaits my arrival."

"Goodbye, Prince," she said politely. "And . . . happy birthday."

Was the little baggage mocking him? He looked sharply at her, suspecting that he heard a faint trace of laughter in her voice. Still, for the life of him, all he wanted was to march over to her and kiss that smug smile off her lips; but oh, no, he was not going to do that. He was going to get on his horse and ride far, far away from her. He was good at forgetting women; he made up his mind to expunge this vexing little redhead from his memory on the spot.

Belatedly, he remembered that he had sworn off helping damsels in distress some years ago.

As he swung up into the saddle and urged the horse into motion, he mentally bade the eccentric Lady Daniela good riddance.

Don Giovanni himself would have been at a loss.

❧ CHAPTER ❧
THREE

Still out of humor with the world after his encounter with the vexing redhead and her unheard-of rejection of him in favor of a rustic, Rafe traveled the rest of the way to Belfort without event, though he was on his guard as they passed the poorer, ramshackle outskirts of Ascencion's sprawling capital.

Nearing the heart of the cosmopolitan Italian city, graceful, wrought-iron street lamps lit the broad, cobbled thoroughfares. People had come out to enjoy the cool of evening. The streets of Belfort rang with laughter and argument from the coffeehouses and taverns they passed. People hailed him everywhere he passed. Dutifully, he waved as he cantered by on the strapping white stallion.

Moving down the street at a trot, the horse coughed under him with the hot, dust-laden night breeze. He patted the animal's warm, damp neck and a puff of dust rose from it. He winced, for his own throat felt caked with fine clay.

Dust coated everything, with the drought in its fourth month. Even the hardy marigolds in the flower boxes of the tall, fashionable city row houses looked wilted. The elegant fountains in every garden square had been turned off to conserve water.

It would get worse before it got better, he thought grimly. It was early July, but soon the sirocco winds would come slithering up from the heart of the Sahara Desert,

49

flattening North Africa, stretching over the limpid jade waters of the Mediterranean, to lie heavily over all of Southern Europe. During those two or three weeks each year, all hell tended to break loose on the island.

As they turned a corner, Rafe caught a far-off glimpse of a fanciful bronze cupola rising over the city roofs, gleaming in the starlight, but instead of heading for his pleasure palace, he was bound for the Palazzo Reale.

He cantered his white stallion into the wide cobbled central square of the city. Here the cathedral and the royal palace faced each other like stately partners in a minuet. Between them stood the famous bronze fountain dedicated to past generations of Fiore kings. Pigeons roosted for the night amid the glorious sculpture work.

Rafe swung down from the saddle and was quickly ushered by the Royal Guards through the gates. Glancing at his pocket watch, he hurried up the wide, shallow steps.

In the imposing entrance hall, he was greeted by Falconi, the ancient palace steward whom he had tormented as a merry youth in these halls. He clapped the frail, formidably dignified servant on the back, nearly toppling him, then quickly caught him.

"Where's my old man, Falconi?"

"Council chambers, sir. I'm afraid the meeting is almost over."

"Meeting?" he exclaimed, already in motion. "What meeting? Devil take it. Nobody said anything about some bloody meeting!"

"Er, good luck, sir."

Rafe waved his thanks and strode quickly down the marble hall to the administrative block of the palace, his heart pounding. Hell, he'd done it again. When he arrived before the closed door of the king's privy council chamber, he paused, bracing himself. Then he threw open the door, making an entrance with an air of supreme bonhomie.

"Gentlemen!" he greeted them, sauntering in with breezy nonchalance. "Good Lord, a full cabinet! Are we at war?" he asked with a grin, shoving the door closed.

"Your Highness," the starchy old men grumbled.

"Hey-ho, Father."

Reading a document at the head of the long wide table, King Lazar glanced at Rafe over the edge of the square-rimmed spectacles perched on his stubborn Roman nose.

King Lazar di Fiore was a large-framed, striking man, square-jawed and hard-featured, with salt-and-pepper hair shorn close and weathered brown skin. He frowned at Rafe, his piercing, dark-eyed gaze boring into him with his characteristic intensity.

Rafe took in that stare, wondering just how badly he had blundered this time.

From boyhood, he had studied his father's every nuance of expression, not only for the benefit of learning to manage men, which his father did expertly, but also because his own young world had revolved, painfully, around trying to live up to the great man's impossible expectations. Finally, he had accepted philosophically that he was never going to be enough in his father's eyes. He would never quite live down The Debacle.

"We're honored you decided to join us, Your Highness," King Lazar remarked, inspecting the document in his hand again. "And no, we are not at war. Sorry to deprive you of that entertainment."

"It's just as well," Rafe said as he dropped idly into his chair at the foot of the table, hooking his arm in lazy pose over the chair's back. "I'm a lover, not a fighter."

The ruddy-cheeked admiral of the navy cleared his throat, swallowing a chuckle. He was perhaps the only man in the room who understood and appreciated Rafe at all, or at least was not offended by him.

The same could not be said for the formidable pair on the other side of the table, Bishop Justinian Vasari and Prime Minister Arturo di Sansevero.

The two were a study in contrasts: the bishop big and bombastic, stocky as a bulldog draped in flowing, brocaded robes; all bark, no bite. He had a round, rubicund face and wild white wisps of hair that stuck out in all directions from underneath his velvet beanie. He was as sure of his God's opinions on all matters as he was gratified by the constant pampering of his gardens at his rich palazzo. Mostly he was known to preach with a rolling, thunderous eloquence, and when he preached against vice and licentiousness, everyone knew to whom he was referring.

In short, the bishop saw the crown prince as the profligate prodigal son of a good and godly father, King Lazar. Fortunately, there was a second son, the cherubic, sweet-tempered, and obedient ten-year-old Prince Leo, who played Able to Rafe's Cain in the bishop's cosmology, though Leo's nurse could well have attested that he, too, was a budding rogue. Bishop Justinian had been named by the king as Prince Leo's legal guardian and had been granted the right of regency, which meant that if God ever smote Rafe down on account of his Roman orgies and drunken chariot races, the bishop would rule for Leo until the boy came of age.

For reasons Rafe could not comprehend, the people of Ascencion loved their fiery, pompous, high-living bishop.

The prime minister was Bishop Justinian's utter opposite, though his opinion of Rafe was the same. Neat, quick, tidy, and discreet, Don Arturo was the consummate courtier. His keen, darting mind was like a silent, razor-toothed barracuda. Fortunately, the don was endowed with an unflinching loyalty to Ascencion. Slight of stature, Don Arturo had hooded brown eyes and a thin, spare mouth that only softened when he saw his sister's children, his little nieces and nephews. He was childless, his wife having died two decades earlier, nor had he ever remarried. His work—Ascencion—was his life.

Were Rafe to repent of his wickedness, the grandiloquent Bishop Justinian probably would have killed the fatted calf for him, but the prime minister, he knew, had more personal reasons to despise him.

Meanwhile, beside Rafe, his Florentine kinsman, the Duke Orlando di Cambio, tactfully slid him the notes he had been taking.

"*Grazie,* coz." Rafe glanced over the page, feeling a little chastened by his cousin's gesture. He knew most of the cabinet would probably have preferred to see Orlando gain the throne rather than he, were it possible.

With the stamp of the Fiori in his ruggedly handsome profile, Orlando, about five years Rafe's senior, looked more as though he were his brother than distant cousin. They were both tall, broad-shouldered, good-looking men and arrogantly aware of their innate superiority. But where Rafe was a dark blond with hazel eyes, Orlando had jet-black hair and ice-green eyes.

Orlando was a bit of a loner, always dressed in black. A successful shipping merchant in his own right before he had left Florence and moved to the land of his ancestors, Orlando now served Ascencion under the Ministry of Finance. He had earned the trust of the cabinet and the king with his able mind and sober, reliable manner; the prime minister liked him particularly. For some months now, Orlando had been included in high-level meetings like this one because he was, distantly, of the royal blood.

"Habitual tardiness alludes to the sin of pride, Prince Rafael," the bishop rumbled, grandly rolling his *r*'s.

"Well, I do apologize for the delay," Rafe said to them

all as he glanced over Orlando's notes. He looked up innocently, hating his own need to give excuses, even if he did have a rather good one this time. "It so happens I was attacked by highwaymen."

The bishop and some of the other advisers gasped, but Don Arturo rolled his eyes.

The king arched a brow at Rafe, who smiled cheerfully in return.

"Were you hurt?" his cousin Orlando asked in concern.

"No harm done. All but one of the thieves are already in custody. My men search for the last remaining fugitive even now."

"Good." The king nodded.

"Attacking a member of the royal family," Orlando said, sitting back in his chair with a look of disgust. "I'll be glad to see them hanged."

"They didn't know whom they were attacking, I fancy. I was in a borrowed carriage—uh, never mind," Rafe muttered, avoiding his father's knowing smirk about the carriage race and the broken axle.

Orlando shook his head regretfully along with the others.

The king cleared his throat. "Well, Rafael, the reason we called you here is because I have decided to take a holiday. I leave tomorrow."

Rafe's eyes widened, his arm falling off the back of the chair.

The man had not taken a break in thirty years of rule.

"Now that that unspeakable Corsican has been penned up again—let us hope for good this time—I have decided to take your mother to Spain for a couple of months to see our grandchildren. I am making you prince regent in my absence, Rafe. What do you say to that?"

Rafe sat there in absolute shock.

He stared at his father and his father stared at him, a

mysterious look of challenge in his piercing gaze, perhaps even a trace of wily amusement in the depths of his wise, dark eyes. "Are you ready?"

"Yes, sir!" he said at once, fervently. His heart gave a violent kick, then raced.

His father held up one hand, halting his euphoria. "But I have one condition."

Rafe wet his lips. "Anything."

King Lazar gestured to Orlando. His cousin rose from his chair, went to the huge carved sideboard by the wall, and returned to Rafe carrying a large wooden tray. A roguish smile flicked over the king's hard mouth as Rafe looked down at the tray.

On it were arrayed five small portraits of women and a small stack of legal papers. Furrowing his brow, he looked questioningly from the portraits to his father.

"It's time you chose a wife, Rafe."

He looked up in horror.

"Go on, pick one," the king said, nodding toward the tray.

"Right now?" he exclaimed, aghast.

"Why not? How much longer do you intend to put it off? We have been waiting for you to make up your mind for three years. It is your duty to produce heirs, is it not?"

"Yes, but—"

"If you want a taste of rule, Your Highness, you must choose one of these young ladies for a wife and sign the proxy wedding papers there."

"Proxy wedding!" he cried, yanking his hand away from the page. "You mean if I sign this, I'm married?"

"Precisely. You see? We couldn't make it much more painless for you than that."

Rafe stared at the paper as though it were a severed hand lying there on the tray.

The king steepled his fingers, giving him a stern look.

"Rafael, your willingness to assume the responsibility of marriage is the only way I can rest assured that I can entrust you with Ascencion when I'm gone."

He sat back in his chair and stared at his father. "You must be joking."

Lazar merely waited.

Rafe shot a trapped, simmering glance at the old men, who regarded him in varying degrees of spite and disdain. No help was forthcoming from their quarter, he saw. He glanced at Orlando, but his cousin was studying the women's portraits.

Rafe couldn't bring himself to look at them. "Father, be reasonable. I cannot just randomly pick someone I'm going to have to look at every day for the rest of my life. I don't even know who these women are!"

"You're thirty years old, Rafe. You've had your time to court suitable women, but you chose to spend that time chasing actresses instead, so we have narrowed the field for you." The king clasped his hands, resting his elbows on the table. "Choose. Then sign. Otherwise, I will leave Don Arturo in command, and you may continue to play. But," he added in a hard tone, "should you make that choice, I will be forced to seriously reconsider your succession to the throne. Leo is still young enough, after all, to be molded for the crown."

Rafe stared at him in disbelief, a knot of dread at the terrible threat forming in his stomach while fury gathered in his veins.

What could he do? He had to submit . . . as always.

Lowering his head, he stared down at the portraits, slowly growing too blind with rage to see the smiling, insipid faces of the approved, voted-upon, politically prudent, royal broodmares.

Puppet.

Prisoner.

He remembered Daniela Chiaramonte, a woman, barely more than a child, standing there on her front stoop as proud as you please, mistress of her own destiny—and he was humiliated.

No, he thought, his heart pounding. For years he had endured his father's domineering. The criticisms and impossible standards. The bullying on one hand and overprotectiveness on the other had all but wrecked his already shaken self-confidence. But this was beyond the pale.

"This," he said in a very calm tone, "is intolerable."

"Pardon?" the king asked ominously, lifting both eyebrows.

Rafe looked up slowly from the portraits with burning fury in his eyes. Suddenly he stood, throwing back his chair.

The ministers gasped. Orlando arched one brow. The bishop narrowed his eyes. Without another word, Rafe pivoted and stalked toward the door.

"Rafe! What the hell are you doing?"

"Freeing myself from *you,* sir!" he shouted, turning. "I am done with you controlling my life! Give the crown to Leo. I don't want it if the price is my soul."

With that, he walked out, trembling with anger. Walking numbly down the hall, peeling his gloves off with shaking hands, he stared straight ahead, his mind a wall of rage. He couldn't believe he had just done it. But bloody hell, they had trained him from infancy to be a king and then expected him to take orders like a lackey! He was done with it.

Let the king disown him if he liked. It scarcely mattered. He had given his best and it had never been enough for the man, but Father had just pushed him too far.

"Rafael!" He heard his father's voice calling angrily from down the hall behind him.

He tensed, stopping at once in spite of himself out of mere habit, like a well-trained hunting dog, an idiot-loyal spaniel. He despaired of himself, knowing that if he didn't keep walking now, he would never be free.

Yet all he could feel was his love for Ascencion keeping him rooted, chained where he stood, cruel mistress, forcing him to humble himself for her, as ever. Still, it was as unprecedented for Father to come after him as it had been for him to defy the king so blatantly in front of the cabinet. In his pride, he could not bring himself to turn around, but he waited where he was, his hands stiff at his sides, his gloves clenched in one fist.

"Rafe, damn you," the king muttered in annoyance, walking to him.

Rafe turned with a bitter expression and met his father, eye to eye.

Lazar pulled off his spectacles and stared forcefully at him. "You choose a poor time to make your stand, boy."

"I am not," he replied in searing quiet, "a boy."

"Do you think I don't know why this is difficult for you?"

"Because this time you are forcing the most important decision of my life down my throat? Because you think me too great an idiot even to choose a decent wife for myself?"

The king was shaking his head impatiently. "No, no. You and I both know full well that the reason you refuse to be snared is because you're still scarred by what that woman did to you when you were nineteen. What was her name? Julia?"

Rafe froze, glancing uneasily at him. His father's gaze was piercing, shrewd.

"It's time to get past it, Rafe. It's been ten years."

He looked away.

The Debacle.

Some people had to learn things the hard way. He, young royal fool, had been one of them, trying to save his damsel in distress. Such an easy target, with his deep pockets and his tender heart.

Those days were gone.

"You should have let us prosecute her, Rafe. By law, she should have hanged. You should have let me take care of it for you."

"I don't need you to fight my battles for me, Father," he said tersely, sickened by the memory of himself at nineteen.

Such a noble young chevalier, so utterly sure of himself, unwilling to flinch before the rumors that his beautiful older woman, his temptress, his prize, had lain with every man in the kingdom and was merely using him. He hadn't cared. He had been sure that if he gave her everything, in time he could make her love him for himself, not for his rank or his wealth or his looks. He had nursed Lady Julia back to health when he'd found her brutalized by some lover. He had satisfied her debts and healed her crushed pride, and for all his tender pains, what was her thanks?

She seduced him, took his virginity, then robbed him while he slept. She had searched his desk, stealing secret government maps which he had been making for his father—maps she then sold to the French, who promptly used them to invade Ascencion.

The House of the Fiori had nearly lost Ascencion to Napoleon, all because the heir apparent had failed to control his adolescent lust for an inappropriate woman.

Not a man in government had taken him seriously since, not his father, not the people, and especially not the cabinet.

"That whore merely beguiled you, took advantage of your youth—"

"I don't wish to discuss it, Father," he said curtly, looking away. "It was my own fault. I trusted the wrong woman."

"And now you'll trust none of them. Rafe, Rafe." Lazar sighed. "You need an heir, Rafe."

"Why?" he demanded. "What's the sudden rush?"

"I'm ill," his father said.

"What?" he breathed, turning to him.

Lazar stared at him, then slowly lowered his gaze. "That is why I am going to Spain to see Darius and Serafina and the children. I don't know how much longer I will be strong enough to make the trip."

"What are you talking about?" he exclaimed. "You don't look sick!"

"Keep your voice down," the king said, glancing down the hall. "No one knows about this except the head physician, Don Arturo, and now you. I want to keep it quiet for as long as I can."

Rafe gaped at him for a moment, incredulous. He struggled to find his voice. "Does Mother know?"

"No. God, no," he whispered, then visibly steeled himself. "I don't want her to worry a moment longer than necessary."

"What's the problem? Does the doctor know what it is?"

He shrugged. "Some sort of stomach ailment. Possibly a cancer."

"Oh, my God," said Rafe, stunned. Then anger filled him. "How can this be? You've never been sick a day in your life! Are they sure that's what it is?"

"Fairly sure. Rafe, what matters is putting our house in order. This is no time for you to walk out on me."

Rafe stared at him, his emotions in chaos. Now that he knew to look for them, he could see the signs of strain in his father's face. Lazar's weathered skin stretched tautly over his cheekbones and there were shadows under his eyes, as though he had been spending sleepless nights.

He could not believe it. His father had always seemed to him as invulnerable and immortal as a god. "Are you in pain?"

Lazar gave a rueful shrug. "I'm fine if I don't eat."

He shook his head. "Father. Why the hell didn't you just tell me this in the first place instead of backing me into a corner like that? I'm damned sorry I lost my temper—"

"I didn't want you to know. You're going to have plenty else on your mind when you're the one with the fate of half a million people on your shoulders." He laid a firm hand on Rafe's shoulder and gave it a squeeze. "Perhaps my methods tonight were a little high-handed, Rafe, but I do want you to wed. Not merely for the sake of the kingdom and the family, but for your own well-being. I sowed some wild oats in my day, God knows, but I don't like what I see happening to you."

Rafe said nothing.

"You're going to want someone who truly cares for you by your side when trouble comes—and it will. I'll tell you honestly, I never could have lasted this long if it weren't for your mother."

Rafe dropped his gaze from Lazar's intense stare and looked blindly at the floor, swallowing hard against the sudden lump in his throat. He feared he might weep like a child on the spot. Some king he would make.

"Yes, sir," he mumbled. Now that he understood the situation, he could not possibly refuse his father's wish. He didn't have the heart. Marry he would, and so be it, though it was akin to a death sentence. "I will do as you ask. But I fear there are no more like her, sir."

His father suddenly grinned. Full of courage even in the face of death, Rafe thought in awe. The king slapped him heartily on the back. "You're right about that. Come on, then. We've got to go over a few administrative details."

Lazar threw his arm around Rafe's shoulders, pulling him back toward the council chamber, though Rafe's mind was still reeling. "You're going to do fine, son. Now, I've arranged for Don Arturo to work closely with you. . . ."

If one day he could be half the man his father was, he would consider his life a success, he thought, still shaken by the news. Yet somehow his mind refused to accept the idea that his father was dying.

Perhaps that was why his thoughts flew to other possible explanations—including sinister ones. Surely the doctors had checked for poison.

If they had found it present, Father would not have accepted the diagnosis of stomach cancer. Besides, who would want to poison the great, the renowned King Lazar di Fiore, the so-called Rock of Ascencion? His Majesty was loved and revered by all.

One thing was certain—Rafe was going to pay a visit to the royal physician and grill him for information. Also, he decided to send his own chef on the ship with his family, for he knew the man could be trusted. He would replace the ship's provisions before they sailed, too.

Fortunately, he knew that if his father really were in danger from some outside source, there could be no safer place for him than under Darius's roof in Spain. His sister's fierce, deadly husband had always been the watchdog of the royal family, the very man who had found the means to turn the French invaders away from Ascencion's shores on that fateful day ten years ago.

Indeed, no matter what threat they faced, they had always been strongest when the whole family pulled together. *A thought to keep in mind when he chose his bride.*

This time, Rafe took his seat at the foot of the table with a grave and troubled countenance. He murmured a stiff apology for his outburst to the members of the cabinet.

Lazar cleared his throat. "My son and I have reached a compromise. His Highness has agreed to select one of the young ladies whom we've approved by the time I get back. The wedding will take place then. I see no need to rush him into a decision now. After all, choosing in too great haste may result in a decision he might later regret. In any event, the prince has many other matters to occupy his mind presently, as I'm sure you will agree."

They muttered grudging assent.

Rafe met his father's hard but encouraging glance from down the long table.

The time was at hand—the time to prove they had all underestimated him. He looked down at his cousin's notes, his heart pounding. He skimmed the page, feeling like a schoolboy before the headmaster, dreading to give the wrong answer. He took a deep breath and lifted his chin.

"Very well, my lords," he said a trifle nervously. "Where do you wish to begin?"

Don Arturo sent him a keen, pointed look. "Where do *you* wish to begin, Your Highness?"

Rafe stared blankly at him for a second.

Those first seconds of full monarchal authority were like taking a huge, green-broke racehorse out for a run in the spring, pure power exploding under him, barely under his control. It was thrilling, dizzying, intoxicating. But years of merciless drills in a hundred different subjects had prepared him for this moment, and his training took over.

When he spoke next, his voice was firm, commanding: "Let us start with this matter of the drought. What is the status of the city's water reserves? And give me an estimate on how quickly we can build more irrigation canals to supply the lowland wheat farms."

The minister of agriculture raised his finger and offered a reply.

Rafe listened intently, willing back his equilibrium. From the corner of his eye, he saw his father lower his head and smile.

≈ CHAPTER ≈
FOUR

Dani awoke with the morning light filtering softly through her bed's threadbare canopy of muslin, which served as insect netting. The light brought into focus the muted, faded tones of the old furniture and the drab stucco walls. She winced faintly at the flaming pain in her arm, closing her eyes again as the pain brought back the night of scant sleep she had passed.

Riding to the village last night and telling the Widow Gabbiano what had happened to her boys had been one of the hardest things Dani had ever had to do. Between her fear for the boys, the throbbing in her wounded arm, and her feverish memory of every word she'd exchanged with Prince Rafael, she had barely gotten the rest she would need for the day ahead.

Today she would make everything ready, and tonight the Masked Rider would effect a daring rescue.

Knowing Mrs. Gabbiano would arrive soon for their foray into the great city, Dani sat up with a huge yawn, eyes watering, then dragged herself out of bed. Even before she could bother checking her gunshot wound, she needed coffee. Wrapping her dressing gown over her cotton night shift, she made her way downstairs, mentally blessing Maria when she smelled the aroma of coffee permeating the first floor.

A good, strong cup of coffee, that's all she asked

from life, she thought as she sat down at the table where the small cup waited for her on the saucer, steaming in the cool air of morning.

The window in the kitchen was open, admitting the fresh, delicate breeze. It carried to her the distant scent of the sea and the pungent smell of the wild mint that grew amid the weeds around the courtyard. The minty flavor of the air reminded her of *him*—that wicked candy man with his peppermints and his sweet, lying mouth and his golden mane, warm butterscotch blond.

She scowled faintly and took another sip of coffee. She wished she had not told him about her philosophy of independence. What an oddball he must think her. Yet it had been important to remove the look of pity she had seen in his eyes, even if only to replace it with male bafflement.

Her thoughts drifted to his invitation to the ball. Knowing she would be busy breaking her friends out of jail, of course she had been forced to refuse. Last night, she had been too dazzled by his looks and charm and his kindness to Grandfather to be properly suspicious, but by the clear light of morning, his flattering desire that she join him for his birthday celebration struck her as odd, indeed.

Offering to send a carriage for her? He'd made no mention of chaperonage. Had he really suggested that he would hand her over to one of his glamorous women to dress her for the party? Good Lord! With his reputation, one had to question the motive behind his seeming generosity.

But then she shrugged off her suspicions as ludicrous. He was used to the fairest flowers of the ton, diamonds of the first water. A man like that would not want a red-headed, tomboy misfit like her—thank God. Such a smooth-talking devil with his angel face and smoky green eyes would be nigh impossible to resist.

Just then, the door that led to the kitchen garden outside

opened and Grandfather walked in. Dani looked up, surprised to find him up and about so early.

"Good morning, my dear!" he said cheerfully.

She smiled at him, overjoyed to see he was lucid today, at least for now. "How are you feeling, Grandfather?"

"Capital, my dear, capital!" he said, his lined face etched with a smile, his raspy voice stronger than usual. "I was just strolling a bit in the morning air and thinking about Prince Rafael. What a fine young man, eh, Dani?"

She glanced skeptically at him, then decided not to contradict him. He looked happy, and if Prince Rafael was responsible for the smile on Grandfather's face, she would not be the one to break his illusions. They had so few visitors.

"Why don't you get him to court you?" he teased.

"Grandfather."

He chuckled, patting her on the head. "And why not? You are cross with him because he's not a man you can boss around like you do the rest of us. But that doesn't mean he would not take good care of you."

"I can take care of myself, as you well know." She sent him a reproachful look and sipped her coffee. "And I'm sure I don't boss anyone around."

He chuckled and wandered back outside.

When he was gone, Dani took her coffee up to her bedroom and finished it as she dressed for her trip into the city in her nicest frock, a demure round gown of flower-printed white cotton. Its short puff sleeves did not cover the fresh bandages that she had wrapped around her injured right arm above her elbow. So, groaning because of the heat, she reluctantly donned a rather frayed and faded long-sleeved spencer of figured blue silk. After Maria helped her plait her hair and coil it on the crown of her head, she was ready to go, but for her bonnet and gloves.

She spent a few minutes stowing all the equipment

she would need for tonight's rescue in a large sack, when she heard Mrs. Gabbiano arrive in her cart. Quickly, Dani checked the contents of the sack one more time. Cradled securely in her black riding breeches and shirt were the three clay-mortar bombs she had made last night, each as big as her fist. There was a flint to light them with, a large coil of hemp rope, her rapier wrapped in old rags, and her spurred riding boots. Finally, she placed the infamous black satin mask in the sack and closed it.

She put on her bonnet, stood before the mirror tying the ribbons under her chin, then slipped on her gloves and went downstairs, carrying the sack with her.

She greeted the tough old peasant woman, Mrs. Gabbiano; Maria walked outside with them. The two older women exchanged worried murmurs while Dani placed the sack in Mrs. Gabbiano's heavy-wheeled wagon. She loaded her horse's saddle in next to it and finally tied her skittish, liver-bay gelding to the back of the cart.

After all her efforts, her wounded arm was pounding by the time she climbed up onto the driver's seat beside the stout, black-veiled widow. She felt a little light-headed with pain.

"Mateo's friend, Paolo, will have his fishing boat ready and waiting to take the boys and me to the mainland tonight," Mrs. Gabbiano grunted the moment they were off.

Dani nodded, aching to think that she must part with them, especially the rascally little Gianni, and Mateo, who had been her closest friend for a decade. She did not speak of her sorrow. "I have the explosives ready. As long as the wardens will let me into the jail to visit the boys with you, then I can smuggle these bombs in to them. They'll be out in no time."

"I hope you're right, my lady," the woman muttered as she slapped the reins over the dapple-gray draft horse's back. Dani fell silent, knowing that Mrs. Gabbiano blamed her for her sons' arrest, though she would never say so.

Traveling north on the King's Road toward the city, they had not gone far when they met a rider coming the opposite way.

Dani's heart sank as she recognized the fat body of Count Bulbati bulging over both sides of the horse's back. The poor animal labored to trot under the man's bulk. Bulbati looked ridiculous as usual in his frilly finery.

"Should we stop?" Mrs. Gabbiano asked under her breath.

"Drive on. Maybe he's in a hurry somewhere and won't have time to chat."

"More than likely he's on his way to see you," she grumbled.

"Lady Daniela! Well met, my fair neighbor!" the unctuous count called, bouncing dangerously astride his horse as he pulled the animal to a halt.

"Good morning, my lord. As you can see, I am in a great hurry—"

"I shall ride alongside you, then, my lady, for I have come to assure myself of your security!" True to his word, Count Bulbati yanked his horse's head around, cursing and bullying the long-suffering chestnut into walking beside their cart. He patted the greasy sweat from his round face. He had small brown eyes with a shrewd, mean-spirited expression and thick, rubbery lips that Dani could not bear to look at, for he was always licking them when he was around her, as though anticipating a dainty feast.

"My security?" she asked, trying heroically to keep the tedium from her expression and her voice.

"Lady Daniela, I heard that there were soldiers searching your property last night and that at last those vile highwaymen who have been plaguing us these six months were arrested!" He paused, peering over at Mrs. Gabbiano in distaste. "Oh, it's the mother of that wolf pack. My good woman, you certainly went wrong somewhere raising those sons of yours. Their thieving has embarrassed the whole county!"

And what of your thieving, you corrupt swine? Dani nearly blurted out, but she refrained, knowing he would only make her life miserable if she provoked him. "On the contrary, my lord," she said in a stinging tone, "bandits or no, those boys—if they are guilty, which has yet to be proven in a court of law—have brought honor to our county. Everyone knows that they only take from the rich and share the proceeds with the poor."

"If you were one of the rich, my lady, I daresay you wouldn't find them half so gallant. I heard the leader remains at large. I wonder who the Masked Rider really is," he said, sending her a piercing sideward glance.

She shivered, a chill running down her spine. There had been moments in the past when she sensed that Count Bulbati had figured out her game and was merely toying with her, angling her into some unknown predicament until he had her right where he wanted her.

"Well," she said stiffly, "I'm sure you are very kind to check on me, but Grandfather and I are fine—"

"I heard Prince Rafael was there," he interrupted, leering at her in challenge.

She looked at him coolly, loathing him. She could feel the sordid innuendo in his words. "That is correct. His Highness commanded the unit."

Bulbati leaned toward her, his saddle squeaking for mercy under the shift in weight. "Did that rogue make improper advances toward you, my lady?"

Dani stared icily down the road. "Of course not, and may I remind you, sir, you are speaking of Ascencion's future king." Archly she reminded herself that that fact had not stopped her from kicking Rafe the Rake where it counted.

Bulbati seemed satisfied with her answer. He straightened up in the saddle again with a smug look. "Actually, my dear, I have news from the city that may surprise you."

"Oh?"

"Oh, yes, a morsel, indeed."

She waited, but it pleased him to gloat with his secret.

"Aren't you curious?" he goaded, glancing at her with an eager lick of his rubbery lips.

She looked away in disgust. "What is your news, my lord?" she asked irritably.

"Very well, I shall tell you. This morning, quite without notification, His Majesty sailed off on a leisure voyage with the queen and little Prince Leo. The royal rogue has been dubbed prince regent for the duration of the king's absence!"

She turned and stared at him, feeling as though she had been kicked in the stomach by a mule. "Are you quite sure of this?" she forced out.

He preened. "The whole island talks of nothing else."

Dani and Mrs. Gabbiano exchanged a glance of dread. The transfer of monarchal power to Prince Rafael boded ill indeed for the boys.

Then Dani noticed the greedy light burning in Count Bulbati's eyes, and could fairly see the gold coins dancing in his head. He was staring off into the distance, no doubt musing that with that royal joker on the throne, he and his ilk could get away with anything they liked, and who would punish them?

Without King Lazar at the helm, Ascencion was going to be in chaos.

"Where did you say you were headed, my dear?" Bulbati asked, breaking into her thoughts.

"I did not say," she replied rather sharply. Must the man

know every detail of her business? They were not far from the count's own driveway now.

"Oh, *well*, far be it from me to pry," he said in bland reproach. "Who am I but your good Christian neighbor, come to look after your safety?"

"I'm going into town," she growled.

"But whatever for?" he whined. "You hate the city, my dear."

She glared at him. "Charity work. I am going to visit the poor. Do you wish to join me?"

His small, piglike eyes shot open. He yanked out his fob watch. "Oh, me, look at the time. I have to be getting back home. It's nearly time for lunch. Perhaps next time, my dear. Oh, here's home. Are you sure you wouldn't like to join me for refreshments?"

"Thank you, sir, but we are in a rush. You may keep all your delightful cakes to yourself."

"Oh, yes, yes!" His eyes lit up.

They bade him goodbye, laughing to themselves as he posted his way on his suffering horse up his own drive. Mrs. Gabbiano shook her head, flipped the reins over the gray's back, and they picked up their pace.

Soon it was sweltering noon under a blaring blue sky, and Mrs. Gabbiano flailed the reins, hotly warning pedestrians out of her path as she negotiated the big, clumsy wagon through the bustling streets of Belfort. Dani wished the cart would stop lurching about, considering that just outside the city she had stopped and strapped the three homemade clay bombs to her thigh.

It was the only way she could think of to smuggle them into the jail. The fist-sized clay balls were packed with enough gunpowder to blow a three-foot hole in the wall of the boys' cell.

Ahead, the piazza looked even busier than usual, while

above them, laundry dried on lines, flapping in the sultry breeze that gusted down the narrow cobbled street.

Just as they reached the square, the cathedral bells began to toll for the noon Mass, but over the resounding knells, Dani heard a banging sound. She looked over at the middle of the square and saw men building a gallows. Chills ran down her spine in spite of the oppressive heat.

An enormous crowd mulled about in the square, abuzz with the news of the capture of the Masked Rider's gang and Prince Rafael's rise to power. The mood in the air was tense. Old men with closed, sun-hardened faces under slouch hats smoked cigars and muttered in groups. Women made their way toward the church for Mass. Children darted through the crowd, screeching and sword-fighting with sticks. There was a long line for water rations, three jars per household per day, doled out under the watchful eyes of soldiers.

Vendors hawked red peppers, zucchinis, oranges, apricots, and grapes from their temporary stalls. An old woman was selling flowers from a basket strapped to the back of a donkey. Carriages rumbled around the four streets that formed the square, the horses' harnesses jangling, but all the while the rhythmic clapping of the hammers rang in the background as the prince's men built the scaffold for her friends and—if she was caught—for her.

Mrs. Gabbiano and she exchanged a grim look, then continued on to the livery stable which the woman's brother-in-law managed. They left the cart and Dani's gelding there. Dani buried the sack containing her equipment under a pile of hay in her horse's stall. Then she and the widow linked arms and marched resolutely toward the jail, hearing murmurs in the crowd here and there from clusters of people who claimed that the Masked Rider would surely come to rescue his gang. Others vowed they would wait in the square to catch a glimpse of the famed outlaw for themselves.

Dani trembled to hear these votes of confidence amid the crowd and did her best to ignore them, focusing on the task at hand.

Crossing one of the noisy streets, a huge, creaking, jangling wagon passed, nearly running them down. Dani jumped back, pulling Mrs. Gabbiano out of the way. As it rumbled by, she saw that it was carrying a bizarre assortment of huge, gaudy mummers' masks. It was heading in the direction of the princes' mysterious pleasure dome. The masks were probably part of the evening's entertainment for his birthday ball, she supposed. The party would probably be the wildest the island had ever seen, considering that Rafael's father had given him a country for his birthday.

Finally, at the edge of the square, the two women crossed the street and climbed the forbidding steps to the entrance of Belfort Gaol. They told the soldiers out front who they were and gained admittance into the dim antechamber, where they pleaded with the warden for a visit.

Mrs. Gabbiano did the talking while Dani stood beside her, her gaze downcast. She concentrated on looking timid and demure, acutely aware, meanwhile, of the bombs snugly secured to her limb. Her heart was pounding wildly, almost with giddy thrill. She couldn't believe she was getting away with this—standing here in the heart of the jail while untold dozens of soldiers were out combing the countryside for the Masked Rider.

"All right, all right, I don't want to hear no bawlin'. You can see 'em," the scarred, surly hulk of a warden grumbled at last, waving off a fly that buzzed around him. He led them down a dank, dark hall. At the end of it, he opened a thick door with a small barred window. "Ten minutes," he growled, banging the door shut behind them.

Dani stood out of the way while Mrs. Gabbiano tear-fully embraced her sons one by one. Poor Alvi's spectacles were cracked, and big, gentle Rocco looked the worse for wear. She could well imagine that the jailers had singled him out, for smaller men were always ganging up on Rocco and trying to bait him into a fight, though he scarcely owned a temper to lose. Mateo, on the other hand, seemed so incensed he could hardly bring himself to speak. Indeed, all the boys were strangely silent.

"But where is my Gianni?" Mrs. Gabbiano asked suddenly. "Where is my *bambino*? I want to see him."

The older boys all looked away.

"What is going on here? Where is Gianni? Tell me what is going on!" the woman cried suddenly, her voice full of panicky maternal instinct. "What have they done with my baby?"

Then Dani and Mrs. Gabbiano listened in shocked, horrified silence as Mateo broke the news. "Last night a man came and took him away."

"Who was it?" Dani breathed.

"I don't know his name. I never saw him before. He was young and the warden called him 'my lord.' He told us he was here on the prince's orders. I think he was one of Prince Rafael's friends."

"Was Gianni released?" she cried.

Mateo glared. "No. The man made it clear that if we didn't tell the Masked Rider's identity, we would never see Gianni again."

With that, something inside of Dani snapped. The cell seemed to grow smaller, crowding her in. She stood there frozen while the unflappable Mrs. Gabbiano grew frantic, crying and wailing to see her child.

Dani barely heard, wrapped up in shocked dread. She had utterly failed to foresee this disaster.

She had asked Prince Rafael to help the child. She had

certainly never imagined that he would separate Gianni from the others and use him as a pawn to root out the Masked Rider's identity. He was more cunning than she'd realized—and more ruthless.

Mrs. Gabbiano brushed off big Rocco, who tried to comfort her.

Dani turned to Mateo. "Where have they taken him?"

"I don't know for certain," her friend said gravely. "There, I think." He pointed to the window.

Her gaze followed the line of his finger. As though in a trance, she walked to the cell window and stared out it while the boys tried to calm their mother.

From the window, she could see the gallows in the square, the fiercely armed soldiers patrolling the crowd. And over the trees, she saw the spun-sugar spires of Prince Rafael's pleasure dome.

As she half-listened to Mrs. Gabbiano's angry crying and her sons' attempts to soothe her, her will turned to steel.

Rafael di Fiore, she thought, *this is war*.

Stalking out of the line of sight of the small window in the cell door, she bade the boys look away, quickly lifting the hem of her petticoat over one knee to produce the bombs and the flint. Her hem fell again. Then she took Mateo aside, leaving the other two to comfort their mother.

"Use these at midnight," she ordered him in a fierce whisper. "Stack them on the windowsill, and when you hear the cathedral bells chime twelve, light the fuses. Turn this table onto its side and hide behind it to protect yourselves from the blast. The rope is to help you lower yourselves down. I will create a distraction below and your mother will be waiting with the cart. You will drive to the coast, where Paolo will be waiting with his fishing boat to take you to the mainland. I have given your mother gold to help you make your way to Naples to your kin."

"What about my brother?" he asked as he hastily hid the items under his straw pallet on the floor. "We can't escape without him."

"I'll get Gianni out of there," she said in fierce quiet, staring at the distant dome and spires.

"No, you won't!" Mateo said in an angry whisper, stalking over to her. "You shouldn't even be here, Dani! You're the one they're after!"

"I can do it." She did not turn to him. She didn't want him to see her fear. "I got you all into this, and I'll get you out."

He began forbidding her to involve herself any further and lecturing her in his usual elder-brotherly way, but Dani wasn't listening. Her thoughts were on her enemy.

She had been in her element last night on the King's Road when she had clashed unexpectedly with Prince Rafael.

Tonight she must travel into his world of glitter and sin. She was going to the ball.

Afternoon shadows patterned the marble floor in the small side gallery where Orlando stood in preternatural silence, his back pressed to the wall, his expression cold as he listened intently to the conversation in the next room.

"As I've t-told you, Your Highness," the royal physician said, stammering with distress, "I tested His Majesty on these five different dates for the ingestion of various poisons, and though the symptoms are similar, no taint in the king's food or drink was found."

"And how do I know that you can be trusted? How do I know that if my father has some unknown enemy, you are not party to the plot?" the prince demanded harshly.

"Are you suggesting a conspiracy, Your Highness?" the old doctor asked in bewilderment. "Am I accused?"

Orlando listened, interested indeed in his reply, but for a long moment, Rafe was silent.

"That remains to be seen. I am taking these files to be examined by some other physicians to study your findings."

"As you wish, Your Highness. By all means, I have done all that is in my power for His Majesty. If I knew of any further procedure to help him—!"

"Has anyone else worked on this case?"

"Only Dr. Bianco."

"Where can I find him?"

"Why, sir, he passed away three months ago."

Orlando tensed in the silence that followed.

"How?" Rafe demanded.

"In his sleep, Your Highness. He had suffered with a weak heart for several years."

"Where are his notes on my father's condition? I'll take them, too."

"Naturally, sir. I will find them for you. You have my full cooperation. . . ."

Orlando slid away from the wall while the old man was still groveling. He turned and stalked silently down the hallway, deserting his post before the prince left the physician's study.

Bloody goddamn.

After years of careful planning, living in bitterness up to his throat, Orlando had not anticipated this twist of events. It was not supposed to happen this way. Everything had gone to hell in a matter of hours.

He had to find Cristoforo before Rafe did. That was all he knew. There was little time to bury evidence.

Fortunately, he had purged Dr. Bianco's case files on the king after he had sent the meddling old man to his Maker. Still, Rafe was on the right track. Soon he might well launch an all-out investigation, and Orlando had to remain at least one step ahead of him.

Orlando nodded pleasantly to a pair of ladies in the main corridor of the palazzo on his way out the front entrance, then asked an attentive servant to have his horse saddled and brought to him. He waited, lighting a cheroot and brooding.

His position could be worse, he supposed, exhaling smoke and squinting against the vibrant sun. The king was not dead, but at least His Majesty and that irksome cherub Leo were out of the way. That only left Rafael, who worried Orlando not at all. The game was far from over. Besides, he was adaptable; how else could he have survived the nightmares he'd known?

When his black stallion was led from the royal stables, he crushed out his cheroot in the sculpted stone urn full of sand left at the foot of the stairs for that purpose, and mounted up. He tossed the groom a coin and rode off, soon passing through the fashionable section of the city with its tall pastel houses to a seedier quarter.

Glancing behind him to make sure he had not been followed, he dismounted before a filthy tavern with a brothel above it. He gave the boy posted out front a murderous look of warning before leaving his stallion in his care, then stalked slowly inside, ready to reach for the knife at his belt in an instant.

The tavern was dim and stank of stale bodies and smoke, vinegary wine and urine. He stalked up to the bar, nodding at the innkeeper.

"Is Carmen working?"

Drying a glass with a soiled towel, the man eyed his fine clothes, met Orlando's icy gaze, then jerked a nod toward the narrow wooden stairs. "Room six, milord."

"Thank you." Orlando set a coin on the bar and walked to the staircase, glancing at some of the thuglike characters sitting in sullen silence in the dark, nursing their ales and cheap gall wines in the middle of the afternoon. When he found room six, he listened at the door, rolling his eyes impatiently upon hearing the young pair rutting vigorously inside.

He pounded once sharply on the door with the heel of his black-gloved fist. "Cristoforo," he said in a low, harsh command. The noise inside stopped. Then he heard worried whispering. He grasped the doorknob and rattled it. "Get dressed. Now."

More frantic whispering from inside.

"I have to go. He doesn't like to be kept waiting."

"But Cristoforo!"

"I have to do as he says, Carmen!"

"Why?"

"Do you think I can pay you on my wages alone?"

"Let him go, Carmen, or I'll slit your pretty throat," Orlando said silkily into the crack of the door. He had no doubt the black-haired young beauty was worth every cent.

"C-coming, Your Grace!" the young chef called in a worried tone over the girl's indignant cry at his threat. "It's all right, I'm coming right away!"

Orlando heaved an impatient sigh and paced in the dingy hallway, the carpet ratty and red under his black boots. He smirked at the sound of beds squeaking inside the rooms all up and down the corridor. A few moments later, the young, wiry underchef Cristoforo came out of room six.

Orlando caught a glimpse of the lovely, olive-skinned Carmen, her nude figure shadowy behind Cristoforo. All of perhaps seventeen, she had a lithe body and red-rouged lips, and he could tell by one glance that the boy had probably never given her satisfaction. Orlando sent her a smoldering look of promise. She scowled at him in reply and slammed the door in his face.

Smirking, Orlando turned to Cristoforo, a tall beanpole of a youth with a shock of bright red hair, mussed. His cheeks were patches of scarlet, considering where Orlando had found him.

"So sorry to interrupt. Your day off, I take it?" Orlando asked gently

"Yes, sir," the lad mumbled.

"Then I don't suppose you know what happened this morning."

"Sir? No, sir."

Orlando stared at him for a moment, tempted to sink his knife into the youth's stomach where they stood. Instead, he clasped him by the back of the neck and walked him toward the stairs, his pace companionable, his grip relentless.

"His Majesty has sailed away on a leisure voyage to Spain, my lad. I would like to point out that you are not among his galley crew. This upsets me, Cris."

His brown eyes flew open wide. "I didn't know, sir! I didn't know! Oh, God, sir! Was there no warning? How are we going to—"

"Shut up," he snarled.

Behind his freckles, Cristoforo's face paled. Indeed, Orlando thought, the boy knew the danger of crossing him or failing him in any way.

"No, His Majesty gave no warning of his plans." Mollified, Orlando flicked a piece of lint off his black sleeve. "Fortunately, I have arrived at an alternative solution."

"Thank God!" the boy exhaled in relief. "It's not my fault, sir, how can I help? What would you have me do? Sir, I'll do anything, just don't—"

"Walk down the steps before I throw you down them," he softly interrupted.

The lad gulped and obeyed. At the bottom, he turned and stared at Orlando. "Sir, y-you're not going to hurt Carmen, are you?"

Orlando smiled. "That's up to you, Cris. Are you ready to help me? Do you think you can avoid another blunder?"

"Y-yes, Your Grace," he croaked in a whisper.

"Good. Then let's start rehearsing exactly what you're going to say when the time comes for you to tell the prime minister how Prince Rafael has been paying you to poison King Lazar."

⊰ CHAPTER ⊱
FIVE

Flaming torchères lined the long drive as the curricle drawn by two prancing white horses joined the queue of carriages waiting to deposit guests before the fancifully carved pink-marble entrance of Rafael's pleasure dome. *Oohs* and *aahs* slipped from Dani's lips as she stared at the peacocks marching with tails unfurled and the albino deer grazing on the park lawn. Then she gazed up, wide-eyed, at the fanciful striped Moorish spires and the bronze cupola, gold against the starry indigo sky.

Straight out of the Arabian nights, it looked like a magic castle all made out of candy, she thought in wonder. Already she could hear the orchestra's lively music pouring out from every arabesque window, could feel the thrumming excitement in the air.

There were jugglers on the lawn, jesters in motley with bells on their tripointed caps. The night hung like blue velvet around her under a jeweled vault of diamond stars, and the sea breeze blew balmy against her face after the day's heat.

She looked everywhere eagerly, unable to help the tingling frisson of pure girlish anticipation that bubbled through her. It was difficult to keep her mind on the seriousness of her mission here tonight.

Earlier in the day, after leaving the jail, she had ridden back home to try to come up with an appropriate means of transportation to the ball. To solve this problem, she had "borrowed" Count Bulbati's fancy curricle and matched horses. Her neighbor never went out at night; she hoped he wouldn't notice they were missing. Then she had gone home to retrieve the one gown she owned that might pass for a ball gown.

Her tiny bodice was of light blue silk. From the high waist fell an overskirt that parted in the front to reveal a white petticoat beneath, which was embroidered with pink flowers below the knee. She was fairly sure her gown was a few years past fashion, but it was nearly fine enough, and besides, the long fitted sleeves covered her lightly bandaged right arm, while the petticoat was long enough to completely conceal the fact that beneath the gown, she was dressed for hard action down to her spurs.

Once she had rescued Gianni from Prince Rafael's palace, she would have to make a quick change in order to go create the distraction in the city square which would divert more soldiers away from the jail, so that Mateo and the others could make their escape. She would need to scramble out of the gown, put on her black shirt and vest and the infamous mask, grab her sword, and ride.

Ahead, she could see that some of the guests were costumed. She was glad she had brought along a blue satin half-mask that matched her gown. It would help her blend into the crowd, because the one thing that could throw her carefully made plans into ruin was if Prince Rafael saw her and remembered her.

Glancing around, she brushed off that worry as best she could. There were so many people present—and so many smart, stunning ladies—she was certain she could slip through the crowd unnoticed. At last, it was her turn to go in. She gave her name at the entrance. The stately old butler lifted a brow, but politely gestured her in.

She passed rows of servants who skipped forward to

take the gentlemen's hats or pointed the ladies in the direction of the lounge, but she passed them all silently, a rush of exhilaration in her veins.

Unaware she was holding her breath, she walked slowly, step by step, into Prince Rafael's pleasure palace.

Dizzy with the music and the wonderful aromas of foods and perfumes, she felt like she was floating. She stared about her, wide-eyed and marveling.

Everything was *so beautiful*. It was like entering a dreamland.

The chandeliers looked like mountains of delicately carved ice. The floor below her was black and white marble, like a great chessboard. The walls were hung with red silk embroidered with golden pineapples. There was particolored confetti raining in clouds from above, and when she glanced up, she saw two girls on trapezelike swings, their slim bodies draped in gauzy trailing silk. They swung slowly over the crowd in huge arcs, back and forth, laughing and sprinkling confetti.

Around her, radiant ladies greeted each other with easy, elegant gaiety, but Dani stood alone. Tilting her head back, she looked up and up and up, past the colored rain of confetti, past the girls on swings. The ballroom lay directly under the famous soaring dome, which she had only ever glimpsed from outside at a distance. From floor to apex, the dome must have been a hundred feet high, she thought in amazement. She squinted in fascination at the distant frescoes painted on the dome and nearly gasped as she picked out the Arcadian orgy depicted, naked nymphs entwined with sporting satyrs and randy gods.

Abashed by the tauntingly obscene images—just the sort of art she would have expected from *him*—she moved her gaze down the sides of the dome.

Girding the bronze base of it, well obscured by shadows,

she could just make out a winding gallery, a kind of narrow walkway from which the crowd could be observed. She saw a lone figure standing there—aloof and above—motionless.

She felt, rather than saw, who it was.

A quiver passed through her limbs as she sensed the menace in this place beneath all its glittering beauty. Her senses vibrated like finely tuned strings at the sight of the prince's dark figure there above the crowd, but it brought her back to her purpose.

Where could Gianni be?

The flow of the crowd was pressing her up along the receiving line. She heard murmurings around her.

"Chloe Sinclair—isn't she divine?"

"Look at that gown! It must cost a fortune."

"The toast of the London stage!"

"I heard they met in Venice when he was on Grand Tour."

The woman holding court at the end of the receiving line was a radiant, sugar-spun confection of a creature, a pink pearl here in the heart of Rafael's magical palace. Dani was awed by Chloe Sinclair's beauty amid her dawning realization that the woman was the prince's mistress—his doxy, his demimondaine—and that she, of the great Chiaramontes, was about to be presented as though to a queen to this creature who had crawled out of heaven knew what London gutter.

Dani looked around in distaste, trying to get out of the way, but curiosity kept her in the line. She had never seen a genuine scarlet woman before.

Chloe Sinclair appeared somewhere between the ages of twenty-five and thirty. Her delicate face was flawless, her hair the gold of bright new coins. She had sky-blue eyes and a perfect little beauty mark just above the corner of her mouth. Her skin's milky whiteness was enhanced by her gown of white silk, but the round, spectacularly low-cut neckline made the traits of her person which had no doubt attracted Rafe the Rake's interest embarrassingly obvious. Dani fought the urge to whisk the shawl from her shoulders and cover Chloe Sinclair's large bosoms with it.

Glancing around, she could see that though many of the guests were bedazzled by Ms. Sinclair's glamorous beauty and fame, a few others here and there looked as appalled as Dani felt.

Really, what was His Highness thinking, appointing a woman of the theater as his hostess? Lord knew how many other representatives from the finest families he had offended with this schoolboyish slap in the face to propriety.

When her turn came, Chloe Sinclair greeted her, her Italian stilted by a clipped British accent. Dani's opinion of Rafael sunk lower when she came close enough to see the burning light of narcissism gleaming in the actress's blue eyes. She seemed drunk on vanity, basking shamelessly in her position as Prince Rafael's hostess. It was all Dani could do to make herself spare the actress a dismissive nod. Ms. Sinclair seemed instantly offended by Dani's lack of enthusiasm toward her. Her wanton-looking mouth stiffened, but Dani looked away and walked on in disdain.

She decided not to waste one more moment indulging her lurid curiosity about the prince's private affairs. Somewhere inside this menagerie of vice, a little boy was waiting for her to rescue him.

She began weaving her way uncertainly through the crowd toward the edge of the gilded ballroom. She passed an absurd fountain spewing arcs of wine from the mouths of silver fishes. She rounded clusters of chatting guests, the women in lavish gowns in every color of the rainbow, though most of the men wore black. A few of the wilder guests were bizarrely arrayed in costumes as though it were Carnevale.

Staring every which way, she dodged footmen carrying trays of wineglasses and lovely antipasti—little pieces of smoked swordfish garnished with the orange pulp of sea urchins, sweet cheeses, snails and caviar, and baby octopus, pink as coral, marinated in pungent lemon. There were fruits—candied figs and apricots, peaches in wine, wheel-shaped slices of oranges covered in sugar-fuzz, garnished with the sweet mint that grew wild on Ascencion.

A footman paused to offer her a thimbleful of his cordials, a sticky-sweet blackberry liqueur, but she didn't dare imbibe, and though the exotic delicacies tempted her, she was too nervous over her mission to eat a thing.

She passed one of the young lords of Rafael's entourage who had cornered a woman against a pillar, smiling as he fed her an oyster from the half-shell, stroking her throat as she tilted her head back to swallow it, her eyes closed.

A whisper of sensuality slid through Dani's veins at the sight of the lovers, but she quickly lowered her gaze and hurried by, hearing him murmuring to the woman that oysters were an aphrodisiac.

Blushing intensely, she stole guilty glances at the other young lords of the prince's inner circle. They stood nearby, edgy and sleek, like fierce birds of prey. Intense and jaded, they monitored the crowd. Dani could not help but notice among them the sullen and gorgeous Adriano di Tadzio, whose dark, seductive beauty put most of the women in the room to shame.

She winced at the memory of the night she had robbed him as the Masked Rider, but if he hadn't been so haughty, perhaps she wouldn't have gone out of her way to humiliate him.

Moving on, she recognized the fair-haired, thin, and amiable Viscount Elan Berelli, who was perhaps the only one of them who could be counted as a decent human being. His big nose, slightly hunched posture, and forward head gave him the look of a friendly buzzard. They said he was being groomed as the future prime minister.

Then she heard deep, worldly laughter from no more than six feet away and froze in her tracks.

Looking slowly over her shoulder, she saw Rafael, towering like a golden colossus amid a cluster of women and men who stared up at him, entranced, hanging on his every word.

Dani stared, too, unable to tear her gaze away. At the sight of him, a tangle of emotions thrashed inside of her like a net full of fish being pulled up from the sea. So, she thought with a strangely anguished longing that her bravado couldn't quite mask, the god had descended to bask in the adulation of his worshipers. Apollo, perhaps.

The most eligible bachelor in the world.

Her gaze took in his sun-streaked hair, his bronzed skin, the white flash of his scoundrel's smile, the strong, dynamic features of his face, carved with indomitable will, but tempered by the gentleness in his eyes, the strength of his innate noblesse oblige. He had thick golden brown eyebrows and a deliciously sensual mouth. On any other man, his sapphire-blue coat would have been foppish. On him, the effect was splendid, the flamboyance of his long hair and jewel-toned coat tempered by the stately reserve of his starchy cravat and the forceful intelligence in his green-and-topaz eyes.

She caught her breath and looked away, his magnificent image emblazoned on her mind.

She cursed herself for admiring a notorious rake, but she had to admit that Prince Rafael was the superior of every man in the room by something more than the happenstance of rank—something intangible. She could feel his effortless dominance in her blood as surely as he stood there. Worse, she was not immune to it.

Ignoring the uncontrollable surge of her reaction to

him, she forced herself back into motion, pressing onward in her quest.

She didn't need his friendship, his pity, or his lavish, unprincipled offers. She didn't need him—or any man. She could take care of herself. She always had.

At last, she came to the edge of the ballroom and slipped away through a salon. She found herself in a dim, empty hallway, and immediately stole down it. At the end of the corridor, she alighted a glistening marble staircase. The steps zigzagged back and forth three flights until she arrived at the top floor. She searched the corridors, calling Gianni's name as loudly as she dared, to no avail. She hurried to search the next floor down and repeated the process, trying every door.

It did not help matters that half of the hallways had trick trompe l'oeil paintings at the end of them. More than once she walked straight into a wall, thinking, thanks to the three-dimensional illusions of the paintings, that the hall continued on, or that she was entering some new room.

No doubt Prince Rafael would have laughed at her, country bumpkin that she was.

When she had exhausted all possibilities in that section to no avail, she returned to the stairs and tried another wing of the palace, repeating the process. Again, there was no sign of the child.

By the time she searched the second floor of yet another wing, she had begun to despair. Perhaps Rafael had moved Gianni to another building. Still, she moved resolutely down the hall, calling his name as loudly as she dared.

Suddenly, from down the hall, she heard a faint, muffled owl's call—Gianni's usual signal. Drawing in her breath, she quickly found the room in which he had been closeted.

"Lady Dan, is that you? I'm in here! In here! The door's locked, Dan!"

"Gianni! Hold on, I'll get you out of there!"

Quickly sliding a hairpin from her coiffure, she leaned down, concentrating on the lock. She tipped her satin half-mask up over her forehead so that she could see better in the dimly lit hallway. Carefully, she picked the lock, frustrated with the time it took her as the moments dragged. Lock-picking was not her forte, but at last she heard the bolt turn. She opened the door and whirled in.

"Gianni!" She rushed to him, grasping him by his thin little shoulders to examine the child with a worried, sweeping glance. "Are you all right? Have they hurt you?"

Suddenly she stopped. The boy was wearing a neatly pressed skeleton suit with knee-length trousers, a little jacket, and an expertly tied miniature cravat. His hair was lightly oiled and combed over to the side.

"Good Lord, Gianni, what have they done to you?" she exclaimed. "You're clean!"

"Yeah!" he said angrily. "The batty old housekeeper made me get a bath and put these patsy clothes on!"

"Take off those shoes," she said at once. "We've got to get you out of here."

"Good, 'cause I'm bored." The boy plopped down on the rug and began pulling the shoes off.

Dani walked away marveling that he was in a better condition than when she'd last seen him. "Not bad quarters you've got here."

"Guess what, Dan? The batty old lady told me this room is where Prince Leo stays when he visits his big brother."

"Really?" she asked, glancing around.

"Yep, he's ten, just like me. I wish I was a prince. How are we gonna escape, Lady Dan?"

His question snapped her out of her surprise that Rafael had placed Gianni in his own royal brother's bedroom. "With this." She pulled the sheets off the child-sized bed, coiled them into a rope, and began tying knots in it, each about one foot apart. Then she walked to the double windows, opening them as wide as they would go. Seeing that her makeshift rope ladder would not yet reach the ground, she pulled down the damask curtains and added them. Then she knotted the rope firmly around the post of the bed and threw the length of it out the window.

"Your escape ladder, my lord," she said grandly, hoping that a playful manner would lessen the boy's fright. Only Gianni wasn't at all frightened.

He peered down, then looked at her in excitement. "Do I get to go on that?"

"Do you think you can hold on tight and climb down all by yourself?"

"Of course! I've climbed trees lots higher than that."

She didn't doubt it. Still, she looked over the two-story height in worry, then crouched down before Gianni and held him by the shoulders, staring into his eyes. "Take your time going down. The rope ladder will bring you to the roof over that balcony, but it looks like you'll have to climb down the rose trellis to reach the ground. Be brave, and please, Gianni, hold on as tight as you can."

He gave her a long-suffering look. "Why do you always treat me like a baby?"

She ignored him. "Brace your feet on the knots. When you get to the bottom, run to those hedges. See?" She pointed. "When you reach the hedges, turn right—which hand is your right?"

He lifted his right hand.

"Good. Follow alongside the hedges. Run as fast as you can and when you come to the wooden gate, go out. Your mother is waiting for you on the other side. She's got the wagon, and that's how you're going to get away. Have you got all that?"

He nodded.

Her frown deepened and she gave his shoulders a squeeze. "Be very careful, Gianni."

He grinned. "I'm not scared!" Spry as a little monkey, he climbed up onto the windowsill, firmly grasping the rope. "You know, Lady Dan, he's not that bad."

"Who?"

"Rafe."

"Rafe!" she exclaimed. "You're speaking of the crown prince! Rafe?"

"He said I could call him that."

"Did he?" she echoed warily. "You spoke with him?"

"Oh, sure. He came here after lunch and had milk and cookies with me. He showed me a good card trick. He was asking me all kinds of questions."

"About the Masked Rider?" she asked worriedly.

"Some," he said. "I told him I don't know who the Masked Rider is. Then, you know what? He started asking about Mateo—and you." The boy laughed in hilarity. "He thinks Mateo's sweet on you. He was awful curious about you, Lady Dan."

She scowled. "That's enough out of you now. Go on and get out of here. You haven't got all night and your mother is waiting down there. When midnight comes, your brothers are going to blast out of jail. You have to be ready to flee."

His small fingers gripped the first knot. "What are you gonna do?"

She glanced over her shoulder, sorely tempted to return to the ball and solve the problem of her taxes once and for all. She had noticed an untold fortune in jewels dangling from throats and wrists. Since Rafael's soldiers had recovered the gold she had tried to steal last night, she still did not have the means to pay Count Bulbati's latest round of taxes. It was as good an opportunity as she could hope for. True, she was a highway robber, not a pickpocket, but soon the guests would be too drunk even to notice if they were robbed. Besides, when the Gabbiano brothers were gone away to Naples, there would be no more highway robberies. She could not pull off her feats of valor single-handedly.

"I just want to go ask some questions about where the king has gone away to," she said, reluctant to let the boy know she was up to thieving again, for she had not set him a very good moral example. "I won't be long."

The child nodded gravely.

"Now go on. I'll be right here watching you." Dani gripped the edge of the windowsill, her heart pounding as the boy moved down the rope, knot by knot. He paused about halfway down. She saw him glance toward the lawn, then he craned his neck and peered up at her.

"What's wrong?"

"Is that a peacock down there on the grass?" he called in a loud whisper.

She glanced over. "Yes."

"Do peacocks really peck people's feet if they ain't wearing any shoes?"

"No, Gianni. For heaven's sake, who told you that?"

"Rafe!"

"Well, he lies an awful lot. Keep going. You're almost there."

A few moments later, the boy reached the balcony, clambered down the trellis, and stepped onto the grass. She quickly threw his new shoes down to him. He grabbed them, paused only to wave at her, then darted across the lawn toward the hedges just as she had instructed. She followed his progress worriedly.

Finally he came to the break in the hedges and disappeared. She waited a few more minutes just to be sure he had gotten away safely, then she gathered the rope ladder in through the window again.

At last, her mission complete, she steadied herself with

a deep breath, smoothed her hair, and folded her hands demurely over her stomach as she braced herself to return to the ballroom.

Cloaked in shadows, his hands resting on the railing, Rafe had returned to the narrow gallery girding the dome's base. Observing his guests, he wondered vaguely how the presence of a thousand people was not enough to dispel his restless, lonely mood.

A party on a night like this seemed all wrong.

He took another long drink, ignoring the inner warning that he'd had too much already.

Twenty-four hours had passed since he'd become the most powerful man on Ascencion, but he felt no change inside himself yet, no easing of the hollowness that he had been so sure would be filled when he grasped his destiny. He was now the kingdom's supreme authority—yet here he was, the star guest of another ghastly party, as though nothing had changed.

Perhaps things never would change for him, he mused, chilled by the thought. Perhaps he would expire of boredom and emptiness. Pleasure he had tasted in every subtle shade, but would he never know contentment?

Sighing as he scanned the crowd below, he saw his mistress holding court near the punch table, dazzling her rapt audience. His friends sauntered through the crowd, keeping their eyes and ears open for the barest whisper of any sort of treachery against the king.

No proof of poisoning had been found in the doctors' files, but even now Rafe was having the royal pantries emptied and every food item tested in the university laboratories by having it fed to cats. He was sure the animals would merely grow fat and happy, for he could not imagine anyone wanting to poison the great King Lazar. No doubt he had merely been seeing too many gothic plays and melodramatic operas lately, but better safe than sorry.

Then he heaved another long sigh, his expression faraway as he gazed down at the festive throng, feeling in no way a part of it.

Maybe Father had been right. He usually was, blast him. Perhaps it was not merely power that would make him happy, but a more settled life as a husband and father. Frankly, though, the prospect sounded deadly boring to him.

He had done his best to try to settle on one of the five young women who had been selected as possible brides for him, but so far all seemed equally undesirable.

The first was a ravishing beauty—with a greedy gleam in her dark eyes that he did not trust. The second was a wit and had even written some published essays on virtuous conduct—but that was the last thing he needed, someone to excise all his endearing character flaws out of him—a moral surgeon of a wife. No, thank you, he thought.

The third was virtuous, a chaste young saint known for her piety, and far be it from him to sully her. The fourth looked sickly and frail. Childbirth would surely kill her. And the last was a big, apple-cheeked butterball of a Bavarian princess with a jolly look about her that Rafe liked immensely, but his friends had assured him that the courtiers and ladies would destroy the girl with their cruel mockery, and he knew they were right.

He frowned to himself. It shouldn't really matter which one he picked, yet somehow he had always thought when he married that it would be for—

What an idiot you are, he told himself, forbidding himself from finishing the thought. Clearly it was time for more champagne.

He was just about to go for a fresh drink to nurse his dejection when he noticed a striking young girl in the crowd moving along carefully, warily—for all the world like a little ginger cat stealing through a garden. He paused, staring at her from a distance with a sudden leap of his heart.

Is that my redhead?

Realizing it was indeed none other than she—the gunpowder girl who could ride standing astride her horse's back—he leaned his elbows on the rail, beginning to smile. *So, the little minx came after all.*

Ha. I knew I saw her looking at me, he thought in amused satisfaction. Well, it was a lady's prerogative to change her mind.

Rafe gazed at young Lady Daniela in heartfelt male appreciation. Her slender figure was clad in light blue, with a dark blue half-mask over her eyes. It did not conceal her identity from him. There was something so unique and rare about her he would have known her in a crowd ten times this size. Her upswept hair glowed a rich chestnut hue in the bright lighting from the chandeliers.

An obvious provincial, she looked adorably out of place in this glamorous, decadent crowd. He shook his head to himself, feeling a curious surge of fondness. Scanning the crowd around her, he saw no sign either of escort or chaperon. Wryly, he lifted a brow. Maybe she had finally caught the hint after all.

One thing he knew—she was out of her depth here, all right. Even now he saw Niccolo, one of his unscrupulous friends, presenting himself to her. In moments, Lady Daniela was backed against the nearby marble pillar before an onslaught of roguish flirtation.

Rafe watched for a couple minutes, his brow knit in consternation, then he smiled for her in the shadows as she extricated herself from Niccolo's attentions and moved on.

He decided he had better whisk her under his wing before one of the others pounced on her. God knew, if anyone around here was going to pounce on her, it was going to be him. Indeed, that sounded like exactly what he needed right now to cheer him up.

He called for Adriano and Tomas, who were sitting in the room behind him, smoking and arguing about horse racing. They quickly appeared at his side. He nodded toward the crowd.

"Do you see the red-haired girl in the blue dress near the palm over there?"

"Who is she?" Adriano asked.

"Her name is none of your concern," he chided with a narrow smile, never taking his stare from Daniela.

"Pretty thing," Tomas remarked, resting his elbows on the rail as he studied her.

"I want her," Rafe murmured. "Bring her to me."

Tomas looked over uncertainly at him, as though unsure if he was serious or joking. "You're sure about that? She looks awfully young. Things are different now that you're the regent, Rafe. You can't just . . ." His voice trailed off.

Rafe held a chilly, reproachful silence, not deigning to explain himself, nor breaking his fixed stare on the girl. He watched her move with lithe grace through the crowd. The caution in her furtive glances as she went sneaking along made him smile faintly to himself. What was the little minx up to?

Ah, but he'd always had a weakness for strays.

"Yes, Your Highness," Tomas said at last, sounding stung, but he withdrew with a slight bow. "Where should we bring her?"

"My bedchamber," Rafe added barely audibly.

"Naturally. Come on," Tomas muttered to Adriano.

Rafe wet his dry lips in anticipation. Would she fight or flee . . . or yield? *A good game, a very good game.*

His friends had only taken a few steps away when Adriano abruptly whirled around.

"What about Chloe?" he burst out with his usual air of torment.

Rafe continued watching the girl. "What about her?"

"She cares for you, Rafe!"

For a long moment, he didn't move, then he merely looked at Adriano, keenly feeling the huge gulf that existed now between him and even his closest friends.

True, he had often felt isolated in their midst, perhaps because of his rank or perhaps because so many of them had no vision for their lives beyond the pleasure of the moment, but at least he had never lacked for company. Now, no matter what comfortable posts he gave his loyal friends in service to Ascencion, he knew they could never contemplate the burden, the weight of responsibility, that rested solely on him. He was only beginning to grasp the full enormity of it himself. He was certainly in no mood to admit to Adriano or anyone else that his new role had him scared as hell.

"I'm waiting," he said coolly instead.

Adriano turned away in disgust. "I don't even know you anymore."

As they walked away, Rafe felt more alone in that moment than he ever had in his life. He didn't move from his spot at the rail, but his gaze fell and with a familiar, hollow feeling in his chest, he wondered if this was the prize he had been waiting for.

Dani had just slipped out of the ladies' lounge, where she had snagged an emerald necklace off a woman who had imbibed so much wine she had passed out on a divan. Slipping the necklace into her pocket, she made her way toward the exit, her heart pounding wildly, when two of the prince's friends stepped into her path.

She drew in her breath, the way blocked before her.

She didn't know the brown-haired one, who was smiling

uneasily at her, but the other was the raven-haired demi-god Adriano di Tadzio.

He looked her over in arrogant contempt. "Is this the one?" he asked his friend.

"Good evening, miss," said the brown-haired fellow with a short, gallant bow, though his smile was a trifle sheepish.

"Come with us," di Tadzio growled, grasping her about the wrist.

Horror flooded her. *My God—I'm caught!*

Before she could react, they each took one of her elbows and began propelling her toward the edge of the ballroom. "What is this about?" she cried frantically— guiltily.

"You'll see." When she tried to yank her arm away, Adriano merely tightened his grip.

She struggled, her heart pounding, the hair on the back of her neck standing on end in sheer terror. People began staring as she was all but dragged away.

"Please don't make a scene, miss," said the brown-haired man apologetically. "That would be embarrassing for all of us."

She fought to compose herself. "Am I under arrest?" she asked with forced calm.

They looked at each other and laughed.

"Am I?" she cried.

"Let's just say there's someone who'd like to make your acquaintance," Adriano growled. "Up the stairs. Walk!"

"Easy, di Tadzio! She's just a girl," said the other in annoyance.

Sensing a possible ally, Dani stopped on the steps and gave the brown-haired young man a beseeching look. "Please let me go. I won't make any trouble—"

Adriano pulled her hurt arm. "Come on, you little slut."

She gasped. "How dare you! You're hurting me!"

"Di Tadzio, there's no need to be rough!"

Adriano ignored the other man and leered at her. "Rough? Wait till *he* gets his hands on you. Then you'll see what rough is. He's a beast with his women, you know."

"Who?" Dani cried, aghast.

"Leave her alone, di Tadzio!" said the other in annoyance. "Ignore him, miss. He's temperamental and he's just trying to scare you. Nobody's going to harm you."

Adriano's gaze flicked derisively over her. "This, over Chloe Sinclair."

Dani said nothing, going cold with fear. She made a mental note of her surroundings and the path they took through the sumptuous corridors. Whatever their plans for her, she was determined to escape. The two men brought her to the third floor, where Adriano opened a door, staring at her with a smirk as the brown-haired man gestured her into the room.

"Please, wait! Tell me what's going on!" She struggled, wedging herself in the way as they tried to pull the door closed. "I haven't done anything wrong! Don't leave me here!"

Adriano laughed apathetically, but the brown-haired man shook his head and pressed her back into the room. "Don't worry, miss. You'll be compensated."

"What do you mean?"

But with a mild look of regret, he closed the door in her face. Crestfallen, Dani heard the lock click from the outside. She listened at the door and heard them arguing idly as they walked away. Her heart sank. She turned around slowly, leaned against the door, and surveyed her cell. She was alone.

Compared to the brightly lit ballroom, the chamber was dim in the flickering glow of one candle. She could make out a couch, a small table, and an armchair. A sitting room of some kind, she thought. A deep, heavy quiet hung in the room. Only the orchestra's music seeped up, muffled, through the floor.

Looking around, she saw a doorway and instantly wondered if she could escape through there. She ran for it, dodging the furniture in the dark, but as she flung into the doorway, she froze, her eyes widening.

Soft candlelight revealed an enormous bed with high, carved posts and a towering Baroque headboard inlaid with mirrors. Rose-colored satin sheets were turned back invitingly, and an opened bottle of wine with two glasses waited on the night table.

"Hello."

She nearly screamed. Leaping back a step, her gaze whipped around the large, dim bedchamber.

The commanding figure of a man sat in a wing chair in the shadowy far corner. As she watched, wide-eyed, he rose and sauntered slowly toward her, but even before she saw his face in the candlelight, she knew that combustible presence, that deep, caressing voice.

She stood mesmerized as Prince Rafael emerged from the gloom, princely and golden and huge, a mighty, fallen angel sauntering toward her from the shadows.

His stare was fixed on her. The candlelight contoured his angular face with shadow and flame, and reached tawny depths in his tarnished-gold hair. Chips of gold glowed in his marble-green eyes, and though his sculpted face was austere, his mouth was voluptuous. She gazed at him, transfixed, as he slowly approached, hands in pockets. Moving casually and with deceptive laziness, he crossed the room to her, advancing relentlessly until she found herself flattened back against the doorframe.

He towered over her, mere inches away, his beauty and sheer size humbling her, his aura of physical strength overwhelming her.

She dropped her head, her breathing shallow and quick.

Flustered, confused, she could not bear to look up at him. Her whole body blushed, going hot, cold, hot again under his unnerving, silent perusal.

Had he found out she was the Masked Rider? If Gianni had been bullied into revealing her identity, surely the child would have warned her.

What should she do? Confess? Throw herself on his mercy? *Grovel—to him? Never!* she vowed, finding courage enough at last to tilt her head back and hold his gaze, though inwardly she quaked. Until she knew for certain she was caught, she would blasted well keep her mouth shut.

"I'm so pleased you decided to come, Daniela. I was having a dismal birthday."

Prince Rafael slid his right hand out of his pocket and traced his fingertip over her blue satin half-mask with a tiny caress down the slope of her nose. His fingertip trailed enticingly over her lips, her chin, and down along the line of her throat. "Do you know," he murmured, "what I want for my birthday?"

"W-wasn't a country enough for you?" she whispered, trembling at his touch.

He smiled faintly with a satyric glint in his eye. She looked away, flustered and blushing, her heart beating rapidly in her throat. Was this his manner of punishing her for her crimes? It was impossible to tell what he was thinking, what he intended, what he knew, but the spell of his potency made her head spin.

"I have a confession to make," he whispered. "I'm a little drunk, I'm afraid, and can't be held responsible for my actions."

"Good Lord!" Paling, she tried to back away from him, but could only flatten herself back against the doorframe. His big, lean body blocked her escape.

He gave her an intimate half-smile. "That said, may I

kiss you? You see, I am really . . . dying to kiss you, Daniela."

"S-sir! Your Highness!"

"A royal command, my lady. I am your sovereign lord, am I not?" he asked softly.

She lowered her head, heart pounding, her cheeks hot with shame. "I—I am not that kind of girl."

"You'd make an exception for me, wouldn't you, sweet?"

"I will *not*." She jerked her chin upward again and glared at him, angry and frightened.

He smiled enigmatically, the calculating intelligence in his eyes churning, layer upon layer of complexity. He lifted her trembling hand from her side and raised it to his lips with flawless self-assurance. He paused, smiling slightly as he held her gaze.

"What I want for my birthday—what I really need," he mused, "is a lovely new mistress. She must have red hair and stunning eyes of aquamarine, and she must know how to make gunpowder. Know anyone who might fit the bill?"

"You are shocking!" she breathed.

"My dear," he whispered, "I have not yet begun to shock you." With that, he dipped his tawny head and kissed her hand—not her knuckles, but the juncture of her thumb—and she gasped as she felt the tip of his tongue flick lightly into the V of her fist. She pulled her hand to her chest and stared up at him in openmouthed bewilderment.

He smiled serenely, a dangerous sparkle in his eyes. "Would you like a drink before we begin? The wine has had a nice chance to breathe and I daresay you look like you could use it." He turned away, strolling to the small night table where the wine waited.

Dani was frozen like a garden stature.

Staring at his broad back that tapered down to his lean waist, she felt faint.

He was toying with her. Surely. He knew she was the

Masked Rider and he was just cruelly toying with her, cat and mouse. *Wasn't he?*

She heard the wine splash softly into one glass, then the other.

"Has the cat got your tongue, my dear? Well, no matter. I didn't bring you here for conversation, did I?" He cast her a roguish wink and held out the glass of wine to her. "Come along, take it."

If he had been Lucifer offering her a glass of human blood, she couldn't have cringed from him more.

Abruptly she found her voice. "What is the meaning of this?"

He chuckled softly and sat on the bed, loosening his cravat. "My, you are young, aren't you? How old are you, Lady Daniela?"

"One and twenty."

"You look sixteen. Eighteen at the most."

Heart pounding, she glanced at the turned-back sheets, the chilled wine, then at him—the confirmed libertine. She blinked in disbelief. *Could it be true? Was she in the clear?* She had seen him up there on that narrow gallery, surveying the crowd. Was that what he had been doing up there—selecting his prey?

She nearly laughed aloud in disbelief. All those beautiful women down there and he had picked her? He must be drunk. But Lord, he was gorgeous enough to tempt her.

As though he had read her mind, he gave her a lazy, knowing half-smile, trailing his wineglass teasingly across his lips, then he took a long drink.

Rather fascinated as he swallowed, she watched the lift and fall of his Adam's apple where he had undone his cravat. His throat was golden, as was the inch or so of his chest visible in the V at the top of his pristine white shirt.

He lowered his glass from his lips and licked them slowly as his gaze moved seductively over her. She leaned back weakly against the doorframe, disturbed by a strange, quivering sensation in her belly. The room was much too warm, so hot it was hard to think. All she could seem to focus on was the simple realization that she was not, thank God, under arrest.

Yet.

He crooked a finger at her, calling softly to her in a velvety murmur. "I'm waiting, ginger cat. Come here and let me stroke you."

His invitation jolted her out of his spell with a small gasp of shock. "Good Lord, I'm getting out of here," she muttered. Spinning away, she marched into the other room on legs that quaked beneath her.

"Only if you can walk through locked doors, I'm afraid," he called after her in wicked mirth. "Go on, shout as loud as you please. No one is going to help you."

She banged on the door. "Somebody let me out of here! Help! Let me out of here!" she yelled, jiggling the doorknob for all she was worth. She suddenly remembered her hairpin, which she had used to free Gianni. She pulled it out of her coif, but try as she might, her hands were shaking too badly to pick the lock.

In the other room, she could hear him laughing. "What's wrong, Daniela?" he called. "Was it that peasant lad that you wanted? My dear girl, why settle for him when you can have me for your protector? Really, have you no feeling for your rank? One takes affront."

She stopped and turned from the locked door, glaring over her shoulder. Now he would insult Mateo as well as her? That did it.

Leaving her hairpin in the keyhole, she marched back to give him a piece of her mind. "What a high opinion you have of yourself, Your Highness! As it so happens, Mateo is my *friend*, and I neither want nor need a *protector*. What a disgusting idea! It so happens I am quite capable of protecting myself, and believe me," she shouted because she couldn't hold back, "you're not such a prize! Furthermore, you cannot simply go around seducing people whenever it strikes your fancy!"

"Of course I can," he said idly, swirling his wine in the glass.

"But why did you have to pick me?" she cried.

He smiled broadly and nodded. "Yes, it is a great honor, is it not?"

"One I would prefer you bestowed on someone else!"

He began unbuttoning his waistcoat, laughing at her as he shook his head. "Ah, my little cabbage, how many virgins do you really think are down there?"

"Cabbage!"

"It's only an expression."

"I have a name!"

"I'm sure you do. Come drink your wine. You'll be glad you did. It's been a while since I've had a virgin," he mused aloud. "What a treat. I was afraid I was going to have to buy one."

"*Buy one?* Oh, you are despicable!"

He gave her an apprehensive frown, yet there was a twinkle in his eyes that made her wonder if this was all a joke to him. "You're not going make this difficult, are you?" he asked. "I should hate to have to restrain you. Ah, well." He opened the drawer of the night table. "There should be some velvet cording in here somewhere. . . ."

Dani suddenly narrowed her eyes as he dug through the drawer and laid a gleaming silver key on the table beside the bed, next to the sweating wine bottle. Aha, he wasn't very bright after all, to have left it sitting out where she could snatch it. Cabbage, indeed!

Rafael shut the drawer. "Well, it's not in here. I must have used it on somebody else."

"Alas," she retorted, smugly noting that he was too

drunk to remember to put the key back where she could not see it. Now all she had to do was get to it. Her path would take her dangerously near him, but having already had difficulty with her hairpin, the key was her best hope.

Holding her elbows behind her back, she swayed nonchalantly toward the bed table. In silence, he watched her edging closer. He looked not at all fooled as to her true intent, but he merely patted his muscled thigh.

"Why don't you come over here and sit on my lap?" he cajoled her softly.

Her cheeks flooded with heat. "Why?"

His voice was wicked, soft. "I want to tell you a bedtime story."

"It isn't bedtime, Prince Rafael," she said with a slight, unwilling smile.

"Delightful," he murmured, watching her. "I believe that is the first smile you've given me." The look in his eyes was changing, the color turning dusky green.

When he called to her again, his voice was velvet, nigh impossible to resist. "Come to me, Daniela. We'll take it very slowly. I promise. It will be wondrous."

She glanced at him from under her lashes, nearly tempted. "I don't know. . . ."

"One kiss," he whispered, and as she held his stare, the playful look faded from his eyes entirely. Leaning forward where he sat on the edge of the bed, he rested his elbows on his knees and interlocked his fingers, staring at her. "You're very beautiful, actually."

"And you are a silver-tongued liar. It was wicked of you to bring me up here." Heart racing, she trailed her fingertips over the slightly dusty surface of the nighttable as she came dangerously near him.

"I know. But I wanted to be alone with you." He watched her with an expression of quiet intensity. "You don't believe me. Why not?"

With another step, the night table was by her hip, the key close enough to grab. "Well, there is Ms. Sinclair," she pointed out.

He dropped his head with a vexed groan. "There are always Ms. Sinclairs."

"Do you love her?"

"That wouldn't be very smart," he said flatly.

"You don't want me, I'm sure. I'm nothing special. Let me leave. Please? You could have anyone else down there. . . ."

He lifted his head and gazed at her for a long moment with a distant, shadowed flickering in his eyes. "You move beautifully, Daniela," he murmured. "You are as graceful as the wind on the sea, and as shy as a dove, aren't you?"

She froze, staring at him, inexplicably frightened all of a sudden, but not in a physical sense.

"It's all right," he whispered as he stood, holding her gaze.

Her heart was pounding. The key was within reach, but she was frozen like a doe before the hunter as he came to her, touching her shoulder, turning her to him. He drew her gently into his arms and enfolded her in his embrace, brushing his cheek softly against her hair. She closed her eyes in the drugging shock of recognition, for the feel of him against her echoed back from a thousand dreams.

She opened her hand upon the lightweight wool of his lapel, barely daring to touch him, while her mind whirled slowly. *He is holding me. Prince Rafael is holding me.* A dream, of course. She would wake tomorrow and forge on alone again, but for now she drank in the warm strength of his arms around her, the heady scent of his cologne.

She heard the soft sound of his sigh above her as he cradled her in his embrace, and she marveled at how natural, how right it felt to nestle against him this way. She felt his large, warm, gentle hands slowly caress her, up the length of her back from her waist. Then he tilted her chin upward with his fingertips.

Her heart hammered in her chest. Her eyes were wide. Her world tilted as Rafael gazed at her.

"I should like very much to kiss you," he said quietly.

Her eyes filled with anguished pleading. She tried to shake her head no, but he only nodded yes, reassuring her with a small, exquisitely tender smile.

She despaired, staring miserably at him. Rafael closed his eyes, lowered his head, and kissed her.

The caress of his lips was as soft as the beat of a butterfly's wings. His mouth was warm and silky atop hers. Her eyes drifted closed and a sigh rose from the depths of her spirit. She felt his lips curve in a smile against her mouth at the shivery sound. He pulled back only slightly.

"That wasn't so bad, was it?" he whispered.

She made a sound of distress in her throat, refusing to open her eyes, despising him for the longing he had released in her with but one chaste kiss. Then he pulled her more firmly into his arms, sliding one arm around her waist to bring her closer to his body. He pressed a kiss to her forehead as though she were a child, then he kissed her brow, her eyes, her cheek, her ear. She swayed dizzily against him, her chest heaving. He steadied her in his arms, holding her as carefully as though she were made of fine china. Ducking his head, he began kissing the curve of her neck, caressing her throat lightly with his other hand.

It was the most deliciously dizzying sensation she had ever experienced, his lips grazing her skin like moist satin, his heated breath tickling under her ear. She took him into her arms, unable to resist, closing her eyes as she held him to her. She touched his long, golden hair in wonder, slowly stroking its velvety length. His strong, long-fingered hands caressed her back, her arms, her sides. Her skin felt fiery, impossibly sensitive. She was weightless, lost in clouds of bliss, and shaking. His caresses turned hot, urgent.

When he gathered her closer still, a shock of pleasure rushed through her at the contact of their bodies pressing together every inch down the length of them both. She heard her own quivery sigh and his hungry growl in his throat. He gripped her buttocks, pulling her up hotly against him. She cried out softly, a dazed, single note of confusion, desire, and need.

"Ah, God, you are so sweet," he panted, kissing his way back up to her mouth.

She felt him trembling as he captured her face between his hands and kissed her mouth again and again, coaxing her lips apart. Confused, she yielded tentatively, and then he showed her what kissing really was. His mouth slanted over hers and she felt his tongue meld with hers, stroking, dancing. Surprise burst through her, and pleasure, and then Rafael was ravishing her with a deep, slow kiss that shattered her where she stood clinging weakly to him.

Little remained of her self-control, but with the small ounce of will she still retained, she was appalled at herself. How could she let herself fall under his spell this way? She tried to turn her face away but he gently brought her back with the soft but authoritative pressure of his fingertips upon her jaw.

"Don't be afraid, sweet," he said in a ragged whisper, smiling slightly, his breathing deep. "It's nicer if you kiss me back, you know."

"I don't want to," she said, a breathless lie.

"You don't?"

"No!"

His soft laugh brimmed with gentle chiding. "Look at me, Daniela."

She dragged her eyes open mutinously and found him gazing down at her with a faint, tender smile. Though his lips were moist and full with kissing, his eyes were like a green sea, storm-tossed with desire.

"What?" she muttered, nearly sulking.

"Has no one ever kissed you before?" he asked very, very gently.

She dropped her head, turning scarlet. How mortifying for him to guess. She stood trembling in his arms, head down. She had never felt more vulnerable. But he touched her under her chin, lifting her gaze to his once more. As his stare moved wistfully over her face, his expression turned melancholy.

"What a lovely, innocent creature you are." He caressed her cheek with one knuckle, his gaze following his touch. Then he slowly shoved his hands in his pockets, as though to stop himself from reaching for her again. He stepped back rather awkwardly and put his head down. "Maybe you would like to just . . . go for a walk with me. I could show you the gardens. They're beautiful by moonlight. We could talk. . . ."

His voice trailed off as she stared at him in wonder.

"Ah, never mind," he said in a low, heavy voice. "What a bloody debacle— I'm truly . . . I'm truly sorry about this, Lady Daniela. You are a lady, but I felt . . . I don't know. I'm sorry. Go, please, you're better off. Take the key on the table. I put it there for you."

"You intended for me to escape?"

"God's truth, I don't know what I intended." He closed his eyes for a moment and when he opened them again, they were full of naked loneliness, his slight smile one of misery. "Go," he whispered. "This hall of lost souls is no place for you."

But she didn't flee when he gave her the chance.

"Maybe no place for you, either," she said softly.

He met her gaze without a trace of arrogance, silent for a moment. "Perhaps I have nowhere else to go."

She felt her reckless heart reach out to him. Holding her breath at her own foolhardiness, she took a step toward him and slid her hand up his chest.

He watched her, his jaw clenched, as though he struggled to hold himself back. Then she heard his breath catch with desire in his throat as she curled her fingers around his warm nape. Pulling him down to her, she kissed his lips gently for a long moment.

He slipped his arms around her waist, pulling her into his embrace and returning her kisses in smoldering desire— desire that exploded in seconds into a raging blaze of passion. She wrapped her arms around his neck, tasting him again and again in glorious abandon. She clenched his hair in her hands, caressed his smoothly shaved face. His answering need was so overwhelming she was barely aware of him maneuvering her toward his sprawling, mirrored bed.

Ever so gently, he eased her down until she sat on the edge of it, her body weak and trembling with the stormy, newfound emotion of desire. He sank to his knees before her, never pausing in kissing her. Slowly his kisses traveled down her neck to her chest. His hand captured her breast and his kisses moved lower. She dropped her head back in bliss, cradling him to her as his warm breath penetrated her gown, molding soft silk to the tautened, sensitive tip. He teethed her lightly through the silk; breathing his name, she arched against him, letting his body slide nearer between her thighs.

"I want you, Daniela. I want you," he whispered. His deft, elegant hands caressed her chest and throat, but she had not even realized he had smoothly unfastened her gown until he began slipping her sleeve down over her right shoulder, kissing the crook of her neck.

In a sudden flash of horror she came to her senses, remembering her bandaged right arm.

Too late.

He had already moved her sleeve lower, and now he saw. He was frowning at her bandaged wound. "Daniela, what did you do to your arm . . . ?" But his voice trailed away.

She stared at him, her heart in her throat.

He furrowed his brow, glanced up into her eyes, then froze with a dawning look of thunderstruck recognition.

Dani's eyes widened with fright at the fury that flooded his dark green eyes.

"You," he whispered as though the breath had been knocked from him.

Everything seemed to move slowly. She pulled out of his grasp, shoved past him off the bed, and ran, yanking her sleeve up over her shoulder again. She had barely taken two steps before he clutched her dress from behind.

"Get back here!" he roared, rising to his feet.

She shrieked, but he didn't let go of her dress, and suddenly it tore at the sleeve. She looked frantically over her shoulder and saw him staring at her gunshot wound, which told him beyond a doubt that she was the Masked Rider.

"You! Goddamn it!" he bellowed. "Not possible!"

"Leave me alone!" she screamed.

When he reached for her, she threw a punch, but he caught her fist and spun her, snatching her arm up behind her back. His grip didn't hurt, but was implacable.

She thrashed before him. "Let me go, you heathen brute!"

"What are you doing here?" he demanded furiously. "How *dare* you come here?"

The grandfather clock in the sitting room began chiming midnight with long rolling bongs. As they struggled, both of them suddenly froze when a huge boom sounded in the distance. The blast rattled the windowpanes and shook the paintings on the walls.

Mateo and the others were making their escape! she

thought wildly. She had failed to create the needed distraction—because she had been too busy in here *kissing him*!

"I said let me go!"

Spinning about face, she brought her knee up hard between his thighs.

He yelped.

"Serves you right, you bad, wicked rake!" she cried as he doubled over to the floor.

With a garbled cry of fury, Rafael grasped for the hem of her skirt, but she yanked away, mere inches beyond his fingers. Grabbing the key off the table, as the final chime of midnight tolled, she fled.

≈ CHAPTER ≈
SIX

With a speed born of pure survival instinct, Dani ran.

Dodging the costumed guests in her way, leaping down the marble steps two at a time, she raced from the halls of decadence as though the devil were at her heels. She fled past the jugglers and the peacocks on the lawn all the way down the drive.

The guards at the gate didn't hinder her exit. Her lungs were burning, but she forced herself onward, running the half-mile down the road to the city, until at last she tore into the piazza, only to find herself in the midst of a full-tilt riot.

Chest heaving, she stood there in her torn ball gown looking around her in disbelief.

The blasts of Mateo's bombs had set off the mob as well. Already suspicious about the king's unheralded exit, the crowd that had gathered for the hanging in the morning had taken the explosion as their cue, rising up with a roar against the soldiers patrolling the square. Dani turned and saw a four-foot hole blown in one wall of the jail. It was still smoking. In the other direction, another fire had been set in a city already parched with drought. People were jeering the soldiers as though they no longer feared their bayonets. Others had begun looting the front row of shops, while another group, in a seething frenzy, was working to pull down the gallows which the prince's men had built earlier that day.

"Stop it! Stop it!" Dani heard herself shouting furiously, but no one listened. She brushed a strand of hair back from her face and looked around angrily.

Any moment now, one of these hotheaded *paisanos* was going to say or do the wrong thing to the heavily armed soldiers and this skirmish was going to turn into a bloodbath—and if those fires weren't put out immediately while they were still a managcable size, the townspeople were all doomed. She could only hope that Mateo and the others had escaped, as planned, and would soon be away on the boat bound for mainland Italy.

Dani kept yelling at the people around her to calm down, but it quickly became clear that the Masked Rider was the only one who might possibly carry the authority with this crowd to command order. Already pushing through fighting knots of people, she made her way to the livery stable where she had left her equipment and her horse.

Quickly she got rid of her ruined blue gown and changed clothes in the stall, hiding behind her horse. She saddled her horse, then swallowed hard as she pulled on the infamous black satin mask, knowing that the moment she appeared as the Masked Rider she was going to be arrested. She had no choice. She had caused enough trouble tonight and she had to prevent the outbreak of violence.

Several moments later, the Masked Rider came galloping out from a side alley to burst into the throng.

"Look!" people began shouting.

Dani's gelding reared, but she managed to keep her seat, shouting in boyish tones at the top of her lungs, "Peace, people! There is nothing to fear. Calm down and go back to your homes!" She urged her skittish horse through the crowd. As tense moments passed, she saw that she was beginning to have an effect. "Don't just stand there! Go help those soldiers put out the fires!" she angrily ordered them.

People fell back from her path, staring up at her, touching her horse as though for good luck as she passed, but the soldiers had also seen her and warily edged closer. She knew her time was running out.

"Listen to me! Go home to your families!" she repeated emphatically. "Behave the way King Lazar would want you to!"

"The prince has thrown him aside!" someone yelled.

"Who told you that?" she demanded. "Do you have proof?"

The man said nothing, merely giving the crowd and Dani a sullen look.

"I thought not. Go home and quit spreading these lies." She moved on. Nearing the newly built gallows, she found a small crowd of young peasant men trying to tear it down. "They can lock you up for destroying government property," she warned.

"Whose side are you on?" one shouted at her.

Before she could answer, a familiar voice reached her. "Dan!"

She looked over and turned ashen beneath her mask to see Mateo shoving through the mob. *Oh, no! Why is he still here?*

Glancing fearfully in the other direction, she saw more soldiers striding relentlessly toward her, still a short distance away. When they came for her, Mateo would be recaptured.

Without a second's hesitation, she urged her horse toward her friend and blasted him with her fury. "What the hell are you still doing here?"

"Waiting for you! Come on, the wagon's just at the edge

of the square!" he hollered, his brown eyes fiery, his dark curls tousled.

"Damn you, Mateo!" She swung down off her horse. "That wasn't in our plan! You know I can't leave Grandfather. Now get on this horse and ride!"

"Do you think your grandfather would want to see you stay here and hang? I'm not leaving you here to die. You're coming to Naples with us." He grabbed her wrist and started dragging her away.

"Let go of me!" she shouted, wrenching her hand from his grasp. "You go, now! Your family needs you! I'll keep the soldiers busy, just get away! Go, please. They're coming—"

And suddenly their time was up. Prince Rafael's soldiers were upon them.

Dani drew her rapier with a cry and stepped in front of Mateo. "Let him go! It's me you want!"

The soldiers refused; Mateo scoffed at her attempt, and the minute her heedlessly brave friend threw the first punch, all hell broke loose. The rowdy and riled Ascencioners began brawling with the prince's soldiers throughout the square.

Mateo was holding his own, but big Rocco came lumbering into the fray to watch his back. Dani was caught in the middle, buffeted back and forth like a buoy in a rough tide, thrown about by the press and crush of the much larger men all around her. Her sword was no good at close quarters. She cast it off, resorting to fists, elbows, and kicks, dodging lightly away from savage blows struck at her.

Suddenly a blow caught her in the face, blindsiding her. She went reeling, tripped back, and landed on the flagstone with the breath knocked out of her.

For a moment she lay there gasping like a fish caught on dry sand, then she groaned as the soldiers came and scraped her up off the ground, clamping her in manacles with the others.

Within fifteen minutes, Mateo, Alvi, and Rocco Gabbiano were back in jail.

This time, Dani was with them.

The ball carried on, the reveling guests oblivious to the kingdom's brush with rebellion in the city square not even a mile away.

Rafe had been apprised of the situation, however, and waited tensely for news. He stood at the railing above the ballroom and threw back a draught of whiskey. He was angry, tense about the riot in progress, with a host of questions about that infuriating redhead swarming in his mind.

Who was she and how the hell had she done it? How had she breached security? The peasant child, Gianni, was gone, of course. Why had she come here, risking her neck to free him? What was her plan? Had she orchestrated the riot?

Impatient for word of her, he pushed away from the railing and walked back into the room, where his friends were clamoring for her blood. Most had been robbed by the Masked Rider. The news that the outlaw in question was a young girl had humiliated them to the point of rage. They had all been bested and wanted revenge. Listening to them chilled Rafe's blood.

"I'll be there to see her hang!" Niccolo said, though he had been flirting with her less than an hour ago, a fact that probably only intensified his venom.

"They had better catch her this time!" Adriano burst out. "And when they do, I hope you are not thinking of letting the little bitch off the hook, Rafe. She's a menace!"

"She's a marvel," he replied in a low voice that went unheard in their raucous outpouring of burned vanity. *The purest kiss he'd ever tasted.*

His own pride smarted along with theirs, but Rafe did not know what to think. Daniela Chiaramonte was a puzzle he urgently needed to solve. She enraged, confounded, baffled him—yet she had wrung from him a great deal of grudging respect, for the girl had nerve the likes of which he had rarely run across in either sex. *And to think, until he had tasted her tonight, she had never been kissed. . . .*

Why, she must think him the greatest damned fool of them all, panting after her like a dog, he thought with a scowl. She probably thought him an utter joke. It would not stand! The girl needed to be put in her place.

"Who is she, Rafe?" asked the scholarly Viscount Elan Berelli, the most prudent and sensible of his friends.

My nemesis, he thought in wry annoyance. "A Chiaramonte. Her name is Daniela."

Elan furrowed his brow and pushed his spectacles up higher onto the bridge of his nose. "Chiaramonte? Wasn't there a Marquis Chiaramonte who ruined himself with drink and gambling when we were boys?"

"I wonder if that was her father," Rafe said with a frown.

Just then, there was a sudden brisk knock at the door. Tomas answered it.

A lieutenant of the Royal Guard saluted, short of breath in his haste. "Your Highness, the fires are out and the riot has been averted. They have been taken."

Rafe stepped toward him eagerly. "All of them?"

"The little child escaped us."

"But the Masked Rider?"

"In custody, sir."

Hearty sounds of satisfaction broke out in the room, as if the young lords' favorite horse had just come from behind to win the derby. Rafe glanced uneasily at his friends, disturbed by the rising savagery in their tones as they urged on one another's anger.

"Let's go get her!" Federico bayed like a hound on the hunt.

"Settle down," Rafe sharply commanded, then turned

back to the lieutenant. "Tell your men well done. Forget the child. He's of no consequence."

"Shall we interrogate the prisoners, Your Highness?"

"Leave that to me. Advise your men that I don't want these prisoners abused . . . and confine the Masked Rider in solitary for the night."

"Rafe!" Adriano hissed in protest. "Don't give her preferential treatment!"

He turned to his friend, lowering his voice. "Am I to let her spend the night with the thugs of the kingdom as her bunk mates? There won't be anything left of her by morning. For God's sakes, she's a virgin."

"A virgin? Throw her to us, then!" Niccolo cried with a drunken laugh, slapping his thigh at his own jest.

Rafe stared at him, then looked at the others, feeling as though he were seeing them for the first time. He thought of Daniela's innocent eyes of clear aquamarine. The louder they crowed for her blood, the more urgent grew his deep-seated impulse to protect her, intensifying to an almost panicked need, especially now that Elan had reminded him of that minor scandal a dozen or so years ago, which he suspected had been the ruin of Daniela's father—and her family fortunes.

He was annoyed as hell at the girl, but whatever she might have done to him or them, she was young and valiant and beautiful—and the note in their voices was ugly.

"We'll teach her a lesson she'll never forget!"

"You'll not touch her," Rafe said in steely quiet, glaring at them.

Some of them stopped laughing abruptly. Others wore sudden, sobered looks of surprise at his curt rebuke.

Warily, he turned back to the lieutenant. "Have the Masked Rider brought to the interrogation chamber at seven tomorrow morning—provided she left that part of the jail intact?" he added dryly.

"Only the west wall was damaged, Your Highness. The masons have already inspected it and said it can be easily repaired."

"Well, that's refreshing. You have your orders."

"Yes, Sire!" the man clipped out, saluting.

Rafe nodded his dismissal, tamping down the urge to have Daniela brought from the rough and dangerous jail immediately. It would be begging for trouble to go too softly on her. Besides, by holding her there overnight, at least he could be sure she wouldn't escape again, nor could his enraged companions get at her. He hoped that when the liquor wore off, their tempers would cool. As for Lady Daniela, it was going to be a long night for his little friend alone in the dark, wondering and agonizing over her fate, but by morning perhaps she'd be more compliant.

He looked over to find Adriano shaking his head at him in disgust. "I can't believe you're taking her side over ours."

"I haven't taken any sides yet. It's for the courts to decide."

"I know you. You're going to find some way to let her off the hook, because you can't resist a tolerable-looking female. Don't get caught up in whatever lies she may have told you—she's a criminal, Rafe! She's a thief! We've been here before, don't you remember?"

"Watch it," he growled, unwilling to admit that Adriano had hit his fears precisely on the mark. It would be all too easy for that girl with her big, innocent eyes and soft, vulnerable mouth to take advantage of him—and yet the fact that he could not predict her next move or control her fiery will excited him intensely.

"Don't you see how she's already started manipulating you? If you help this little wench, she's just going to take you for whatever she can get. Just like Jul—"

"Do not speak that name in my hearing," he warned

fiercely, cutting Adriano off just as the door opened and Don Arturo burst into the room, followed by several of the other old counselors.

"Oh, for God's sake," Rafe muttered under his breath. "What are you hags doing here?"

"There are fires and a riot in the city tonight, Your Highness!" the prime minister announced, marching over to him with the air of a man clearly prepared to take charge. "We thought you should know—if you're not too busy entertaining yourself!"

"The fires are out and the riot has already been put down," Rafe said with elaborate patience, ignoring the insult with stalwart diplomacy. "Return to your homes."

"I should think not!" he exclaimed in self-righteous indignation. "Your Highness, you have been in power mere hours and have no experience with political crisis. The cabinet will manage everything from here on in. His Majesty would expect no less of us. Run along and enjoy your party. After all, it is your birthday," he added under his breath, glancing at the other old dons.

They scoffed knowingly.

"My lord, he's going to let that filthy bandit woman off the hook, even though she robbed us all and gave away our gold!" Adriano whined to the prime minister. "Can you talk reason to him?"

Don Arturo looked up at Rafe shrewdly. "Yes, I heard the Masked Rider was captured. A female, you say?"

"A Chiaramonte," Rafe warned softly. "Don't any of you see that everything she's done has benefited other people? I saw her house, her dress. She didn't spend a cent of that gold on herself, and I daresay you all could spare it."

"The law does not care for motive and circumstance, Your Highness," said Don Arturo, pouncing on this new development with a fighting gleam in his eyes that said he would take any reason to combat Rafe now that the king had gone. "It is your duty, as I'm sure you are aware, to hang this lawbreaker."

"I know my duty," he said in a low, stoic tone. He also knew that his father's counselors were just waiting for him to make one wrong move so they could take power from him before he wrecked the kingdom for his father.

Just then, Orlando joined them, slipping into the room with a grave nod to the men, then he sent Rafe a questioning look. Orlando was family: The presence of at least one sure ally bolstered Rafe's confidence.

"Gentlemen," he said, lifting his chin, "rest assured that when I have heard all the facts, I will decide Lady Daniela's fate. Until then, I am hardly going to send a lynch mob after her. You all just need to calm down," he added in annoyance.

"*Calm down,* while justice is being trampled underfoot?"

"That is a gross exaggeration."

"I think not!" The prime minister drew himself up to his diminutive height. "If you fail to uphold the law *yet again*, Your Highness, do not count on me as your ally!"

Rafe absorbed this and was silent for a long moment, staring at the floor. "Don Arturo, you disappoint me." He lifted his sober gaze to the prime minister's face. "I had hoped you could rise above your personal grudge against me for the good of Ascencion, but I see now you still blame me for your nephew's death. I know he was like a son to you, but I wasn't the one who killed him."

A stunned silence dropped upon the room.

Even Rafe's wilder companions looked shocked. Giorgio di Sansevero had been a friend to them all, and his name was too painful to mention.

Everyone was staring at Rafe.

Don Arturo trembled with ire. "You were there. You could have saved him, but you didn't, and to my thinking, it's the same as if you were the one who cut him down in cold blood. You knew as well as anyone that dueling was against the law, but you didn't stop him. No. Instead, you were his *second*," he said bitterly.

"He was my friend. I could not refuse his request."

"He would be alive here today if you had done your duty. He was a boy," the man wrenched out.

"As was I."

"You could have stopped him. He looked up to you like they all do!"

"I tried to stop him. Giorgio wanted blood and I wasn't about to tell him how to live his life."

"Dueling is against the law!" he cried again in anguish. "You ignored the law then, and it seems that you will ignore it now! Who will have to die this time for your entertainment?"

"How dare you?" Rafe bellowed, taking a step toward him.

"Gentlemen, gentlemen," Orlando broke in smoothly, pushing his way between them. He gave Rafe a hard look, then turned to Don Arturo. "Let us behave like civilized men."

The duke's interruption diverted some of the angry tension that vibrated in the room. He looked around at the others. "My dear Don Arturo, His Majesty left Prince Rafael in governance of Ascencion for a reason. Of course His Highness knows his duty. There is no question of that. For duty's sake, loyalty's, indeed, for his very pride's sake I have no doubt that my cousin will serve justice. When this woman has been condemned to death, the people will rest content that he is as trustworthy a leader as King Lazar himself."

Rafe looked over at him in bafflement. "Are you daft? The people love the Masked Rider. If I hang that girl, they'll hate me even more."

Orlando looked taken aback, then smiled patiently. Rafe felt his anger climbing at his cousin's easy manner. Rafe liked Orlando, but kin or no, he could never quite bring himself to trust the man.

"If you don't hang her, Rafe, who's going to mind your authority?" Orlando asked reasonably. "I really don't see that you have any choice."

"I damned well do have a choice," he said forcefully. "I am the prince regent, am I not? A fact you all seem determined to forget." With a look of disgust, he turned away from them, racking his brain.

Hang Daniela? he thought as the reality of it sank in. He would sooner smash some priceless Hellenistic vase or burn the Mona Lisa. How could he destroy someone so young, so much better, finer of spirit than himself? He had wanted to wrap her sweet skin in silk and cover her body in kisses, but now he must send her to the executioner. He flinched at the thought. He was the supreme judicial authority on Ascencion in his father's absence and he alone had the power to save her. Yet they were right. Who would respect his authority if he let her go?

He would continue to be naught but a joke in the eyes of the world, playing the fool again for a woman. Besides, what kind of precedent would it set for future criminal cases if he pardoned her? *Ah, ginger cat, what a bind you have put me in now.*

"Leave me," he murmured, needing time alone to think. "All of you."

"Your Highness—" Don Arturo began.

"Goddamn it, I will be obeyed," he uttered low, in fury. Out of all patience with their defiance, he whirled around to face them, his voice a whip. He took a step toward them in regal wrath. "Get out of my house, all of you!" he thundered as they scrambled toward the door as though a lion had been unleashed in the room. "Elan, go downstairs and tell that damned orchestra to put their instruments away. Get these people out of here! The party is over. It's over. Do you hear me, you useless, lazy bastards?" he shouted at his friends. *"The party is over!"*

Rafe stood in place, his chest heaving.

They were gone in a moment and he was alone.

He raked his hand through his hair, noticing that it shook slightly with fury and, if he was honest, with a trace of fear. He felt woefully inadequate for the burdens now resting on his shoulders. Riots. Fires. Droughts.

Courtiers rallying against him. Friends who were suddenly transformed to barbaric strangers—or had they always been that way and he too lulled by pleasure and music and boredom to notice?

Shaken, disappointed in everyone he knew, including himself, he walked over to the liquor cabinet and poured himself a small glass of whiskey. He tossed it back and felt it burn a fiery path down to his belly. He wiped his mouth with the back of his hand, then his grim gaze fell upon the tray where the portraits of the five princesses were arrayed. His friends had been making witless jokes all evening about them.

He stared at their meaningless faces.

Daniela Chiaramonte must obviously hang. No doubt.

He had felt this bullheaded, disastrous need to save a damsel in distress once before. He would merely ignore it, he resolved, for he knew his own idiotic chivalry was not to be trusted. Daniela was not the sort of woman one dared rescue. She would probably slice his hand off if he reached out to help her. No. He would let her go to the gallows just as he should have let Julia go to debtor's prison all those years ago. She had brought it on herself. Adriano was right. They were both thieves.

With a sudden, strangled growl of pain, he struck out, sweeping the five princesses off the tabletop. The frames went crashing to the floor. He looked up from their scattered, vacant smiles and met his own tempestuous glare in the elegant mirror.

I need answer to no one, she had said, so wild and free with the starlight on her hair. *It is merely the choice I have made.*

Rafe dropped his chin almost to his chest. Now he, too, must choose.

Dani huddled in total blackness on a moth-eaten pallet on the floor, hugging her knees to her chest. With her forehead resting on her bent knees, she hadn't realized she had finally dozed off until the lock banged in the iron door of her windowless cell.

The clanging noise roused her instantly, still half-immersed in her longing dream about the beautiful water dancing in Rafael's fountain in front of the pleasure dome. In her dream, she had been unable to get to it, though she was straining on her knees, crawling, weeping for it in helpless frustration, aching for that towering silvery plume of sweet water. It was just out of reach, for the chain around her ankle had stopped her a few feet short of it, but all she longed for was to plunge her mouth and hands into it to slake her agonizing thirst.

The dream fled as she woke, but the thirst remained.

She clambered to her feet as the guards unbolted her cell. Quickly she put her black mask on again because she didn't want them to see the fear written all over her face. When the door swung slowly back, she threw up an arm to shield her eyes against the morning light. Blinded, she felt huge hands seize her arm, unchain her ankles only, then yank her out of the cell.

"Where are you taking me?" she rasped, her throat dry and thick.

"Shut up." The warden shoved her ahead of him down the dank stone corridor.

She stumbled toward the light, chains clanking. Soldiers and other wardens materialized out of the gloom. Dizzy and weak, she was aware of a corridor, slashes of shadow and sun striping the flagstone floor, six uniformed guards marching her to some unknown place, sunlight gleaming on their bayonets.

She heard the soldiers' boots striking the flagstones sharply, but the sound of their brisk, snapping strides could not drown out the chanting and roaring of a distant mob. She listened, knowing the mob had something to do with her, but she couldn't make out their words.

"Bring in the prisoner."

The yeoman of the tower lowered his ceremonial battle axe, stood aside and opened the massive door at the end of the jail's long corridor.

The guards shoved Dani into a dim, stuffy chamber. She tripped, landing on her knees with a strangled curse. From behind the black mask, her glance swept the room.

It appeared to be an interrogation chamber or audience room of some kind, and was lined with more of the prince's heavily armed Royal Guards, posted every ten feet around the perimeter.

There were high windows and a vast fireplace, the hearth empty. Against the longer wall ahead was a rough wooden throne on a raised stone dais, and on it sat the unmoving figure of a man.

The hairs on her nape bristled: She knew him.

The hazy light from the high windows fell behind him so only the prince's immense silhouette was clearly visible in the gloom of the hot chamber. Elbows on the chair's arms, fingers steepled in thought before his face, he did not need to move or even speak to make the imperial power of his presence felt. The aura of authority around him was palpable, eloquent in the expansive planes of his shoulders and his hard-lined jaw, edged with sun. His gaze was like a physical weight and in his stillness, he was as dangerous as a rogue lion in the shadows, idly flicking its tail, silent, keenly watching.

Fear spurted anew in her veins. She could well imagine how angry he must be with her. There was such a thing as male pride, of which he had more than an ordinary share, and she had bruised his—royally.

As her eyes adjusted to the dimness, she saw the prince was dressed entirely in black. After his finery of the night before, the severe clothing somehow only enhanced the effect of the hardened seducer. His loose-sleeved shirt hinted at the steely, sculpted arms and shoulders beneath, while his waistcoat snugly spanned his hard chest and molded his lean waist. His riding breeches were crafted of expensive-looking black leather which appeared both comfortable and soft; his glossy hessian boots shone.

He watched her with a cool, hooded gaze.

With an idly impatient gesture of one black-gauntleted hand, large and graceful through a dusty beam of sunlight, the prince caused the guards to search her, then he linked his fingers thoughtfully again before his seductive mouth.

The battle-hardened yeoman stepped forward at the un-spoken command, pulled her to her feet, and began briskly patting her sides. But when he ran his hands over her chest, his sudden grunt of surprise turned to a yelp of pain as, re-flexively, she brought up both clasped, manacled hands and swung at him. "Get your hands off me!"

She didn't know where her burst of strength came from.

Whirling clear, she smashed the guard in the face, then spun and leaped to catch another full force in the chest with a well-aimed kick. When another guard stepped too near, her knee came up hard between the man's thighs.

The soldier dropped, but in the blink of an eye a bayonet

was pointed at her throat. She froze and stood stock-still, chin high, chest heaving.

Then, from high on the throne rolled a low laugh pierced by slow, insolent applause.

"Don't you laugh at me!" she cried, hurting her parched throat with her shout.

When he spoke, his deep voice rumbled with gentle yet ominous indulgence: "Remove the mask."

Tensed with anticipation, Rafe watched the yeoman round her warily. From behind the black hood, her fierce eyes tracked the man, snapping blue sparks.

Cautiously, the yeoman moved toward her. The girl cursed as the mask slid away. At once, a cascade of wavy chestnut tresses tumbled free to her shoulders and blazed in the slanted sun.

The men gasped and she all but hissed at them like a little cat, backing them off.

His men slunk back to give her space, responding instinctively to her unmistakable air of inborn command. Seemingly satisfied with their distance, Lady Daniela then turned her sharp, wary gaze to Rafe.

He sat motionless, his elbow on the chair arm, his curled fingers idly obscuring his lips, his heart pounding recklessly. One glance, and he wanted her just as urgently as he had the night before when he'd spied her in the crowd. Just as hotly as the first night he had met her in her threadbare salon.

She . . . *woke* him. His senses, his mind, his slumbering heart. Her beauty made him catch his breath like a splash in the face of icy water from some mountain stream, so cold it was painful, and yet exhilarating and crystalline pure.

Joan of Arc came to mind, with her hands bound before her, that irresistible saucy chin jutting high, a smudge of soot on her cheek, and her aura of angry pride shining

around her like the morning light. The loose black shirt
and vest she wore disguised her virginal curves, but her
shocking breeches followed every line of her trim calves
and thighs and gracefully turned hips. She was lean and
wiry like a fine, fast filly.

When Rafe's gaze flicked back up to her face, Daniela
held his stare with bold, cool poise, neither intimidated
nor impressed. And he, who knew all there was to know
about women, still had no idea what to make of this one,
who seemed little more than a child. She was not a ravishing beauty like the lovers in his past—if they were
roses, she was a proud and wild tiger lily. They glared like
so many cold chips of diamond beside the burning simplicity of a whole and perfect fire opal. There was so much
more than beauty there: blazing spirit, tumultuous life.

Father had been right, Rafe thought with a slight, de-
vious smile as he stared at her. He would need someone he
could depend on by his side, and he could imagine no
more staunch and fearless ally than the valiant Masked
Rider.

A sleepless night of soul-searching and agonizing over
both their fates had resolved him.

With one last outrageous scandal to shock the world, he
was going to change his life, live up to his dying father's
hopes, amaze Ascencion with his brilliant leadership, and
produce an heir to carry on the royal line. Her fiery beauty
proved the spark that had ignited him. Moreover, he was
going to break his father's domination of his life and assert
his own control over his destiny. Standing there defiantly
before him, with her blazing aquamarine eyes, *she* was his
declaration of liberty.

Of course, it would have been a fatal revelation to let her
know how important she was to his plans. When women
sensed an opening, they seized it, he well knew. Proceeding
with caution, he had decided just what he was going to say

to get what he wanted yet keep her in line, for she was a handful, all right.

Oh, he had made up his mind about Daniela Chiaramonte. And as he gazed at his future wife, he had a feeling from the bottom of his rake's soul that he was the one who was doomed.

⪎ CHAPTER ⪎
SEVEN

Dani did her best to keep her chin high and her shoulders flung back in a defiant pose, but inwardly she quaked, more afraid of Rafael alone than his whole squadron of burly guards. With an almost bored flick of his hand, he dismissed his men. In a moment, they were alone, staring at each other in hostile silence.

The tender lover of the previous night had vanished inside this remote, brooding autocrat. His harsh, angular face seemed carved of granite. "I am displeased, Daniela. Most seriously displeased."

"Go on, hang me! I don't care!" she cried desperately, rattled and on the defensive. "I'm not afraid of you!"

"Hang you?" he asked blandly. "Let us think on this, my dear. Hanging seems much too light a sentence for the . . . pains you've given me." He shoved up from the throne and walked casually down the three steps from the dais, approaching her.

He walked past her to the long rectangular table in the center of the room and pulled out one of the rough-hewn chairs, gesturing. "Sit."

She kept a wary stare fixed on him as she walked over and lowered herself to the plain wooden chair, rather grateful for the invitation in her weakened condition.

"Hands on the table."

Again she obeyed, burning with angry shame. It was terrible to be humiliated by her own actions in front of a man whose respect and admiration she secretly longed for. The longing itself shook her—but she had never known another person like him, so vibrant and magnetic, so exciting to be near.

He pushed in her chair with ironic chivalry, then bent over her shoulder, planting his hands on the table around her body, hemming her in. His face was but a hand's breadth from hers. She could feel his warm breath near her ear. She closed her eyes and held perfectly still, helpless before her total physical awareness of him.

"You lost this at the ball," he whispered, skimming her cheek with the tip of his nose as he placed a small object on the table before her.

She dragged her eyes open and found herself staring down at one of her silver spurs.

"You left it in my bedchamber," he added silkily.

She huffed at his innuendo and turned away, blushing crimson, but at least she managed to hold her tongue.

With a slight, arrogant smile, as though he knew precisely his effect on her, he pushed away and walked languidly around the table. On the other side of it, he pulled out a chair, spun it lightly around backward, and straddled it, lowering himself. He folded his arms over the chair's back, rested his chin on his arm, and stared soberly at her.

"Tell me everything."

"I can't talk until you give me water," she croaked.

Studying her, he frowned and nodded, getting up. He walked to the door, asked quietly for drinking water, and returned a moment later with a pitcher and a tin cup, pouring as he crossed the chamber to her. He held the cup out to her and she took it warily from his hand. He folded his arms slowly over his chest and watched her drink in lusty greed. She basked in the heaven of water filling her mouth, rushing down her parched throat, but her eyes opened when she felt him stop her with a firm hand on her arm.

"Slow down. You'll be sick," he murmured, reaching across the table.

She lowered the cup and peered longingly into it in order to avoid looking at him. When she glanced up at him hesitantly, she found him staring at her wet lips. She looked away, dizzy with the memory of his deep, slow, drugging kisses last night. Oh, he was a wicked man, somehow making her want him even when she knew he was about to send her to the gallows.

Resting both her elbows on the table, she buried her face in her hands.

A long moment of silence passed and neither of them moved, she sitting at the table with her head in her hands, he standing across from her, watching her with relentless patience, his arms folded across his broad chest.

"Why did you do it?"

She drew a deep breath and lowered her hands, watching her fingers as she interlocked them. "Two hundred souls count on my lands for their livelihood, Your Highness. When the drought struck and ruined our crops, I saw that if I did not come up with the money from somewhere, they would starve. I tried other ways. I sold off all my mother's jewelry. But I could not sell myself to that swine Count Bulbati, so I invented the Masked Rider. But," she admitted, swallowing a fraction of her pride, "I never intended for it to go this far."

"It was a witless thing to do. You do realize, Lady Daniela, that I am bound by law to hang you?"

She steeled herself and lifted her chin. "If you are expecting me to grovel for mercy, Your Highness, don't waste your breath. I have been aware from the start of the consequences of my actions and I am prepared to die."

He stared at her. "Good God, are you always like this?"

She shrugged.

"My foolish urchin, your life is in my hands and so, might I remind you, are the lives of those peasant boys to whom you seem so inordinately attached."

Her wary gaze flicked back to him at his mention of the Gabbiano brothers. "What about them?"

He rested his hands on the back of the chair across from her. "Tell me this. The eldest—Mateo. Is he in love with you?"

"What? No!" she scoffed, blushing instantly.

"I want the truth."

Her scowl turned to a look of confusion. "I—I don't know. I hope not."

He pulled out the chair and sat down, skimming his fingertips restlessly over the nicked and scarred surface before him. "Yesterday, the man was willing to hang rather than reveal the Masked Rider's identity. I questioned him myself and all he continued to do was insist that *he* was the Masked Rider. He was willing to die in your place."

"Well, I'd do the same for him, but it's not that kind of . . ."—she hesitated with an uncertain frown—"love. The Gabbianos are like brothers to me."

He leaned forward and asked conspiratorially, "You mean your noble Mateo has never declared himself?"

"Good Lord, no! I'd run him through if he tried, and he knows it!"

He appeared to fight a narrow smile. "Then is it safe to presume you are not in love with him, either?"

"Love," she declared, "is for fools."

He studied her with a mystified gaze. "Aren't you a little young for such a policy, my dear?"

"I am not your dear; I am not your anything!" she burst

out, feeling trapped and blushing intensely at the hungry way he was staring at her. "Are you going to tell me my sentence or are you going to stand there tormenting me? Because I don't see what this line of questioning has got to do with anything!"

"Obviously, it's a matter of critical importance." He gave her an aloof smile. "Forgive me, we royals must be as blunt in these matters as horse breeders. Too much is always at stake for the niceties, you see. Questions of legitimacy are a part of royal life."

"And what has that got to do with me?" she retorted.

"Well, for example, when you bear my sons you will have to do so before a small audience. Another case in point—after our wedding night, proof of your virginity will have to be shown to the elders of the council—"

Dani didn't wait to hear the rest.

She shot up out of the chair, only to be stabbed by a bolting pain in her stomach from gulping the water. She let out a small yelp and fell back down to her seat again. Clutching her stomach, she doubled over in her chair.

Rafael was by her side in an instant, down on one knee, steadying her with a large, firm hand on her shoulder. "Shhh, breathe deep. It'll pass." He stroked her back in long, soothing caresses, slowly quieting her spasms as the pain dispersed. "Thata girl," he whispered. "You're a tough one, Daniela Chiaramonte. God knows you'll make one hell of a queen."

"What are you talking about?" she rasped, her face searing red.

"Did I forget to mention? You are going to marry me. That is your sentence."

She stared at him blankly. "You must be drunk."

"Sober as a churchman."

"Are you out of your mind?" she nearly shouted.

He smiled—charmingly.

"I will not marry you! No! *No!*"

"Of course you will, my dear. Come, Daniela—here I am, down on bended knee for you. I lay my kingdom at your feet." His tone was jaunty, his eyes twinkling. "It appears I have rendered you speechless."

Ohhh, a joke. Yes, that was it. Now she understood. She wanted to strangle him until that boyish grin wilted off his fine mouth. "Don't you dare try to charm me, Rafael di Fiore." Wretched with nausea and fury and disbelief, still holding her stomach, she glared at him, her hair hanging lankly in her face. She could not believe a woman could look such a wreck and receive a marriage proposal from the catch of the century.

"First you shoot me! Then you have me dragged to your room and try to seduce me! What kind of perverse game are you playing with me now?"

"*Tsk, tsk,* Daniela, so suspicious." He smoothed a lock of her hair behind her shoulder, touching her as though he owned her already.

She felt herself starting to panic in earnest. "You're not serious."

"Oh, yes, I am."

"I can't marry you! I don't even like you!"

"That's not what your kisses told me last night," he whispered with a knowing smile.

"Do you think I'm such a country bumpkin that I can't see what you're doing?" she demanded, narrowing her eyes. "You're trying to make a fool of me!"

He lifted his eyebrows. "Why would I do that?"

"To get back at me for robbing your witless, shallow friends! I know you're going to hang me or worse, so just quit this cruel game—"

"Quiet," he said firmly, cupping her face in his black-gloved hand with a touch so soft it brought tears to her eyes. He held her gaze in steady reassurance and solid confidence. "This is no jest. You've got yourself into some serious trouble here. Let's just say it amuses me to help you. Naturally," he added, as his touch on her face turned to a light caress, "I expect you to help me in return."

She stared at him, slack-jawed with disbelief. "How?"

"Oh, several ways," he whispered, stroking her cheek with his knuckle. "You have the proper lineage. You are, I daresay, in sound health for bearing me sons."

"Sons?" she echoed, paling. Dear God, he *was* serious. His princess? His queen? She did not know the first thing about being a queen. Her head swam as she gaped at him. True, she had the great Chiaramonte name to boast of, but she had never even been presented at court due to her family's financial plight.

"I apologize if my offer lacks romance, but I am not of a sentimental nature," he said with a breezy shrug, lowering his hand. "Besides, you said love is for fools, which I can attest is true. You told me at your villa that you intended never to marry, but I'm afraid you forfeited your freedom when you took to lawless behavior. You see, Lady Daniela, the plain fact is I have a use for you."

"A use—for me?" she asked weakly.

He nodded. "Fortunately, criminal though you are, you were never dangerously violent. We both know the Masked Rider is loved by the people of Ascencion. You are something of a national heroine, while I, on the other hand— well, the commoners are less than enamored of me. They are only commoners, I know, but I desire my people to care for me as they care for my father. You, my lady, are just the instrument I need to win them over. This will serve as your dowry." He lifted her black satin mask from the table and dangled it before her eyes.

Wide-eyed, she looked from it to him. "His Highness wishes to use me . . . for my influence with the people?"

He was watching her reaction closely, a flicker of some

mysterious emotion in the green depths of his eyes, but his tone remained light. "Yes. That sums it up rather neatly."

"I see," she said, dropping her gaze, her mind reeling. "What exactly would my role involve?"

He shrugged cynically. "You need do little more than stand by my side, wave to the crowd, and look happy."

But he had mentioned sons. She studied him, debating. Of course, as the crown prince, it was one of his chief duties to produce heirs, she knew, just as it was his future wife's raison d'etre to give them to him. She had long harbored an abnormal fear of childbirth, but at the moment, the notion of actually bearing his children seemed so impossible, implausible, unimaginable, and unreal that it did not really frighten her.

What frightened her was the thought of having an unprincipled, unreliable, and utterly charming rake for a husband—and worse—far worse—falling in love with him. Becoming his thrall, his slave.

"Be wise, Daniela," he murmured, watching her emotions war in her face. "This is no place for your pride."

She rested her forehead in her hand and glanced mistrustfully at him. "What about the Gabbiano boys? The only way I can agree to this is if you let them go free."

"*What?* Don't be absurd!" he retorted, his self-assured facade slipping as he scowled angrily. "I'm not about to let them walk away clean when we both know they are guilty under the law! Do you want to make me a laughingstock?"

"Then I'm afraid we have no deal. Every crime they committed was on my orders. You can't spare me and lock them away for the rest of their lives."

He stared at her incredulously. "God, you are a brassy wench." He pushed up from his crouched position before her and walked away, shaking his head.

In the silence that followed, there was nothing to do but watch him coursing relentlessly back and forth across the chamber, his long-legged strides eating up the ground, ending each pass with a clean, soldierly pivot. It was a strange and acutely unpleasant sensation, knowing that the man held their lives in his hands. She hoped she had not just sent them all to the gallows, herself included, but loyalty demanded all for one and one for all.

The prince eyed her now and then with a wariness that might have been shock or hostility or both. At the far end of the room, he stopped in profile to her. Hands on his hips, he turned and eyed her dubiously. "Banishment."

Dani absorbed this. "They will be free?"

"As long as they never set foot on Ascencion again."

Slowly, she lowered her head, saying nothing.

"It is more than generous," he warned. "Banishment, Lady Daniela. It is my final offer." He paused. Tapping his lips with one finger in thought, he began striding toward her. "As a matter of fact, I have a couple of conditions for you in return." He leaned down and planted both hands on the table across from her, probing her with an even stare. "First, you must give me your word that you will desist this playing at Robin Hood. You have put yourself in foolish danger quite long enough and I will not have my wife making a spectacle of herself. No more Masked Rider."

For a moment, she said nothing, her mouth pursed tautly. Already the commands had begun, she thought, man and wife—master and slave. She would have liked to wrest a promise of fidelity from him in exchange, but she might as well whistle down the wind. There was no point asking him to be faithful when he was only proposing a marriage of convenience designed to save her neck and win him his people's affection. She supposed she should reconcile herself to it now that Rafe the Rake would never change. He had said it himself: *There are always Chloe Sinclairs.*

"And your second condition, my lord?" she asked, her voice edged with resentment.

His stare intensified, boring into her, scanning the very depths of her. "Second, if you are my wife, you must never lie to me. I can forgive anything but deceit. Fall to human frailty, disappoint me, walk out on me, break my heart. But never—ever—lie to me."

She knew the moment he said it why Rafael demanded this. With sudden, jarring uneasiness, she remembered the old half-forgotten story of how a beautiful woman spy at court had seduced and tricked him when he was just an innocent youth. The country had nearly been plunged into war with France. The whole kingdom knew the tale, perhaps the world. Now the fierceness in his eyes captured her, made her hold her breath. He had granted her every demand, asking only for honesty.

For the first time, she wondered if he had been deeply hurt by the traitorous woman. Had he loved her? There was no question in her mind that he must have been humiliated by his all-too-public blunder. She thought of his countless women and his careless disregard for them, hiding behind his impregnable wall of charm.

"Honesty, Daniela. Can you give me that?"

"Yes, Prince Rafael," she said faintly, her heart pounding as it sunk into her mind that she was getting in far, far over her head this time. "Yes, I can."

"Then we have an agreement?"

She swallowed hard. "Yes, it appears that we do."

"Good," he said smoothly, revealing no reaction. "I will send servants to care for you and a physician to tend the wound on your arm."

"Thank you," she replied in a ridiculously calm tone.

Walking over to her, he slid a small key out of his waistcoat pocket and reached for her hands, unlocking her manacles. He took them off her and shoved them away, then examined her wrists, his thumbs gently caressing the chafed, pale skin.

He lifted his gaze from her wrists and looked into her eyes in silence.

For a second, he held her wide-eyed stare, looking every bit as awed as she was by the enormity of their decision. Then he quickly veiled the stark emotion in his eyes and released her hands, turning away.

"Wait here. I'll be back in a moment to take you to the palace."

"As you wish, my lord," she breathed, her heart pounding at the mad recklessness of it all. Her mind in a whirl, she lowered her head and listened to his soft footfalls as he crossed the stone floor. *God, what have I done? I don't want to be a wife and I can't be a mother!*

Too late now.

There was a pause.

"Daniela."

She looked up, her face ashen.

One hand on the latch, Rafael searched her eyes from across the chamber. "I will take care of you," he said. Then he opened the door and went out.

He took her home with him like some bedraggled stray cat he had found in an alley, bringing her not to his pleasure dome but to the Palazzo Reale. Prince Rafael was making some kind of statement by taking up house there, Dani believed, but she wasn't sure what his message to Ascencion was.

When they arrived at the massive, sprawling rectangle of golden brick with its mansard roofs and elegantly carved windows, he led her by the hand through the gilded maze of soaring marble halls into the finest private block of the palace, where the royal apartments were located.

On the third floor, he installed her in a huge, airy suite decorated in rose-plush velvet. It had a sitting room graced with a milk-white fireplace mantel carved with swans and a balcony off the bedchamber with a distant view of Belfort.

He left her in the care of a mild-tempered old physician to tend her gunshot wound belatedly, along with a battalion of busybody maids in starched caps and aprons to wait on her. The maids took one look at her in her grimy black clothes and immediately began drawing a bath. Others prevailed upon her to tell them what she wanted to eat, anything at all, as though they feared she might blow away with a gust of wind if they didn't fatten her up for His Highness on the instant.

Tomorrow, Rafael had told her, the royal couturiere,

who had made her reputation dressing his sister, the ravishing Princess Serafina, would spend the day with her to create a wedding gown as rapidly as possible, for the madman wanted the wedding to take place in three days' time! The dressmakers must also begin work, he had said, on the extensive wardrobe she would need for her new life as crown princess. Then he had left her in the hands of the servants, laughing as she angrily backed away from the doctor and servants poking and prodding at her.

By the time they had finished with her in their quest to turn her from a tomboy into a princess, her arm was freshly bandaged, her skin was scrubbed with rose-scented soap, her hair was washed and combed rather violently through. She had nothing to wear but the pristine white cotton shift and the paisley silk dressing gown they had given her. She had eaten a prodigious amount of food, served to her on shining silver platters.

Between courses, they let her send word to Maria and Grandfather about what had happened to her, for they had surely worried enough. Once the message had been sent off, Dani felt much better, but by three in the afternoon she was exhausted from her long ordeal.

Gazing out from the balcony, she nibbled a piece of chocolate almond biscotti and finished a cup of coffee sweetened with as much sugar as she pleased—luxury upon luxury—then dragged herself back inside and slid into the huge bed, curling up under the crisply cool linen sheet.

She doubted she would get any sleep in spite of her fatigue, for the butterflies in her stomach would not stop their ceaseless fluttering, nor could she stop thinking about her wedding and the intimate rite that would follow—her deflowerment by Prince Rafael. What would it be like? Would he kiss her whole body? She buried her heated face in her pillow with a whirling sensation in her heart and a tickle low in her belly. She curled up more tightly under the sheet as a surge of fear routed her desire, because kissing, she knew, was not where it ended.

Would it hurt dreadfully? How would she find the strength to force herself to submit to the painful, disgusting, and terrible invasion of his body in hers—especially when she knew it could well lead to her death in childbirth, just as it had for her mother?

Yet she had given him her word. She would have to let him do it to her.

What mattered, she told herself, was that she had managed to save the Gabbianos. Besides, if she survived the ordeal of the birthing, perhaps as crown princess she could do good things for Ascencion, like rid the kingdom of corrupt swine like Count Bulbati, who had driven her to crime in the first place. What King Lazar and Queen Allegra were going to say about their son's choice of brides filled her with dread. She supposed she would have to cross those bridges when she came to them. At the moment, she was exhausted.

Gazing down at the patterns of sunlight on the pretty Persian carpet, lulled by the afternoon sun, and worn out by her ordeal of a night in jail, gradually she fell asleep.

When she awoke it was morning.

She sat up suddenly in surprise, abruptly remembering her new world. She rubbed her eyes and was staring about her in amazement when suddenly the door opened and the stout, matronly head maid peered in.

"Oh! Good morning, your ladyship. Just in time for breakfast! There is a gift here in the next room for you. Would you like to see it now?"

"For me?"

A smile wreathed the plump woman's face and she

nodded encouragingly. Dani slid out of the enormous cano-
pied bed and padded lightly toward the maid, who held the
door open with her body. Warily, Dani peeked past her into
the next room, then gasped.

Eyes wide, she walked into the sitting room, which had
been transformed while she slept into a fantasy garden. It
was filled with countless bouquets of flowers. She walked
dazedly into the room, intoxicated by the delicate floral
perfumes. Roses wrapped in sprigs of baby's breath starred
the room—scarlet, pink, peach, and white; there were regal
orchids of deep purple, camellias with succulent snow-
white petals, curly snapdragons and the praying hands of
demure lilies, resplendent blue irises and bunches of
daisies, yellow and white, and a voluptuous red hibiscus
blossom alone in a slim crystalline vase, a mysterious and
strangely erotic bloom. Lifting the card gently from the
nearest arrangement—two dozen pink roses, delicate buds
mixed in with unfurled blossoms in all their summery
glory—she inquired to see who had sent her such a stunning gift. All it said was *R*.

"R!" she exclaimed softly, casting a breathless glance
at the maids as her face turned as pink as the roses.

The women smiled, glancing at one another.

"R," she whispered again to herself. Exceeding generosity from a man who was only using her, she thought, and
suddenly an impish giggle bubbled up from the depths of
her heart and escaped her lips. Startled, she clapped a hand
over her mouth to stifle the joyous, girly sound.

"Come, my lady. You are due for another feeding," the
head maid chided. "You're as thin as a twig!"

Dani smiled, feeling foolish but too happy to care. "It
was awfully nice of him to send me the flowers, don't you
think?"

"Oh, yes, miss," the maids agreed, hiding their smiles.

"I wonder why he did that." She danced back into the bedchamber and let them put her dressing gown on her, giving herself over to their will.

Maybe he was reaching out to her through this lovely gesture, she thought in sparkling wonder. Perhaps there was more sincerity in his offer of marriage than she had dared to hope before. Maybe he had sensed that she was not the kind of person who would ever lie to him. That was what he wanted, wasn't it? Someone he could trust.

She was no great beauty, but she was unquestionably loyal to those she loved.

The brisk uniformed women herded her back into bed as a younger maid brought in an elegant silver tray and served her breakfast. Within moments the couturiere sailed in and introduced herself while her assistants and seam-stresses began setting up for the full display of gowns and fabrics in every shade of the rainbow.

Dani ate breakfast sitting up in her sprawling bed, with the sharp-eyed couturiere sitting in a chair nearby, explaining various gowns and fabrics to her while she consumed a leisurely feast and cheerfully decided that robbing Prince Rafael had been the best mistake of her life.

They took a break for lunch, by which time she was bored senseless of hearing about silks and satins, muslins and velvets, laces and taffetas, and especially of hearing the mantua-maker complain that she had only forty-eight hours left to concoct a wedding gown worthy of a royal bride.

Dani kept glancing at the door, hoping in spite of herself for a visit from *R* so she could ask him if the *R* stood for rake, rogue, or Rafael. In any case, she was sure he knew what looked well on a woman and she would not have minded hearing his opinions on some of the gowns the couturiere had suggested.

To her own surprise, she was quite looking forward to his meaningless flirting and teasing mischief, but he never showed. She began to worry that there had been some mistake. Had he forgotten about her? Would the wardens come to throw her back in the jail?

Surely this was all too good to be true. Maybe he had changed his mind—or rather, come to his senses. As the sun strolled across the sky into afternoon, Dani learned she was not allowed to leave her suite. Wearing her first new mint-green day dress, which the seamstresses had brought ready-made and had efficiently tailored to fit her so she would at least have something to wear, she only got as far as the hallway before her keepers herded her gently back into her flower-crowded rooms, but not before she glimpsed the Royal Guardsmen posted in the corridor outside her apartment.

Whether they were there to protect her or make sure she didn't escape, she was not sure, but as the day wore on and her nervous boredom escalated, she began to wonder if she was still a prisoner after all. Troubled, she walked out and stood on the balcony, frowning as she gazed out over the royal park toward the city and the distant sea. A few minutes later, one of the maids came looking for her and announced with a teasing sparkle in her eyes that her ladyship had a visitor.

Rafael? she wondered as her heart skipped a beat. She spun around and hurried back through the bedchamber to the sitting room, feeling her cheeks flood with heat. She felt his combustible presence resonating through the pink-and-gilded suite, heard his deep, pleasing voice from the other room as he briefly questioned her servants, making sure all her desires had been met. The butterflies in her belly promptly came back even before she entered the room.

When she stepped into the doorway, she saw him standing on the other side of the room, inspecting one of the bouquets he had sent her. His back was to her, his hands clasped behind him, his tall, elegantly athletic form flattered by the flawless blue cutaway coat and buff linen pantaloons he was wearing. His dark gold hair was drawn back in the usual queue, which arrowed neatly down between his wide shoulders.

Light seemed to fill her being as her gaze traveled over him. A smile broke over her lips and she rested her hands on her waist. "Well," she said archly, "if it isn't the mysterious *R*!"

At her greeting behind him, Rafe abandoned the plentiful roses as he flashed a mischievous grin, turning around to face her. But when he saw the stunning young female standing in the doorway, his eyes widened and he nearly lost his tongue.

Smiling brilliantly at him, her cheeks glowing, her vivid aquamarine eyes shining with kittenish playfulness, his fresh young bride-to-be dropped him a delicate curtsy. "Thank you for the flowers, Your Highness."

"Good God!" he exclaimed, staring at her. "You are ravishing."

Still holding the curtsy, she swept her startled gaze up to his. He strode across the small room to her in an instant, lifting her to stand erect before him.

"You marvelous creature, let me have a look at you." She blushed as he strolled in a circle around her, his gaze purely drinking her in. "My, my, I shall have to reward Madame well for this."

"You are teasing me," she said, throwing him a scowl.

"I am not. Your dress, your hair . . ." He felt the fine mint-green silk of her gown between his fingers, tugged one of the curled ringlets framing her face in roguish affection, then suddenly threw his head back and laughed in delight, clapping his hands together once loudly. "You are perfect, Daniela! Truly perfect." Abruptly, he seized her hands and began pulling her toward the door. "Come! It's time to separate the wheat from the chaff. By God, you are going to help me cut loose the dead weight around here!"

"What do you mean?" she asked, hurrying to keep up with his long, cheerfully brisk strides. "Where are we going?"

"I want you to meet my friends."

She planted her slippered feet on the ground and stopped. He turned to her in question, still amazed by her transformation. Whether it was her fine new clothes and stylish appearance that flattered her so well, or adequate food and a good night's rest, he did not know. He had merely come to check on her, not wishing to leave her stranded alone in her rooms all day, but now all he could think of was showing her off, throwing her in everybody's faces, as it were, after he had spent the past thirty-six hours defending his decision to marry her. One look at her should be enough to quell their objections permanently.

Daniela Chiaramonte had been made for him.

She held her ground, giving him a pleading look. "I don't want to meet them. They are going to hate me!"

He stared at her coral-pink lips. "Hmmm?"

"I robbed practically all of them, Rafael."

Ignoring her words, he leaned down, helplessly drawn, and tasted her lips with a soft kiss.

She closed her eyes, going still under his light, caressing kiss, then abruptly she pulled back, scowling up at him again. "Did you even hear me?"

He smiled wistfully at her, holding in check sweet visions of how he would rather have spent his afternoon.

"All I could hear was angelic strains of song, my dear. Did you not hear them, too?"

She narrowed her eyes at him, but a smile tugged at her bewitching mouth.

"Listen," he whispered, leaning toward her again. He slipped his arm around her slim waist and pulled her gently to him, kissing her tenderly once more. "Did you hear it that time?"

Dreamily, his bride opened her eyes and gazed up at him. Lifting her hand, she cupped his cheek. "You are a lunatic," she said softly.

With a sudden good-natured growl, he grabbed her and picked her up in his arms, tossing her bodily over his right shoulder. He laid a jovial slap on her backside while she shrieked and swung her slippered feet. "Come, my dear! It's time to meet the court."

He strode energetically down the hall, carrying her like a marauder making off with his prize.

"Put me down! Put me down!"

"Do you ever wonder what might have happened if I had been the outlaw and you had been the princess?" he asked, noting with a grin that she really wasn't fighting very hard. He turned his head to bite her hip through mint-green silk before setting her gently on her feet outside the door to the salon where he'd left his friends.

She was laughing, her face red from being held upside down, and he felt himself flooded with a wave of intense desire. He could hardly believe his good fortune that soon without guilt or taint or compunction he could take her to his bed, enjoy her, keep her entirely to himself—his wife. Her laughter was quickly stifled by the heat in his stare. She took a step backwards from him, her eyes turning wide and uncertain and shy. He smiled faintly, wondering if anyone had ever told her before how adorable she was, for she seemed entirely innocent of her own allure.

He bridled the passion in his gaze before it sent her fleeing in fright. "If anyone in there is rude to you, they're gone from this court. Understood?"

"You would make your friends leave for me?" she asked, looking awed.

He traced the delicate curve of her cheek with his knuckle. "I have many friends, but only one wife. No unhappiness shall touch you under my roof, Daniela. I will look upon any insult to you as an insult to myself."

"You are more than kind," she said rather faintly, then cleared her throat and assumed a more businesslike air, "but I can take care of myself, you know. I'm not sure I am comfortable being placed in the middle between you and them."

At the moment, he felt prepared to slay dragons for her, but perhaps he was coming on too strong. "My lady, suffice it to say that you are my choice, and I am their lord. Think of it as a test of their loyalty to me."

"Oh," she said, nodding gravely. "All right."

"Ready?"

She smoothed her dress. "I suppose. I will try not to embarrass you."

He gave her a reassuring smile. "Just be yourself. I'll be right beside you." A surge of protectiveness moved through him as he opened the door for her.

She seemed to brace herself, then forged in with a queenly stride. Rafe watched her hungrily, full of quiet pride in her as she entered the room ahead of him. Her flowing, graceful walk held him fascinated, her light skirts swirling around her slim, neat legs, until she took a seat in a wing chair in the center of the room. Her spine was straight as she sat primly, her head high, her work-reddened hands folded demurely in her lap.

Rafe sauntered in behind her and stood guard behind

her chair, leaning on the back of it in a casual pose, his narrowed eyes full of cool warning as he bade his friends approach her, introduce themselves, and congratulate her on their happy news.

Elan liked her at once, Rafe saw in relief. His cousin Orlando treated her with polite reserve, but the haughty Adriano and the ever-sarcastic Nic were deferentially courteous only because Rafe was standing menacingly behind her chair. Daniela did not offer any of them her hand; this pleased him. She handled herself with lofty, commanding poise, saying little. After presenting a few of the others to her, Rafe was satisfied.

He placed her hand on his arm and led her from the salon, glad to have her to himself once more. As they walked down the hall, he noticed she looked a trifle shaken.

God knew he had hundreds of urgent tasks to handle, but all that seemed to matter at the moment was being with her—preferably far away from the prying eyes of the court. He slipped his arm around her slight shoulders and gave her an affectionate squeeze. "You did well."

She glanced up at him uncertainly. He grinned with sudden inspiration.

"Come! There's something I want to show you." Seizing her hand, he tugged her down the hall, cajoling her with his softest, most irresistible smile when she protested.

Within an hour, they were aboard his sleek thirty-foot sloop, cutting through the placid waves out into the harbor. Rafe felt free. Standing at the wheel with his shirtsleeves rolled up and his long hair loosed and blowing in the evening breeze, he was aware of Daniela watching him furtively as she poked through the contents of the picnic hamper. One of the servants had handed it off to him before he had abandoned his staff, guards, and the stragglers of his entourage on the shore.

He glanced up past the sails at the violet-blue sky, where a few early stars had poked through. Before them, the western horizon was golden and pink, like a cherub waking. The yacht rode low in the water. When they had sailed perhaps a mile out from the island, he tied the wheel in place and climbed up into the rigging to lower a few of the sails, slowing them to a gentle, rocking crawl.

Daniela watched him and ate a peach.

He smiled to himself as he tied off the topsail and jumped down to the glossy, polished deck. Judging by her impressed look, she hadn't suspected he knew how to sail without deckhands to order around, he thought in amusement. But, a prisoner of his rank and his own reputation, this boat had been his sanctuary: here was the only freedom he had ever really known. He savored the solitude the sea offered. Moreover, he was constantly surrounded by flatterers, but the vastness of the eternal ocean reminded him of his own insignificance and thus kept him humble.

As he sat down on the deck beside her near the bow, he wondered what she would say if he told her he had never brought a woman aboard before.

She offered him a cube of cheese impaled on a cutting knife. He declined with a wave of his hand, then looked around for the bottle of the light young wine he'd brought up from the compact but well-stocked cabin. He found it, then dug about aimlessly in the hamper for the corkscrew, frowning. She handed it to him with a small smile. He took it from her and stole a kiss.

"Sometimes when I was a boy," he said as he stuck the corkscrew in and began turning it, "I used to dream of packing my belongings on this little boat and sailing away forever. Running away from home. I wanted to be an explorer in the Congo and the Far East, but I was stuck here—fortunately." He looked askance at her, his eyes sparkling.

"I would have surely died of malaria or been eaten by cannibals upon setting foot in the jungle, eh, coddled rich boy like me?"

She was laughing at him.

"What?"

"Only *you* could find cause to run away from such a life. No doubt it was *torment* being adored by everyone—the future king, born with the silver spoon in your mouth, the apple of your mother's eye—"

"Now, now, it was no bed of roses!" he protested, laughing with her at his own expense. "I had my trials and tribulations, like anyone."

"Like what?" she retorted as he pulled the cork free.

"It so happens a great deal has always been required of me. I have been drilled on a hundred subjects related to statecraft since I was old enough to walk," he announced over her scoffing.

"Such as?" She reached into the hamper, then turned to him, holding up two glasses.

He poured the wine. "Rhetoric, history, logic, composition, philosophy, languages—dead and living—algebra, finance, military engineering, architecture, comportment, ballroom dancing—"

"Ballroom dancing!"

"One doesn't want to trip over one's feet when one lives in the public eye." He finished pouring the wine and replaced the cork, setting the bottle aside.

She handed him one of the glasses, then folded her arms over her bent knees, smiling at him. "What else did you have to learn?"

"Learn? No, not learn, my dear—*master*," he corrected her as he clinked his glass lightly with her own in a cursory toast. "My father would have it no other way. 'You must be the strongest, the smartest, the best, Rafael,'" he said, affecting his father's stormy countenance. "'No weakness.' That was the motto I was assigned."

"Fairly rigorous," she remarked as she took a sip of wine.

Watching her, he did the same, wondering how it would taste on her lips.

"Why was your father so strict?"

Rafe lowered his glass. "Well, he believes, as I do, that the only effective means of rule is by example. If men sense weakness or inferiority in a leader, they will fall on him like wolves on a wounded calf." He noted her grimace and gave her a smile, determined to keep the tone light. "To wit, I was given every tool possible with which to make myself into a model human being. How did I do?"

"I'm not sure," she replied with a wily grin that charmed him utterly.

Smiling, he wondered if she was aware that she had sidled up infinitesimally closer to him. He was sitting with one hand braced behind him. Now her shoulder nestled into the space beneath his arm, as though she were slowly relaxing into him by degrees. He made no move toward her for fear of scaring her away. She crossed her dainty ankles and flexed her stockinged feet. She had slipped off her shoes.

"Tell me more about what it was like growing up as the future king. Was it very hard?"

"Well, there were the academic subjects—reading, writing, and so forth; the social graces; the athletics—which I enjoyed tremendously, by the way; and the fine arts—those I did not master," he added. "I have no artistic or musical talent whatsoever, but I do have taste, so Father couldn't fault me on that."

"I mean how did it *feel*?"

He stared dubiously at her for a moment. "It was fine."

A chestnut curl fell coyly by her cheek when she tilted her head, smiling skeptically at him.

"I don't know. Everyone was jealous," he admitted, gently tugging the curl like a spring; then he released it and watched it bounce back up into shape. "The first law of survival which you must understand in your new life as princess, Daniela, is that every living soul in the court has an agenda. Because of what you can do for them if you choose, they'll laugh at your every joke and praise your every thought, but you never know who your real friends are." He chucked her softly under the chin and gave her a wink. "Except for me, of course."

She smiled warmly at him. Her eyes were as clear as the water, and she was as unafraid as a child. A flicker of guilt for bringing her into the dangerous world of the palace slid through him. She was unprepared for it, such an innocent. He would really have to look out for her.

He lifted his glass to her with a smile and they drank, then they were silent, merely sitting side by side and basking in good company with the evening breeze on their skin as the sun sank lower in the west.

His mind continued to revolve on the topic she had brought up. He spoke abruptly, still staring at the waves. "You know the history, I'm sure, about how my father's parents were assassinated when they were just a few years older than you and I are now. My father was just a boy at the time, and he was the only one who escaped alive."

She nodded sadly. "A horrible, tragic blot on Ascencion's history."

"Yes, it is. Well, my father suffered a ghastly childhood in exile after their deaths. His experiences hardened him, and he thinks that is the source of his effectiveness as a king. And so he worries constantly that my life has been too easy. 'They're going to eat you alive, Rafael,' he is very fond of saying."

"Ah, how nice that he has such faith in you," she said wryly.

He turned and looked at her, taken aback that she understood him precisely. "That's exactly right," he exclaimed. "He thinks I'm an idiot. They all do."

"Well," she said, "you're not."

"No, I'm not," he replied.

She gazed at him, smiling a little, both of them caught up in the rare instant of crystalline understanding and warm connection, then Daniela lowered her lashes and seemed to hesitate to speak. "You will be a great king, Rafael. Anyone can see that."

"Ah," he muttered, looking away.

For a moment she was still, then she rested her hand on his shoulder and caressed him slowly, tentatively. He closed his eyes, lowered his head.

It felt wonderful, her touch. He didn't want it to end.

Believe in me, Daniela. The thought whispered through his mind. *Please, I just need someone to want me for me.*

"His Majesty may be a hard man and I'm sure it isn't easy for you, being the object of all his hopes for the future of Ascencion, but he is your father and I'm sure he means well."

"I've lived in his shadow all my life," he barely whispered. "Nothing I ever do is good enough for him. Just once, I wish he would look at me and say, 'Well done, Rafe.' Why should I care what he thinks of me? And still, I do. But every time I try to assert myself in action, all I can think about is what happened when I was a stupid lad, and I'm sure you know that story, too. Everyone does."

Daniela rested her head on his shoulder, sliding her arms around his neck. "Everyone makes a mistake now and then," she said softly. "One mistake isn't the end of the world, Rafael. Maybe your father has forgiven you; maybe it's only you who can't forgive yourself."

"Why should I? I was a fool. Maybe I don't deserve to rule Ascencion."

She caressed his tensed back. "Did you love her?"

"I don't know. I thought so at the time, but maybe not, because it didn't feel like this." Alarmed by the soft sincerity in his own voice, he quickly forced a careless, charming smile and looked over at her, but she lifted her hand to touch his lips with her fingertips.

"Don't do that," she whispered, her gaze grave and innocent. "It's not necessary with me. I am to be your wife."

He stared at her, realizing that in the same manner that he had unmasked her, she had just laid his soul bare. Slowly she lowered her hand.

For a moment he couldn't find his voice, and then it came out a bit hoarsely. "How is it a provincial little girl like you can understand an international scoundrel like me?"

"We're not that different. Rafael, there's something I want you to know." She stroked his hair as she spoke softly. "You've told me what it was like growing up at court amid those false, smiling courtiers, and I understand it's not your habit to trust the people around you. You don't have to trust me, either, if you don't want to. I wouldn't blame you. But you spared my life, I am in your debt, and the fact stands that I would never betray you. I promise you that."

He stared at her, thinking of the loyalty that had stopped her from ridding herself of her senile old grandfather when she could easily have placed him in one of the kingdom's charitable asylums. The same loyalty that had lured her to his pleasure palace to rescue the boy, Gianni, though she risked discovery and arrest. The same loyalty to the two hundred peasants who lived off her land, which had driven her to crime in the first place in order to feed them.

It was a frightening moment, realizing that he believed

her words, and that he did not want to hold her at arm's length—realizing, indeed, that for the first time since Julia, a woman had gotten under his skin.

She laid her hand gently on his cheek and caressed him, and he came back from brooding on his fear to gaze into her aquamarine eyes.

She was so simple, so genuine. He was safe. He knew it, felt it.

Abruptly, he wrapped his arms around her waist and pulled her against him, shutting his eyes and burying his face in her hair. His heart was pounding. He felt the fervent, sudden need to shower this woman with everything she had ever wanted, fulfill her heart's desire, give her anything, everything. Then it struck him that he had become accustomed to buying his women's affection with material possessions, shiny baubles costing fortunes—worthless, in the greater scheme of things, and all he had been willing to give.

Daniela deserved something real from him. He pulled back just far enough to stare again into her jade-blue eyes.

The golden light of sunset had turned her rich chestnut hair to brilliant sienna and polished her porcelain skin to a delicate hue of creamy peach, but as he gazed at her, her cheeks filled with a wine-pink blush. She looked away.

"You confuse me so," she said barely audibly.

"How?" he murmured, turning her face toward him again with a gentle touch and holding her in a deep gaze.

"You say you are only using me to win over the people, and then you look at me . . . like that."

"Like what? Like I want to kiss you?" he whispered, smiling faintly. "Because I do."

She appeared not to know what to say. Resolutely, she turned around and sat facing forward between his spread thighs, her back to him.

He realized her shyness had just caught up with her. He wrapped his arms around her waist and set his chin on her shoulder.

"I am no expert on comportment, Your Highness, but I don't think this is proper," she said, holding herself stiff and prim as he cuddled her.

"Proper?" He chuckled. "They're calling you the bandit princess, and I'm still Rafe the Rake. I would say, my little cabbage, that we passed 'proper' long ago."

"Don't call me a cabbage," she mumbled.

"What do people usually call you, then?"

"Dani."

He smiled and gave her a squeeze around her waist. "Well, that suits you. It's a hellion's name, all right. You can call me Rafe, if you like."

"I don't wish to call you Rafe."

"No?"

"It is a scoundrelly name." She looked over her shoulder at him archly. "I shall call you Rafael, like the angel."

"Hmmm, an optimist, are you?" He sifted his fingers gently through her hair, then massaged her scalp and neck and thin shoulders until he felt the tension easing from her.

She sank back against his chest with a luxurious sigh. "That feels wonderful."

"I should probably warn you I'm rather gifted with my hands." He nuzzled her ear and felt her tense again as he explored the curve of her neck with little nibbling kisses, but as he continued massaging her shoulders, again she slowly relaxed. "You have such pretty arms," he said, caressing his way down them to her wrists. Then he gently took her hands, linking his fingers with hers. "Are you uneasy with this?" he whispered, pausing, feeling as careful with her as though he were still just a youth with his first lady love.

"No," she said quietly.

"Good." With his fingers still threaded through hers, he drew her hands back and pinned her arms ever so gently behind her for a moment, gazing down her gown's neckline at her creamy, lifted chest. Her breasts were small but delightfully pert, firm. He wondered if he could fit her whole breast in his mouth. She'd like that, he thought with a narrow smile. He fixed her hands behind his waist and reached down to caress her slim sides.

"It's getting dark," she said rather breathlessly. "Shouldn't we perhaps be getting back?"

"I like being on the water at night. You can't see, you can only hear the waves and smell the salt, and you have to feel your way back to shore . . . feel your way through the dark," he whispered as he ran his hands slowly over her flat belly and upward to her breasts. "A man has to know exactly what he's doing."

She arched back against him with a soft catch in her breath as he cupped her small, fine breasts in his large hands. Her generous nipples turned hard under his lightly circling thumbs.

"Rafael," she moaned breathlessly, flexing against him so that her breasts seemed to swell wantonly into his hands. Her arms were wrapped behind his neck. "We . . . can't. We are not married yet."

"You're in no danger, my love." He slid his hands back down her belly and began stroking her thighs. "I don't wish to deflower you tonight. Tonight I just want to learn what you like."

"But I—I don't know what I . . . like. . . ." Her voice trailed off on a dreamy gasp of pleasure.

"Well, then," he whispered, "let's find out."

With her head cushioned on his chest, she turned her face to him, seeking his mouth in innocent ardor. He lowered his head and parted her lips with a languorous stroke of his tongue, savoring the taste of her. She reached up, caressing his cheek as they kissed in slow, soulful intensity.

While she ran her fingers through his unbound hair, Rafe continued kissing her, deftly inching her skirts upward over her exquisite legs. His heart pounded as she let his hands roam up under the gathered layers of silk gown and muslin petticoat. He groaned when his fingertips came to the edge of her white stockings and found warm, ineffably tender skin. His groin flooded with heat and his body turned rock hard in an instant, but he fought to hold his throbbing need in check, unwilling to push her too fast.

She was so fragile and small, so precious in his arms. She was so different from everyone he knew, the hardened, calculating creatures of the court. Dani might think herself tough and independent, but he ached to protect her nearly as fervently as he longed to give her pleasure. Inexperienced as she was, he hoped to lessen her anxiety about their wedding night by letting her glimpse the joys that lay in store for her.

Under her dress, he explored her skin, gently kneading her hips and stroking her soft, flat belly, devouring her mouth all the while. He caressed the reticence out of her, until there was no tension under his hands, only rising, supple warmth, turning swiftly hot and frantic.

Behind his closed eyes, he smiled to himself as his leisurely pace made her restless. She arched and writhed slightly between his legs in virginal frustration, an impatient moan in her throat. Her hips lifted with sweet craving as his right hand glided down her belly. He knew just where she wanted to be touched and was glad to acquiesce.

When he stroked her tenderly and found her core soaked with silky wetness, throbbing under his fingertips in pure feminine invitation, he felt his tight rein on self-control fly apart. He went still, warring with himself, growing drunk on her sighs of urgent need.

"Rafael, Rafael . . ."

Heroically, he conquered himself and kissed her earlobe. "Dani. Would you like to watch?" he whispered in wicked softness, sliding her skirts higher with his other hand.

"No! I couldn't!" she panted, scandalized.

"Watch."

Her chest heaved. "No! Don't . . . make me."

A satyric smile curved his mouth, for he heard the eagerness in her voice. Perhaps it was time for the little Masked Rider to have a new adventure.

"Why not? Is it sinful?" he whispered. "Don't you like it? Do you want me to stop?"

"Rafael," she pleaded, melting back against him.

"Watch me touch you," he murmured as his fingertips began to circle. "There's nothing to be ashamed of, my darling. You're allowed to do everything with me. I only want to fulfill your desires. Watch me pleasure you. Look at how beautiful you are . . . your sweet body. I love to touch you. You're like a goddess, Dani, like Artemis of the moon, the huntress, free and untamed. You are the changing moon, my wild, virgin love."

"Oh, Rafael." She turned and kissed him ardently.

Inexplicable burning wetness rose behind his closed eyes for an instant at her purity, then quickly fled as their kiss ended.

He kissed the curve of her neck, moved by her shy uncertainty as she lowered her head and observed him touching her, panting slightly. She wrapped her hands around his bent knees on either side of her and leaned back weakly against his body.

She was so ready, he thought in agony, his hardness chafing against her back through their clothes. It would have been so easy to lay her down and take her now, here on the warm, glossy planks of the deck, that still held the heat of the sun, but he repeatedly shoved temptation aside, vowing to prove his respect for her by making their wedding night her first time.

"Is this too hard?" he asked as he touched her.

"Perfect," she breathed, arching wildly.

He smiled against her neck. His thumb deftly teased her jeweled center while his middle finger gently stroked inside her tight, fluid heat, and as he kissed her ear and the back of her neck, in mere minutes she gave in completely. Her fingers dug into his breeches-clad thighs as she gasped with amazement, then moaned her delight, laying her head back on his shoulder as she moved with his touch.

Victory enraptured him. He gathered her tightly in his arms before her feminine groans of bliss had barely ended. He turned her to face him and held her with an almost savage sense of possession. She wound her arms around his neck and clung to him, her sweet body limp.

"Oh, Rafael," she whispered, with wonder tinging her voice. She buried her face against his neck for a moment, then lingeringly kissed his cheek. "I think—I think I must have needed that," she confided as she slowly caught her breath.

Taken aback, he burst out laughing softly and hugged her helplessly. "Absurd little darling," he whispered.

"I mean it," she protested in full gravity.

"I know," he said, chuckling, those strange, brief, nostalgic tears rising again in his eyes as he buried his smile in her hair. *This is what I have been missing.*

Fullness. Contentment. For the first time in ages that he could remember, he felt like he was really there, *with* her in this moment, not just making an appearance, going through the motions. He felt as though she had given him back everything Julia had robbed him of—his innocence.

She sighed and laid her head on his shoulder, closing

her eyes with a blissful little smile, while Rafe glanced up at the cool blue moon. He held her tenderly, his soul mate, neither of them speaking or moving, both listening to the cadence of each other's breathing and savoring the warmth of having been found.

≈ CHAPTER ≈ NINE

Dani felt like she was dancing on air as they walked back up into the Palazzo Reale, her hand clasped in Rafael's. If they passed footmen and courtiers and ladies, she noticed them not at all. She only had eyes for Rafael, glancing constantly at his classically chiseled face and needing, perhaps, just a little reassurance that the wonderful, wicked thing he had done to her was no cause for belated regret.

He walked her to her apartment and kissed her goodnight in the little sitting room packed with flowers. Their perfumes intoxicated her like the bottle of wine they had finished.

"I don't like saying goodbye," she murmured, a bit tipsy and loath to release her arms from around his neck.

"Would you like me to stay with you tonight?" he whispered, running his hands up her sides in sweet coaxing.

A shiver of temptation ran through her. Pulling back, she looked up at him with a smile. "You'd better not."

He gave her a charming little sulk. "But I want to."

"Don't pout, dearest. You'll see me tomorrow," she said teasingly, reaching up to cup his clean-shaved cheek.

"It's already tomorrow. It's half past two."

"Then you'll see me today. Later."

"Ah, very well." But instead of letting her go, his hold around her waist tightened and he brushed the tip of her nose with his own. "So, will you show me that trick of yours sometime, riding the horse standing up?"

"Maybe, when I get to know you better."

"I like the sound of that. Hmmm, I wonder what presents I can send you tomorrow," he mused as he stole another little kiss, nipping playfully at her lower lip. "What would you like?"

She smiled dreamily, closed her eyes, and laid her head on his broad shoulder. "I don't need any presents. I can't think of a single thing. I'm happy."

"Then you must let me make you happier still. Name your heart's desire."

She pulled back to smile archly at him. "Well, now that you mention it, if you're really determined, my roof at home needs fixing."

He groaned.

"Maria could use help caring for Grandfather, and some of the peasants have been asking for months for some repairs to their houses—"

"Can't you think of anything for yourself, woman? You're supposed to ask for diamonds or something. I'll gladly take care of this tedious roof business, but must you thwart my every attempt to spoil you?"

Laughing, she hugged him again. "You are too good to be true, Rafael."

"I'm true," he said softly, nuzzling her cheek.

"Then that's enough for me. There's nothing else I want."

"Oh, really?" He gave a sudden, mischievous half-smile in the dark. His caressing fingers dipped flirtatiously between the cheeks of her bottom, and deeper, pressing muslin petticoats against her. "I don't think that's *quite* accurate," he remarked pleasantly as she protested with a shriek and tried to squirm away from him.

He caught her around the waist and stopped her from fleeing, stroking more insistently. Trapped in his arms, laughing and scandalized, she blushed crimson as his slow, wicked touch sent jolts of mad desire zooming through her anew.

"I think there is something very definite that you crave, my dear, and I think I know just what it is."

"Go away, you incorrigible rake! I'm falling asleep on my feet."

"All right," he relented. "But I shall put you to bed first."

With that, he swept her up into his arms and carried her into her bedchamber, kissing her soundly before laying her down on her bed.

She stared up at him as he bent over her, his hands planted on either side of her, his massive shoulders looming in the dark. His long dark gold hair hung down, shadowing his angular face, but his eyes were luminous in the gloom. He looked like Lucifer, come to her in a dream to seduce her.

She held her breath, staring up at him as his gaze moved hungrily over her face and her body. Then he met her eyes without a trace of a smile but with a hot male aggressiveness that made her shrink back deeper into the mattress.

He was so much larger than she, so richly endowed with raw, rippling, physical power.

"I am burning to make love to you," he whispered, starkly holding her stare. "I have longed to feel you under me since the first moment I saw you. But," he said with a sudden, more tender smile, noticing the startled fright in her wide-eyed stare, "I can wait. One more night I can wait, if I must, love. Not a moment more. And then . . ."— lightly he traced the curve of her face, "Heaven."

She swallowed hard. She had felt so close to him all evening, she wondered if she ought to tell him now about her great fear of childbirth, though she knew it was her duty to give him a son. But when he looked at her with his gaze so full of admiration, she could not bring herself to reveal her weakness.

Golden, magnificent Prince Rafael thought her fearless and brave. She did not have Chloe Sinclair's great beauty; she only had her character to adorn her, and she was vain enough to wish to hide it from him that she was actually quite a coward.

He leaned forward, kissed her chest, then, giving her a final smile, pulled out of her arms and walked wearily to the door. She came up onto her elbows and watched him stride away, still a little frightened but thrilled merely by his bold, proud walk. Her gaze moved appreciatively over him, from the powerful breadth of his shoulders down to his lean waist and taut buttocks. She rolled onto her side and propped her cheek in her hand, watching him.

He paused at the door and glanced over his shoulder at her. His white smile was wolfish in the dark, his eyes glittering. "You look good enough to eat, Daniela. Are you sure you don't want me to stay?"

She sent him a drowsy, sensual smile. "Goodnight, Rafael."

"Ah, well." With a long-suffering sigh, he gave her a sketch of an ironic, gentlemanly bow, then went out, closing the door quietly behind him.

Sighing in delicious contentment, she lay back with a smile on her lips, unable to come back to her senses even though she knew she was in deep, sweet peril. *You're an oddball, a tomboy, a misfit,* her better sense clamored, trying to warn her back from the precipice toward which her emotions were irrevocably stampeding. *You could never hold a man like him.* But she was falling gloriously in love and it felt too wonderful to stop.

Soon she drifted to sleep, dreaming of Rafael . . . and heaven.

If the royal golden boy had caused a scandal with his intention of marrying the so-called Masked Rider, Orlando knew the next day that there was much more to it than a mere outrageous lark, for today the prince set out—almost deliberately, it seemed—to make enemies. Orlando could not guess what he was up to—a fact which in itself alarmed him, since he had always rather taken Rafe the Rake as a joke.

Today the prince began his casual war on the court by setting the lovely Lady Daniela on his knee just before the fiscal meeting began, and keeping her there for the duration—flaunting his chosen bride in their faces in defiance of his father's will.

The ministers were infuriated at this utter flouting of decorum: Rafe answered them with a bland invitation to leave if they didn't like it.

Only the bombastic Bishop Justinian had done so with a thunderous refusal to perform their wedding ceremony until the king had approved the match. Then, in a whoosh of satin robes, he had exited grandly

Lady Daniela had flinched at the bishop's holy ire, still innocent of how the prince was using her to make his stand. The girl was clearly uncomfortable, but Rafe refused to let her flee, holding her firmly yet gently on his lap and whispering in her ear.

Her wide, blue-green eyes still wore an expression of naive uncertainty, but Orlando noticed that the more the old men nagged and badgered Rafe about various matters, the more the girl's countenance changed from a blush of maidenly embarrassment to a scowl of brazen defiance, until at length she appeared quite content to stay just where she was, at Rafe's bidding, his little ally.

The lover and the fighter, he thought, shaking his head to himself.

Rafe's light caress on her hair seemed all that stopped the lovely, feral redhead from lunging across the table and lashing out at the men who would dare treat Ascencion's future king without the pomp and obeisance due his rank. Rafe and Daniela's united front against the ministers silenced the old men until at last they simmered down to work with little more than a few obtuse grumbles.

The younger men, particularly Adriano and Nic, exchanged disgusted looks with Orlando, but dared not let Rafe see them.

Orlando caught Adriano's glance and held it for an extra second or two, then the beautiful young man looked away, his high-boned cheeks flushing. Orlando smiled to himself, biding his time. He knew the weak link in the chain that was the prince's inner circle. Adriano was jealous, mercurial, emotionally fragile. It didn't surprise Orlando that Rafe's most ardent follower was so hostile to Lady Daniela.

The ostensible reason for the girl's presence at the meeting was to take notes, since Rafe could not be bothered to do it himself, but it was distracting how the prince sat at the head of the table with the pretty girl on his lap and could not seem to keep his hands off her. Lounging like some pagan emperor on his throne, signing the fate of millions with one hand, while with the other he was constantly caressing her back, toying languidly with her hair, nuzzling her cheek.

Lady Daniela listened intently to everything with an intensity and a clarity of expression that impressed Orlando. From time to time, she leaned to Rafe and whispered something in his ear, remarking upon what was said, Orlando guessed. Everyone could see that her words commanded his acute attention, but not even the fierce Lady

Daniela was brash enough to dare speak her thoughts aloud to the king's cabinet.

The meeting dragged, argument after argument. Don Arturo was being downright tedious, unable, especially after this latest insult, to concede the smallest point to Rafe, who remained tranquil but would not budge from his veto of the new tax the prime minister was arguing.

Still, he stroked Daniela as though she were a beautiful red tabby cat on his lap.

The way his hand traveled back and forth, slowly, indulgently, possessively, from her arm to her shoulder was maddening to Orlando. Quite without intending to, he kept envisioning them making passionate love. A woman like that, he kept thinking, would give herself completely but only to one extraordinarily fortunate man, and then in his mind's eye he saw her surrendering instead to *him*. Some of the old ministers looked a bit hot under the collar as well, with the foreplaylike exhibition.

The pair seemed to have an unspoken communication all their own and the chemistry between them made the room sizzle. Everyone was uncomfortable, realizing, perhaps, that Rafe was merely tolerating them and didn't really need them anymore.

All he seemed to need was Daniela and, perhaps, a bed.

When the gentlemen took a short break at half past ten, some of them gathered at the end of the hall, cursing the prince as an arrogant lech, but Orlando was not convinced it was mere sexual desire that had prompted his kinsman to keep the girl with him so faithfully.

There was something deeper in it.

Daniela and Rafe conferred together quietly after the old men had left the room. Furtively, Orlando watched them. He saw her steal the traces of checked anger from Rafe's face with a touch on his cheek and a gentle kiss.

Perhaps he was the only one who really saw and felt

how changed **Rafe** was under the new influence of Lady Daniela, Orlando thought. One thing was certain: He didn't like what he saw. It was bad enough that the tide of public opinion had already begun to turn in Rafe's favor with his sparing the valiant Masked Rider. Now the girl looked prepared to pick up a sword to defend her golden savior, while his shrewd, marble-green eyes seemed to look out upon the world with a new, mysterious, and disconcerting focus.

The prince's yawning ennui was gone. His air of careless bonhomie had vanished. With none of his usual idle banter, Rafe had said few words, but those he had spoken were quiet, full of discipline, impact, drive.

Disgusted by the couple so urgently in love, Orlando turned away and joined the others in the hall, wondering what the hell would become of his plans if Rafe lived to get his soon-to-be wife pregnant.

By the look of them, that wouldn't take long, and he didn't know if he could arrange the prince's demise that quickly. Thus far, the oblivious Rafe had passed through his lethal traps miraculously unscathed. If he sired a son on Daniela, the throne would fall to their child, not to Rafe's younger brother, Prince Leo. Orlando could not allow that to happen.

He glanced over his shoulder at them in the other room, then narrowed his eyes as they kissed, thinking themselves unobserved. Orlando turned away with a heart full of envy and hate. With his dark good looks, his wealth and title, and his connection to the royal house, he'd had many beautiful women, but no one had ever kissed *him* that way.

Not that he had much use for gentleness with a woman. His loving usually left welts on soft skin; he reveled in secrets and perversity. His women were carefully selected and to these he bestowed rewards of shuddering shame in exchange for the cries of pain that were his delight.

Still, he did not understand the arcane bond between the prince and his newest plaything. The strange power of it frightened him. Perhaps it was time to turn Rafe's fair little ally against him, he mused. The beauty of it was, he wouldn't even have to lie.

The cabinet reconvened after the break, but the afternoon session was cut short when Lady Daniela suddenly had her fill of Don Arturo's condescending manner toward Rafe. She interrupted the prime minister in the middle of his snide explanation.

"That will do, sir!" she uttered, rising from Rafe's lap to stand, leaning toward the man in blazing fury, her hands planted on the table.

Don Arturo gaped at her, but when Rafe stifled a laugh, hiding his mouth behind his fist, the prime minister's temper snapped.

"You shouldn't even be in here, little miss! Who do you think you are?"

"A patriot and your future queen, sir, that's who," she belted right back at him.

Rafe laughed in delight, but the ministers gasped.

Daniela Chiaramonte wasn't done. "You're the one who shouldn't be here if this is how you speak to your country's sovereign lord. I never saw such insolence in my life! You're supposed to be serving Ascencion, not sewing discord. Why are you deliberately undermining His Highness?"

The peaceable minister of agriculture attempted to intervene. "Don Arturo is not undermining His Highness, your ladyship—"

"The devil he's not," she spat, her eyes blazing aquamarine

"Daniela," Rafe purred from behind her.

"Yes, my lord?" she replied, still fixing Don Arturo in her kittenish glare.

"Would you excuse us for a moment?"

"As you wish, my lord," she said stiffly, but she turned to him before she exited and asked him privately in a tone of agitation, "Your father wouldn't take this from them. Why should you?"

"Go, my sweet," he murmured gently, kissing her hand.

Orlando's gaze swept the council chamber as he felt the tension climbing with every second. He had a feeling that the moment the lady left the room, all hell was going to break loose.

Daniela nodded stiffly to him, then walked out, shoulders thrown back, her chin high. Rafe watched her until the door had closed. Then he turned back to them with fire and brimstone in his eyes.

"Don Arturo," he said calmly. "Gentlemen of the cabinet. You are *fired*!" he roared, slamming his fist on the table before him.

Listening outside the door, Dani's eyes flew open wide at Rafael's furious bellow. When the prime minister challenged him, he went on the rampage, by the sound of it. Everyone in the other room was shouting, but Rafael's deep, commanding voice thundered over theirs.

Oh, Lord, what have I started? she thought, paling.

Just then, the frightfully dignified palace steward came marching down the hall and saw her eavesdropping. His wrinkled face drew into a lordly frown.

Chagrined, Dani withdrew from the door. She supposed any moment now the dismissed cabinet members would come gusting out of the council chamber in anger and she certainly did not want to get caught in their exodus. She could scarcely believe she had lost her temper so completely as to have yelled like a quarrelsome fishwife at Don Arturo di Sansevero, the king's most venerated official, for heaven's sake. Yet she was delighted that Rafael finally refused to tolerate the man's insolence any longer.

With mixed feelings at the knowledge that she would probably be cast somehow as the villainess in all this when the king and queen came back, she hurried off toward her apartment in the hopes that there, at least, she might manage to stay out of trouble.

Sweeping down the hall past one of the main salons, Dani heard trilling laughter from an artfully cultured so-prano voice. Halted by curiosity, she peered through the wide-open doorway into the salon and saw Chloe Sinclair elaborately arranged on a striped cream-and-gold couch with her pink silk scarf draped over its scrolled arm and her dainty feet tucked under her. The woman was radiant with laughter, dimples winking, the afternoon sun gilding her champagne-blond hair.

At her feet and seated on ottomans around her sat an ar-dent group of worshipers, dashing blades who hung on her every word and offered lavish compliments. Young ladies sat demurely by, gazing wistfully at her as though they only wished they could be a fraction as dazzling as she.

Dani's heart fell. If ever there had been a feminine equivalent for the prince's celestial beauty, it was surely this bright, sugar-spun fairy queen.

What is she doing here? She must have come to see Rafael, but . . .

Dani didn't know how to complete the thought without growing furious at the implications. After all, she was marrying Rafael tomorrow.

In the brief second that she stood there, the English diva's sky-blue eyes flicked to her. Recognition caught in her eyes and turned at once to hostility. Chloe's laughter died down, but she looked right through Dani and turned away again, redirecting her diamond smile to one of the young bucks at her knee—cutting Dani as thoroughly as though she had slammed the door in her face.

Clenching her jaw, Dani turned from the salon door and

forced herself to keep walking until she was in her rooms. Angrily, she paced back and forth in her apartment, arms folded over her chest, waiting for Rafael to come to her. Obviously he had called an end to the meeting downstairs, so when the fighting was over she expected he would come and see her.

Unless he allowed himself to be distracted by that arrogant theater woman! she thought. There was no use denying it. She was outlandishly jealous and petrified of the famous diva's hold on Rafael. Chloe Sinclair had the beauty and sophistication worthy of a royal prince and, seeing her, Dani felt all the more like a tomboy-oddball misfit.

Some of the flowers in the sitting room were already wilting. She reached to snatch a dying rose impatiently from one of the bouquets and yelped with pain as she pricked her finger on a thorn. She abandoned the sitting room and paced back into the bedchamber, sucking her pierced finger until it stopped hurting. Restlessly, she went out onto the balcony, squinted against the high sun, and counted the dragging minutes.

He must come, she thought. He had promised her that later today he would take her personally to the docks to say goodbye to the Gabbiano brothers, who were being deported to Naples that afternoon.

A few minutes later, one of her maids came to the edge of the balcony and said she had a caller. Dani all but ran into the other room, but in the doorway she drew up sharply in surprise.

Dressed all in black, Orlando stood admiring her flowers.

The Duke Orlando di Cambio had the Fiori family resemblance. Raven-haired, darker complected, and somewhat older than Rafael, aside from his coloring, he looked astonishingly like the prince. He was carrying a small leatherbound document box. As she stepped into the room, he turned to her and offered her a smile that did not quite reach his cryptic, ice-green eyes.

"Lady Daniela." His voice was deep and quiet. He bowed to her. "His Highness is preoccupied at the moment and asked me to check on you."

"Is he?" She felt the blood draining from her face.

Preoccupied, was he? Anger flooded her, out of all proportion. She did her best to hide her reaction from his kinsman, not wishing to make a fool of herself in her jealousy.

Orlando cast a quick glance toward the heavyset maid standing at attention in the doorway, then looked at Dani again. "Shall we take a turn down the hall and talk a bit?"

"As you wish."

Orlando gestured toward the door. "After you, my lady."

She was almost too angry to notice where they were going. All she could see in her mind's eye was Rafael and his silvery English beauty. *Name your heart's desire, Daniela. Anything you want,* she thought angrily, remembering his attentions last night. How did he propose to fix her roof if he was busy fawning on that theater woman?

Simmering, she kept in step with Orlando's long strides as they walked down the empty marble corridor. At the far end of the hallway, a small potted lemon tree basked on a sunny balcony whose French doors had been left open to admit the breeze. The wispy curtains billowed gracefully. They headed for it.

Orlando was silent, his head high. He had a wider brow and a slightly hooked, aquiline nose, but he even carried himself rather like Rafael, she thought. Before he detected her anger and she humiliated herself with revealing the cause, she strove to be civil and make conversation.

"I was not aware that His Highness had any cousins," she remarked coolly. "I thought all of the Fiori except

Rafael's father were slain in that unspeakable butchery of King Alphonse and Queen Eugenia."

"Rafe and I are distant cousins," he replied. "The di Cambio line left Ascencion a hundred years ago and resettled in Tuscany after some absurd family argument."

She was curious about the history of the renowned family she was about to join, but he seemed disinclined to speak more about it or himself, and she was in no mood to press him. They arrived at the balcony and he swept his hand before her, inviting her to step outside. Cautiously, she moved past him.

The lemony scent from the little potted tree filled the sun-warmed air. The balcony overlooked the broad graveled drive that led from the huge black gates of the palace grounds up to the grand front entrance. She could see soldiers posted here and there below, carriages coming and going on the kingdom's business.

Orlando balanced the document box on the railing and stared at her. "Lady Daniela, the truth is I have come to speak to you about your impending marriage. You said back there in the council chamber that you are a patriot, and I do believe that's true. I believe you want what's best for Ascencion and for Rafael."

"Of course I do."

He hesitated and looked off toward the horizon, frowning. "I fear my cousin is on a reckless course. Please understand that my first loyalty must be to Ascencion and King Lazar. What I have to tell you, I'm afraid, won't be easy to hear."

It couldn't be harder, as the moments dragged, than knowing her fiancé was even now dallying with his beautiful mistress. She thrust the thought angrily aside and folded her arms over her chest. "What is it?"

Orlando looked at her again, his expression grave. "I fear that by marrying you, Rafe is jeopardizing his future and may well cause another rift in the royal family like the one that drove my ancestors away from Ascencion a century ago."

Taken aback, she stared up at him.

"I am fond of Rafe, you understand, but everyone knows he misbehaves. He's good-natured and doesn't always take matters as seriously as he should. I'm not sure he realizes the consequences he may have to pay if he marries you. I've tried to make him understand, but he won't listen, so in the prince's best interest, I had to come to you."

She felt her blood running cold. "What consequences?"

"Well, to put it plainly: The likelihood is that King Lazar will disinherit him and name Prince Leo his successor to the throne."

"What?" she cried. Immediately she thought of Rafael's words last night on the boat when he had talked about his strained relationship with his father.

"Just before the royal family sailed for Spain, the king threatened Rafe in front of the whole cabinet with the loss of the crown, in favor of Prince Leo."

"I can't believe His Majesty would really carry out such a threat," she said in horror. "Do you? Rafael would be crushed."

"Well, he has caused his family a great deal of embarrassment."

She winced. "I still don't believe King Lazar would disinherit him because of me. I may be poor, but I'm from a good family—"

"You were arrested for highway robbery, my lady. That point rather thrusts your pedigree into the background. Do you really think Their Majesties will accept a known criminal as the mother of future Fiori kings? They will see you as a taint in the royal bloodlines, no better than if you were Chloe Sinclair."

She looked sharply at him. He gave her a regretful smile, a trace of calculation in his ice-green eyes.

"They can dissolve the marriage, Lady Daniela, and they will. Believe me, they have the power."

"But you don't understand, I owe Rafael. He spared my life and freed my friends! I gave him my word. I can't go back on it."

"If you owe him, all the more reason to refuse him. Marry Rafael, and you wreck his life. Is that what you want?"

"Of course not. Why do you people treat him like a child? He's a grown man and I'm the one he wants!" she cried, more plaintively than she had intended.

There was a silence. Orlando's steady, pitying gaze seemed to ask, *Then why is he right now with Chloe Sinclair?*

"My dear child," he said at length, "I hate to see you get hurt. You're so young. It really is unscrupulous of him."

Her mouth quivered with hurt. "What do you mean?"

He shook his head. "I've seen him do this thirty, forty times. These affairs of his last a week, maybe a fortnight. Come, surely you've heard about his reputation."

"It's just talk," she attempted.

"No, it's not," he said sadly. "It always starts out as though he has found the love of his life. Expensive gifts, pretty compliments, smooth talk. Seduction. And then he gets bored, I'm afraid. Chloe Sinclair is the only one who has been able to hold his interest for more than a month, and I think we can both guess why. You're not like that," he said, his gaze and his tone both softening. "You deserve better than that. Don't allow yourself to be dazzled or you will end up looking the fool. He may be the crown prince, he may be my cousin, but as I am a gentleman, I'll stand here and tell you, Lady Daniela, that when it comes to women, Rafael di Fiore is a cad. Surely this is not news to you. He gets away with everything because he knows how to draw women in. You'll be under his thumb before you know what happened to you, and by then he'll be on to some new plaything."

She stared at him, holding back tears by sheer dint of will. Every word he'd spoken came as though he'd read it verbatim from a diary of her secret fears. A lump was forming in her throat as Orlando added, "I hate to be the one to break the news, but I think it's safe to say you are just another of his whims. I'm sorry."

She shook her head briefly and turned away, her heart pounding. She felt sick to the pit of her stomach. She had known. Oh, she had known he was too good to be true.

"I'm afraid there's more," Orlando said gently, opening the document box.

In sudden revulsion, she half-feared it contained bribe money to make her agree to give Rafael up, the final insult to her pride, but when he nodded for her to look inside, instead she saw five small portraits of young women. "Who are they?"

"These are the young ladies from among whom the prince was ordered to choose his bride." He went on to describe briefly the bargain King Lazar had struck with his son, giving him the helm of Ascencion during his absence in exchange for Rafael's promise to settle on one of the girls in the portraits. "This is the main reason I believe Rafe will be disinherited if he marries you," Orlando said soberly. "He didn't like his father ordering him to marry—taking away his freedom. Nor did his pride like it that these girls had already been selected without anyone consulting him. You see, I fear he is marrying you as a slap in the face to the king."

"Oh, God," she whispered in horrified shock. She lowered her head and shut her eyes, hating herself in that moment for her provincial naïveté.

What a stupid fool she was, walking right into that rake's silky trap. How could she have thought that a golden god like Prince Rafael would want a scrawny red-headed tomboy like her—a criminal—when he had nearly half a dozen princesses to choose from for his wife and Chloe Sinclair for his lover? How could she have failed to see at once that his sole intention was to shock the world and infuriate His Majesty?

He had only been pretending last night, she realized. God, what a fool she had been, playing right into his hands! She shuddered at the thought of the liberties she had allowed him to take with her person, all against her better judgment. She had trusted him last night, body and soul, and he had been toying with her all along, the same way he had been toying with her the night of the ball when he had ordered his friends to procure her for his lecherous amusement.

What a hypocrite he was, extracting her promise of honesty in the jail when, meanwhile, he had been standing there lying to her about his own true motives.

I hate him, she thought. She suddenly missed Mateo desperately, her one true steady friend. She missed Grandpapa and she wanted to go home.

"I have no doubt that in the king's eyes, Rafe's marrying you will be the last straw," Orlando went on. "The throne will go to Leo. What will become of Rafe, I don't know. What will become of Ascencion, however, that is the real question."

Dani lifted her head, opening her eyes again. She crossed her arms over her chest, roiling with terrible hurt and fury as she stared out over the city. "If Rafael is such a despicable cad that he would do this to his father and to me, why do you want to see him ascend to the throne anyway? Maybe he doesn't deserve it."

"He has been trained all his life to be king. He's not incompetent, he just lacks maturity. Hopefully, that will come in time. Besides, the only option is Prince Leo, who is but ten years old. A minor on the throne jeopardizes the stability of a country."

She closed her eyes, struggling to think over the chaos of her emotions. "I don't know what I am to do, Your Grace. I can't simply refuse him. My friends are still in custody. If I go back on my word, Rafael will be furious. God knows, I don't want to marry such a cad or bring down King Lazar's fury on myself, but if I refuse him now, he could still send the Gabbiano brothers to the gallows. Even when they move to Naples, they will be watched, at least for a time."

"That's true. Well," he said, drawing a deep breath, "considering that the wedding is to take place tomorrow, maybe it is too late to call it off. Perhaps our only hope at this point is to procure an annulment when the king and queen return."

She glanced at him uncertainly.

"Do you understand what is required to obtain an annulment?" he asked in a delicate tone.

She shook her head.

"It means you must not . . . yield yourself to him. If the prince gets you with child . . . well, there is nothing more dismal than a king's unwanted bastard," he said in a low, rather bitter voice.

"I understand." She looked away. That much of it was cause for relief, she thought, staring with a downward, dispirited gaze at her hands lying limply on the railing. Vulnerable hurt throbbed in her, but at least now she needn't worry about dying in childbirth.

A few moments passed in silence. Dani glanced over her shoulder toward the hallway to see if Rafael had come back yet from his tête-à-tête with Chloe Sinclair. It would not do for him to see Orlando and her together, lest he suspect something.

"I confess, I didn't know what to expect from a female highwayman," the Florentine duke remarked. She looked over and found Orlando watching her. "Perhaps by law you should have gone to the gallows," he murmured as he reached out and brushed his knuckle down the curve of her cheek. "Still, you are quite a find."

She pulled away with a scarlet blush, confused by his improper caress.

"Give him up when the time comes, and I'll make it my business to protect you from the king and queen's wrath. Your willingness to lay no claim on Rafael will help me bargain with Their Majesties for your freedom. I can see to it that you are granted immunity for your crimes. If, at that time, you are still pure, well . . ."—he gave her a cool, enigmatic smile—"perhaps you and I can reach an arrangement of our own."

"Don't be indecent," she forced out, shocked by his proposition. "When Rafael and I are married, you will be my kinsman, too."

He slid her a dark, knowing smile, locked the document box, and walked away.

"*How* can you think to attach yourself to that scrawny little country wench?" Chloe spat, her blue eyes narrowed and cold. She paced back and forth across the salon, her gauzy gown swirling around her legs. "Do you really think *she* can satisfy you? Well, let me tell you, loverboy, the thrill will soon wear off! She's just like the rest of them. She's going to bore you out of your skull, and you're going to come crawling back to me—but when you do, all you're going to get is a door slammed in your face! Do you think I need you? I can have any man that I want!"

Rafe sighed.

"I can!" she shouted, taking another enraged step toward him. "Anyone! Nic, Orlando, even the king if I want him!"

"For God's sake, have a little decency," he muttered, unimpressed by her threats.

She trilled a brutal, nervous laugh. "Does that scare you, Rafie? Afraid I'll have more fun in your papa's bed? I'm sure I would. He's still as virile as a stallion. The king is a *real* man, not like you."

"And in thirty years of marriage, he has never once cheated on my mother. Pretty as you are, Chloe, I don't think he's going to break his record for you."

She sneered at him. "You little mama's boy. I should seduce him just to spite you. I'd wager he needs a good lay, because the queen's nothing but a tired old hag."

She would insult his mother now? he thought, checking his anger. "Ah, what a shame you think so, for Her Majesty has such a high opinion of you," he said lightly.

His sarcasm flustered Chloe only for a heartbeat. "I know your mother hates me. She hates every woman who tries to get near you."

He shrugged. "She's merely a superior judge of character."

"And you're still tied to her apron strings! Maybe I'll take Orlando instead. What do you say to that?" she flung at him.

"Sleep with the gardener if it soothes your vanity, my dear, I'm sure I don't give a damn. It's not as though you were chaste when I met you."

"Bastard!" she hissed, but to Rafe's surprise, she still didn't throw her dalliance with Adriano in his face.

He knew something had been going on between his old boyhood friend and his mistress for some time, not that he particularly cared. He'd have to be blind not to notice. At nearly every social event, Chloe and Adriano could be found snickering together, making nasty remarks about people to each other behind their hands. The stunning pair were inseparable, constantly clinging to each other, doting on each other in a way that appeared mere abundant affection, but which Rafe had rather indifferently assumed was more.

"Maybe I will," she went on. "Your cousin is *so* handsome and I hear he really knows how to satisfy a woman—"

"Frankly, I don't care whom you take to your bed, so long as you understand that you are no longer welcome in mine," he said sharply, out of patience with her.

She flinched, then fell silent, staring at him in reproach.

"You'll bore of her," she promised bitterly, then turned her back on him and walked over to the striped couch, where she sat. She crossed her arms under her sumptuous breasts, exhibiting them to best advantage, and glared straight ahead with a furious pout on her pretty lips, ignoring Rafe—or pretending to ignore him.

He stood by the window rubbing his temples. All her screaming had given him a headache, or perhaps it had been the sheer savagery of her attack.

You'll bore of her. Hell, maybe she was right, for all he knew. Half an hour ago, when Chloe had stopped him in the hall and stiffly asked to talk to him, he had walked into the salon full of resolution to end his affair with her before marrying Daniela.

But from the moment he'd stepped into the room, he had received an education on why and how exactly Chloe Sinclair alone had managed to hold him for four months. The reason, he had discovered, was that she knew exactly what to say and do to maneuver him however she liked. Though her manipulation was transparent, the fears she wielded against him were real. From the moment he had shut the door, she had played on his self-doubt like a spoiled child banging on the same key of a harpsichord, over and over again.

She's using you. It's obvious. You don't even know her. She'd promise you anything to save her neck—and gain a crown for good measure! You're so stupid, Rafe! You can't trust her. What makes you think this girl is any different from the others? You'll be bored of her in a fortnight.

Maybe Chloe was right. He was already deep in the red-head's power. He marveled, chilled now to think of the things he had revealed to her last night about his deepest fears. She could use any of that against him. Maybe he had thrown himself into this rashly and too fast. How could he ever really trust his own judgment when he had blundered so often in the past?

But he had made public his intention to marry Daniela. He had declared it before the council, and marry her he would. To back out now would be to lose face entirely.

He looked over, jarred from his tangled thoughts, when he heard a sniffle. His heart sank, seeing that Chloe had started to cry.

She lowered her head and rested her fingers on the bridge of her nose, two teardrops spilling in unison down her cheeks, on cue. "Why do you make me say such ugly things? I hate you. I love you. I only want to make you happy."

He stared at her, knowing he was being manipulated by the tears, but helpless all the same. He couldn't stand to see a woman cry—and Chloe knew it. She probably even believed that she loved him, but he had long since known that the only person in Chloe's world was Chloe. Still, he felt miserably sorry for hurting her.

When she sobbed again, he walked over to her, crouched down next to the couch where she sat, and wordlessly handed her his monogrammed handkerchief.

She took it and dabbed at her tears.

God, what am I doing? he wondered heavily, suppressing a sigh. He thought of Dani and was afraid.

He lifted his lashes and coolly studied his mistress.

With her endless appetites and bewildering mood swings, Chloe Sinclair was a self-avowed bitch, but at least they were used to each other. She knew not to expect too much from him, and God knew they were compatible in bed. Maybe it was too soon to sever ties with her. After all, as long as Chloe got what she wanted, easy things like fine presents and lots of attention, she didn't give him any grief. She didn't shake him, trip up his defenses.

Gingerly, he rested his hand on her thigh and caressed her comfortingly. "Don't cry, sugar-sweet," he murmured. "Everything will be all right."

She sniffled prettily and eyed him askance, sulking. "I'm not important to you. You don't care about me."

"You know that's not true."

"You wouldn't marry her if you loved me!" she said, fresh tears rising to glimmer in her large blue eyes.

"I have a duty to my family and to Ascencion," he said softly. "You know that. It's all a matter of bloodlines. I told you that my father was hounding me to choose a wife."

"But what's so great about her?"

The pleading insecurity in her big blue eyes took him aback. He knew Chloe had not felt threatened in the slightest by the five princesses in the portraits. But when it came to Daniela, she pouted and lowered her head, a long, graceful swath of golden hair falling forward to veil her rosy cheek. "Are you in love with her, Rafe?"

It was a question he didn't know how to answer, but he had no desire to reignite her fury. "Sweetheart, I've only known her for a few days," he replied evasively.

She huffed a bit but did not explode. Slowly he exhaled with relief.

His answer felt like a shameful betrayal of Dani and left

him feeling even more like a heel, but his adolescent impulses rebelled against the surge of guilt.

Hang it all, society recognized his right as a wealthy male to keep a mistress if he chose. Daniela surely knew that, too. Every man of fashion had a lady on the side. Only the Rock of Ascencion was the model husband, and everyone knew Rafe the Rake wasn't the man his father was.

"Listen," he said, caressing her thigh again lightly, "we don't need to make a decision about each other here and now. Maybe we should think about it for a few days."

Head down, her sapphire gaze slid askance to his. He saw her calculating what she might be able to get out of him for this.

He continued petting her and spoke soothingly. "You go back to your townhouse and just relax for a few days. Pamper yourself a little and see your friends while I get through this wedding, all right? I'll come and see you soon."

"Promise?"

Guiltily, he nodded.

Then she sighed and gave him a melting look. "All right. You know I can deny you nothing. But first . . ." She slipped her arms around his neck, nuzzling his cheek. "Oh, Rafe," she breathed into his ear, causing him to shiver, "let's make love. Right now. I miss you, Rafe. I need you. I never got to give you your birthday present."

His whole being protested when she kissed him, parting his lips with her tongue. He tensed, too much a gentleman to brush her off, but determined to extricate himself from her clutches without rousing another temper tantrum or more tears.

She sighed, ending the kiss, then lay back against the couch's cushions, toying with the ribbons on her dress, frisky invitation in her eyes. "Play with me, Rafie."

Shaking himself out of a stare, he forced a smile of regret. "You could tempt a saint, sugar-sweet. Unfortunately, I'm scheduled for a couple more meetings this afternoon." He glanced at the clock, but didn't deign to tell her that the promise he'd made was to escort Dani to the docks to say goodbye to the Gabbiano brothers. He was already late.

"We'll be quick."

"*Cherie,* there are some pleasures I refuse to rush," he whispered.

"You incorrigible charmer, I think you are just putting me off." She gazed at him with wistful adoration in her eyes. "I'm sorry I hurt you, Rafe."

He stared at her, realizing that he wasn't all that hurt . . . which was just another proof, perhaps, that he had known better from the start than to let himself truly care about the spoiled, cosseted beauty.

Perhaps he had chosen her deliberately because she posed no threat to his defenses, unlike certain redheads of his acquaintance. For the life of him, he could not imagine Dani ever saying deliberately cruel things to anyone. The thought brought another severe wave of self-disappointment washing through him and filled him with the need to get away from his mistress at once.

Suavely bending to kiss her hand, he took his leave of Chloe and left the salon.

Late, damn it, he thought, hurrying down the marbled hall. That was all he needed—for his bride to hate him, too.

A short while later, he stood apart from her and her lowly devotees on the wooden docks, tapping his riding crop against his boot, irritated and impatient with the long hug she was giving that dullard giant whom she called Rocco.

Dani's cool, distant courtesy toward him when he had

arrived to take her down to the port to say goodbye to her precious Gabbiano brothers had told him, loud and clear, that she knew he had met in private with Chloe. She did not speak a word about it, however, merely giving him the cold shoulder.

He didn't even have the heart to try to charm his way back into her good graces, he merely bore her silent rancor glumly. With every passing moment, he grew angrier at himself for not having had the mettle to break it off with Chloe. His bride looked utterly lovely in her new cerulean-blue walking gown, he thought, gazing longingly at her. She had on a charming bonnet with a couple of the pink roses he'd sent pinned to the brim, and her short gloves were white.

Next, she hugged the bespectacled middle brother, then bent down and hugged the freckled child Gianni for quite a long time. After him, she embraced their widowed mother, who had chosen to go with the boys.

Watching their tearful goodbyes made him feel like an ogre for sentencing them to this. He pulled his candy tin out of his pocket and took a peppermint, sucking it as he sulked. If nothing else, it kept his mouth busy to prevent him from shouting out, *All right, all right, they can stay!*

His merciful impulse was promptly quashed, however, when his wife-to-be released the child and turned to her lifelong devotee, the noble Signore Mateo.

Rafe narrowed his eyes and scrutinized the pair together, searching for signs of a more-than-friendly affection. Daniela took Mateo's arm and together they turned away, walking to the edge of the dock, apparently deep in some urgent conversation.

Rafe's temples throbbed. Then he noticed the little scamp Gianni grinning at him, and scowled as the child waved. He forced himself to pace back toward the coach to wait, shocked down to his glossy bootheels to discover that he hadn't even married the chit and already he was turning into a jealous husband.

"I need you to do this for me, Mateo," Dani pleaded, staring up into her friend's stormy dark eyes. "You're the only one I can trust."

"You know I will, but why get involved with these people?" he asked angrily, the wind riffling through his thick curls. "I will come back the moment I can and rescue you."

"How many years have I been telling you that I can take care of myself?" she whispered, then glanced warily over her shoulder at her royal fiancé. Rafael's broad back was to her as he stalked toward the coach, the evening sun gilding his dark-gold hair. She turned back to Mateo. "Furthermore, you will not come back here. You know if they catch you here again, you'll hang! Use your head. Your mother and brothers need you."

He stared at her sorrowfully, then hung his head. "I failed you. It's my fault you were caught and now you're forced to submit to him! It's a disgrace—"

"I'll be fine, Mateo. I can hold him at bay until the king and queen return. If you really want to help me, do as I'm asking—go to Florence and learn what you can about this Duke Orlando di Cambio."

"Why do you want to know about him?"

"He says he wants to help me, and that if I cooperate, my marriage to Rafael can be dissolved when the king and queen come back, but there's something about him I just don't trust. He's as slick as oil and he walks around the palace as if he owns it. Now, will you do this for me or are you going to be a mule?"

He sighed, shaking his head. "You know I'll do it."

"Good. But be careful. I don't know the extent of Orlando's power in Florence. He seems possibly dangerous."

"I'll be glad to spy on him for you—if the prince's guards will let me out of their sight."

"Tell them you're going to look for work," she suggested.

He nodded his assent.

Inwardly, she blessed her saints, for although half of her purpose was to learn more about the mysterious Orlando, the other half was to give Mateo some useful mission to stop him from attempting to come back and rescue her, in his usual misguided bravery.

"The nobles of Florence ought to know Orlando. You might try talking to their servants. I was able to learn, also, that he owns a shipping enterprise with docks and warehouses at the mouth of the Arno River at Pisa."

Just then the ship's bell clanged, summoning him. A few of the Royal Guards approached to escort him to the boat. Dani and Mateo stared at each other in distress.

"Mateo." She winced. "I'll miss you." Overwhelmed with sorrow at the hard goodbye, she moved to embrace him, but he held up his hand, looking away.

"No. If I hold you, I'll never be able to let you go. Besides, he'd probably blow my head off," he muttered, jerking a nod toward the land where Rafael waited, pacing, head down.

"I'm sorry," she whispered, not knowing what else to say.

"For what? Being born a duke's daughter? That wasn't your fault." Clenching his hat in his hands, he squinted toward the horizon. "Go to your prince, Dani, but never forget he doesn't deserve you any more than I do. I doubt there will be any annulment."

"Mateo, he's only using me."

He gazed at her. "I don't think so." With that, he gave

her a kiss on the forehead, turned around, and slowly walked up the gangplank, his shoulders squared.

The sailors drew it up after he was aboard, and soon the ship set sail.

Dani was still standing on the docks alone after the frigate had disappeared from sight. She kept her paisley shawl wrapped around her, though the evening air was balmy. She had not felt so alone since childhood.

She heard footfalls nearing her. The docks' boards creaked as Rafael approached.

She did not turn to him. He came and stood behind her, offering the warmth of his body and a comforting caress on her arms. She would have liked nothing better than to turn in his arms and cry her eyes out, but instead her posture stiffened with the still-fresh wounds from all that Orlando had revealed to her.

Her temporary bridegroom was an amoral cad, but she would not wreck his life for him. Nor would he weaken her, with all his practiced sweetness.

She had never needed anyone. She never would.

Rafael wrapped his arms more snugly around her waist and lowered his chin to her shoulder. "How are you doing?" he murmured.

"I'm fine," she said in a low, prickly tone, wishing he would not be kind to her.

"They'll be all right," he whispered tenderly, giving her a caring squeeze around her waist. "We'll make sure of it."

Gathering her composure, she turned around and gazed up into his green-gold eyes, so full of gentle concern as he frowned down at her, his thick, golden eyebrows knit.

"That Mateo . . ." he said with a taut nod, his jaw slightly clenched, as though he were forcing himself to admit it. "He seems like a good man."

She stared up at him. He cleared his throat and glanced away, giving his cravat an embarrassed tug. His admission was a final, unsought generosity that she had never expected in a thousand years. It cut straight to her heart, and she hated him for being able to weaken her so.

"Yes," she forced out in reproach, "he is a prince among men." She brushed past him and stalked to the coach, shaking. Taking her seat inside the vehicle, she saw him standing where she had left him, looking baffled by her curt reply.

Tilting his head, he sent her a questioning, hurt glance. She dropped her gaze to her lap, her shoulders bunching up defensively. She felt wretched all of a sudden to know she had been mean to him. It was unlike her, but he made her feel so vulnerable, so confused and lost.

Sliding his hands into his pockets, Rafael seemed to shrug off her remark to himself, like a man accustomed to moody women. Furtively, she watched him as he came walking toward her.

He really was the most excellent looking man, she thought bitterly. Her gaze traveled up his muscular legs in dark blue pantaloons to his lean waist and broad shoulders. Peeking from behind her bonnet's brim at his classical face and gorgeous lips, she could recall exactly the taste of his peppermint kiss.

Her body tensed and she tore her gaze away.

He sat down wearily across from her in the coach and signaled the driver with a knock on the wood. They heard the coachman urge the team. The harnesses jangled and the vehicle rolled into motion.

A tense moment of silence passed between them.

"Is there something bothering you?" His tone was ginger.

She glared out the window. "No."

"Dani," he said, gently chiding.

"I want to go home," she said with a pitiful catch in her

voice. She could feel him gazing at her, but she refused to look at him.

"Your home is with me now."

"It is not!" she burst out. "There are people who are counting on me! I have a duty to take care of them! I haven't checked in on them in days. I haven't seen my grandfather or Maria—"

"Dani," he murmured soothingly. He leaned forward, bracing his elbows on his knees. He took her hands and held them in his own. "You are to be my wife, the crown princess. Your duty is to me now and to Ascencion. I've already sent a staff of the best nurses in the kingdom to help Maria with your grandfather."

"You did?"

"Yes."

"Well, he needs me!"

"Darling, hush now, everything's going to be all right. I venture to say this is just a case of prewedding nerves."

She looked away from his gentle yet troubled gaze, realizing she was being churlish. For some reason—pride, perhaps—she could not bring herself to ask about Chloe Sinclair. Rafael probably didn't even know he was doing anything wrong; like Orlando had said, he was like a lovable, wayward child. There was no use making the coming days any more unpleasant than they were already going to be.

"We'll get through this," he told her. "You're not going back on your word, are you?"

"It is madness, Rafael. You do know that, don't you? You should not be marrying me. What is your father going to say?"

"'Congratulations,' I should think."

She rolled her eyes at his nonchalant smile. His gaze was veiled, mysterious, and his green-gold eyes were as full of intelligence as any she'd ever seen—not childlike innocence.

Just like Orlando, this man had tricks up his sleeve, she thought. She decided the two of them were equally awful.

"My father doesn't run my life, Dani," he remarked as he released her hands and sat back again, crossing his ankle over his opposite knee and lounging against the Moroccan leather squabs. Bracing his elbow on the window ledge, he watched the landscape rolling by and spoke in a musing tone. "Oh, he may be a bit peeved at first, granted, but when he knows that the future of Ascencion is safe, he'll forget all his fury. Mark my words."

"And how do you intend to assure him of that?"

"By siring a son on you, of course."

She gasped and stared at him, but said not a word—she dared not. Nor could she think how she was possibly going to resist on her wedding night, less than twenty-four hours away, when this wicked, fallen angel came to her bed . . . offering heaven.

≈ CHAPTER ≈
TEN

"You have lost your mind. Do you know that?"

Hours before his wedding, Rafe stood before the mirror, giving his cravat a tug; then he checked the cut of his striped waistcoat in the mirror. "Most definitely," he agreed. His mood was buoyant. It was a fine, clear day and soon he would marry the girl that he, not his father, had chosen.

He had taken his life in hand.

Arms folded over his chest, Adriano was leaning by the mirror, still staring at him. "Rafe."

Rafe ignored him and nodded to his valet. The man held up his gleaming white coat so that Rafe could slip his arms into the sleeves. He shrugged it on.

"Excellent, Your Highness," his valet murmured, straightening it on him.

Rafe nodded, inspected himself in the mirror, and flicked a thread off the gold epaulet.

"Your dress sword, sir."

Rafe accepted the long silver blade, sliding it into the jeweled sheath at his hip

According to the reports brought to him every half hour, his little bride's progress was coming along more slowly, her ladyship fighting and balking every step of the way. By the sound of it, her final transformation from bandit to bride was proving a difficult one, painful for everyone involved.

"Rafe," Adriano said again, cutting into his thoughts. "Tell me you're not really going to go through with this."

Rafe flashed him a grin.

Adriano glared. "What about Chloe?"

Rafe clapped him suddenly on the arm, blithely deciding on the instant that he wouldn't be needing Chloe after all. Dani was really all that he required. "I've got a smasher of an idea, di Tadzio. You can have her."

Adriano stared blankly at him. *"What?"*

"You seem to have an inordinate interest in the woman. She's all yours. A hint—don't fall for the tears. She weeps at the drop of a hat. That's what the theaters pay her for. I think she fancies Orlando a bit, though. Be warned."

"It's not like that between Chloe and me," he said flatly.

Selecting a cologne from his expensive collection, Rafe gave a chiding laugh. "You flirt with her. I've seen you. Don't misunderstand—I don't mind in the slightest. I give you my blessing. Frankly, I thought you had already indulged—not your fault, of course. Chloe can make herself hard to resist, I know," he said easily, waving off Adriano's protest. Suddenly sensing danger for his shy little bride, Rafe turned to him. "You know Chloe is angry about my marriage."

"Of course. I just came from her townhouse. She is distraught."

Rafe's gaze hardened. "Keep her on a leash for me, di Tadzio, will you? I mean it. I don't want her mauling Daniela."

"Rafe." Adriano stood and met him eye to eye. "Don't go through with this. God, what's happened to you? You used to be so amusing. For weeks you've been a bore."

"Tell me how you really feel, di Tadzio," he said, chuckling as he walked away.

"Chloe loves you!" Adriano exclaimed, following him. "Marry one of your father's broodmares if you must, but she's the one you belong with. Yes, she and I spend a lot of time together, but all she talks about is you. 'Tell me about Rafe when you were boys.' 'Will Rafe like this gown?' If I take her out to a café, 'We must bring Rafe here!' 'Do you really think Rafe cares for me?' "

Rafe rolled his eyes.

"Frankly, I think you're making a big mistake."

"A mistake?" He grabbed Adriano by the arm and pulled him over to the balcony, thrusting the French doors open wider. "Look."

Below them in the sunshine, a cheering throng sprawled as far as the eye could see. "A royal wedding. The Masked Rider, no less! You're missing the whole point, di Tadzio. Look at them down there. They're eating this up!"

Adriano's gaze moved slowly over the throng. "I see you learned something from your years of chasing actresses," he said softly. "You've become quite the showman."

"You witless ornament, you understand nothing!" Angrily, Rafe turned Adriano to face him, shoving him by the shoulder. "If Chloe was under the delusion that I was going to marry her, she's the one who's out of her mind. Daniela Chiaramonte was born and bred to be queen, and you can tell Chloe I said so."

Adrian looked at him in cool hauteur for a moment. "I'll do that, Your Highness."

Something about Adriano's insolent stare infuriated him. "You really ought to try her, di Tadzio. She's even better on her back than she is on stage." He kept going. "What's the matter? Afraid she's too much woman for you?"

Adriano muttered a foul epithet at him and left the room. Rafe stared after him, his anger ablaze, then he noticed Elan's glance slide from the slammed door to him.

"What?" he snapped.

Elan's face assumed its most diplomatic look. "Your Highness, Adriano is . . . how shall I say? Ah, never mind."

"You think he's right? Is that it?" he demanded, shoving aside a vague, uneasy flicker of recognition. Some things were better left ignored. Still, he was angry at himself for yelling at so fragile a creature. God forbid that he had just set Adriano off again on one of his ghastly suicide threats.

"No, nothing like that." Elan came toward him with a fresh glass of wine, which he gave to Rafe. "For my part, I think this is the best move you've made."

Placated somewhat, Rafe took a drink, then nodded. "Damned right it is. She's my choice. She's what Ascension needs. She's tough. She's beautiful and good, and above all, she's loyal." He was determined to believe in her. At least he was trying. "She's what I need, and if my father doesn't like it, he can leave the bloody throne to Leo for all I care."

Elan lifted his glass, regarding Rafe in amusement. "To the bride."

"The Masked Rider. Let's pray her virgin blood is the only type shed tonight," he muttered under his breath.

They clinked glasses and drank.

Dear God, prayed Dani, her face white behind her gauzy veil, *please don't let me fall flat on my face getting out of the coach. Don't let me make a fool of myself, that's all I ask.*

The splendid state carriage, drawn by six white horses, floated to a halt in front of the cathedral amid a sea of seething humanity that stretched in every direction as far as the eye could see. The Royal Guard in full dress uniform held the roaring crowd at bay along the wide steps. Dani held on to her grandfather's arm for dear life. His Grace, the Duke of Chiaramonte, looked terribly dignified with his heavy white mustache and his newly cleaned and pressed military uniform. He was humming tunelessly under his breath in his gentle, raspy tenor, but he seemed lucid enough.

"Didn't I tell you you should get Prince Rafael to woo you?" the old man said with a sidelong grin.

"Grandfather."

"Must have been my telling him about your talents, Dani, mark my word," he said with a wink. "How many young ladies out there can stand astride a galloping horse's back?"

"Oh, Grandfather."

Her composure was stretched thin from a whole day of being poked and prodded and fussed over by the snobbish royal couturiere and the hairdressers and various experts in protocol. She had fought the torturers every step of the way, but by the time they were through with her, she had to admit she would do her temporary husband no discredit.

Crowning her carefully curled hair and securing her veil in place was a tiara of glistening brilliants formed into rosebuds. It was the richest thing she had ever seen. Her gown was a masterpiece of elegant splendor. A long train of shimmering gold satin lamé, embroidered at the bottom with seashells and flowers representing Ascencion, flowed back luxuriously over her shoulders, secured in front between her breasts by a jeweled brooch depicting the lion rampant of the royal house. Her white satin petticoat had creamy Brussels lace over it and rows of folds trimmed with gold ribbon. Her long gloves and slippers were of white satin.

The perfume of the pale roses in her nosegay filled her nostrils, every inch of her skin was kissed by the pearly silk chemise she wore beneath the heavy gown, and her ears rang with the wild pealing cadence of the cathedral's bells, the slamming boom of the cannons, and the crowd's ceaseless cheering.

One glance around the square proved that Rafael had scored innumerable points in the hearts of Ascencioners everywhere. Dani had never guessed that the Masked Rider was so well loved. The royal rake's past excesses were forgotten in the ecstasy of the day. The people's faith in his honorable nature, it seemed, had been restored by his gallant show of mercy toward her and her friends. They did not realize they had played right into his hands. He was, she decided, more Machiavellian than charming, as princes went.

Just then, the coach door opened to reveal one comfortingly steady face. The friendly buzzard, young Viscount Elan, Rafael's best man, stood at the ready, giving her a bolstering smile. He helped her grandfather gingerly out of the coach, then turned back and offered her his hand.

The time had come.

Dani trembled and held her breath. Gathering all the poise she possessed, she ducked her head coming out of the coach, pausing with one foot on the step to steal a glimpse at the surging crowd, like a dizzying mosaic made of living colored tiles, and the towering gray cathedral, and the white flash of the circling birds with the sun on their wings.

The mob roared when she emerged. Swallowing hard, she looked at Elan, grateful for the sincere welcome she read in his eyes.

"Please tell me he's in there," she whispered over the crowd's roar. "Please tell me he came and that this is not some horrific jest."

"My lady, your bridegroom awaits you," he murmured with a fond look, then he gave her back to her tall, gaunt grandfather, bowing to him. "Your Grace."

Grandfather nodded. As they marched toward the entrance of the cathedral, Dani could smell the frankincense pouring out from the great doors, could already hear the pipe organ's jubilant polyphonics in a dazzling tapestry of sound, punctuated by the trumpets' proud hail.

Clinging in fright to her grandfather's steadfast arm, she could see nothing inside the church during those seconds while her eyes adjusted from the sunshine to the pious dim. As her eyes adjusted, she recalled praying in this cathedral dozens of times before, but never had the central aisle appeared so long.

Adorned with a narrow white carpet strewn with rose petals, it seemed to stretch a mile before her, and at the far end of her walk there waited a man.

The prince's tall, powerful silhouette was bathed in the multicolored light streaming through the rosetta window.

Dani stared at him from behind her veil, then looked around slowly. The cathedral was packed to the rafters with the highest nobility in the land, all wearing their pro-scribed court costumes in the style of the previous century. She was sure they must be cross with her for giving scarcely any notice of the grand event. She wished she could tell them it was Rafael's fault.

Even the choral galleries were jammed full. She did not want to wonder what all these haughty aristocrats, courtiers, and ladies truly thought of her.

The pipe organ's song blared to its crescendo and faded into silence. A hush fell. Elan looked over at Dani and gave her a firm nod.

On cue, Grandfather started down the aisle like an an-cient knight advancing relentlessly on an enemy. The organ music resumed with a subdued, stately hymn that sounded like Vivaldi.

Dani kept her gaze fixed on Rafael. Feet planted shoulder length apart, hands clasped behind his back, he stood coolly at the foot of the altar, where, in a sea of flowers, countless priests stood fanned out in a half-circle behind the red-robed Cardinal whom Rafael had imported from Rome, going over the bishop's head after his refusal to marry them. The candlelight played gorgeously over their rich robes of ruby and garnet, sapphire and gold.

How in the world had he brought all of this together so quickly? she wondered as they walked slowly down the aisle. The man had but to wave his hand and what he desired came to be.

She ceased trying to make herself believe it was real then.

Of course this wasn't really happening to her. In all likelihood, she thought, keeping her chin high and her walk slow, she was probably still in jail, in solitary confinement, hallucinating all of it.

A third of the way from the altar, she could see her groom more clearly. *Golden, magnificent Rafael.* He was so beautiful her knees went weak.

He was splendidly arrayed in the full-dress uniform of the Royal Cavalry, of which the crown prince was always the honorary commander. He was wearing a black-cinched white coat with shiny gold buttons notched up to his suntanned throat, dark blue breeches, and a jeweled saber. His tawny mane was neatly tamed, but encircling his proud brow was the simply detailed circlet of solid gold that proclaimed his status as master of all the land.

His golden green gaze moved softly, possessively over her, then he held out one white-gloved hand to her as she came closer. She barely noticed her grandfather's teary-eyed smile as she rested her hand on Rafael's and went with him to the altar.

The wedding itself was a blur. The only moment that pierced her complete, overwhelmed daze was when she and Rafael knelt, side by side, on the velvet-cushioned prie-dieux to receive the Holy Eucharist. She sneaked a sideward glance at him and spied him praying. His eyes closed, head bowed, sword at his side, he was like a medieval knight consecrating himself for battle.

She looked away quickly, moved to the core by his chivalrous beauty.

Suddenly, after a seeming eternity of prayers, Gospel admonitions that he must be a faithful husband and she an obedient wife, assorted Bible readings, songs, and amens, the wedding was done. Dani could barely even remember saying her vows, she had been so numb throughout. The genial-looking cardinal beamed at them, nodding his permission that Rafael could now kiss the bride.

When he turned to her, the holy knight she had glimpsed vanished. The wicked little smile he sent her was pure rogue. He took a step toward her, mischief in his eyes.

"Oh, no, you don't!" she breathed. Eyes widening, she pulled back, certain he was going to half-ravish her in front of the thousands of people just because that's what everyone expected Rafe the Rake to do.

But then, quizzically, his scoundrel's grin softened to a tender smile of reassurance. Gently, he took the edge of her veil between his fingertips.

"This is the last mask that shall ever hide you from me, my darling wife," he whispered. Then he lifted the gauzy netting over her head and took her face between his gloved hands.

Dani was aware of every living body in the church leaning forward as Rafael lowered his mouth to hers. But as his lips softly caressed hers with exquisite warmth, she forgot them all, everything.

She did not quite hear the thunderous applause when it broke out, nor the cardinal's proclamation as she reached for her husband's shoulders to steady herself, weak and whirling inwardly.

Smiling against her mouth, he went on kissing her. And on and on and on . . .

The lavish feast that followed took place in the banquet hall of the royal palace with Rafe presiding over the head table. His wineglass dangling between his fingers, he leaned back idly in his chair, sated and at ease after the meal. His mood was expansive. He sloshed the wine in the glass, making it whirl lightly.

Rafael di Fiore: married man, he mused. As his gaze moved over the heads of his guests at their large circular tables—there were about four hundred of his loyal friends, key nobles, and their wives gathered noisily together—he found himself filled with a deep, pleasing sense of pater familias. All that was lacking now was a row of adorable, obedient, and robustly healthy little Rafaels sitting at his table. That would come soon enough.

"Everyone must be married," he declared. "I shall make it a law."

"Then I am moving to China," Niccolo announced.

Elan smiled. A few of the others laughed. Most had resigned themselves to his marriage to the girl who had plagued them so relentlessly, accepting it with humor once their tempers had cooled.

"What could be better than this?" Rafe went on, musing aloud. "A fine meal. The cool of evening wafting in through the open doors. Laughter from the throats of friends who would gladly lay down their lives for me, and here, at my right hand," he said, capturing Daniela's fingers gently, "my sweet and lovely wife."

At his light touch, Daniela glanced anxiously at him, then immediately dropped her gaze to her untouched plate. She looked like she wanted to bolt for freedom.

He smiled faintly, watching her creamy apricot complexion grow tinged with a light cherry hue. His intrepid bride was visibly flustered but did not move her hand away. Oh, no, he thought in wry approval, her pride forbade it. He turned his hand to stroke hers lightly with his fingertips, listening to the fanciful, gracefully airy melody from the harp, flute, and violin trio who played nearby.

How will she be in bed? he wondered, watching her, but he could already guess and the knowledge moved him and aroused him intensely. *A trembling ingenue with the soul of a wildcat.*

He curled her hand over his fingers and lifted it to his lips. He brushed a lingering kiss over her knuckles and held her nervous gaze. When she peered up at him from under her cinnamon lashes, he gave her a soft, reassuring smile.

"You haven't touched your plate," he murmured. She had been visibly overwhelmed all night, startled every time somebody addressed her as *Your Highness*. "Not hungry?"

She wet her lips with a shy flick of her tongue, shook her head. "I . . . can't."

He set down his wineglass and enfolded her small hand between both of his. He leaned toward her, elbows on the table. Holding her hand close to his lips, he studied her face.

"Have I told you how beautiful you look tonight?" he murmured.

She tried to pull her hand away, scowling lightly. He held it more tightly, his smile widening.

"Don't make a display of yourself in front of all these people, I beg you," she whispered.

"What people?" he asked softly. "I only see one person. One . . . lovely young woman who shines like the silver moon, the princess of all the skies. My wife." He kissed her hand again.

She looked at him skeptically, then her gaze flicked back nervously to the throng.

"You'll get used to it, darling," he said, his tone intimate. "You'll soon learn to ignore them."

"How do I get used to you?"

"Well, I wouldn't want you to get too used to me. I would never want to bore you." Eyes dancing, he stroked his thumb over the back of her hand. "Darling, you and I merely need a little time to get to know each other better. Don't fear me."

She lowered her gaze and was very still.

"What is it, Daniela?"

She gave a small shrug.

Rafe stared at her. A wave of protectiveness washed through him the likes of which he had not felt since he was a boy. Her shyness, her painful vulnerability, struck him as unutterably endearing.

"Are you tired?" he asked gently.

She nodded, still blushing, still refusing to meet his gaze.

He reached to caress her cheek. "Why don't you go up to bed?" he suggested as his heart began to pound.

Slowly, she looked at him and searched his face, new desperation in her remarkable aquamarine eyes. Leaving his hand atop hers, he leaned toward her and kissed her satiny, glowing cheek, ignoring the cheers when he did so, the thunderous clanking of dinner knives on crystal goblets.

"There is nothing to fear," he whispered into her ear, nuzzling her cheek gently. "I promise."

She turned to him, her great eyes brimming with bottled turmoil, youthful wretchedness written all over her pale, guileless face. He stared at her, wanting her from the core of his soul. He had been patient; he had been good. Tonight he would claim his reward.

"Very well," she said barely audibly. She began pushing back from the table, looking anywhere but at him.

He sprang at once from his chair and was behind her in an instant, pulling out her chair from the table, giving her his steadying hand as she rose. She kept her stare riveted to the floor, her cheeks positively crimson as he escorted her from the table and down the few steps from the dais. In the corridor just outside the banquet hall, they stopped. She lifted her chin and searched his eyes with an expression of virginal panic.

"You need some time alone. I understand." One hand resting in a gallant pose behind his back, he bowed to kiss her hand one last time.

She nodded once and pulled her hand from his grasp.

It was a good thing he had forbidden the court from carrying out the ancient tradition of escorting the royal newlyweds to their bedroom, he thought in tender amusement as he watched her flee from him, her gauzy, pale gold train billowing out behind her. He shook his head to himself, smiling faintly as she hurried down the dim corridor. She'd probably swoon of shame when he merely handed off the blooded sheets to the palace steward, for it was necessary to provide this traditional evidence of the bride's virginity.

It's about time, ginger cat, he thought. *It's about time.* He had a feeling that tonight he was in for the game of his life.

Shaken to the core of her heart, Dani fled down the hallway, fighting tears. What was he doing to her? Cruel, despicable man! Why must he toy with her when she knew he had only married her for his secret agendas? *"Darling?"* Why was he calling her darling? She'd rather be called a cabbage than that. She did not want to see kindness in his golden green eyes. Why was he making this so hard on her?

She clung to the facts. She knew what she knew about Rafael di Fiore. He was a womanizer, a rakehell with endless appetites, and this marriage was a travesty. Why, just a few nights ago, he'd had her, a total stranger, dragged to his room—brought to him like a midnight snack!

Well, he could do his worst, but his charm was not going to work on her! she thought in a vengeance as she gained the stairs, servants whisking out of her way, showing her the path. He would not succeed in stealing her heart, no matter how tender his gazes, how gentle his words.

Gaining the opulent chamber she had been assigned, she tore free of the bridal gown with a maid's help. Ripping the tiara out of her hair, fighting her way out of the corset, she finally felt like herself again when she was wearing nothing but a plain chemise. She sent the maids away. At last she could breathe.

She went to the balcony and inhaled deeply of the cool night air. She lifted her fingertips to her temples, her head throbbing.

The last thing she wanted was Rafael di Fiore trying to tell her how *beautiful* she was, she thought with an inward sneer. What a pack of lies! Chloe Sinclair was beautiful, not her.

Forcing a deep breath, she shrugged some of the tension out of her shoulders, gazing out over a splendid view of the city, the elegant mansard roof of the palace sloping gently away from the small balcony.

The celebration in the city was still in full swing, judging by the distant noise and lights, with the occasional fireworks going off. Farther away, she could see the moon's silvery dazzle upon the sea that embraced their island home.

What a day. She didn't know how she had gotten through it, especially those last few moments and the agony of exiting the banquet hall, knowing, to her mortification, that the moment she excused herself from the table, every soul in the room knew where she was going and why.

A grueling day—and the night was still to come.

She looked fearfully over her shoulder at the bed, then she peered at the door. *I am never going to be able to resist him.* He was so beautiful and knew just how to beguile a woman. She wanted him too much . . . and she was going to wreck his future if she gave in to her desire.

Cad that he was, she couldn't ruin his life. Not when she had glimpsed his vulnerable side and knew how much he loved Ascencion. She didn't want to be the reason he lost the one thing he truly cared about.

Not stopping to heed her own scoffing observation that he would no doubt have a key, she padded over swiftly and locked the door.

Turning around, her gaze swept the room and suddenly landed on her riding boots, which had been tucked neatly in the corner with her folded breeches and shirt on the velvet-upholstered chair. She had forbidden the servants to throw her black clothes away. Now she was rather surprised that they had obeyed her.

Before she quite knew what she was doing, Dani was across the room, slipping into the black breeches and shirt. With trembling hands and no idea what she meant to do, driven by sheer survival instinct, she pulled on her riding boots. She felt stronger already, infused with hope that there was some way she could save them both. Her heart pounding wildly, she ran to the open window.

With a hard swallow and one backward glance which might have been a painful twinge of conscience, she stepped out onto the balcony and climbed over the edge, peering down. The roof had many levels, turrets poking up against the dark blue sky here and there. It was easily negotiable. She studied the situation quickly and saw that she need only slide down, drop perhaps four feet. Lower, there was a handy platform from which she could continue her descent and escape. Should she?

Never lie to me.

Mateo and the others were safe. Rafael di Fiore was only using her. Her mind was made up.

She was getting the hell out of here.

Over sherry and cigars in the billiard hall that had been the devil's den of their youth, Rafe resisted his friends' attempt to get him drunk, knowing Daniela's innocence. But by the time he pulled himself away, laughing, he wasn't exactly sober, either.

"Enough, you evil influences on my virtue," he said, laughing. "I have business to attend to this evening—"

Catcalls thundered around him. At last, he was allowed to leave amid a lewd salute involving pool sticks and humor more befitting a pack of twelve-year-olds. He bade them adieu amid cries of, "Send in the women, send in the whores! The married man has finally gone home!"

Laughing to himself as he trudged down the hall alone, he wondered if they would ever outgrow their antics and sighed to think that these were the men he had entrusted to high positions in government after disbanding the old council. Fortunately, they knew when to be serious. They hadn't laughed like that in a long time.

Tonight marked a new start, he thought as he nodded to a servant who bowed to him. He climbed the stairs wearily, still trying to absorb the fact that he was married. He hadn't expected to feel any different, but he did.

Outside the bedroom door, he paused as he laid his hand on the knob. There was no telling what he'd find when he opened the door. She could be sleeping. She could be crying. She could be waiting to hurl a dagger in his chest, for all he knew.

With a smile and a sigh, he started to turn the knob. His smile flattened to a look of displeasure but no real surprise.

Locked.

Wearily, he found the key in his waistcoat pocket and unlocked it, pausing before he went in, half fearful some strange booby trap awaited him. He quickly scanned his memory for some of his favorite practical jokes from boyhood. A bucket of water above the door to dump down on his head? A wire for him to trip over?

She wouldn't dare.

Bravely, he pushed the door open and peered in. The chamber was dark, the curtains billowing gently over the open doors to the balcony. He squinted his eyes as his gaze moved to the bed. A luminous pile of white satin. He frowned with another disturbing surge of the tender chivalry she aroused in him. Had his poor little bride collapsed in exhaustion without even bothering to undress?

"Daniela?" he said softly, closing the door behind him.

But when he walked to the bed and touched the puff of silk and petticoats, his eyes widened. There was no girl in it.

He whirled, staring around the room. She was gone. Shocked even as he cursed himself for not expecting this, he strode toward the balcony just as the thin little cry reached him from beyond, somewhere in the darkness.

"Heeeelp!"

⊰ CHAPTER ⊱
ELEVEN

A bead of sweat rolled down the side of her face as Dani clung with all her strength to the turret that was less than fifteen feet from the balcony.

Her vision had adjusted to the moonlight, and by its blue glow she saw the glint of anger in her husband's eyes, but his face assumed that maddening look of wry amusement as he rested his hands on the balcony's railing and regarded her with polite interest.

"Whatever are you doing out there, my dear?"

"Oh, don't be a beast now," she pleaded angrily, glancing at the ground God-knew-how-many feet below while she kept her arms wrapped tightly around the small turret. "I'm s-stuck. I'm going to die."

"Don't be morbid, Daniela," he said cheerfully as he stripped off his coat, then swung his leg over the rail. "I am your husband and I shall save you."

"Be careful!" she said, as it registered in a corner of her brain that this good cheer from him under such circumstances probably meant he was infuriated with her.

"Nonsense, I shall tell our children all about this night," he continued as he slid with nonchalant grace down the curve of the mansard roof and stood at its edge, considering his next move. "And our children's children. And our children's children's children." He jumped.

Dani gasped.

He landed, left foot first, with agile grace on the same small, flat perch she had used. She blinked, staring, her heart pounding.

"In fact," he said as he stepped across a ravine, "I shall have it written into the annals of Ascencion's history. Better yet, I'll declare it a holiday. Roof-climbing day, what?"

She suddenly gasped in horror as he teetered on his feet for a moment, laughing.

"You're drunk!"

Pressing himself flat against the turret as he came around to her, he looked up indignantly. "I am not. That wouldn't be very gentlemanly of me, would it? You being a vestal virgin and all. How the devil did you get up there?"

"You lunatic! I cannot believe you're drunk! You're going to get us both killed!"

"Tut, tut, my dear, I've done much stupider things than this and survived intact. Why did you climb up on that turret? I believe the direction you wanted was down."

She pursed her mouth. "I was trying to come back."

"Were you?" He passed a keen glance over her face.

"P-please, Your Highness. I don't know how much longer I can hold on."

He grinned up at her suddenly with a twinkle in his eyes that dimmed the stars. "Will you hold me as tightly as you're holding that turret?"

She squeezed her eyes shut. "I despise him, God. I despise him." She heard him laugh. She shot her eyes open. "This is not funny!"

"Ah, right. Here's what we're going to do. Give me a moment." With his much larger stride, he was able to straddle the gap in the roof that had caused her dilemma. He anchored his left foot against the angle of the roof, while his right remained planted on the narrow rim around the turret. Balanced precariously over the distant earth, he reached up his hands for her.

"You've got to be joking," she croaked as he firmly grasped her hips.

"Let go," he commanded, suddenly no humor in his voice.

"You've got nothing to hold on to. You'll fall! Go back inside!"

"Don't be frightened, sweetheart," he coaxed. "Let go. Come with me. Slowly."

"Rafael."

"It's all right. Just let go. I won't let you fall."

She closed her eyes at his gentle tone, but even though she was willing to obey, her arms would not come unclamped from the pointy turret. "I can't."

"Hush," he said. "Come. I won't let you get hurt. You've got to trust me, darling."

She swallowed hard. "A-all right. I'm going to start letting go now."

"Good. Be still in my arms."

She knew any sudden movements could upset his balance. Cursing herself for putting them both in this position, she raked her fingers down the roof as his grip around her hips tightened, lowering her, inch by inch. She prayed frantically in her mind.

She could feel the enormous strength in Rafael's arms, shoulders, and chest as he eased her against him. His movements were slow, careful, and balanced, executed with a grace which she could only conclude had been developed over years of training in fencing, for the whole kingdom knew he was an accomplished swordsman. With his great leg strength he held them both miraculously steadfast over an abyss.

She could do nothing but wait, her heart in her throat, as

he pushed off from the rim around the turret and leaned backward, pulling her and himself over the void.

They both fell upon the small flat perch to relative safety. She lay there panting in frightened relief, thanking God countless times in her mind.

"I wonder if that earned me a kiss," he mused aloud.

She looked at him, her eyes narrowed. He smiled roguishly, a few gold strands of hair falling free against his angular cheek. "No?"

"We're not inside yet."

"Can't blame me for trying," he remarked. "Must be those little breeches of yours. Really torment a man's imagination, if you don't mind my saying." He lay back on the roof, folding his arms under his head. "Beautiful night. You know, girls have risked their lives trying to get into my bedroom, not out. You are the first. You are indeed the first," he repeated more softly, his faraway stare fixed on the moon.

She gazed at his profile, his absurdly long lashes, his imperious nose and broad forehead. A wave of shame for her cowardice rose in her. "I'm sorry, Rafael."

"Well, my little cabbage-head, I suppose you are forgiven."

"I am?"

"I told you there is only one thing you could do that would anger me."

"Lie."

"Yes."

"Rafael?"

"My mother calls me Rafael, you know." The moonlight slid across his cheek as he turned to gaze at her. The golden stubble of his day's beard gave his classically handsome face a rough edge that rather pleased her. He reached out his hand and cupped her face. "You have beautiful eyes. What is it?"

She didn't pull away, but at his flirting, she utterly forgot what she had meant to say. His thoughtful look turned to a smile.

"I can feel you blushing under my palm," he murmured, then he pinched her cheek. Judiciously, he pulled his hand back and folded it under his head again.

Dani stared out over the distant sea. "Do you charm all your women this way?"

He paused. She sensed him stiffen as though her softly uttered question stung him, but his tone was dry. "Well, I don't always rescue them from plunging to their deaths, but generally speaking, yes."

"This is your system, then."

"No. I don't have a system. For seduction, you see, is not a science. It is an art. And you, my dear, are in the hands of a Michelangelo."

"Are you going to—well, never mind, of course you are. How stupid of me—"

"What?"

"Never mind."

"What, Dani?" he whispered, looking over at her with a slight, wicked smile. "Am I going to seduce you?"

"No! That wasn't my question!" she gasped in mortified shock.

"What's on your mind?"

She dropped her gaze, blushing to the roots of her hair, but she had to try to ascertain if he was at all serious about her. "You—you are going to keep your mistress, of course. Ms. Sinclair?"

She knew he was staring at her but she could not bring herself to look at him. Her voice was hollow and strained, her words tumbling out fast in the awkward silence. "Perhaps it would be easier if we just went inside now and got it over with—" she started, but as she shifted to get to her feet, his iron grip wrapped around her waist, and the next thing she knew, she was on her back and he was covering her mouth in kisses. A few strands of his long hair fell forward, brushing her face like silk, and his hand cupped her cheek and caressed her neck, her hair. It was glorious.

Worse, her arms went at once around his neck as if of their own accord and she held him with an indescribable sense of pained joy. Slowly she understood that he desired to part her lips, and slowly she gave way, opening her mouth.

He breathed her name then gave her a deep, slow kiss full of feeling, stroking her tongue with his own. There was nothing in her world in that moment but Rafael. His mouth on hers, his hands on her skin, the rock-hard musculature of his shoulders and back under her palms as she clutched him to her.

Deeper and deeper he kissed her, moving partly atop her, his big body warm and lean. His left forearm pillowed her head, but she felt his right hand wandering down from her neck, exploring her body. He laid his hand on her midriff, and she wondered if he could feel her heartbeat pounding in the core of her.

She felt a small tug on her shirt and realized he was unbuttoning it. She tore her mouth away from his. "Rafael," she breathed as his hand slipped inside her shirt and cupped her breast. She groaned, arching her head back, eyes closed.

Never had she dreamed a man's touch could be so incredibly warm, so tender. Rafael's kiss lingered at her throat, lips like satin and his day-beard like soft, scratchy sand. Only his hand moved inside her shirt, gently caressing her breast.

She did not realize she was holding her breath as he trailed his thumb and forefinger along her nipple, teasing it to aching arousal before gently kneading her soft flesh again in his large warm hand. Moments passed, but she had lost all track of time. She groaned again when his touch left her skin—an anguished sound at the denial.

"Soon, my pet. Patience." Gentle amusement warmed his deep whisper, but it was enough to remind her that she was supposed to somehow resist.

Obediently buttoning her shirt again, he rested his hand on her midriff and looked down at her. Panting, she opened her eyes and stared up at him dazedly. His smile was faint, and an odd sort of world-weary wisdom shone in his eyes under his long gold-tipped lashes. In the black sky behind him, the moon sat cool and white, like a dove perched on his shoulder.

He rested his cheek on his fist, his elbow braced on the roof's rough surface. She realized her hands were still clasped behind his neck. She realized, too, that she had no wish to let him go.

"You see?" he murmured, drawing circles on her belly with his fingertip. "Nothing to fear."

She wasn't sure of that, but she gave him a drowsy smile, deep under the spell that his kisses had cast on her. "You dodged my question with consummate skill."

"I didn't dodge it. I wanted to kiss my wife. Is that so wrong?"

"Well? What is the answer? Or don't you want to tell me?"

He lowered his lashes and toyed with a button on her shirt. "It is a concession I am loath to make."

"You are in love with her," she said with a cold twist in her middle.

"Not by a long shot," he declared. "It's the principle of the thing."

"What principle?" she asked dubiously.

"Well, if I were to obey you in this matter, then you might take it into your head that you can bully me around like those peasant boys of yours—"

"I'm sure I have never bullied anyone!"

"On the other hand, if your reason for making this request was that you wanted me all to yourself in a . . . jealous sort of way, I don't see how I could refuse." He gave her a winning little smile, but she narrowed her eyes at him again.

"Has anyone ever told you that you are, oh, just a trifle arrogant?"

"Me?" he exclaimed, his eyes teasing her. His voice softened and he sifted his fingers gently through her hair. "I have already removed her from the palace, Daniela. I will not shame my wife."

She looked away, disappointed that he did not offer to break off the affair entirely. "Well, thank you for that courtesy," she said stiffly.

"Are you sure you don't want me to yourself? You'd better speak up now or hold your peace. I mean it. You'd better claim me if you want me." He grinned at her, baiting her.

"What good would it do me?"

"You never know."

I might as well want the moon, she thought, but instead of answering, she only touched her knuckles gently to the hard line of his golden, scruffy cheek. He smiled seductively and gave a slow, heavy-lidded blink, visibly enjoying her touch.

"Rafael?"

His deep murmur caressed her. "Yes, Dani?"

"Were you shocked that I tried to escape?"

"No."

"Were you shocked that I came back?"

"No."

"No?" she echoed, surprised by his answer because her own decision to return had taken even herself off guard. Her conscience had stopped her from going any farther. The man had spared her and her friends' lives. She owed him better than to run away without explanation, especially when she knew that he had been betrayed before.

"You gave me your word. A moment of fear is understandable under the circumstances, but you gave me your oath and I know you're not a coward."

She looked away, hiding her distress. "Rafael?" she asked more quietly.

"Yes, Dani?" he answered with a small, contented sigh.

"I'm sorry I punched you," she whispered. "And kicked you. Twice. Even if you did deserve it."

"Sorry I shot you," he answered, giving her a glum look.

"Well, you had due cause," she admitted gravely. "I did rob you."

He turned and stared at her, bafflement in his eyes.

"What?" she asked.

He shook his head, then began laughing, low and husky.

"What is it? I don't see anything funny—are you mocking me again?"

"Hush." He leaned down and kissed her lips, still laughing softly. "I do believe I am smitten with you, Princess Daniela di Fiore."

"Spare me your gallantries, Rafe!" she retorted with a blush, but her slight smile told him she was pleased.

Pushing up, he stood and leaned down to offer her his hand. "Come on. Let's go inside."

The thought of going into the bedroom with him nearly unnerved her, but she couldn't stay out on the roof for the rest of her life, she thought, so she joined him. They climbed back carefully to the balcony. Rafael never let go of her hand. She saw it was fortunate indeed that he had come along to rescue her, for although it had been easy enough to slide down the curving mansard roofs, going back up would have been impossible for someone of her five-and-a-half foot height. Rafael, however, at about six-foot-three, was easily able to vault the slick surface, either lifting her ahead of him then climbing up after her, or going up first and pulling her up by her hand. The climb taxed even her wiry athleticism, but he was dauntless.

When at last she gained the balcony's railing after him, he opened his arms to her, inviting her playfully to jump into his arms. Intrigued by her husband's enigmatic smile in the dark, she let go of the railing and reached out to him, her heart skipping a beat with the mad risk of total trust, but he caught her in his embrace.

He didn't put her down. Instead, he turned around, pressed her back gently against the wall, and lowered his lips to hers, parting them. His slow, savoring kiss spoke louder than any words that it was going to be a memorable night, but fear whispered through her. Danger was mounting by the moment.

His two-handed grip on her backside tightened and he gave a low, throaty laugh that drove her wild. Immediately she clamped down mentally against the surge of desire. They were too near the bedroom—too near the bed—but his wet, hot kisses were like candy, and she was eagerly devouring them. She couldn't seem to help it, no more than she could stop herself from caressing his chest, freeing his hair from the queue, running its silken lengths through her fingers.

She wanted him so much, wanted to touch him everywhere, as he had done to her that night on the yacht.

He secured her against the wall, lifting her thighs to his hips, one then the other, coaxing her to wrap her legs around him. Despairing of safety, Dani obeyed, and when he seemed satisfied that he had her body securely twined around him, only then did he come up for air from the drowning kisses he was giving her.

Breathing heavily, he gazed at her. "Hello," he whispered.

"Hello," she panted, blushing.

"I have an idea," he murmured. "Let's go see what's in

here." Holding her with his large hands cupping her backside, he moved away from the wall and walked slowly into the bedchamber.

Her mouth went dry. "Rafael . . ."

"Yes, darling?" he murmured softly, nuzzling her cheek.

Her heart was pounding furiously. "I don't—I'm not ready."

"Hush," he breathed, rocking her slightly in his arms as though she were a little child who merely needed quieting. "You will be."

"Rafael."

He kissed the tip of her nose. "Dani, my angel. My little firebrand with the hair of flame. Don't be frightened. I'm going to take very, very good care of you. Remember what I gave you the other night?"

"I remember."

"There's much more than that in store for you now."

"There is?" she whispered, her voice going hoarse with longing.

He crossed the room and gained the bed on his knees, where he laid her down under him and began kissing her slowly, deeply.

He lifted her legs and wrapped them securely around his compact hips again. She shuddered at the hard warmth of him between her thighs.

"Don't you like it?" he whispered against her skin. "The feel of our bodies together. Do you feel how perfectly we fit together, Dani? It isn't always like this, you know. There are poor matches, and there are good ones."

"Rafael." She could barely utter his name, staring up at him in pleading.

Oh, she was failing fast.

He smiled softly. "Dani." Watching her face intently, he began unbuttoning her black shirt with one hand. "We're one of the good matches. Can't you feel it?"

She wondered how many times he had said this to other women. The worst part of it was she wanted to believe that he meant it only for her.

She swallowed hard and strove for a reasonable tone. "Now, Rafael—"

"Dani," he echoed more hoarsely. He slid her shirt down over her shoulder and began kissing there while his deft fingers unbuttoned it the rest of the way down her chest and belly. "How lovely you are. How innocent. Don't be afraid."

"I think you should stop now."

"Now?" He lowered his head and kissed her throat, moving south in a leisurely fashion. "No, not now, my precious. Now I shall give you pleasure such as you have never known."

"But I don't—want—any," she attempted, shoving at his shoulders.

He merely laughed against her midriff, then nipped her lightly beside her navel.

"You bit me!"

"Did I? Well . . ." His voice was lazy and slow as syrup. "I could eat you up like a sweet peach, darling. Maybe I will."

"I really think that's quite enough—"

"I may never get enough of you, actually." His warm, wet mouth moved with leisurely slowness over her skin, rounding up over the curve of her breast, then he captured her nipple, kissing, sucking with a depth of soul that robbed her of her wits. "Mmm," he purred as he suckled her.

She writhed, her heartbeat racing. "Please!"

"Please, what, Dani? What would you like me to do? This, perhaps?" He slid his hand between her thighs, rubbing softly.

"Stop it!" she groaned, squirming frantically as she

tried to escape his gentle, fiery touch. "You know that's not what I meant! Get off of me! Please!"

"Hush," he whispered, "let me pet you. I only want to make you feel good. Dani, I'm going to make you feel so good."

"I feel fine. You must stop—"

He reached for the fastenings of her black breeches, gave her a coy little smile, and yanked the knot in the draw-cord free. Suddenly her breeches hung loose about her waist.

"Beautiful," he whispered, pulling slowly, exposing her skin inch by inch as he slid the breeches down her hips. He lowered his head, nuzzling her chest and throat. "Ah, Dani," he breathed, "I want you so badly."

Moving lower, he kissed her quivering belly, then paused. Straddling her thighs, he rose up onto his knees over her and began unbuttoning his shirt down his chest, button by button.

There was a fleeting opportunity to try to escape. As Rafael undid his cuffs, Dani curled upward, starting to flee, then he let his fine white shirt slide slowly off his shoulders. It whispered back off his skin, falling upon the coverlet, and Dani promptly forgot to move, riveted, staring at his naked chest.

He was beautiful. Utterly, extravagantly beautiful.

She drew in her breath at the noble and majestic sight of him, the silky skin of his broad shoulders and powerful arms glistening in the moonlight like warm, sculpted marble. Her gaze traveled in awe over his splendid, sunkissed chest and exquisitely carved belly.

Mute with awe before him, her heart sank. How on earth was she going to resist? She hadn't a chance, not a prayer.

She was only human. Besides, she could never escape such massive strength. If he wanted her, he would have her, and that was the end of it.

But Rafael di Fiore would never take a woman against her will. She knew this from the marrow of her bones.

She lifted her gaze slowly, sorrowfully, dazedly, from his flawless, classical torso to his austere, angular face and found him watching her.

They stared at each other.

I can't ruin your life, she thought. *You are too wonderful to throw it all away on me.* She felt a spontaneous impulse to tell him how comely he was, how perfect and full of masculine grace, but she bit her tongue. He knew, she thought, growing increasingly lost by the second. Oh, he knew.

Staring down at her, he reached out and took her hands. Lifting them one by one to his lips, he pressed a sweet kiss into each of her palms. Then he laid her hands on his chiseled belly, inviting her without a word to touch him.

With a small, hopeless groan of want, she gave in to the seduction of his stark male beauty, exploring him, marveling at the velvet heat of his skin. She ran her hands slowly up his midriff to his chest, learning him, stroking him. He quivered like a stallion under her hands.

His sculpted chest heaved, lust glittered in his eyes, and his dark gold hair spilled like luxurious sin to his shoulders. He looked wild and elemental and very, very male.

Entranced, she molded her fingers over the muscular curves of his shoulders, then raked her nails slowly down his brawny arms.

He closed his eyes, lowering his head while she went on touching him. The ends of his hair dusted the clean, sweeping architecture of his collarbones. She bent upward and smoothed his long hair behind his shoulders, then became caught up in playing with his hair, running her fingers through it as she lifted her face and kissed the crook of his neck. He tasted faintly salty, smelled of brandy and expensive cologne.

She lingered like that, eyes closed, her hands tangled all in the glorious golden chaos of his hair. She promised herself she would stop in one more second, one more second . . .

She was not quite able to believe it was happening. Prince Rafael—in her arms, in her bed—her husband, if only for a while. In a haze of sensuality, she brushed her lips over the place on his neck where she could feel his pulse slamming inside his artery.

Eyes closed, he tilted his head back in total surrender, her name on his lips.

With the drums of instinct pounding in her blood, she parted her lips and gave him a kiss on his neck such as he had given her, teething his warm, tender flesh, sucking it hungrily.

"Dani. Ah, God, Dani," he breathed, "what a fool I've been."

"Why?" she asked, nuzzling his throat, seeking another intriguing place to bite him.

"I thought I knew what pleasure was. But nothing . . . nothing prepared me for this, for you. You make me feel . . . everything."

Moving back a small space, she raised her gaze to his enraptured face and knew she had never seen anything so powerfully erotic as him in that moment. Despair surged through her, entwined with her desire. She closed her eyes in defeat at the bewildering surge of longing within her, to open herself, body and soul, become one with him, to take him inside herself so she need never be alone again.

Loneliness, wild and dark, rose in her like a crushing ocean wave. It defeated her and she gave in, hating herself, but she needed him too much. Her caress slid down his chest as she lay back again, her body trembling.

Rafael lowered his chin and lifted his gold-tipped lashes heavily, his green-gold eyes smoldering.

"My turn," he whispered. He caressed her cheek, then

his fingertips trailed under her chin, down her throat, and skimmed lightly down her chest. He parted her unbuttoned shirt and gazed down at her breasts. He gently cupped them for a moment, then pressed his thumbs over their crests, pinching ever so lightly, teasing them to turgid arousal until she was gasping.

Then he covered her with his body. Kissing her lips again and again, he eased his warm, bare, velvety flesh down upon her and thrust his tongue hungrily into her mouth.

She went rigid, however, when she felt his hand inching down inside her loosened breeches. Reason flung back to her as she realized this was swiftly going too far. She had to save him. She had to stop him. *But he was going to be so angry.*

She clutched his great shoulders. "Rafael——"

"Kiss me," he whispered in silken command.

She felt a mysterious, steely hardness pulsing fiercely against her abdomen, and when she realized what it was, she tore her mouth away from his, trapped beneath him.

"Don't, don't," she panted feverishly. "Don't do this, darling. Don't. We can't."

"We can. We shall," he breathed, smiling at her in debauchery, his eyes glittering feverishly. As his lips lingered against hers, his hand inside her breeches moved.

She gasped. "No! Please, Rafael——"

"Yes, Dani. God, *yes.*" He cupped her mound and slowly slipped his finger inside her.

She cried out with a gasp of sweet shock, then somehow she found the strength to fight, bucking off his touch.

"Dani, calm down! I'm not going to hurt you, sweet——"

She ignored him, thrashing as fully in earnest as that night on the King's Road when he had captured her in the woods. He won as easily now as he had then. His left hand clamped like a manacle around both her wrists, pinning her hands to the bed above her head. Quickly he moved his thigh across her legs, blocking her before she even thought about kicking him in the groin a third time.

"Calm down," he ordered gently. He was panting slightly. "Dani, angel, I'd never hurt you, don't you know that? You belong to me now." He brushed a light kiss over her brow, and she nearly sobbed with wanting for it to be true. "Mine to protect. Mine to take. Was I not gentle?"

"You're a brute and I want you to let go of me!" she said through gritted teeth just to get rid of him. Fighting tears of furious frustration, she began thrashing uselessly again.

"Dani, stop it," he said crossly, stilling her struggles. "You know I've every right to this."

"But I don't—want—this!" she cried.

He laughed softly, nuzzling her cheek. "You promised never to lie, *ma chère*. Dani, my sweet, it's our wedding night and this was part of our bargain. An important part, as you well know. Give in to me, darling. Lie back and let me love you," he breathed.

"Don't do this to me, Rafael!"

His laugh was low and wicked. "I like when you moan my name like that," he murmured as he began kissing her ear. "Don't tease me, Dani. Because I can feel your wetness drenching my hand and I've a pretty fair idea of how much you are enjoying yourself."

She closed her eyes, reeling with his heated kisses. "I hate you."

He laughed softly, a debauched, seductive sound. "That's not what you'll say in the morning. Now, here's what we're going to do. First, I'm going to finish undressing you. And then I'm going to make love to you nice and slow, Dani," he said as he began pulling her shirt off her. "Nice and gentle for my virgin bride. There will only be pain the first time, my love, and after that, I promise you, a world of pleasure awaits."

"Please, no," she said in a dwindling whimper.

"Hush," he whispered. "It's natural to be nervous your first time because you don't know what's going to happen, but you must trust me, darling. I can ease your fear if you'll just relax—"

"Stop touching me!"

An angry scowl knit his thick, golden eyebrows. "Damn it, you have a duty to Ascencion and to me! Quit playing games."

"I'm not playing games. I'm not!" she whispered, but he paid no attention, slipping her black breeches down around her hips. She slammed her head back against the pillow in impotent fury.

He began and he was gentle, as promised. She could not stop him—or perhaps the dark, hungry, wanton core of her that needed so badly stopped her from fighting as she should have.

Holding both her wrists fast under his left hand, with his right he slid her breeches farther down her thighs, caressing everywhere he went. His fine, strong hands moved warmly over her sensitized skin, his touch smooth and sure. He leaned down to kiss her mouth, but she had the moral fortitude to at least refuse his kiss, turning her face away, then she uttered a helpless groan of mingled misery and pleasure as his fingers stroked the small, dense tuft of hair concealing her womanhood.

Maybe Orlando was all wrong, she thought desperately. Maybe the king wouldn't mind this match. Maybe she could give herself to Rafael in jubilant abandon and keep him and there would be no consequences.

Fool.

His touch was light and delicate, full of practiced finesse. She tried to writhe away, but his fingers only pushed deeper with gentle pressure while he whispered, *"Hush, baby, hush."*

She groaned angrily as he pleasured her, wild for him yet desperate not to fail him. His caress was slow, slow and rhythmic-deep. Lightning danced along her nerve endings as he drove her inexorably toward the summit. Her heart was pounding.

When she gasped in a shock of pleasure like a pearl diver breaking the surface, he claimed her mouth in a ravishing kiss. . . .

Swept away, Rafe kissed her, his entire body shaking with lust. He moved down to suckle her breasts as he pushed her breeches farther down her legs. She was feverish under his hands as he caressed her everywhere. He had to have her. He couldn't wait much longer. He had never before experienced such an onslaught of barbaric possessiveness over a woman, such total, urgent, bewildering need.

Touching her as deeply as his fingertip could reach, he wanted to make her come seven thousand times. He wanted to take her, own her, love her until he was empty, and as he held her pinned down, tasting her, he knew with a kind of dread that he could never get enough of her. Knew she could enslave him with his own need for the purifying, gemlike flame of her love.

Then she shuddered under his touch with another infuriated moan of pleasure and tried to bite his tongue in retaliation for making her feel it. He was too quick for her, laughing darkly, but her fight ignited primal fires in his blood.

"What's this, my dear? You want it rough?" he whispered raggedly. "I can do that for you if it's what you really want."

"Let me go! I hate you," she growled, raking her nails down his back with a commanding touch that spoke anything but hate. His ginger cat had claws.

"I noticed," he said with a half-smile as he grazed her

pebble-hard nub with a feather-light touch of his middle fingertip, back and forth, driving her crazy. "May I kiss you here?"

She groaned, thrashed, her slim hips lifting for his caress even as she refused him.

"You're right. I should quit wasting time." He rolled atop her, braced himself on his hands over her, and pressed his pelvis slowly between her thighs. *Bliss.*

"Feel what you do to me?" he whispered, dragging his erection, like a great stone temple pillar, over her mound with a stroking motion of his hips.

She gasped, moaned at the burning contact. *"Please."*

In wild possession, he arched over her lithe body, knowing his greater strength would deliver him this victory. Chivalry, honor were forgotten under the violent rule of instinct. Nothing mattered but making her his own in the most physical way possible, again and again and again. "I want you now." He released her wrists, not caring if she struck him, for no blows could deflect him. He reached down and freed his aching sex, pulsating and huge in his breeches for her. Until he was buried to the hilt inside her tight heat, every moment was an eternity of pain.

"No, no," she was moaning as he eased between her thighs and cradled her in his arms.

He tried to calm her, stroking her hair. "Breathe, love, my sweet wife. Fighting me will only make it hurt," he whispered, panting. "I don't want this to hurt you, my darling. Oh, God, let me in."

Her fear and desire both at fever pitch, she squeezed her eyes shut tightly, grimacing. "Rafael!"

As he guided himself to her glistening threshold with a hand that shook slightly, it came to him through a thick haze of need that she had started crying.

He stared down at her, his pulse like a field of racehorses. She had not cried when she had been arrested, held in jail, interrogated, forced to say goodbye to her lifelong friends, nor when the prime minister of the land had yelled at her. She had not even cried at her own wedding, but she was crying now. His fierce little outlaw girl was crying and shuddering under him.

In fear.

He paused for about two seconds, staring down at her in bewilderment, whereupon his wits came out of nowhere, whirling back to him like the Furies. *Dear God, he had simply overpowered her and was seconds away from—*

Scorching need blazed through him.

No! he roared silently, squeezing his eyes shut in fury at the denial. With a curse on his lips, he pushed off of her and tore himself away from the bed, fighting to get his lust under control. He felt like someone he didn't know. *What had she done to him? Damn her! What was happening to him?*

"Get out," she said in a shaken voice a moment later.

Hands on his hips, chest heaving, he looked over at her. She had scrambled out of the bed and now stood against the far wall, wielding his dress sword, her black shirt hanging open over her white chest, the breeches riding low around her waist, giving him a glimpse of her flat belly.

A jolt of lust made him want to risk her blade, but he merely looked at her. For the sake of his battered pride, he hoped it did not show in his face that he was scathingly ashamed, though he was too angry to repent just yet.

He had no idea what had come over him. He had never forced himself on a woman in his life. Indeed, he had killed two men in duels in the past for the same. Yet any apology he might have uttered stuck in his throat.

How could he have read her so wrong? He'd heard her denials, but he knew she was merely shy, and he could have sworn her body had been begging for him. He felt baffled, lost. Why did she not want him? She was his wife.

"I said get out."

He turned to her. "I'm not going anywhere."

That was all he needed—the court talking about him getting thrown out of his new bride's bedchamber on his wedding night. He could not figure out what had happened. Women simply did not tell him no. She was legally his own, practically his possession. He had saved her neck and she had no right to deny him. She would not best him tonight.

Not in the bedroom. Never there.

"I mean it! Get out of here!" Her eyes snapping blue fire, she advanced on him, the sword at a dangerous angle in her hands. She stepped up onto the bed and walked slowly across it, coming down off the other side, moving in on him until her blade was under his chin.

He smirked at the blade, then at her. "What are you going to do, Dani? Stab me?"

She was shaking slightly. "I should. I ought to kill you now and do this kingdom and the women of the world a favor!"

"Don't speak for the women of the world until you become one of them, little Dani," he said in a soft tone.

"What's that supposed to mean?" she shouted, her cheeks flushing.

He glanced disparagingly at her boyish garb. "It means you're just a scared little girl who doesn't know what she's missing. But never fear," he whispered. "I'll make a woman of you yet. How dare you refuse me after all I've done for you?"

"I'm trying to help you!" she wrenched out.

"Help me? What on earth can you mean?"

"I found out about your five princesses!" she burst out. "If I resist you, then our marriage can be annulled when your father comes back. You can wed one of them and then you won't lose the throne! You'll lose the kingdom all for my sake, Rafael! I won't let that happen! Ascencion needs you!"

He stared at her in dark, incredulous fury. "Who has been talking to you?" he asked in a murderous tone.

"It doesn't matter who told me. I truly don't wish to be difficult. What matters is that you spared me and my friends, and now it's my duty, in turn, to protect you!"

"Your duty . . . ? Damn it, Daniela, you are my wife! Obeying me—bedding me—is your duty!" he thundered, taking a step toward her, his expression fierce. "For once in your foolish young life, you will do as I say! Now, I command you as your sovereign and your lord, *tell me who has been talking to you*!"

"Orlando!" she cried, and backed away, flinching at his wrath.

He froze. *"Orlando?"*

"He said he doesn't want there to be another rift in the royal house. He told me about the king's threat to leave Ascencion to Prince Leo if you don't do what he says. Rafael, if you don't marry one of those girls, you'll be disinherited. I don't want you to lose everything all because you spared me and my friends. I don't want to be responsible for ruining your life!"

"Wait one moment." In light of his history with women, he wasn't quite ready to believe in her noble excuses. She was the girl, after all, who had said she would never marry anyone ever. "*When* did Orlando tell you all this?"

She swallowed hard. "Yesterday."

"Yesterday," he echoed as his fears began to materialize. "And you knew what you were going to do—refuse to give yourself to me? You knew that yesterday? Concocted this plan with my cousin?"

She stared at him in silence.

"Come, Dani. Out with it." His heart was pounding and there was a sick feeling in the pit of his stomach. "You're telling me you went before God today and gave your word—in front of the church and all those people—you made me a promise and it was a lie? Were you lying up there today?"

"You don't understand!" she cried, tears filling her eyes.

"I think that I do." He stared at her.

Perhaps lust and ravaged pride were clouding his brain, but all he could seem to think was that it was Julia all over again and he had walked right into a trap made of heartless, female wiles.

She looked so innocent, so young.

He was such a fool.

"An annulment, eh? You intended to deceive me even before you set foot in the church," he said bitterly. "Maybe you've been lying from the start. Of course you have. In the jail. You would say anything to save your own pretty neck, wouldn't you? And Mateo's," he spat.

"That's not true! I was in earnest! I am trying to protect you, Rafael!"

"You're protecting yourself, you lying little thief!" he roared. "You gave me your word. Everyone warned me not to trust you."

"I care for you!"

"Do you?" He lifted his chin, staring at her in searing fury. His tone was calm, polite. "Then get in that bed and spread your legs and prove to me you're not a liar."

"Don't you dare talk to me like that," she warned him. "I am not one of your theater trollops."

"Damn you," he whispered, his shoulders slumping. "You used me."

"*I* used *you*?" she echoed in amazement. "You're the one using me! You made that perfectly clear. You told me right to my face that the only reason you were marrying me was to use me for my sway with the people. Now I find out you're using me to strike at your father—a man whom I personally happen to admire."

"I am not using you to strike at my father. I am sick and tired of being controlled. Nor will you control me! Damn you!" he wrenched out in anguish. "You were supposed to have been on my side."

She opened her mouth to answer, but no sound came out.

"I see now you think me a joke, just like everyone else does," he said softly. "You were the one who was supposed to believe in me."

"I do believe in you, Rafael. That's why I stopped you tonight." Tears brimmed in her eyes. "If you consummate our marriage, you will never be the king. It's me or Ascencion. I won't let you make the wrong choice."

"Really?" he said cynically. "Well, all I know is that I gave my pledge of honor this day before my God and country, and I'm not breaking it for you."

"Stay back!" she shouted when he took a step toward her.

"I'm not going to touch you, *wife*," he muttered in contempt. "I merely need to use the tip of the blade."

"What for?"

He didn't answer. Giving her a cautious glance, he took the end of the blade between his right forefinger and thumb. Holding it steady, he brought up his left hand and nicked his thumb on the point before she could stop him.

"What did you do that for?" she demanded.

He winced as blood rose to the small wound. Squeezing the cut so that it bled even more, he walked to the bed, turned down the covers, and wiped his blood on the sheets.

Slowly lowering the sword, she looked at him in bafflement.

"Was it good for you?" he asked sardonically as he quickly stripped the sheet off the bed and carried it toward the doorway.

She just stared at him, her brow furrowed.

Sending her a smug look of victory, he went into the other room, opened the door, and handed off the blood-stained sheet to the palace steward, who was waiting discreetly in the hallway.

Catching on too late to what he was about, Daniela came running. "Rafael! Stop!"

He quickly closed the door and blocked it with his body, folding his arms over his chest and smirking at her.

She stared at him in shock. "Proud, willful man! What have you done?"

"No annulment now, my love. Did you think I was going to just let you make a fool of me in front of all Ascencion? You're stuck with me now, my girl. The proof of your deflowerment has already been submitted. So I propose we go back to bed and finish what we started."

She gaped at him in amazement. "Arrogant, unscrupulous blackguard! You would cut off your nose to spite your face!"

He arched a brow at her.

Marveling at him, she shook her head in angry disbelief. "You are such a child."

"I do have a certain boyish charm," he drawled, perversely delighted that he had exasperated her as thoroughly as she had him.

She narrowed her eyes. "Your so-called proof settles nothing. A doctor's examination can still prove I am chaste when your parents return, and the marriage can still be annulled. I will not yield! If you want me, you'll have to force me—and I know full well that you won't."

No, he wouldn't.

Irked by her accurate assessment of the situation but smiling tautly, Rafe considered his next move carefully. It seemed he had only one option.

Slowly, he walked toward her, pressing her blade gently aside.

Watching him, her eyes huge in the dark, she let him get near, too proud to back down when her fight was up, he supposed. He took her lovely face between his hands and lowered his mouth to hers, giving her a slow, light, seductive kiss.

"I won't have to force you, Dani," he breathed silkily. "We'll see how long you can hold out."

She moaned barely audibly under his kiss. Her slim, warm body melted against him, undoubtedly against her own volition. She had been left as hungry for release as he. Her need engulfed him, but the lady had made her wishes clear.

"You know where to find me, darling. But this time, you're not getting it until you ask me nicely," he whispered. With a heated, slight smile, Rafe pulled out of her arms, turned, and walked away into his adjoining room.

She was still standing where he'd left her with a lost, dreamy look of aching desire when he shut the door between them.

But he didn't lock it.

⚜ CHAPTER ⚜
TWELVE

The next afternoon they were due to make their first public appearance as man and wife. The occasion was the christening of a majestic new ship of the Royal Navy. Under an azure sky, the little whitewashed, red-roofed port town was festooned to welcome them. The open area around the quay was jammed with people who had come to catch a glimpse of the royal newlyweds. Dani wondered if everyone who had come to congratulate them could see that they were not speaking to each other.

Behind the raised dais, the blue harbor served as a backdrop. Graceful ships with furled sails bobbed gently in their berths behind them. Standing at the podium, Rafael made a brief speech to the people while Dani stood by his side, smiling fixedly with placid pride and listening attentively to her husband as he mesmerized the crowd with his deep, mellifluous voice, holding them captive with his golden charisma.

It was excruciating to stand here in public with him when privately everything between them was in shambles. But, by God, she was determined to uphold her end of their bargain in this sense, at least. She would do her part to help him win the love of his people. Only, she was already beginning to see that he really didn't need her assistance.

They *wanted* to believe in him. They wanted to love him. All they needed was a decent overture from him to show that he cared—and anyone could see that if there was anything the rakehell prince cared about, it was Ascencion.

He spoke beautifully. Despite the simplicity of his conservative clothes, there was a splendor about him which she could not help but admire. The sea breeze carried to the crowd his eloquent words affirming the future. Dani felt the way the whole throng seemed to drink in the sight of them together, sending a wall of cheers back to him when he had finished.

Dani clapped for him, too, as the wave of deafening applause rolled over them, heady, intoxicating even to her shy sensibilities.

When he turned, threw a grin at the crowd over his shoulder like an accomplished showman, then smashed the bottle of champagne against the ship's mighty hull, they went wild, their roar punctuated with impassioned cries of, *"Viva il principio! Viva la principessa! Viva Ascensione!"*

Rafael's smile as he waved back at them was dazzling beyond the sun's glint on the waves. Then he turned to her and held out his hand, meeting her gaze in silent, forceful instruction, with a flash of hostile, heated lust in the green depths of his eyes. She understood what she must do, however, and rested her hand tremulously atop his. With a sweeping gesture, he presented her to the thundering crowd.

She kept her chin high while the world stared at her and applauded in jubilation, for what reason, she could not guess. She certainly didn't feel she deserved it after the debacle of the previous night.

Their visit to the port town was not long. Tonight there was an ambassadorial reception which Dani was already dreading. The next few days were booked full of similar social events and public appearances which she had no choice but to attend. Like Rafael, she was public property now. When they got into the carriage, it was necessary to wave until they had passed through all the areas where people lined the streets to hail them. At last, their cavalcade turned onto the King's Road not far from the place where she had once robbed him. The carriage sped through the woods' green shadows, heading back toward Belfort.

Across from her, Rafael sank back against the squabs, drew off his gloves, and pressed his eyes with one hand.

She wanted to tell him how moving and eloquent his address to the crowd had been, but she decided not to risk opening herself to conversation when it would probably just turn into another argument.

The tense, awkward silence went unbroken all the way back to the Palazzo Reale, Rafael staring hungrily at her, as though daring her to meet his gaze and know his desire, but she kept her nervous gaze riveted out the carriage window.

When they arrived at the palace, Dani got out of the carriage and hurried at once to her apartment without saying a word to anyone. She couldn't stand the tension anymore that was bunched up inside her muscles. She needed activity.

She ran up the marble stairs, locked the door inside her apartment, mistrustful of the look she had seen in Rafael's eyes. She half-feared he might come up and try to coax her into bed again if she lingered, so she moved quickly, changing her clothes to a smart riding habit.

A fast, vigorous gallop was just what she needed. She missed her horse, who was even now stabled in the royal livery. She would have liked to ride the expensive white Arabian mare that had been one of Rafael's wedding gifts to her, but since she wasn't going to be keeping Rafael or his gifts, she did not want to get used to such luxuries. Her skittish, liver-bay gelding was good enough for her.

With her veiled, brimmed hat and riding crop tucked

under her arm, she dashed out of her apartment again, waving off her maids impatiently. She was bounding lightly down the marble stairs when Rafael stepped into her sight at the bottom of the staircase.

She froze. A jittery feeling immediately sprang to life in her belly.

They were alone.

As he stared up at her, a dangerous half-smile curved his hard mouth. "Don't you look pretty," he said as he idly sucked a peppermint. He began walking slowly up the steps toward her, his hands in his pockets.

Intensely aware of him and ill at ease, Dani swallowed hard at his approach, then made up her mind to walk loftily past him as though he didn't exist. She lifted her chin and forced herself to proceed down the stairs.

He stepped into her path at about the middle of the staircase. She took a sideways step; he followed, arching one golden eyebrow at her. She stepped back the other way; again, he blocked her, smiling coolly.

"Remove yourself, please, Your Highness," she said caustically through gritted teeth.

"You have not yet kissed your husband good morning."

"I am not kissing you, Rafael."

"All right, then, I'll kiss you." He leaned toward her to kiss her cheek, but she lifted the riding crop at an angle across her face, gently barring his way, though his nearness made her shiver and the scent of his candy triggered delicious memories of his kiss.

He seemed to know his effect on her. He grasped her hips, caressing her. "You look like you're ready to go for a ride, Daniela."

"That's right." She attempted to push him off her. "I'm on my way out."

"Just kiss me once, then I'll let you pass," he murmured.

"I've heard that before," she replied dubiously.

"One kiss." He paused. "Or would you prefer I kiss someone else?"

She narrowed her eyes at him. "Do you actually think you can make me jealous?"

"I'm hoping. Give me one kiss and I'll be good," he whispered.

"And then will you go away?"

"If you still want me to."

"One kiss," she repeated, her mouth watering at the thought.

He held up one finger, which he then touched to her lips. Reading her wary acquiescence in her eyes, he rested his fingertips gently on her cheeks and lowered his head, brushing his satiny mouth over hers in tantalizing softness. Dizzily, she held on to his waist to steady herself. His kiss alighted with greater intent on her mouth. She closed her eyes and parted her lips.

It was useless.

Passion burned too brightly between them like an iridescent flame. Heat flooded her as he ravished her mouth. He gave her his swiftly dissolving peppermint and took it back again, tearing his kiss away.

With barely restrained force in his touch, he moved her so that her hip abutted the wide, carved-marble banister. He cupped the back of her thigh through her skirts, urging her in wordless coaxing to sit partly on it. Laying her back against the wide flat railing, he leaned over her and devoured her mouth with wild, ravishing kisses. He cupped his hand around her thigh, gently lifting her left leg, as well, to rest on the railing.

She braced herself there with one hand behind her, the other on his shoulder. Her heart raced with wild, reckless thrill while he ended the kiss, slowly lowering himself to his knees on the next step down. She had no idea what he was doing, but she did not possess the strength to protest when he slid her skirts up and parted the slit of her white muslin pantalettes. She tilted her head back in helpless welcome when she felt the pad of his thumb stroke her, and then she gasped as his wet, warm mouth covered her in a fiery burst of icy-hot peppermint bliss.

"Oh, my God," she moaned. It was all she could do not to fall down the steps.

She heard his throaty laugh at her reaction to his debauchery. Then he used his tongue to caress her with the candy before it dissolved entirely, along with her wits. He slid his middle finger into her as he blew gently on her aroused flesh, sending a fresh wave of icy-hot sensation to rack her body with wild pleasure.

She leaned back weakly on her elbow on the wide marble railing, her other hand still clinging to his shoulder, her riding crop hooked under her finger and trailing down his back, the tasseled tip of it dusting his muscled rear end in tight breeches.

Her chest heaving, she gazed down in an utter, wanton haze of lust at his blond head between her thighs. He licked her in circles lightly, with exquisite finesse, and he said, *"Mmm,"* against her flesh, as though he were feasting on soft, melting chocolates and could not get enough. She stroked his sleek, golden hair while he applied himself to pleasuring her with naughty little flicks of his luscious tongue and his fingers moved in and out of her teeming passage.

God forgive her, but even this shocking decadence wasn't enough. Nothing would ever be enough but to feel Rafael inside of her, taking what she so longed to give.

He seemed to sense when she grew rigid, poised on the edge of release. She cried out in anguish when he pulled back and gazed up at her, looking tousled and lusty as a wanton god. One glance into his eyes told her that his control was hanging by a thread. His left hand caressed her thigh, his royal signet ring gleaming gold.

He wiped his glistening mouth on his wrist as he held her stare feverishly. "Are you ready now to ask me nicely, love?"

His challenging whisper slammed her back to reality. She stared at him, appalled.

"Absolutely not," she forced out with knee-jerk defiance.

"Ah, what a shame," he breathed, regretfully brushing her skirts back down.

She could only stare at him in disbelief, stunned that he would leave her in torment.

Smiling at her, cool anger turning his eyes steely green, he stood and began walking up the steps past her. "Cheer up, Dani. If I have to suffer, so do you. Let me know if you change your mind."

Dazedly, she moved away from the marble railing and stood unsteadily on the steps. She was shaking with tumultuous emotion and unfulfilled desire. Slowly, she sank down and sat on the step, unaware that he had stopped at the top of the staircase, clenching and unclenching his fists, and now forced himself to turn and look down at her.

She wrapped her arms around herself and lowered her head in despair. All the fight drained out of her. She hated him—needed him. Needed him so much. How could he leave her like this, feeling so empty and alone, ashamed of her own wantonness?

Yet this was precisely what she had done to him on their wedding night, she realized. She heard slow, heavy footsteps as he came back down the stairs to her. He crouched down beside her and leaned close, kissing her cheek.

"I'm sorry, baby, my precious, I'm sorry." His whisper

was raw. "Let me take you upstairs, angel, please. Please. I need you so badly."

Flinching with want, she tried to pull away from him.

He slid closer. Lifting his hand, he stroked her cheek, her hair. His hand was shaking. He closed his eyes and rested his forehead against her temple. "Dani, please, this is killing me. You're my wife. Don't turn me away. You're all I think about. You're the only one I want—"

"I am afraid," she said barely audibly.

"No. No fear," he panted, grazing his lips against her cheek back to kiss her earlobe. His hand covered her knee. "I'll make it good for you—"

"Afraid to have a child!" She closed her brimming eyes in fierce anger. "I'm afraid to have a child. I'm afraid."

He stopped.

There, she thought. She had said it.

Finally blurted out the truth, the core of fear in the center of all her bravado.

"I am terrified," she said. "I am a coward." She felt him staring at her.

"I don't understand."

She drew a deep, shaky breath but still could not look at him. "Even if by some miracle your father doesn't disinherit you, the annulment must stand because I cannot give you an heir. You must find someone else, Rafael. I can't do it. I cannot."

He was silent for a very long moment. "Is it . . . your health?"

"My health is sound."

"I'm sorry, I'm still not sure I understand."

She turned to him at last. "Have you ever seen a woman die in childbirth?"

"No."

"I have. That day in the jail when you asked me to marry

you, I knew you would have to have an heir and I thought then that I would face it when the time came. But if I can't even keep you as my husband, I don't want to risk dying for you—not that way! I meant it when I said I would've taken a swift death at the end of a noose rather than to die that way—in blood, and terror, and screaming. Such screaming as I never heard in all my days—"

"Easy, there. Easy," he said, laying his hand on her shoulder with a frown of gentle concern. "Dani, not all women die in childbirth. You're young, strong."

"My mother died birthing me, Rafael. Grandfather says she was narrow-hipped, the same as me." Hearing the frantic note in her own voice, she struggled to appear calm.

"But Dani—" His voice broke off and he stared at her. The self-assured Rafael seemed flustered and completely routed by her awful, unwomanly confession.

It was so terribly awkward. But then, ever the prince, he smoothly rose to the occasion. He put his arm around her shoulders and drew her close to him protectively, pressing a kiss to her hair. "Darling, I would never let anything happen to you," he whispered. "I know you're afraid. I wouldn't want to have to go through that myself, but we all must face our fears. I promise you, you'll have the best physicians—"

"No doctor can control nature, Rafael!"

His soft kiss lingered at her temple. "No, my love, only God can do that. But I cannot believe that God would take you away from me now that I've finally found you."

"Found me?" she said bitterly. "You only wed me to use me, Rafael."

He met her eyes intensely for a moment, as though there were something profound that he had to confess as well. But his mouth was grim and pale, and he said nothing.

Rising to his feet, he raked a hand through his hair and walked away.

For three days, Rafe put his work between himself and the world. Except for the arduous state occasions when they were required to stand together, eat together, dance together, and play the blissful newlyweds, it was easy to avoid his wife, for he spent most of his time in the administrative block of the palace while she was confined, on his orders, to her pink suite on the third floor.

He ached with want and with a love that terrified him, but in spite of everything, he refused to get rid of her. Doing so would have been tantamount to admitting to Don Arturo and the bishop and Adriano and everyone else who had warned him against this that he had made a mistake in marrying her, and he was not willing to do that. He had made his vows before God and country. He had to save face, and the plain truth was, hang it all, that he wanted to keep her.

Why, he didn't know.

The memory of her sweet giving that night on the boat, her innocent face flushed with passion and her blue-green eyes filled with sensual bliss, haunted him as the days dragged by.

So supremely self-assured, he had sought from the start of their acquaintance to seduce her, but he was the one who had been seduced. And he hated it.

It was Thursday, late afternoon, when his stomach growled, reminding him he had forgotten again to eat lunch.

Considering the report he had just finished reading, the thought of eating struck him as a trifle unappetizing, in spite of his hunger. No poison had yet been found in the foodstuffs from the royal kitchens, according to the university scientists and physicians whom he had instructed to examine it for any taint. Their methods seemed to him satisfactorily meticulous, and so far all the cats were healthy, but the mere thought quashed his already diminished appetite.

Instead, he moved on to the next order of business, calling his secretary to show in his next appointment.

The fat-bellied Count Bulbati sailed into the small, stuffy salon with his pug nose in the air, clearly a man who did not take Rafael di Fiore seriously.

Rafe could spot the type at a hundred paces.

Ten minutes into their interview, however, Bulbati's smug disdain had crumbled. Then he began to sweat. Profusely.

Rafe continued to grill him casually and without pity, knowing the man had bothered Daniela. Sooner or later, he knew he was going to have to go crawling back to her, and he wanted some kind of meaningful gift to lay at her feet when that time came.

The ledger books from Bulbati's jurisdiction under the Ministry of Finance lay open on his desk.

"A very singular mode of wooing, my lord," Rafe growled as he looked up from the neatly doctored columns of numbers. "Did you really think you could get her to marry you by starving her out of house and home?"

Bulbati swiped at his pale, doughy face with a handkerchief. His sweat made the whole room stink. "I cannot fathom why Lady Daniela is accusing me—"

"Look, you revolting mound of flesh, I've had it with your dodging my questions. You and I both know you are guilty. These accounts have been altered and you're the only one in a position to do that and to profit from it! You are looking at fifteen years or more in prison, my lord!"

"Your Highness, you don't understand!" Bulbati squealed.

"I'm allowed to skim a small portion off the top for myself! It's all right, you see. He knows about it—" The count suddenly stopped himself with a look of horror.

Staring at him, Rafe sat back slowly in his chair and skimmed his jawline with his knuckles. "Well, this is very interesting. Who has given you permission to embezzle funds from Ascencion's coffers, my lord?"

Rafe did not show it, but he was a little shocked. He had the feeling he had just opened a veritable Pandora's box of trouble. *Open those books and you will find the real criminal,* Daniela had said that night at her villa, shooting straight to the mark in her usual Robin Hood fashion.

Bulbati closed his eyes, his pasty skin turning a sickly green color. "Oh, what have I done now?" he said to himself. "Caught between a rock and a hard place. Oh, dear, oh, dear me."

"I'm waiting."

Bulbati turned a suddenly desperate expression on him. "Your Highness, you don't understand. He will kill me!"

"Think about life in prison, my lord. That is what you are facing. You have embezzled from the king; you have abused your office, not only to line your own pockets, but to try to get your hands on an innocent young lady. Your actions are dishonorably vile and your words prove you a coward. If you hope for pity, you will find none here, at least not until you begin to cooperate."

"If I tell you, I will be in mortal danger!" he whispered, mopping his brow with his damp handkerchief. "I will need constant protection!"

"From whom? I'm not going to play a guessing game with you, Bulbati. Name this mystery man or you are done for."

Sweat poured down Bulbati's face, dampening his frilly cravat. He tugged at the lacy bow as though he couldn't breathe. "Please don't cross him, Your Highness. It's better just to put it under the rug. I'll pay back all the money—"

"His name."

"I'm not the only one working for him, you know, a-and it isn't just the Ministry of Finance! He is more powerful than you know! He has influence in every branch of government."

"Give me his name, damn it!" Rafe bellowed, slamming his fist on the desk.

The man stared like a startled feeder hog, slipped his thick fingers into his waistcoat as though trying to still his heart, then closed his eyes and seemed to gather himself.

"Orlando."

Rafe sat in complete silence for a very long moment.

It was difficult in that moment to say what he felt. Numb. Reeling. Blank. Then anger flooded him.

"You lie."

"N-no, Your Highness! It is the truth!"

"You expect me to believe you, an honorless swine, over a duke of the royal blood?" Rafe rose slowly from his chair, glowering. "How dare you accuse my kinsman? Take it back! Where is your proof?"

"I—I have no proof. I am telling you the truth, Your Highness. It's true!"

"It is a lie!" he roared, slamming his fist down on the desk, but the reflex of wanting to believe the best about someone he cared about was not working this time. Horror ran like poison in his veins—not the horror of surprise, but worse, that of recognition. Still he fought it. "Guard!" he barked.

Bulbati was already scrambling up from the creaking chair and waddling hurriedly toward the door as the Royal Guardsmen posted outside the salon stepped in.

"Keep this man in custody overnight, but for now, get

him out of my sight. We'll see if he changes his story to-morrow," he snarled.

"Yes, sir," they answered, and took the count away.

The door closed behind them and Rafe closed his eyes, his temples pounding. Hands on hips, he paced to the window and stared out at the long shadows stretched across the park lawn, nearly blind with fury and utterly routed.

He did not know what to think.

In the two years since Orlando had moved from Flo-rence and established himself on Ascencion, Rafe had often sensed that the man was not exactly what he seemed. But Rafe had always felt a bit sorry for his strange, brooding, solitary cousin, who had no immediate living family and no real friends that Rafe knew of. He had supposed Or-lando was a trifle jealous of him, as most men were, regret-tably. But if Orlando's rancor ran deeper than surface jealousy, Rafe was not sure he wanted to know it.

Ever since he had found out that Orlando had gone be-hind his back to talk to Daniela, Rafe had been wary of his cousin, inevitably. Even if his kinsman's intentions had in-deed been to protect him and the family, Orlando's private talk with Dani was a breach of trust. That had been a per-sonal matter, but this accusation from Count Bulbati had more profound and far-reaching implications.

Strangest of all was Bulbati's repeated statement that Orlando had vast power and would actually kill him if he revealed his name. Rafe frowned to himself. Surely that sloppy swine was lying.

Why, he had seen Orlando that very morning and had read nothing unusual in his cousin's attitude. The duke had been present for the meetings of Rafe's new, woefully green cabinet. He had been glad of his cousin's presence, since Orlando was older and had more experience than any other man he had appointed.

Orlando had behaved naturally and Rafe had shrugged off his uneasiness, for if he didn't trust his own family, whom could he trust? Mulling on it now, that seemed like a hopelessly naive philosophy.

Julia would have laughed at him for it.

His arms folded over his chest, Rafe lifted a fist to his mouth as he stood, brooding and motionless, at the window.

He did not like the train of his own thoughts. He had deliberately avoided becoming a suspicious and untrusting man, because that would have meant that Julia, in her treachery, had won, but this time, he forced himself to imagine the most diabolical scenario. It would not do to be taken by surprise.

Father was ailing. Stomach cancer. *Supposedly.* As crown prince, he was the heir to the throne and so far had no sons. *Orlando had convinced Dani not to sleep with him.*

If both he and Father were dead, the succession of the throne would fall to Leo, with the bombastic Bishop Justinian as his regent.

The bishop disapproved heartily of Rafe but was zealously devoted to the king and to Leo, as well. No, he thought, the priest was no traitor. However . . . if Leo was in power, hypothetically, and Bishop Justinian died before the boy-king came of age, who, then, would become Leo's regent?

The question made Rafe mildly ill.

He wanted to think it would be Darius Santiago, his fierce brother-in-law. But Darius had lived in Spain for four years, was out of touch with what was happening on Ascencion, and was, when it came down to it, a warrior, not a statesman.

Prime Minister Arturo di Sansevero might be chosen— but then, Rafe knew who Don Arturo's favorite was.

Orlando.

And if Orlando got control of Leo, who could say if the child would ever live to see the age of eighteen, when he would come to power?

The line of his own thoughts sickened him. Surely, *surely* he was blowing everything out of all reasonable proportion. After all, there was no evidence yet that Father's illness was anything other than the stomach cancer which had been diagnosed, and as for him, there had been no attempts on his life.

None at all.

Suddenly unable to stand still, Rafe pivoted and left the room, striding out into the hall in a rush of determination to have a talk with Orlando's superior, the old, white-haired Don Francisco, venerated head of the Ministry of Finance for the past twenty years.

Rafe's heart was full of foreboding, but he moved with caution, not wanting even to think how the equation might change if and when Dani became pregnant. If she bore him a son, Leo would not succeed to the throne, Rafe's heir would.

He checked the flow of rage that gusted through him to contemplate that he might have brought Dani into danger by marrying her. Hadn't Orlando sought her out in private once already?

On his way to the royal livery, he ordered more guards posted around her, specifying that they were not to let her out of their sight for a minute.

He said nothing about his cousin, deciding not to put them on Orlando's trail yet, for the simple reason that if his crafty cousin was indeed guilty of something, he didn't want to give Orlando any prior warning that witless Rafe the Rake was finally on to him.

Since he did not want his visit to Don Francisco to be noted by the world at large, he took an unmarked coach to the old man's elegant city palazzo.

Rafe sent his footman to the door while he waited in the carriage, but the servant came back reporting that the old financier was not at home, having gone out on a fishing trip, making the most of the temporary recess of the cabinet which Rafe had ordered in his foolish fit of anger, firing all of his father's trusted advisers.

He stifled a sigh and scratched his forehead.

An inspiration came to him. He ordered the coachman to take him to the wheelwright's large, noisy shop where his phaeton was being repaired.

They were just about to close for the day, but when he arrived, the wheelwright and his apprentices fell all over him in their efforts to serve their royal patron. The master wheelwright led him over to his phaeton, which was being given a final polish before being returned to him, the repairs complete.

When Rafe asked to see the broken axle which had been removed, the man's cheerful countenance turned puzzled.

"Of course, Your Highness," he said, looking at him oddly. He ordered a couple of his apprentices to bring it from the pile of broken wheels and other carriage parts in a corner of the stable yard behind the sprawling shop.

Rafe waited restlessly, glancing over his stylish vehicle. It was merely a tickle of ominous intuition, but he wanted to examine the axle, just to assure himself that no one had tampered with it.

Miraculously, he had walked away from the carriage accident without a scratch, but if he had been one jot less of a skilled driver, and if he had not leaped out of the thundering vehicle at the last minute, he could have been thrown from the twisting phaeton or pinned under its splintered halves and dragged while the team kept running.

Collecting his note for fifty thousand from the loser of the wager, he had laughed off the mishap at the time and merely steadied himself with a swallow of whiskey, but now the full knowledge of what could have happened chilled him.

He turned when the lads came back a few minutes later, then went stock-still as they reported that the broken pieces of the axle were gone. Missing. Vanished.

The carriage-maker looked flustered at this news, embarrassed in front of his royal patron, and yelled at them. "Are you blind? Excuse me, Your Highness. I'll find it myself."

But as sunset cooled the sweltering shop, the master wheelwright didn't find the axle, either.

Rafe walked out of the shop amid their profuse apologies.

The evening was filled with beautiful waning pink light, but he stood on the sidewalk with knots in his stomach, staring down the street to the left then the right, dazed, struggling merely to get his bearings. He rested his hands on his hips and tried to gather his thoughts. Clearly he had come out of his sleep not a moment too soon.

He began walking to no place in particular. He waved off his coachman and ignored the constant stares of people in the street. For once, couldn't he just walk down the street like anybody else, until he had figured out what the hell was going on?

He barely acknowledged the citizens who called to him, bowed, curtsied everywhere he went—all these people who were counting on him to take care of them when he couldn't even adequately protect his young wife under his own roof.

He could barely think. He was too furious. Head down, hands in his trouser pockets, he walked until twilight turned the city pearl-gray, not even noticing where he was going.

When his fury smoothed out to a calmer, slow-burning anger, it left him with a kind of despair. He had failed. So soon, he had failed.

He saw he was going to have to send for Father to come back because he didn't know what to do. God forbid he should do the wrong thing. He was not afraid of Orlando, but he was petrified of blundering. The stakes were too high to be left to someone like him, a stupid, overgrown adolescent.

Rafe the Rake, he thought, hating himself. He was nothing but a gaudy showpiece.

But damn it, even Father would have been hard-pressed to know what to do in this situation, he was sure. Well, what *would* Father do? he demanded of himself.

Confront him head on, he thought at once. *Hit him like a battering ram.*

But that wouldn't work. If Orlando had been sitting there smiling at them for the past two years, a face-to-face confrontation would be pointless. Obviously the man was a consummate liar. So where did that leave him?

Hell, even Darius would know what to do better than he. Darius would have handled it by playing just as dirty as Orlando until he had gathered proof of his guilt, then he would . . . do what? Rafe wondered, racking his brain. Knowing Santiago, he would probably mete out his own justice, simply cut the man's throat, and wipe his hands of the matter. But Rafe was not the professional government assassin that his brother-in-law had been trained to be.

Besides, his mother had raised him to use violence only as an absolute final measure. Because he would be king, she had taught him to use his strength gently, lest he turn into a tyrant and harm those whom it was his God-given duty to protect.

The lamplighter, ladder under his arm, walked past him, not even recognizing him, Rafe noted gladly. The blue-uniformed man merely went about his business, lighting the gas lamps in the fashionable neighborhood that he had wandered into.

Ambling along the sidewalks, enjoying the calm cool of night, Rafe took a peppermint out of his pocket tin and sucked it, head down, hands in pockets.

Passing in solitude beneath a lamplight's feeble sphere of golden light, he suddenly heard a carriage jingle to a halt next to him amid tinkling laughter, while a familiar male voice called a halt to the smart black team.

"Whoa!"

"Rafe? Darling, is that you?"

With a depressed sigh, he turned and looked up slowly to find Chloe and Adriano seated side by side in a dashing cabriolet, the black leather hood raised over them.

"Well, if it isn't the married man," Chloe drawled.

"Rafe? What are you doing out here?" Adriano asked in puzzlement.

"Dear me, he looks lost."

"Is everything all right?"

Rafe merely lifted his gaze heavily to his friend's, then glanced at Chloe.

Under her frilly parasol and elaborately brimmed hat, his ex-mistress's delicate face glowed by the lamplight, but her artificial smile faded as her gaze took in his grim expression. "My God, darling, what is wrong?"

Adriano frowned at him, too. "Has something happened?"

"Get in this carriage right now," she ordered, sliding over on the seat to make room for him as the mockery fled her perfect face.

He didn't move.

He had not visited Chloe since he'd met Daniela, but he knew he could have her back in a heartbeat. He was in no mood to be plagued with guilt on top of everything else. Society recognized his right as a wealthy male to keep a mistress if he chose, and if his wife's sensibilities, insecurities, and fears were going to stop her from fulfilling his needs, why should he not seek his pleasure elsewhere?

But as he gazed up at the stunning, blue-eyed blond, he knew he shouldn't get into that carriage, because he knew just where it would take him.

And yet there was a great comfort in the familiar escape into self-indulgence, just as there was in the welcoming darkness of night.

Without another word, he stepped up into the carriage with them.

⊰ CHAPTER ⊱
THIRTEEN

Chloe's eyes welcomed him with sultry knowing as their hands accidentally brushed. She slanted him a glance as he sat down next to her. There wasn't much room.

Squeezed between them, Chloe moved partly onto Rafe's lap and draped an arm around each of their shoulders, Adriano's and his.

"Isn't this cozy?" she purred. "My two favorite boys." She kissed Adriano's cheek, then Rafe's, and whispered, "Whatever's wrong, my love, you know your Chloe can always make you smile."

He looked at her, holding her hungry stare with a surge of unfulfilled lust. A mocking smile of triumph flicked over her fine lips and he looked away. She leaned toward him and brushed a light kiss on his ear.

"Miss me?" she whispered.

He pulled away, hating himself and despising Daniela for driving him to this. She should have given in. She was his wife.

At his nape, Chloe's long fingers tickled him as she began playing with his hair, while Adriano urged the horses into motion.

They rode for a few moments in silence, then he noticed Chloe smiling to herself like a cat over a bowl of cream. Her gloating look made him realize she had probably heard from Adriano that he had not been spending his nights in his wife's bed, but in his old boyhood rooms in the west wing. But she was too shrewd to mention it.

She merely continued toying with his hair, lightly tickling his neck with her touch until he could not think in his haze of need. He kept his face turned away from her, watching the neat, narrow houses slide by.

The cabriolet passed through the open solid-wood gates and rolled down the dark, private alley beside Chloe's townhouse to the quaint stone carriage house in back. The vehicle had barely stopped in the courtyard behind the house when Chloe swept her hat off and tossed it aside, pushed back slightly against the seat, and pulled Rafe toward her.

With a low, hungry groan, he went willingly, claiming her mouth in a harsh, ravaging kiss. Despair pounded in his veins, in his heart, but he ignored it. He dragged his hand down to knead her large, round breasts, her skin lily-pale in the dark. She sighed, stroking between his thighs with one gloved hand. With the other, she did the same to Adriano.

Rafe clutched her, hardening instantly under her palm. Adriano set the brake, tied off the reins, then turned to them, touching Chloe's hair for a moment as Rafe kissed her. She pulled her mouth away, breathless, a wanton smile on her plump lips as she petted Rafe and reached out to Adriano.

"My favorite boys," she whispered.

Rafe glanced up, panting with want, as Adriano climbed into the narrow compartment in the back. Leaning down to caress her face, Adriano began kissing Chloe's mouth and gently taking down her pinned-up hair.

Rafe's gaze moved over her sinuously arching body. He tugged the plunging neckline of her gown lower still, freeing her breasts to feast on them. He slid off the seat and knelt on the floorboards between her spread knees.

There wasn't much room, but he no longer cared, no more than he cared that she was unfastening di Tadzio's black trousers, licking her lips in anticipation.

It wouldn't be the first time they had shared a woman, but it had been a very long time and Rafe wondered if he was a bit too sober for this tonight.

"Perhaps I am intruding," he murmured in the dark, panting. After all, he had given her to Adriano on his wedding day.

Chloe glanced down at him as she caressed Adriano's hip. "Nonsense, darling." She reached down to run her fingers through Rafe's hair. "Why don't we all go inside and have a drink?"

"No, you two go," Rafe said, glancing uncertainly at his friend. "I'll just borrow your carriage to get home, if you don't mind."

"You're not going anywhere," Chloe chided, lifting one dainty foot and rubbing it between his thighs.

He flinched with aching want and closed his eyes.

"Go with him, Chloe. He needs you. It's all right," he heard Adriano whisper. Rafe dragged his eyes open and saw him kiss her forehead. "I should leave anyway."

"But why? My darling, stay." She pouted. "Rafe doesn't mind."

Rafe looked away, scratching his eyebrow. *I really ought to go,* he thought.

"No, dearest. Treat him well," Adriano whispered softly, caressing the curve of her face with one fingertip.

Rafe didn't know what was going on between them. If Adriano was in love with her, he had merely to say the word and Rafe would bow out. But when Chloe sat up and thrust her big breasts under his face, his mouth watered and his mind was made up. If he didn't get laid very, very soon he was going to go stark, raving mad.

She made much of wriggling past him as she got out of

the coach, coquette that she was, dragging her hip against his erection. Rafe eagerly followed her down from the vehicle, throwing his friend a grin over his shoulder.

"Thanks, di Tadzio. I owe you."

"Don't mention it," he said with a short, rather wistful laugh.

Adjusting himself briefly, Rafe sprang up the back steps, catching only a glance of Chloe's skirts swishing around the corner ahead of him in the brightly lit hallway of her elegant townhouse. He ignored the startled butler, chasing her as she ran from him, giggling. He caught her halfway up the stairs, hooking his arms around her hips from behind.

Flushed and breathless, she turned in his arms and gazed up at him with an almost girlish adoration. He bent his head and watched her fingers pluck the fastenings of her dress free.

From the courtyard below, they heard wheels grinding over cobblestone as Adriano turned his team around and left. Rafe glanced briefly toward the sound.

"It was cruel of you to scare him away," Chloe whispered.

"He'll live."

"He adores you, and he is so gorgeous."

"You're too greedy, Chloe," he said with a darkly chiding smile. "Rest assured, I'll wear you out tonight all by myself."

"Well," she whispered with a teasing smile, "you can try. Come." She captured his hands and started to lead him the rest of the way up the steps, but when his gaze swept the staircase, suddenly he knew it was no use.

Dani filled his mind. Dani, whom he needed so much he could nigh weep with unfulfilled yearning. Dani, his wife, whom he loved with an ardor that scared the hell out of him. His fear was the only reason he was here. *Adultery.*

No idle game anymore.

This is wrong. Even if he was in his rights, it was wrong.

He was supposed to be setting the example for his people, not sinking to the level of whatever he could get away with. He didn't want to hear his conscience's feeble whisper, but it came through, loud and clear.

Go home, Rafe. You can't do this anymore.

If ever there had been a day for drawing lines of loyalty in the sand, this was that day. And if ever he was going to grow up and be a man, the time was now.

"Hurry, darling. Don't just stand there!" Chloe urged in an eager whisper.

Standing on the staircase, he closed his eyes and hung his head, loathing himself. In that moment, he was unable to walk away from Chloe, and equally unable to take another step toward her bedroom.

She came back down to him uncertainly. She stroked his chest. "Are you all right? Come upstairs, Rafe. I've got a special treat in mind for you."

Trying to gather his wits, he shrugged off her embrace resentfully when she tried to slip her arms around him.

"What's wrong, lover?" She was ruthless, gently caressing his throbbing rod through his clothes. "I'll make it better."

He grasped her wrist hard, though he barely had the strength to restrain her.

"Stop it," he said through gritted teeth. "Let's both just stop it. You know I shouldn't be here. I don't even want this."

"But you need it," she whispered. "Nobody can satisfy you as I do."

You're wrong, he thought. *You leave me empty.* To his despair, he knew that no woman would ever satisfy him again but Dani. Need for her agonized him with a longing that was more than physical. She was the only woman he dreamed of . . . the only one who wouldn't have him.

The hell she wouldn't, he thought in a sudden flood of angry decision.

He would not let her do this to him. He would not stoop to this dishonor. He had gone before God and pledged fidelity, and so be it.

He stepped back woodenly from Chloe's embrace, his heart pounding, groin throbbing. "I'm sorry, Chloe. It's not going to happen. You know as well as I do that it's wrong. I won't be back. Goodnight."

Rage came into her eyes, but without another word he turned and walked away.

"Rafe, you blackguard! Get back here!" she yelled furiously behind him. "Don't you dare walk out on me! Where the hell do you think you're going?"

Walking resolutely to the door, he paused but did not look back. "Home," he said. "To my wife."

And she would be his wife before the dawn, more than in name only.

He was fed up with waiting, out of patience with her wrong-headed denials. He was sick of playing the gentleman.

While Chloe spewed a stream of epithets at him, Rafe raked his trembling hand through his hair and stepped out into the dark coolness of night. Relief at his narrow escape slid through his veins as he went down the few steps and set out in the direction of the Palazzo Reale.

Where is my husband?

It was past eleven and no one had seen him in hours. With a sinking suspicion of his whereabouts, Dani had been unable to sleep. To distract herself from her angry suspicions, she had begun exploring the palace.

Presently, she was walking alone in the royal portrait gallery, a long rectangular room with walls sheathed in red silk. The footmen must have thought she was mad when she ordered them to light all the candles so she could study the pictures, but she was past caring. The hem of her new light blue walking gown dusted over the highly buffed parquet floor as she strolled, hands clasped behind her back, studying her husband's ancestors and wondering if she ought to try to memorize them in chronological order.

It seemed wasted effort if she was going to have her marriage annulled, but there was little else to do when she was confined to the palace, her every move shadowed by a unit of now six Royal Guardsmen. At first it had been only two.

The portrait gallery had entrances on either end of the long hall. At both, her unsmiling uniformed guards had squarely planted themselves. She wondered if the rest of her life was going to be this way, so closely guarded in her own home—if this was to be her home.

Wandering to the far end of the windowless gallery, she stood gazing up at the large painting over the hearth, hung in a resplendent, gilded frame.

It was a portrait of the royal family, made on the occasion of Princess Serafina's wedding to Count Darius Santiago ten years ago. The royal bride, Rafael's sister, was the most breathtakingly perfect-looking woman Dani had ever seen, a genuine Helen of Troy.

Now, there, she thought dismally, *is a princess*.

In the portrait, Princess Serafina had rose-white skin, a tumbling mass of jet-black ringlets, and laughing, joyous violet eyes. Beside her, her uniformed bridegroom was every bit as beautiful as she, but his intense midnight stare and hawklike face held not a trace of a smile. Still, the way his hand covered hers so gently made it clear that the fierce-looking Spaniard probably turned to putty in that laughing goddess's hands.

To the bride's right stood her darkly handsome but stern-looking father, King Lazar, his jet-black hair silvered at his temples. He was modestly dressed for so great a legend, or for a man all Ascencion believed could walk on water.

On the other side of the newlyweds sat Queen Allegra, light-haired and gracefully maternal, on a red velvet stool, holding the then-infant Prince Leo. Known for her humanitarian efforts, the queen appeared the embodiment of nurturing, motherly wisdom.

Dani gazed at her wistfully, wondering how her own life might have been different if that stranger, her mother, had survived.

Papa would not have fallen apart, gambled away their family fortunes, and drunk himself into an early grave, she thought. She would have been raised as a proper young lady, not a wild tomboy. Perhaps if she'd had a mother, her own womanhood might not have felt so foreign and threatening to her. As it was, how could she mother Rafael's children when she'd never even had a mother of her own?

Her gaze moved pensively over the portrait. Nestled in the queen's arms, the baby Prince Leo gazed out sweetly from the painting with cherubic, rosy cheeks and a tuft of black curls sticking straight up, comically, from his head.

Rafael stood behind his mother in the portrait, his white-gloved hand resting protectively on her shoulder. Though the artist had captured the roguish sparkle in his eyes and the trace of his cocksure grin, his proud, hard face was even then carved with the same air of innate command as the king's, but he had his mother's coloring and something of her thoughtful expression.

Dani stared up at the portrait for a long time, despairing that an oddball misfit like her would ever fit into the warm and loving picture that the royal family made.

Just then, she heard voices at the entrance to her left. She turned and saw her guards admit Duke Orlando.

She suppressed a tired sigh, forcing a polite expression as he strode toward her with a darkly charming smile.

"Ah, Daniela, there you are!" he said in an amiable tone. Not content with the familiarity of addressing her by her Christian name, when he reached her, he caught her hands in his, greeting her as though they were the best of friends. He angled his square chin downward and smiled at her.

She supposed she ought to be grateful. He was the first person who had been friendly to her in days.

"I have been looking for you everywhere," he said.

"Oh?"

"Yes. I've been worried about you."

She tilted her head in question. With a firm, slight smile, he tucked her right hand through the crook of his left arm, coaxing her to walk with him.

"I wanted to make sure you're doing all right," he murmured, lowering his voice.

"I'm well enough," she admitted. "Thank you for asking."

He cast her a shrewd look askance. "Have you kept all the things we talked about in mind?"

"I can think of little else."

"Hmmm," he said, sounding skeptical.

She looked at him in question. His dubious glance slid to hers.

"What is it?" she asked.

Judiciously, he pursed his handsome mouth. "Forgive me for speaking indelicately, my lady—but I just inspected the, er, bedlinens that were collected on your wedding night. I know you are a wily woman, however, and that the proof isn't necessarily authentic. I had to make sure we still understand each other."

"Aha, you're checking up on me." She pulled her hand from his arm and walked away, then her glance fell to the nearby portrait of King Lazar as a young man. It suddenly struck her that the likeness between the king and the Florentine duke was astonishing.

Why, Orlando looked more like the king than Rafael did! she thought. Odd that the family resemblance should be so strong in a distant cousin.

He caught up with her then and stopped her, pinning her with a hard warning look. "What happened, Daniela?"

She stared at him blankly for a second, suddenly remembering something he had said to her at their previous meeting: *There is nothing more dismal than an unwanted royal bastard.*

Her eyes widened.

No! she thought in amazement. She quickly dropped her gaze to hide her shock. Her heart was racing. *Could it be true? Could Orlando be King Lazar's bastard son?*

Maybe this was a family secret that nobody was supposed to know, she thought, her heart pounding.

He is older than Rafael . . . the king's true eldest son.

Her suspicions suddenly called everything Orlando had said to her into question.

She had mistrusted the duke instinctively, enough to send Mateo investigating him, though all Orlando's arguments to date had made good, logical sense. It would be hard on any man to see the royal heritage that might have been his go to his universally adored younger brother. She suddenly doubted the authenticity of Orlando's brotherly concern over Rafael's future. *He* was the one, after all, who had wanted her marriage to Rafael annulled. Perhaps he had something to gain by keeping them apart.

"Daniela, I am asking you what happened," he repeated through gritted teeth.

She stole another glance at the king's portrait, then at him, astonished anew by the likeness. "What do you think happened, Your Grace?"

His ice-green eyes narrowed under his long black lashes. He took her chin between his forefinger and thumb and lifted her face with a punishing grip. "Don't think to toy with me, girl."

"Sir!" one of her guards said harshly. A pair of the uniformed men came striding toward them.

Orlando dropped his hand.

"Your Highness?" the guardsman asked.

"It's all right, gentlemen, I can take care of myself," she said, casting a shrewd glance from the guard to Orlando, who stood there simmering.

"I want an answer."

"It's none of your business," she replied as the guards bowed and withdrew. "And don't you ever touch me again."

"It is entirely my business!" he hissed. "Did you give in to him?"

She said nothing, blushing with embarrassment at the immodest topic, her heart pounding with anger at his insolence.

He held her in a penetrating stare, then a slight, cruel smile broke across his face. "No," he whispered. "You are still pure. I can smell it. God, you please me."

She gasped, blushing crimson, and pivoted on her heel, stalking away from him.

He followed her with a soft, cruel laugh. "Where are you going, Daniela? Don't you want to stay and chat with your kinsman?"

"Get away from me!" With every step, she grew more convinced that he was her husband's brother and that he coveted her merely because she belonged to Rafael.

She gained the main, white marble hallway, Orlando a step behind, her guards hastening to catch up, marching in formation at a respectful distance.

Just then, Adriano di Tadzio turned the corner ahead of

her and came stalking down the hallway with his usual look of haughty contempt. In spite of the fact that the man clearly despised her, she fled to him.

"My lord, pardon me!" she called rather desperately. "Have you seen my husband?"

He stopped, tall and gorgeous, and looked down his excellent nose at her. "Oh, yes," he said in hauteur. "I most certainly have."

"Where is he, please?"

"Hello, Adriano," Orlando murmured in a taunting drawl, swaggering up slowly behind Dani.

Adriano gave him a look of heated loathing. "Your Grace."

"Have you seen Rafael?" Dani repeated. Though Rafael had been avoiding her for days, at least Orlando would stay away from her if the prince was near.

Adriano tore his hostile gaze away from Orlando and looked at Dani. "Yes, actually, I have."

"Where is he?"

"I don't think you really want to know, Your Highness." He said her new title with disdain.

"Don't be a boor, di Tadzio. Just tell me where he is!" she pleaded.

"Well, if you insist." His gaze flicked to Orlando, then to her. "Rafael is in bed with his mistress." He smiled coolly. "Sorry."

Dani's eyes widened. Her jaw dropped and her heart fell.

Adriano studied her with a slight smile, and Orlando began laughing softly again.

"Are you sure?" she asked in a small voice as hurt rushed up to constrict her throat.

"Very sure. If you will excuse me."

She turned away, stricken, reeling, barely aware of the low-toned exchange between the two men.

"Where are you headed?" Orlando murmured.

He shrugged. "Nowhere. To my rooms."

"I'll join you."

Both dark, handsome men bowed to her with elegant, lordly courtesy as she turned away and walked swiftly down the hall, heartsick and dazed with pain. As she blindly made her way back to her apartment, her emotions fluctuated from despair to dread and back again with protean fluidity, but by the time she reached her apartment, quietly shut the door, and crossed to the balcony to stand in the sultry night air, she was shaking with anger—at herself.

She was the one who had chosen to believe Orlando over Rafael.

She was the one who had driven her husband into the arms of Chloe Sinclair.

And she was the one who was going to lose him if she didn't come to terms with her fears and admit one simple fact, she thought as she braced her hands on the rail and hung her head: that she was hopelessly in love with the man.

Roughly, she brushed a tear away and sniffled. She had never needed anyone before, but the thought of losing Rafael, of letting that wonderful man slip through her fingers, made her want to die. She stared down at the place on the roof where he had saved her.

You have to claim me if you want me, he had teased, but she knew now he hadn't been jesting. *No,* she thought, lifting her chin with an infusion of stubborn, angry pride. *I will not lose him to that theater woman. He is my man and I'll fight for him!*

If he lost his kingdom for marrying her, well, that was his own fault. She had tried. And besides, he had never seemed overly worried about that possibility.

Orlando could have been making it all up. Between Rafael and Prince Leo and Princess Serafina's brood of six royal grandchildren, there was no way Orlando could hope to gain the throne, she reasoned, but some people just could not bear the happiness of others. Maybe Orlando was one of them. To think she had almost let him ruin her marriage to the man of her dreams! Well, Orlando and Chloe Sinclair both could do their worst—she would not lose her prince to their scheming.

Squaring her shoulders, she pivoted and walked back into her bedroom, staring at the bed where she had slept alone since her wedding night. She knew where his old, boyhood apartment was located in the west wing, but she realized with a sinking feeling that there was no sense going there tonight.

Tomorrow, she vowed, she would seduce her husband. But would he still want an oddball tomboy-misfit when he had the ravishing Chloe Sinclair at his beck and call?

She went over to the mirror of her vanity and peered into it just long enough to acknowledge that she was . . . pretty . . . in her own wary yet warm, simple way. She touched her face, gazing in the reflection at her eyes, which he had called beautiful. Then she left the mirror and climbed into bed.

She lay on her stomach, staring toward the balcony, where the light curtains billowed on the limp breeze. She closed her eyes, determined to fall asleep so that tomorrow might come all the faster.

Forgive me, Rafael, she thought. *I made a mistake. I should have believed in you more.*

And maybe I should have believed a little more in me.

"You really must learn not to blush like a schoolgirl every time you see me," Orlando remarked as he and Adriano strolled down the hall.

The younger man sent him a glare from beneath his black forelock, then quickly looked away. "I think I hate you," he mumbled.

Orlando smiled. "I'm sure you do. You've got to pull

yourself together, my boy. You're the only one suffering these paroxysms of guilt. Chloe found it entertaining, and I certainly don't waste my energies on regret. I thought Chloe said you had been with a boy and a girl before," he added dryly.

"Not like that."

Orlando cast him a knowing smile. "Wasn't it nice to finally get it the way you need it?"

"Would you shut up about it before someone hears you?"

Orlando paused, lifting a brow at his snapping tone. Adriano glowered at him again, then walked on.

He shook his head to himself in amusement. The boy was a wreck.

It had happened on Rafe's wedding night. Orlando had gone to comfort Chloe for purposes of his own. When he had arrived at her townhouse, he had found Adriano already with her, both of them distraught. So he had comforted them both. Anyone close to the prince, after all, was a possible weapon that could be used against him.

Orlando slid into motion again and quickly caught up to him. When he arrived at his side, Adriano glanced anxiously down the dim, empty hall, then looked at him again.

"You're mad to jest about it. What if someone finds out?"

"You mean Rafe."

"Anyone!"

Orlando smirked dryly. "Sorry to inform you, Adriano, Rafe knows. Trust me."

Adrianoe turned and stared at him, looking appalled. "What do you mean?"

"It's called turning a blind eye. He could have thrown you to the wolves a long time ago if that was his choice. Instead, he has clearly put you under his protection." He studied Adriano for a moment, almost pitying his torment.

"I think it's safe to say that as long as you don't irk him too badly, you're in the clear."

"I'm sure you're wrong, I'm sure he doesn't know. I couldn't bear for him to know," he whispered.

Orlando supposed that was true. Adriano di Tadzio was as fragile inwardly as he was gorgeous outwardly.

He had heard stories around the palace about three different episodes in the past where Adriano had been yanked back from the brink of self-slaughter by none other than the bright, shining, golden Rafe, who was, himself, the cause of his suffering.

"I wouldn't worry if I were you," Orlando said almost gently. "Everyone around here has something to hide. Are you going to invite me in, by the way?"

They had arrived at Adriano's rooms.

Adriano put his hands in his pockets and blushed, studying the floor. Orlando waited coolly, watching with interest as the beautiful young man tore himself apart with his inner war.

"I don't think it would be wise," he finally said, though his dark eyes glittered like those of a starved man. "Not here."

Orlando shrugged with a mild smirk. "Suit yourself. I'm sure we'll meet again." He began drifting off down the hall.

"You're not—you're not going to tell anyone, are you?"

"Get some sleep, di Tadzio. You worry too much. By the way, was Rafe really with Chloe tonight, or were you just saying that to be a prick to Daniela?" Orlando called, sauntering down the hall.

Adriano gave a short laugh. "He's with her."

"Not all day, surely? No one has seen him in hours."

Adriano tossed his forelock out of his eyes. "The last I heard, he disappeared into the city after an appointment with someone from your department."

Orlando stopped. Turned. "The Ministry of Finance?"

"Yes."

"Do you know who it was?"

"Some vile little fat man. Don't know his name. In some kind of trouble, apparently. He's accused of embezzlement, I think."

"Was he arrested?"

"Rafe questioned him, but the fellow wouldn't cooperate. Elan told me they threw him in one of the holding cells in the palace basement for the night. I guess they'll try again tomorrow to make him talk."

Orlando's heart had begun to pound. "Rafe interviewed him personally?"

Adriano nodded.

"That's odd," Orlando remarked in a carefully casual tone. "Well, good evening, di Tadzio."

"Ciao," Adriano muttered as he went into his suite.

Orlando stood there in stunned amazement for a second, trying to absorb it.

The time was upon him.

The time to act. Now.

Tonight.

His heart leaped. The blood roared in his veins. If the prince was on his trail, there wasn't a moment to lose. He began striding quickly toward the stairs.

He had to find out at once exactly how much Bulbati had told Rafe. At heart, he believed Bulbati feared him too much to reveal anything, but he had to be sure. He always liked to be meticulously prepared for the worst.

Without another minute to lose, Orlando went to the palace basement where Bulbati was being held in the highly secured cells.

He got through the staunch Royal Guardsmen by explaining that, as Bulbati's direct superior in the Ministry of Finance, he had every right to question the man about his activities, and so what if it was midnight? The Royal Guardsmen hesitated; he employed his usual blend of charm, manipulation, and arrogance.

Perhaps they saw a bit of his father in him, he thought in bitter amusement as they finally stepped out of his path and admitted him.

The air was dank but cooler under the palace, in the bowels of the earth. Torchlight flickered on the rough stone walls of the curving stairwell. Orlando slid off the leather strap tying back his queue and let his long black hair fall free to his shoulders as he slowly descended to the cell below where Bulbati was being held.

"Is someone there?" the count called. "You can't leave me to starve here! I demand some proper victuals!"

Orlando's broad shadow loomed large as he crept silently along the wall down the short aisle. All the cells were empty, save one.

"Prince Rafael? S-sire, is that you?" Bulbati stammered, seeing the shadow approaching.

Orlando saw the count's pale, plump hands wrap around the iron bars down the way.

"Oh, God," the count whispered as he came into the man's view.

Orlando smiled serenely at him.

Bulbati began backing away. "I didn't tell them anything! I didn't, my lord!"

"Did you give them my name?" he asked gently as he took a key out of his breast pocket and twirled it in his fingers in silent threat.

It wasn't the key to Bulbati's cell, of course, but Bulbati didn't know that.

"No!" the fat man choked out in horror, cowering in the corner of his cell. "I told them nothing!"

"For some reason, I don't believe you, Bulbati." He slid his knife out of its sheath.

"I didn't, I didn't, I didn't, oh, please, please, please, my lord," Bulbati whispered as Orlando lifted the key toward the lock, then glanced at him.

With a wide-eyed, panic-stricken expression, Bulbati's jaw was working noiselessly. Sweat poured down his face. He clutched his chest, gasping as though he couldn't get breath.

"Did you give them my name, you filth?" Orlando asked again. "Tell me now before I lose my patience."

"Help me!" Bulbati gasped out. Suddenly he fell onto the floor, his face tomato-red.

Orlando lifted a brow and stared at him curiously, then shook himself. "Did you tell them, Bulbati?" he demanded once more, unamused by this display.

But Bulbati didn't answer, merely gurgled, his bulk lolling on the floor, twitching violently.

"Bulbati!"

Scowling, Orlando crouched down and peered through the bars at him.

The twitching stopped. Bulbati's body went rigid and stiff. Strange small choking sounds came from his throat; his wide eyes stared blindly. Orlando waited but Bulbati did not move again. Orlando reached through the bars and poked him: no response. Not so much as a blink.

Suddenly Bulbati's body disgorged its contents from both ends.

Wincing in disgust, Orlando swept to his feet. Well, the count wouldn't be telling any secrets now. He stared at Bulbati, then suddenly laughed. He had never *scared* anyone to death before.

Marching back up the torchlit corridor, he stifled his laughter and assumed an angry expression. "Guards!" he bellowed, pointing down the aisle as they came running. "What the hell is going on here? Bulbati is dead!"

"My lord?" the first asked in astonishment.

"Go see for yourselves! The man is lying dead in his cell. I demand an explanation!"

He watched them scramble to survey the situation, heartened by this unexpected boon. Perhaps his charade could continue a little while longer. His spirits lifted, eager for the night's work. Finally it was time to throw the net around golden, laughing Rafael, who was, without even knowing it, the sun and center of King Lazar's cosmos.

Time to make a new use of the young chef Cristoforo.

Orlando left the guards in chaos behind him, bounding lightly up the circling stone stairs with a leering grin, leaping them two at a time.

⊰ CHAPTER ⊱
FOURTEEN

Orlando located Cristoforo, the young underchef, in the same brothel where he had found him before. Once more, he plucked the skinny lad out of pretty Carmen's bed, then tossed him into his black carriage, binding his wrists and ankles with ropes to avoid any mishaps, and was presently driving, hell-for-leather, to the prime minister's elegant palazzo in the west end of Belfort.

The drive was not long, but Orlando's urgency made him impatient. At last, the black coach rolled to a halt before Don Arturo's sprawling home, which he had visited many times, cultivating the prime minister. Having lost his precious nephew Giorgio in that duel years ago, the old man had taken Orlando under his wing like the son he'd never had.

Not that his true father had any suspicion of whose son he really was, he thought in a bitter pulsation of hate. He jumped down from the driver's seat and walked back to open the carriage door. Barring Cristoforo's exit, he studied his human instrument of deception with a hard warning stare.

"You know your lines, I trust?"

"Yes, Your Grace," Cristoforo gulped, then gingerly added, "Is it not too late to call on him, sir? It's p-past midnight."

He smiled blandly. "Don Arturo would not wish me to

delay in bringing such shocking and terrible news to him as you have to tell, my dear boy."

The tall, lanky lad shuddered and looked away, staring out the window, his thin shoulders hunched.

"Don't do anything foolish, Cristoforo. I will be back directly to fetch you." With that, Orlando checked his ropes one more time, then locked the carriage door from the outside and proceeded up to the house.

As he walked toward the graceful entrance, he meditated on his pretense and felt himself changing, chameleonlike. By the time he banged on the prime minister's door, his expression was one of anger and frantic dread. He paced back and forth across the small front patio in feigned agitation until the old butler, in nightcap and dressing gown, opened the door and held up a candle.

"Good heavens, Your Grace! Is aught amiss?"

"Wake the prime minister," Orlando ordered at once.

"Sir?"

"For the good of Ascencion, get him, man! We are in a state of emergency!"

Staring at him as Orlando shoved the door open and strode into the foyer, the butler paled. "Right away, sir."

When the butler had scurried off to wake Don Arturo, Orlando went back outside and ordered Cristoforo out of the coach. Holding him roughly by the arm, Orlando propelled the youth into the palazzo and shoved him into Don Arturo's reception room.

"Wait here until I come for you. Do not fail me," he murmured in warning, then locked him in.

He returned to the foyer with just enough time to glance into the mirror, reassembling his countenance into a look of angry discomposure before the venerable Don Arturo came shuffling into the foyer in his dressing gown.

"Orlando, what are you doing here at this hour? What has happened?"

"Don Arturo!" He strode to him. "We must speak privately, sir, right away."

The older man frowned, his single bushy eyebrow moving up and down like a black bar across his forehead. "Very well. Calm down, boy. Step into my study."

"I have news pertaining to the king's illness. Dire, most terrible news," he said in a struggling tone the moment the door had closed behind them.

"What is it?" the prime minister asked, pausing behind his desk rather than sitting down. Above the fireplace mantel was a portrait of the nephew who had died in the duel.

Orlando rubbed his forehead as he shook his head. "Sir, I barely know how to say it." He lowered his hand and met Don Arturo's anxious stare. "I have evidence that the king's illness is not stomach cancer but may actually be the result of . . . poisoning."

"What?" Eyes widening, Don Arturo slowly sank into his desk chair.

"I found a young chef of the royal kitchens who claims that someone of our mutual acquaintance bribed him to administer poison in His Majesty's viands. He says the poisoning began over eight months ago!"

"Whom does he name?"

"He can tell you himself, sir, for he is here."

"In my house?" he exclaimed.

"Yes, I will bring him in. Then you can judge for yourself whether or not you believe him, for I know not what to think. He is waiting in your reception room."

"Orlando, wait! I need a moment to absorb it all. My God. My poor, dear king. A poisoner?" Don Arturo looked up at him shrewdly. "How did you find this vile creature and what on earth convinced him to confess to you?"

"Cristoforo came to me of his own free will and told me everything, confessing his part in the crime because he sought my protection. With His Majesty having left Ascencion, the lad is no longer needed. Now the one who hired Cristoforo is trying to kill him in order to conceal the plot."

Don Arturo leaned forward, his voice dropping to a tremulous whisper. "Whom does he name, Orlando?"

Orlando gave him a distraught look. "Who has the most to gain by the king's demise, my lord? It pains me to say it, sir. I think you realize of whom I am speaking."

"Rafael," he answered, as though he barely dared breathe the name.

Orlando closed his eyes and nodded.

Don Arturo covered his mouth with his hand and sat back, stunned into silence.

Orlando gave him a hard look, inwardly rejoicing at the man's look of instant credulity. "I will be right back with the chef."

Don Arturo gave no reaction, staring at nothing with a stricken look on his lined face.

Orlando exited the study without another word and walked down the hall to retrieve Cristoforo, exulting with private glee. Unlocking the door of the reception room, he opened it and stuck his head in.

"It's time," he grunted, but as he scanned the room, he saw no Cristoforo . . . only an open window.

He cursed and ran into the room, crossing to the window. He caught only a glimpse of Cristoforo running full speed before the lad disappeared around the corner down the block. The little whore from the brothel was with him! They were fleeing, hand in hand. Carmen must have followed them from the brothel and helped him escape.

Snarling, Orlando leaped over the windowsill and dropped effortlessly to the soft ground below. He slid his knife out of its sheath and raced after them with long swift strides.

The boy dodged the nightwatchmen rather than seeking their protection. He must have realized that the guardsmen would merely hand him over to Orlando. The young lovers left the main thoroughfare, ducking into a maze of dark, narrow alleys. Orlando plunged into the squalid backstreets after them.

The only sound was their pounding footsteps reverberating off the close, high walls, and the roaring of his pulse in his ears, the quick, hot want of blood. He needed the boy more or less alive, but he knew what he wanted to do to the girl.

Ahead, they separated, Cris darting to the right, Carmen to the left where the alley split. Hot on their heels, Orlando veered to the right, going after Cris.

He was a bit out of breath from the chase, but he laughed in spite of himself to see that Cris had just flung himself into a dead-end alley.

The lad stood staring at the brick wall straight ahead, then whirled around to face Orlando.

Orlando bent over, resting briefly with his hands on his thighs, then he straightened up, his chest still heaving, and stalked slowly toward the chef. Cristoforo backed away. He cast panicked glances about him at the garbage piled along the sides of the alley, no doubt seeking a weapon of some kind.

"Time to go back, Cris," Orlando panted.

"No! I won't do it!" he shrieked. "I don't want to!"

"But you shall. You will tell Don Arturo everything, just as we discussed."

"Shall I tell him you're the one who wanted the king dead, you evil bastard?" he shouted, starting to cry.

"Poor little boy," Orlando said, snickering.

"I never wanted to hurt anyone. You forced me!"

"We made a deal, Cris. A simple business transaction. You sold me your soul, don't you remember?"

"The deal is off. I won't do it. It's bad enough what you made me do to the king. I won't send his son to the hangman!"

"Rafael is a fool. He deserves to die."

"Well, he's not evil and mad! He's not you!" Cristoforo screamed out. "Why are you doing this to them?" Weeping copiously, he backed away into a garbage heap.

Orlando was staring at him with dark, gathering anger as he realized that, with the boy's escape attempt and his hysterics, Cristoforo really could not be trusted any further. He had driven the boy to the breaking point, beyond his own ability to control him. If he brought Cris back to tell his tale to Don Arturo in this state, he might well blurt out the real truth.

He knows too much.

Orlando was suddenly furious with the wasted effort. He loathed inefficiency. He took another slow step toward the lad, tightening his grip on the knife's hilt. Cris stared at the knife, mesmerized. His unmanly bawling stopped abruptly.

"You disappoint me, Cris. You really do."

"No. Please. I am unarmed," he whispered.

Orlando moved closer. Suddenly something hit him in the side of his face, stunning him momentarily. He jerked away from the hard blow as the broken bit of brick bounced off him to the ground and rolled. He knew without looking that the girl had thrown it at him, but instantly Cris bolted.

Orlando ignored the pain and leaped after him, blood running into his left eye from the gash on the side of his forehead. He reached out and grasped the back of Cris's coat and put his foot out, tripping him from behind. Cris fell with a sob.

Orlando bent over him and cut his throat, then leaped over his still-convulsing body to chase after the girl.

Because he had been preoccupied with Cris, she had a head start, and on her own, Carmen moved faster and more covertly. Orlando chased her down a series of blind alleys until he realized he no longer heard her footsteps ahead of him.

The streetwise little whore was obviously used to fending for herself, he thought. But he'd get her. She didn't have a prayer.

A flicker of motion above made him look up to see her hastily climbing an old rickety peristyle, from which she jumped onto an outer balcony and scrambled onto the roof. He leaped up onto the peristyle, beginning to climb it, but the wood snapped under his greater weight and he tumbled down to the alley again with a vicious curse as Carmen scampered away into the darkness.

He sprang to his feet on the ground with a large splinter in his fisted hand and looked up the side of the building where she had gone. Just before she dashed out of sight, eluding him over the rooftops, Orlando hurled his knife at her by the hilt with a mighty heave of his arm.

The blow missed. The knife bit into the clay stucco of the house and stuck there, vibrating with the impact. *"You little bitch!"* he roared. *"You can't escape me! I'll find you! I'll drink your blood!"* His deep scream reverberated off the alley maze like a demon's curse.

Glaring, his eyes nearly red with rage, he looked up at his knife sticking out of the side of the house up by the eaves. He did not attempt to retrieve it.

It was a murder weapon, after all.

Raking a hand through his hair, his body shaking with exertion and fury, he turned around and began walking back slowly the way he had come. He hated that little whore and when he caught her, she would not have an easy death, he vowed.

He tried to assure himself that Carmen would be too petrified to go to the authorities, for who would believe a whore against a duke of the royal blood? But just in case, he decided to make the Royal Guardsmen and the city police aware of her and the lies they could expect from her if she tried to contact them. For his part, he knew he had to go back to the prime minister's house and tell him *something*. He had left the man standing there in his dressing gown when he had gone tearing off after Cristoforo.

He searched his mind for what to say as he trudged through the waking city back toward the west end. He had to proceed carefully, for above all, he needed Don Arturo behind him in order to gain power. How could he account for his vanished witness?

But he'll believe of his own accord because you're giving him what he wants most in the whole world, he mused after a moment's consideration: *the head of Prince Charming on a silver platter. Yes,* he thought with an icy smile. The prime minister was all too willing to believe.

Dani was having the most splendid, wicked dream. It seemed as though the door had clicked and a wedge of light had angled in. Another click as it closed, and she sank back into deeper layers of sleep, only to feel the mattress bow under a new, graceful weight, as though someone large and strong were sliding into her bed with her; then the dream changed. Her breathing deepened. She felt large, warm, gentle hands slide up under her scoop-necked night rail and begin moving slowly over her body as she lay on her stomach, one arm tucked beneath her pillow.

Rafael.

Her body softened; pleasure washed in a warm wave down the length of her. She felt kisses down her spine, a clean-shaved face brushing against the rising curve of her backside. Then the warm, tickling delight of his fine mouth, dusting more kisses down the backs of her legs, which seemed to part with a will of their own at the teasing sweetness of his play, but she came fully awake only when he gently spread her bottom cheeks with his deft, warm hands and plunged his tongue into her, stroking her with a kiss.

Thrills of shocked bliss zoomed and spiraled through her body. She sucked in her breath and arched up onto all fours. Without pausing, he curled his hand around the front of her thigh and caressed her ultra-sensitive jewel with his fingertips while he explored her sex with his tongue.

She reached down behind her and ran her fingers through his dark gold hair. His powerful arms and chest were bare. At her caress, he glanced up and sent her a smoldering look, his enticing mouth against her pale skin. Then his gold-tipped lashes lowered again and he bent his head and continued pleasuring her.

She was soon beyond shame, barely able to hold a coherent thought but for the realization that, with his bag of wicked tricks, he could have had her anytime he had wanted. Then reason fled. Sensation was all.

He continued seducing her.

When she moaned loudly with desire, he began kissing his way up her spine again, holding her firmly by her hips. He worked her night rail up over her head and pulled it off her, then covered her with his body, pressing her into the mattress under his weight. His chest was hard and hot against her bare back.

His muscled body was so large he seemed to surround her on all sides, dominating her; kissing her ear, he was a firm but gentle master. She could hear him breathing heavily, felt the soft, chafing broadcloth of his breeches against the bare skin of her backside and the massive evidence of his need as he ground his throbbing groin against her.

She arched her head back as his fingertips lightly caressed her throat, moving down to tease her nipples. She moaned with want, her body undulating under him. In that moment, he ruled her utterly.

"Ask me nicely," he breathed.

She whimpered his name, knowing if he left her in unfulfilled torment again, she would die. His signet ring gleamed in the moonlight as he ran his hand over her fevered skin.

He kissed her shoulder. "Ask for it."

She closed her eyes and gave him her surrender. *"Rafael, Rafael,"* she breathed. *"Take me."*

"Turn over," he ordered in a ragged whisper. Pushing up off of her, he permitted her to roll onto her back while he finished undressing, staring at her body all the while.

Naked with her a moment later, he cupped her breasts and moved down to kiss them. She cradled his head against her, closing her eyes.

"I love you, Rafael," she said very softly. "I don't want to lose you."

Slowly, he rose over her and looked deeply, solemnly into her eyes, into her very soul. "You will never lose me. "

"Rafael." She caressed his chest with both hands, then slipped her arms around his neck. "Make it so they can never part us."

He closed his eyes, bent his head, and parted her lips with his own. Kissing her all the while, he gently eased her legs wider apart and lay between them.

He murmured to her softly as the time drew near. She grew nervous at the sheer size of him. She watched his face, every nuance of his expression as she lay in his arms, trusting him as she had never trusted another living soul. She gave everything. She let him stoke the fire in her until she was ablaze, and when the time came, she opened herself completely, giving, yielding, as he eased in, whispering to her like a man gentling a wild horse.

He told her, softly, raggedly, when it would hurt, and she cried out as he thrust deeply into the core of her, but there was the ecstasy amid the pain, for she knew he was hers now, hers forever.

And then he began to make the hurt go away.

"My love," he whispered, pressing fevered kisses to her brow. "My love. I needed you so much. I've missed you." The warm, virile smell of his skin mingled with her faded day's perfume and with the musky smell of sex that thickened the air. Stroking her arms and shoulders, Rafael caressed her breasts until her nipples strained rigidly under his palms.

Shyly, tentatively, she sought his mouth in the darkness as the pain slowly receded. She opened her mouth wider, consuming his slow, luxurious kisses. He fed her with his kisses, plunging his tongue deeply into her mouth until she caressed it with her own, sucked it hungrily. His hands traveled down her sides, following her curves down to her hips.

"So sweet, so tight," he whispered. He stroked her, cupped her backside in both his hands, kneading her flesh, then his hands slid lower, drawing her legs apart even wider.

"W-what are you doing now?" she whispered in sudden alarm, still sounding a bit distraught from his rending her.

"Now I'm going to finish it, my darling," he murmured, panting. He was trembling with restraint, his passion held in check. He kissed her shoulder while she slid her arms around him, bracing herself, not sure what was to come.

Pulling back gently from the tight sheath of her body, he thrust inside her again, again. He groaned with pleasure as he took her; he moved faster, seemingly unable to stop. It was like being caught in a summer storm; he was hard and steamy-slick, covered in sweat.

Surely she would be split in half, she thought, but she closed her eyes with a grimace, held on to his massive, sculpted arms, bit her lip, and silently endured the ramming of his warriorlike body into hers, forfeiting herself to his rage of love.

Then something peculiar happened. She was not sure exactly when the pain began turning to pleasure, but suddenly a burst of bliss beamed forth like a burning, sweet star in the place where he had once kissed her with the peppermint.

Startled, she dragged her eyes open and stared up at him. His eyes were closed and now he slowed his pace to a deep, languorous rhythm, savoring every moment as he took her in long, slow strokes. A diamond drop of sweat rolled down the side of his face, which was etched with tantalizing bliss.

"Oh, God, yes," he groaned, hanging his head. His golden hair fell forward in a silky curtain around her.

She moaned abruptly a moment later, then her rigid body began softening under him. The fullness of having him inside her ceased to be discomfort. Fascinated and amazed, she closed her eyes, relaxed under him, and let passion flow through her veins like wine. She shivered and clutched him to her, gasping with undreamed-of pleasure. She was aware of nothing else but the sensations that were sweeping ever closer, and then they crashed through her body and she cried out against his skin, holding on ever so tightly to him.

He was whispering wildly to her. In a state of bliss, she was rigid, pulsating: She felt as though she had been born for this moment.

He claimed her mouth, rising on his hands above her as

the last of his control flew asunder. He took her with urgent, vigorous strokes, then gave himself up to the dark wave of his release as it came roaring up from the depths of him. A barbaric growl tore from his lips: His mighty body went rigid and he gripped her in a savagely tight embrace. Pinning her fixedly under him, his hips lunged, his manhood pulsed with completion inside her and filled her womb to brimming, leaving him spent.

Over his broad shoulder, Dani stared up at the bed's canopy above her, her eyes wide. He collapsed heavily on her with a soul-deep sigh. She enfolded him in a soft, nuzzling embrace.

After a long moment, he slipped his still quite rigid sex out of her body. She grimaced faintly, but found, to her surprise, that the pain she'd expected was nothing compared to a gunshot wound.

Rafael glanced down at her, his golden mane tousled, his eyes heavy-lidded. He was still breathing deeply, but the man looked thoroughly satisfied. Dani smiled softly, filled with the sweetness of the knowledge that, indeed, they belonged to each other now. With a brief mist of tears in her eyes, she reached up and cupped his beloved face.

Even if she died in childbirth, he was worth it.

He pressed a lingering kiss to her palm. "There's something I must confess, Dani," he murmured.

She said nothing. She already knew about his visit to Chloe Sinclair's and wasn't sure she wished to discuss it.

"The truth is, I didn't marry you because you were the Masked Rider." He stared down at her. "I didn't really need to use your sway with the people. That was just the excuse I gave you for my proposal. It was much more than that, but I didn't know how . . . I didn't dare tell you . . ."

"What is it, Rafael?" she asked, taken aback.

"I knew from the moment I saw you that you were

the one I have been looking for all my life," he whispered. "I would have found any excuse to make you mine, Daniela di Fiore."

He kissed her and she closed her eyes, quivering at his words. He ended the kiss and they were silent. When he caressed her face lovingly in the dark, she looked at him again, loath to ask, but she had to know.

"Did you go to Miss Sinclair's tonight?"

"I was there," he admitted quietly, his eyes registering a flickering pang of guilt, "but nothing happened. I swear it on my honor, Dani. I ended it with her and left. Then I came straight home to you. You are my wife."

"You left?" she asked in a small voice, longing to believe.

"Yes, my love. A man needs more than the pleasures of the flesh." He trailed his fingertip along the line of her jaw and down her throat and whispered, "You alone satisfy my soul. Will you forgive me?"

"Yes, Rafael, but . . ." She paused for a moment, struggling with her doubts. "I know I cannot leash a man like you, but if you ever stray, you will lose my trust."

"I know that," he said soberly. He laid his hand on her midriff and, leaning closer, kissed her forehead. "Please do not fear it anymore, because there is nothing I treasure more than you and this trust of yours that I've finally won. I would sooner lose my kingdom, my life. I learned my lesson tonight, Dani. You are the only one."

Lying on her back, she turned her face to him in the darkness. "I believe you, Rafael." She gazed at him. "My heart is in your keeping."

"And I will hold it as gently as a baby sparrow in my hand, my sweet one." He leaned down and kissed her, then he yawned suddenly and stretched like a lazy lion, all lordly pride and tawny velvet.

He gathered her into his arms with a playful little growl. Cradling her, he stroked her hair, gazed into her shining eyes, and whispered, "Sleep, Princess."

With a soul-deep sigh, she rested her cheek against the satiny warmth of his chest and, for once in her life, obeyed.

❧ CHAPTER ❧
FIFTEEN

"Let me tell you, Your Highness, I could get used to this," Dani sighed in luxurious contentment as she sank deeper into the bathing tub of blue-veined marble that was big enough for two people.

Rafael sat across from her, resting his head back, his eyes closed, his arms slung over the rim of the tub. At her words, he opened his eyes and sent her a slow, lazy smile. "Royalty has its advantages."

As he reached for a slice of almond biscotti from the silver tray that held their breakfast, she watched the play of sculpted muscle in his arms and chest with his simple movement. Beads of water sparkled on his bronzed skin in the slanted morning light that filtered through the high windows of the prince's private bathing room.

Their bath was an inexcusable decadence in light of the drought, but Dani had awakened sore enough from her deflowerment to allow herself a little pampering.

Rafael washed down his biscotti with a swallow of dark, strong coffee, then noticed her smitten gaze and smiled, leaned toward her in the water, and kissed her cheek with boyish sweetness, then resumed eating. She lifted her crossed ankles and rested them on his muscled thigh.

"I have been thinking about this business of your father

possibly disinheriting you for marrying me, and I think I have a solution," she announced.

He lifted his eyebrows. "Now, that's my national heroine talking. By all means, let's hear it. I need all the solutions I can get."

"I think if we work together the way you originally suggested that mad day in the jail—if we reach out to the people of Ascencion—travel around meeting them face to face, for instance—everything would be different."

"How do you mean?"

"They want to love you, Rafael, but so far they only know you by your notorious reputation in the scandal sheets. They need to know the man you really are. You could see the places where the ordinary people live. I'll take you there. Then you can get to know them, talk to them. Find out what their fears are and their dreams for themselves and their children. Between the two of us, I'm sure that we can find a few practical ways to help them, and if we do that, I know they will fall in love with you, as I have. Since Ascencion is your father's first priority, then perhaps he will see what we can accomplish together for the good of the island, and he'll give our marriage his blessing."

He was staring at her.

"What do you think?"

Snapping out of a dazed look, he shook his head at her. "You are my needle in a haystack, you amazingly brilliant, beautiful woman." He leaned toward her and kissed her soundly. "Let's do it."

She smiled against his mouth. He lingered, brushing his nose against hers.

"Daniela?"

She stole a quick kiss and murmured, "Yes, sweetheart?"

He smiled softly at the endearment and caressed the line

of her jaw with his fingertips. "I take it you have made peace with the matter of childbearing."

She lowered her lashes and nodded shyly.

He lifted her gaze to his with a gentle touch under her chin. "You know I won't let anything happen to you. Besides, it could be weeks, even months before you become pregnant. But when the time comes, I swear to you, you'll have the finest doctors, midwives, experts—"

"Will you be there with me?" she whispered pleadingly.

His eyes widened. He considered for a heartbeat, staring at her. "If it's what you want, yes. Yes, I will."

"If you are there, I know I'll be too proud to cry."

He linked his hand through hers beneath the water, drew it to his lips, and kissed it. "Then I will be there for you, Daniela. Always."

She wrapped her arms around his neck and held him tightly.

From entwined embraces and sweet, small kisses, they began washing each other playfully, lovingly, when all of a sudden their caresses were interrupted by an ominous knock at the door.

"Rafe!"

He frowned toward the door. "Elan? What the devil do you want? I'm busy! Privacy is the one luxury royal life does not afford," he added in a rueful aside to her.

"Sorry, Rafe, but I thought you'd want to know—I've just been given some rather shocking news."

"What is it?" he called impatiently.

"Ah, Your Highness may wish to hear it privately."

"Our wife is entirely in our confidence, my lord. Spill it," he ordered Elan through the door, casting Dani a roguish grin.

"As you wish," Elan called through the door. "Count Bulbati was found dead last night in his cell."

Dani gasped at the news about her unpleasant neighbor.

With a question on her lips, she glanced from the door to Rafael. At once, she saw that his smile had faded. His face had gone hard and grim.

"I'll be right there," he said in a steely tone. He brushed his knuckle reassuringly over her cheek as he rose from the bath, but his eyes were far away, their green-gold depths churning with veiled anger under his silky, gold-tipped lashes.

He stepped out of the tub and reached for a towel, his magnificent body streaming with water, glistening bronze in the morning light.

"What's going on, Rafael?"

"It's a long story."

Warned off by the aura of threat around him she made no move to follow him out of the tub, watching him as he toweled himself dry. Slipping into his dark silk banyan, he tied it loosely around his lean waist. The voluminous silk flowed gracefully around him as he strode back to her and leaned down, cupping her face between his hands. He gave her a last, lingering kiss. The passion between them sparked to life. Dani quivered under his kiss, parting her lips for the lush caress of his tongue on hers.

Ending the kiss, he held her in a smoldering gaze. "I'll see you as soon as I can."

She smiled wanly at him. He pressed another kiss to her forehead and rose, turned, and marched out to his adjoining room in a swirl of dark silk, like some pagan warrior-chieftain of old with his golden mane spilling damply over his shoulders.

An hour later, dressed in one of her pretty new muslin morning gowns, her hair coiffed, her body not as sore after the soothing bath, Dani was making an earnest study of a manual on court protocol when one of her maids came into the doorway of the sitting room holding a gleaming silver tray.

Dani looked up from the tedious book. "Yes?"

"A letter's come for you, Highness."

"Thank you. Bring it, please."

The servant obeyed. Dani plucked the folded letter from the polished salver and nodded her dismissal. She unfolded the fine linen paper and scanned the authoritative, flowing handwriting with interest.

To Her Royal Highness Principessa Daniela di Fiore, lately Lady Chiaramonte

From Mother Superior Bernadetta Rienzi of the Sisters of Santa Lucia.

She read the heading in amazement. *Sister Bernadetta?* Why, she remembered that terrifying, black-robed dragon lady from the second convent school that had tossed her out for misbehavior! She had not seen the woman since she was eight years old.

Why on earth would Sister Bernadetta be writing to her now? Probably to scold her for something, she mused wryly, then read on.

Dearest Princess Daniela,

As my former pupil, you were always a bright girl. It was unfortunate that you could not finish your education with us.

"Ha," she snorted aloud. "Unfortunate for whom?"

I understand that as the Masked Rider you have often lent your help to those in need. Forgive my brief greetings after all these years and my presumption upon our past acquaintance, but if you are still in the habit of coming to the rescue of those in danger, know that now

*there is one who craves your aid most desperately and
whatever protection your influence allows.*

Fascinated, Dani narrowed her eyes.

*The young unfortunate in question is a ruined girl
who has occasionally come to seek aid of our charities.
Her name is Carmen. Last night she appeared on our
convent's doorstep in a state of terror, claiming that she
had witnessed a terrible murder and that now her own
life is in danger. The victim, according to the girl, was a
chef in the royal kitchens. We have kept her safe through
the night in the convent, but beyond God's grace, I know
not how to protect her, if her tale is true.*

*Because of her present, unmentionable mode of life
and the identity of the killer whom she saw with her own
eyes, she fears to go to the city guards. Because of your
past deeds as the Masked Rider, you are the only one
she will speak to. If you are willing to hear the girl out,
please come as quickly as possible to the convent of
Santa Lucia. Blessings of the Holy Spirit upon you.*

*Your sister in Christ,
Mother Superior Bernadetta Rienzi*

Without a second's hesitation, Dani grabbed her gloves
and bonnet and marched out of her apartment in search of
Rafael to let him know where she was going. The moment
she left her rooms, her six burly guards fell into step behind her. The palace steward informed her that he was in
the council chamber with his young cabinet.

She walked in on their tense conversation about the
death of poor plump Count Bulbati. Rafael sat at the head
of the table. Elan, the sarcastic Lord Niccolo, and the
haughty Adriano were all there, with a few others.

Adriano shot her a prickly look from beneath his glossy black forelock. She ignored him and brought the letter to Rafael. When she arrived by his side and greeted him with a murmur, offering him the letter, he captured her hand, bringing it to his lips in habitual gallantry as he scanned it.

She watched him tensely as he set the letter down and scratched his forehead in thought, frowning.

"I'll go with you," he murmured to her, then looked at his men. "Nic, Elan, Adriano, come with us. The rest of you can go. We'll reconvene this afternoon."

"Rafael, this girl has obviously been terrorized. She's not going to want to tell her tale in front of all of you," Dani protested in a low tone.

He rose from his chair, laid his hand in the curve of her lower back, and steered her toward the door. "I know. But I have a feeling I know who she's going to name as the culprit."

"You do?" she asked, glancing up at him, wide-eyed. "Whom do you suspect?"

He shook his head. "Let's just wait and see."

To her consternation, he called for his weapons in the hall. She stared in foreboding while he buckled on his sword and pistols. She was taken aback by the smooth but grim expertise with which he handled them. Then she followed him as he stalked outside. While his hooded gaze swept the sprawling courtyard around them, he gave her his hand, assisting her into the coach.

His three friends followed in a second carriage. Dani's guards took to their horses and rode in formation around the stately royal coach.

They spoke little in the carriage. Dani was confused. She wanted to ask him about Count Bulbati's death, but gathering anger had begun to thrum in his big, lean body. The brooding, dangerous aura around him discouraged conversation. Her sense of foreboding grew. Ducking his head slightly, his expression restless, Rafael watched out the window.

When they arrived at the convent, Mother Bernadetta greeted Dani, but they did not waste time on pleasantries. The nun, tall, brisk, and firm, walked with her hands tucked into the slats of her black habit. She was broad-shouldered for a woman and carried herself like an aged warrior-queen. Dani found it no surprise that they had clashed wills when she had been a student here.

Mother Bernadetta led Dani in at once to see the girl while Rafael and the other men waited gravely in the re-ception room near the entrance.

Carmen was a pretty, black-haired girl with olive-toned skin and wary, dark eyes. She was pitifully young for her harsh trade, perhaps sixteen or seventeen, but the air around her was old beyond her years. Dani closeted her-self with the girl and gave her some comforting words and reassurances, then asked her to speak her tale in front of the prince as well as her. Carmen agreed with a hesi-tant nod.

Dani squeezed the girl's hand in silent encouragement, then rose and quietly went to the door, calling Rafael in.

World-weary as she seemed, the young girl grew a bit starry-eyed when the tall, golden prince walked in, straight out of a fairy tale. He did not seem to notice, either thor-oughly used to that reaction from females or too sharply focused on his own thoughts. He sat down beside Dani, rested his elbows on his bent knees, and lightly clasped his hands, giving the girl an intent, sober look.

He had the air of a man who would take care of every-thing; Dani was proud of him.

Then Carmen haltingly told how the young journeyman chef Cristoforo had been taking bribes so that he could af-ford to visit her. The man she described as contacting

Cristoforo from time to time had long raven hair, icy green eyes, and wore fine clothes, always of pure black. She had not known nor cared to ask why the stranger was paying Cristoforo. She only knew that her "friend" was frightened of the man.

Dani felt Rafael tense beside her when Carmen told about how the black-clad man had come last night and taken Cristoforo away in a coach.

"Before Cristoforo left my room, he begged me to follow because he was afraid something terrible would happen to him. He said he would pay me. So I did," she said, her dark eyes grave. "I ran the whole way, though I could barely keep up. I watched where the coach turned and took shortcuts—I know the city like the back of my hand. That's how I know whose palazzo they went to." She looked from Dani to Rafael. "The prime minister's."

Rafael's eyes flickered but his face was impassive. "Go on."

Carmen wrapped her arms more tightly around her thin body, hunching down in her seat as she went on to tell of the boy's escape from Don Arturo's house and the terrible chase that ensued. "I knew the man was going to kill him then. So I picked up a broken piece of a brick and threw it as hard as I could."

"Did you hit him?"

"Yes, Your Highness. I hit him right here," Carmen said somberly, pointing to her left temple by her forehead. Her hand trembled. "He had blood running down the side of his face. He was horrible. But the blow didn't stop him for long. He . . . did it, then."

"Killed your friend?" Dani asked softly.

She nodded, head down. The old nun went to Carmen and embraced her against her large, matronly bosom. "There, there, child."

Rafael rose from the couch, bowed to the girl, and left

the room. Dani murmured comfortingly to Carmen, then went out into the hall and found her husband conferring with his three friends in muted tones. As she walked toward them, they exited briskly after he had spoken to them. Tall and kingly in the midday gloom, Rafael looked over at her from down the stuccoed hall as she approached.

"I think we both know whom she accuses," Dani said. "Do you believe her? I confess I have no idea what to make of all this."

"I do," he replied grimly. One large hand resting on the hilt of the sword at his side, angry calm glowing in his eyes, he looked more than ever like an archangel on the warpath. "Get the girl, would you? You and she are going to a place where I know you'll be safe until I've taken Orlando into custody."

"Are you going to arrest him for the boy's murder?"

"Among other things. I've had some of our agents out looking for him since last night. I think he may also have had something to do with Bulbati's death."

She started to turn away to get Carmen as he'd asked, but then she paused, glancing at him in trepidation. "Rafael, has it ever occurred to you that Orlando might not be who he claims?"

He turned to her with a look of distraction. "Hmmm?"

"Am I the only one who has noticed that Orlando looks exactly like the king?"

"What?" he exclaimed, staring at her with a riveted expression.

"I hate to cast aspersions on your father, but haven't you ever wondered if Orlando might be something closer than a distant cousin? Is it not feasible that he could be your brother? Half-brother, that is."

"A bastard? But my father would never . . ." His voice trailed off and his stare turned haunted.

"It could have happened before His Majesty married

your mother, Rafael. Do we know Orlando's age?" Dani cringed slightly in the awkward silence as Rafael shook his head dazedly. "Well, I'll go fetch the girl." She turned and started down the hall, but then she stopped and hesitantly turned once more. There was no use holding back the rest. Casting off her uncertainty, she walked back to him. "I probably should have told you this before, but I didn't want you to be angry."

He searched her eyes in question.

She braced herself for his reaction. "Rafael, Orlando has been propositioning me."

If his wrath had been contained before, at that moment it rushed to the surface. His eyes turned the color of an angry, churning sea. *"What?"*

"It started the afternoon he came to talk to me privately. He said that after our marriage was annulled, he would take me under his protection if I so desired. I refused him flatly, of course," she said hastily. "But then it happened again last night while you were . . . out."

A look of pained guilt flooded his face.

"Well," she said awkwardly, not wishing to reproach him since he had already said he was sorry, "I'll go get the girl."

Soon they were riding in his carriage, surrounded by Royal Guardsmen on horseback. His three friends followed in the vehicle behind.

The streets of Belfort were crowded as they crossed the city.

Except for conferring briefly with the Royal Guardsmen before their cavalcade left the convent, Rafael had remained utterly silent and tense.

Furtively, Dani watched him as he brooded. Realizing Carmen was staring anxiously at her, she gave the child a slight, reassuring smile. Just then, they heard shouts outside and their driver called a halt to the team. Dani stole a glance from behind the pulled canvas shade and saw an imposing figure on a black stallion.

"You are the princess's guards, are you not, my good fellows? Is Her Highness traveling out today?"

It was Orlando's voice, pleasant, blasé. Dani exchanged a wily look with her husband. Quickly she realized that since Rafael and she had spent so much time apart, Orlando must have assumed she was alone.

"Allow me, dear husband," she murmured, sending him a conspiratorial look.

Rafael smiled at her and gestured to Carmen to duck down out of sight.

Then Dani pulled the shade near her seat and leaned out with a cordial smile. "Good day, Your Grace."

"Daniela." Under the shadow of his low, black top hat, his vivid eyes glowed.

The guards watched keenly, immediately sensing that she would only greet him with Rafael's permission. The armed men were wise enough to remain silent and let him pass.

Orlando smiled at her and urged his stallion closer at a stately walk. "Well, you've been allowed out of your cage at last, I see. My congratulations. You look radiant, as ever," he murmured, tipping his hat.

The gesture was slight, but Dani knew what to look for, and when he lifted his top hat slightly, she saw the large, purplish bruise on his temple.

"Oh, my dear cousin," she replied with a sympathetic frown, "whatever did you do to your poor head?"

It was all the signal that Rafael needed.

Without warning, he flung open the coach door, drew his sword, and sprang at Orlando, leaping across empty space at him with a barbaric roar.

⊰ CHAPTER ⊱
SIXTEEN

Before Rafael's onslaught, Orlando's startled horse reared and shied. The two men grappled fiercely while the six Royal Guardsmen joined the fray with a huge cry.

Pandemonium broke out.

Dani tried to see the fight, but the driver sent the coach surging forward, away from the violence. Nearly hanging out the window, she saw that Orlando somehow held his seat. She saw him kick Rafael squarely in the chest. The prince fell back a step, then Orlando spurred his horse and charged, tearing through the cluster of guards. He rode his horse straight into one of the narrow shops, clattering through the arcade to the next street.

"Get him!" Rafael roared. He was already shoving one of the guardsmen aside, commandeering the man's horse.

She held her breath, staring as he swung up into the saddle, every movement graceful with angry precision.

He glared at his men as he jerked a nod in her direction. "Protect her. Take her to my house. Half of you come with me. I want him alive!"

"Rafael!" She began getting out of the coach with an offer to ride with him on the tip of her tongue, but he looked sharply at her and seemed to take in her intention with a glance.

"No, Dani. Stay!" he ordered. "Help the girl. She's our only witness."

With that, he gathered his reins, spurred the horse, and rode away with three of the Royal Guardsmen, their progress slowed by the crowd that had rallied in the street when their fight broke out.

"Are you all right?" Dani asked Carmen quickly.

The girl nodded, then she heard more arguing just outside the coach.

"You have the carriages, man, give me your horse!"

"Rafe'll need us!"

She looked over quickly and saw Elan, Adriano, and Niccolo taking her remaining guards' horses. They were eager, full of gusto, as though it were a fox hunt instead of a chase for a deadly killer.

"Hell, I didn't bring my weapon," Adriano said suddenly, patting his hip.

"Here." Niccolo tossed him one of his pistols and he caught it by the handle out of the air.

"Be careful!" Dani shouted. They didn't look back.

She watched them disappear down the street after Rafael with a heart full of foreboding.

Thunder and dust whirled around Rafe as he and the three Royal Guardsmen charged up the King's Road about half a mile behind Orlando.

He rode low over the big bay gelding's neck, keeping the pace vigorous but careful not to wreck the animal's wind, for there was no telling how long this race would go. His every muscle was taut with slow-burning anger.

Sweat ran into his eyes and made the dust from the road cling to his skin. He squinted against the westward sun, intensely focused on the black-clad horseman in the distance.

Orlando had tried to lose them in the city, but when they had split up to surround him, the duke had bolted. Rafe could not guess his cousin's destination, but he did not mind chasing him clear to the other end of Ascencion, so long as Orlando continued in this direction, far away from Dani. He could not have gone forward without a sense of certainty that she was safe.

He was so fixed on the rider ahead that he barely heard the faint shouts some distance behind him on the road. When the voices reached him dimly over the pounding of hoofbeats, he stole a moment's glance over his shoulder and saw his friends galloping after him.

He lifted his arm in salute, acknowledging that he had seen them, but he did not slow to wait for them because he was not letting Orlando out of his sight.

Then he settled into the grueling pace.

Orlando led them nearly twenty miles up the King's Road. Streaking past the turnoff to the port, he made his way toward the wooded, mountainous north. Seeing this, Rafe realized Orlando had no scheme to flee Ascencion, though he might have been able to save himself by doing so.

Perhaps he hoped to hide in the wilds.

With the sun slowly sinking behind the mountain crests that rose before them, they rode into the western shadows.

Rafe suddenly realized where Orlando was headed when he caught a glimpse over the trees of the crumbling medieval citadel that had been the stronghold of the di Cambio dukes so many ages past. He furrowed his brow. *But that place is an old ruin.* The horses were laboring at a hard canter when Orlando abruptly turned into the woods, disappearing from view.

Within moments, they arrived at the mouth of a vestigial road which had nearly been reclaimed by nature. It was overgrown with tall grasses and vines of ivy draping from the trees.

With a glance that swept the terrain, Rafe decided to use the tactic again of surrounding his cousin. For that, he would need a few more men, but his friends weren't far behind. Besides, if he didn't wait for them now, they would likely miss the turnoff that Orlando had taken.

"Stay on him!" he shouted at his men.

"Where the hell's he going, Sire?" one of the guardsmen yelled.

"To the old di Cambio fort! Don't let him out of your sight! Remember, I want him alive!" He waved the three Royal Guardsmen on ahead while he pulled up at the edge of the road to wait for his friends and instruct them.

Their arrival would prove a further advantage, Rafe calculated. Orlando had probably counted only the three guardsmen and him in pursuit.

The sight of his friends' faces was a welcome prospect as they pulled up their blowing horses where he waited impatiently.

"How do you want to do this, Rafe?" Elan asked quickly, wiping the sweat off his brow with his forearm.

"We'll surround him. You and Nic go around to the south of the citadel—"

Suddenly the most horrific, bloodcurdling screams Rafe had ever heard pierced the air, screams of man and beast. It sounded like slaughter. Rafe swore and turned his horse as the piercing, awful sounds continued.

"Careful!" Elan barked as they urged their nearly spent horses dashing off in the direction of the bone-chilling screams.

The woods were not deep. Instead, the overgrown road led through them only about fifty yards. On the other end there were open, scrubby fields surrounding the ruins.

"Hurry!"

"I don't think there's anything we can do for them, by the sound of it," Niccolo said under his breath.

Even now the terrible screams had begun to fade.

They came to the edge of the woods. Ahead, the brown

road wound through the parched green field, up to a rise about a hundred yards off.

"I don't see anyone!" Adriano said, angrily scanning the open field.

The sounds, hellish groaning now, were coming from just beyond the rise.

"Oh, Christ," Rafe whispered, staring at the road ahead where there was a gentle undulation in the rolling hills. His horse was spooked by the terrible sounds of suffering, but he forced the balking animal forward.

They rode forward cautiously, keeping the horses to a trot.

When they crested the rise, they all froze for a second in sheer horror, then leaped off their horses and ran to the edge of the spiked pit. All three horses and two of the men were already dead, impaled on metal spikes rising from the ground, in this barbaric defense structure resurrected by Orlando from an age of darkness.

Rafe slid through the dirt to the last surviving Royal Guardsman, but the gurgling man died as he reached him.

Then there was only silence.

Eerie, chill silence, with the crumbling hulk of the black citadel towering over them, not a quarter mile away through the trees.

"Oh, my God," Rafe said after a long moment, staring at the bodies.

The others were perfectly silent.

He looked over at them with a hard expression, realizing that any manner of evil, insane devices might be waiting to snare them in this place. They were his closest friends and he could not bear to lose them. He wanted to turn back because he knew they might not all make it out of this alive, but if he did that, he might never get this close to capturing Orlando again.

All of Ascencion was at stake. He could not think as a friend. He must think as a king.

Elan had taken his spectacles off and turned away, looking like he might well puke. Adriano was white, as if he still couldn't believe what he was seeing. Niccolo had climbed out of the pit, his face a rictus of rage, and was staring toward the citadel.

"There!" Niccolo suddenly cried. "Get down!"

A bullet slammed into the dirt near Rafe.

They dropped, the dead momentarily forgotten. Flat on his stomach on the edge of the pit, Nic took aim with his pistol.

"What are you doing?" Rafe asked him evenly.

"Save your fire. You'll never hit him from here," Adriano said with unnerving calm.

"You're right, di Tadzio," Nic muttered. "Excellent point."

Rafe watched the brown-haired, brawny Nic slide back down into the pit with a look of pure, cold rage, as though his wits had snapped. Nic climbed over to the dead captain of the guardsman and wrenched free the rifle strapped to his back.

Rafe said, "I repeat, I want him alive."

Angrily, Elan turned to Rafe with a wrenching stare. "Even now you want to spare him?"

"Especially now," Rafe said in a low, bristling growl.

Nic dropped down on his stomach at the rim of the pit and took aim with the rifle. "Arrest me, then, Rafe. Because I say he dies." He squeezed the trigger.

There was an agonized, demonic squeal from the shadows at the base of the fort.

"You hit him!" Elan gasped.

The black stallion bolted out from the place where Orlando had concealed himself in the brush, the duke clinging to the saddle.

"He's still up! Did you hit him or not?" Elan pressed.

Niccolo didn't answer, but merely reloaded.

"No, you hit the horse," Rafe murmured, watching as the excellent black stallion finally stumbled, fell, somersaulting violently while Orlando dove to the side, tumbled, and sprang up, running back to the cover of the trees. "Let's go. He'll be on foot now."

All strode back to the horses and mounted up.

Rafe's stare tracked Orlando until the man sped into the cover of the woods. "Elan, Nic, you go that way," he said, pointing left. "Di Tadzio and I will take the right. We've got to close him in. Avoid gunfire in favor of swords. Leave the rifle, Nic! Let's try and avoid accidentally shooting each other. Is everybody all right?" he added, glancing quickly from one face to the next after the carnage they had witnessed.

They murmured grimly in the affirmative.

"Good. Let's get him." He nodded to Adriano and they wheeled their horses away while Elan and Niccolo cantered off in the opposite direction.

They rode past the black stallion, dead with a seeping bullet wound in its neck, then plunged into the darkening woods.

Rafe's pulse pounded in his ears as they stalked Orlando, slipping stealthily through the trees. Adriano kept abreast with him about twenty feet to his right.

The woods were alive with the sounds of twilight, the breeze, the rustling leaves, the chattering birds. At the sound of a twig snapping, Rafe jerked his head, leveling his weapon, but three ghostly deer merely bounded by in a line, tearing through the brake.

He glanced over questioningly at Adriano through the semidarkness, sweat trickling down his cheek. The other man shook his head, indicating that he saw nothing so far.

Rafe realized Orlando's black clothing would help him blend all the more easily into the growing shadows.

They pressed on.

Time had lost all meaning in the riveting tension, so Rafe did not know how long they had been hunting Orlando when suddenly two gunshots roared from some distance away and there was a shout. Immediately Rafe and Adriano drove their heels into their horses' sides, sending the animals lunging forward through the undergrowth.

Another shot boomed, its echo rippling across the hillside.

Rafe prayed it was Niccolo doing the shooting. But when he and Adriano burst into a small grove by a stream, they found Nic flattened on his back. He tried to sit up as they jumped down from the horses and ran to him. Rafe swallowed hard, seeing the dark stain spreading across the front of Nic's brown waistcoat.

"He dropped out of the trees," he gasped out, his eyes round, his face ghastly white. "He ran! He could be anywhere."

"Don't try to talk." Rafe quickly took off his coat, covering Nic with it. He ripped off his cravat and used it to try to stanch the flow. "Where's Elan?"

Shaking violently, Nic whispered, "I don't know. His horse threw him." He began to choke.

Rafe pulled him up to a sitting position. Nic leaned weakly against Adriano.

"Stay with him," Rafe ordered.

Adriano nodded as Rafe swept to his feet and scanned the grove. He drew his sword and thrust his way into the brake in cold fury. There was a place where the twigs were crushed and broken. Elan's spooked horse had probably forged the path.

"Elan!" He sliced vengefully through a mound of thorns, casting an enraged glance up at the branches overhead. *"You savage,"* he said under his breath. "Elan!"

He dreaded what he might find. It was bad enough that

the sarcastic, wisecracking Nic was down. Rafe refused to admit to himself that he knew Nic was going to die. He could only think that without Elan's brains and steady, cautious nature to balance his own recklessness, he had no idea how he would go on.

"Elan! Answer me, damn you," he added in barely a whisper.

"Rafe!" came the viscount's thin cry from a small distance to the left.

"Elan! Where are you?" Rafe shouted, his heart pounding anew as he looked around frantically. "Are you hurt?"

"I'm here!"

Rafe whirled around as Elan picked his way through the thorns.

"Nic's down, Rafe."

"I know." He saw that his friend was covered in cuts, his spectacles skewed, but he appeared to have sustained no serious wounds.

"My horse dashed. Orlando dropped right out of the trees in front of us and opened fire. He hit Nic. I think he only missed me because I was on his left."

"Did you see which way he went?"

"Towards the citadel, I think." He looked around, at a loss. "My horse is gone."

"Forget the horse." Gesturing to him, Rafe led the dazed viscount back to the grove.

Adriano glanced up as they joined them. Seeing Elan, he let out a long breath of relief, then looked back down at Nic. "He's unconscious."

Rafe looked down bitterly at his friend's wan face, etched with pain. Then, with his eyes narrowed and thunder in his heart, he scanned the tree line.

"Both of you, stay with Nic," he said. "I'll finish this."

"You are out of your mind if you think I'm going to let you go after him by yourself," Adriano said quietly. He looked up at Rafe with searing intensity from under his black forelock.

"It's between him and me."

"Rafe," he said, "you don't even know what Orlando is."

"And you do?"

Adriano did not answer for a moment, a flash of guilty shame in his dark eyes which he quickly hid. "I have my suspicions," he mumbled.

"What do you mean?" Elan asked him.

Adriano merely looked at the viscount, then stared at Rafe.

"Stay with Nic," he repeated. "Those are my orders." With that, Rafe walked away, the sword light and ready, humming in his hand for blood.

"Orlando!" he bellowed, his roar echoing in the deepening gloom.

Shoving branches aside with his sword, he marched on, too angry to feel the slightest fear.

The woods were growing thicker, more tangled.

Moments passed.

Rafe's frustration escalated to rage. "Come out and *stand*!" he roared.

"What's this? Does the king's golden boy actually dare to fight me one on one? Man to man?" drawled a voice nearby.

Rafe whirled.

"Where's your army, Prince Charming? It's dark, and you're all alone." Orlando was leaning against the fat trunk of an oak, his arms folded over his chest, smirking coolly at him. "What an innocent you are."

"Who are you?" Rafe demanded, bringing his sword up as he closed in on him warily.

Orlando merely smiled.

"Have you or have you not been poisoning my father?" Rafe ground out.

"*Your* father? Ah, you must mean the saintly King Lazar . . . that God-appointed shepherd of the flock who has never committed a sin, never cheated on his wife. You love your mama, don't you, Rafie?"

"Answer my question," he said through gritted teeth. "Have you or have you not poisoned the king?"

"Why, of course not, Rafe. You did. Just as you had your minions murder that useless young chef last night, before he could give away your plot. Don't you remember?" Orlando smiled, his teeth flashing white in the dark. "What's this? You look confused. Well, just ask Don Arturo. He knows the whole story."

"I want plain answers! You are trying my mercy," he said, bringing his sword up under Orlando's chin.

The man flicked a contemptuous glance toward the blade, then sneered at him. "I don't want your *mercy*, Rafe. Don't you see? Your *mercy* only makes me hate you more. Such a gentleman. Such a prince. But your mercy cannot sound the depths of my hate."

Shocked by his sheer venom, Rafe shook his head, holding the sword steady. "What did I ever do to you?"

"You were born, to start."

"What did my father ever do, that you would poison him?" he demanded angrily.

Orlando laughed in soft bitterness, leaf shadows playing over his bruised face, so like Rafe's own. "*I* was born, I suppose."

Rafe stared at him, holding his breath. "Are you my brother, Orlando?"

"Merely your killer," he answered, lifting a pistol into Rafe's face.

Rafe threw himself forward, knocking Orlando's arm upward as he squeezed the trigger. The bullet flew wild as Rafe bowled Orlando over. They landed in a heap at the wide base of the tree, tripping on the large gnarled roots.

Drawing back with his grip wrapped around his sword hilt, he smashed his fist into Orlando's face.

It did not knock him out, as Rafe had hoped, but it unbalanced him.

His chest heaving, Rafe stepped back, wielding his sword in both hands now. "Get up," he growled.

Orlando held up his empty hands. "Are you going to strike me down, Your Highness? You can see I've no weapon."

"Draw your sword."

"What's this? Does the gallant prince wish to duel?"

"Draw your sword, you coward!"

Orlando stared at him. "You'd better think twice about this, Rafie, because if I had you in this position, I would not for an instant hesitate."

"I already know you don't fight fair. Now stand," he snarled.

"Very well, very well." Orlando climbed to his feet, dusting himself off, chuckling. "But know that after I kill you, coz, I shall take for my prize the fair Daniela's maidenhead."

In answer, Rafe lunged viciously just as Orlando slid his saber from its sheath with a sinister whisper of metal. Their fight was wild. They engaged, then Rafe flung him back.

"How is it you still haven't managed to bed your own wife, Rafe? Ladies' man like you," Orlando taunted him.

"You should see yourself," Rafe answered with a disgusted smile. "You are truly . . . pitiful."

"Doesn't she fancy you?"

"Oh, I think she fancies me plenty," Rafe said, slicing with his blade, his smile widening wolfishly.

Orlando sneered. "Since when?"

"Last night," he replied smugly, edging closer.

Orlando froze for a moment. "Do you mean to say the little bitch finally let you mount her?"

Rafe's fury flared anew at the insult to his wife, but he

quickly checked it. Losing his temper would only give his foe the advantage. "Why, Your Grace," he answered coolly, "a gentleman never discusses such things."

Orlando grimaced with ugly fury and charged with renewed force.

Metal met metal, shearing sparks.

The clash of their swords rang through the woods, blow after blow, both men seeking blood. Then they circled, having tested the bounds of each other's skills. The tips of the two blades danced in lethal opposition, weaving small rings in the air around each other, as each man tried to deceive the other into leaving himself open.

Orlando's sword suddenly darted at Rafe in a straight thrust at his breast. Rafe smoothly passed his blade under the oncoming sword, deflecting it with the forte.

With timing honed in endless practice, Rafe saw the withdrawal of his enemy's blade and sensed the start of his covering action. He lunged. The lightning-fast riposte drove past Orlando's defending blade, biting deeply into the man's right shoulder until it struck bone. Orlando roared like a wounded beast, falling down on one knee in agony.

Rafe pulled back from the thrust with a barbaric growl of satisfaction. Orlando glanced down at his wound.

"Yield," Rafe ground out, his chest heaving as he held Orlando at bay. He longed for recompense for Nic, but he checked his vengeance. Orlando had much more to answer for.

Staring down at his wound, Orlando slowly lifted his head, his eyes nearly red with rage. "I will never yield to you." He supported his faltering right-hand grip with his left and spoke in a voice from hell. "I'm used to pain. You're not." He staggered to his feet. "But you soon will be."

Orlando attacked again, drawing on a strength that Rafe could only guess came from demonic hatred. Still, Rafe was expert enough a swordsman to parry every ferocious thrust and swing of the razor-sharp blade—until his heel caught on the oak's swollen, gnarled branches.

It was just enough to knock him off balance. Immediately Orlando lunged. Rafe allowed himself to fall to escape the blow, but to his horror, he lost his grip on his saber in the instinctive response to catch himself, breaking his fall with his right hand.

He reached frantically for his sword, feeling the shadow of Orlando's blade above him, poised to deliver his death blow.

"Goodnight, sweet prince," Orlando said with a leering grin.

"Don't move."

There was a click. The sound of a pistol being cocked pierced the silence.

Grasping his sword, Rafe looked up and saw that Adriano had come out of nowhere and was standing with his pistol resting against Orlando's temple.

Rafe sprang to his feet and wrenched the sword out of Orlando's hands, throwing it aside. "Good timing, di Tadzio."

"Don't mention it, Rafe." Adriano held his ground unflinchingly.

With Adriano's gun to his head, Orlando began to laugh with a sneer. "Well, well, if it isn't the prince's pretty bitch-boy."

Adriano thrust the gun against Orlando's cheek. "Let me kill him, Rafe. You don't need him. Let me kill him for Nic and those men back in the field."

"I think somebody's nervous," Orlando chided in a singsong voice as he slid a glance casually from Adriano to Rafe. "What's the matter, love? Do you think your friend would find the truth about you a bit hard to, shall we say, swallow?"

"Rafe." Adriano gulped. His dark eyes were wild, desperate. "Don't listen to him."

"Let's get out of here," Rafe muttered gruffly, lifting his sword toward Orlando. "Turn around and walk with your hands behind your head."

"But wait, coz," Orlando said, "I think there's something you should know about your little friend di Tadzio. You see, there's a compartment in Chloe's bedroom with a peephole in the wall—"

"You're a liar!" Adriano shouted savagely. "Don't listen to him! Don't listen to his filthy lies!"

"—and from there, your pretty boy watches you screwing Chloe. She lets him watch. Every actress loves an audience, you know—"

Rafe was frozen in midmotion, completely taken aback.

"No, I didn't! I would never do that!" Adriano all but screamed.

For an excruciating moment, Rafe could not bring himself to look at his friend. He stared at nothing, then abruptly shook off Orlando's accusation.

It was of no consequence whatsoever at the moment.

"Shut up, Orlando," he said. "You're a snake, all right, but you're not slippery enough to get out of this. Ignore him, di Tadzio."

"Let me pull the trigger on this son of a bitch, Rafe. He deserves it. You know he does," Adriano said through gritted teeth.

"Calm down," Rafe ordered him curtly as Orlando laughed.

Refusing to meet Rafe's gaze, Adriano stared at Orlando with murder in his eyes. "It's a lie."

"I know that," Rafe said, striving for his most matter-of-fact tone. "Now let's get the hell out of—"

"My dear Adriano, how can you turn on me like this after all we've shared?" Orlando interrupted in a silky tone.

"I hate you," Adriano was whispering. "All I have to do is pull this trigger."

"Too bad he wants me alive, eh?"

Rafe turned on them both. "Orlando, for the last time, shut the hell up! We're getting out of here. Di Tadzio, just ignore him! He's only saying these things to rattle you and to divide the opposition. Don't play into his hands!"

"Oh, you're the only one he wants to play with, Rafie," Orlando murmured with a smile.

"*You son of a bitch!* I'll kill you!" Adriano screamed, shoving the gun harder against his cheek while Orlando laughed like a madman, as though bullets couldn't hurt him.

"Go on, Adriano," the duke coaxed in a caressing voice, "tell Rafe what you want to do to him. He might just let you, you never know."

"*Jesus Christ,*" Rafe muttered.

"I might *look* like you, Rafe, but you're the one he burns for."

"Orlando, leave him alone." Rafe still could not bring himself to look at Adriano, but he held his kinsman's cold stare, eye to eye. "I don't know what you're trying to do to him," he warned softly, "but stop it. Now. This is between you and me—"

"It's between me and the world, Rafael," Orlando snarled. "You're nothing. You're a joke. It's between me and God-Our-Father."

Adriano was nearly in tears, shaking, frantic. "Don't listen to him, Rafe. Please, it isn't true. I swear, I'm not like that. It's a vile, filthy lie—"

"Shut up, di Tadzio!" Rafe burst out, turning to him. "He's lying. I know that. Forget it. I don't care! What do you mean when you say our father?" he demanded of Orlando.

"Rafe?" Adriano asked, looking over at him slowly, brokenly.

Unwilling to be the first to break his stare with Orlando, Rafe looked over uneasily and met Adriano's eyes. He read pure torment there. He dropped his gaze, wanting to die, striving to think of something reassuring to say, for he was half-afraid his friend would turn the gun on himself.

"You know, you really ought to try him, Rafe," Orlando drawled in the moment's silence. Sliding Adriano a glance askance, he added, "I did. And he was divine."

Rafe thought then that Adriano was going to pull the trigger. But he did not. Instead, his whole tense demeanor dropped. His finely chiseled face went blank, and he lowered the gun from Orlando's temple without a word.

"Fine," he said to Orlando. "You win."

He turned and began walking away, leaving Rafe to hold Orlando at sword point.

"Adriano! Where are you going? *Gesu*," he muttered under his breath, simply cringing. "I know, Adriano. I have known for years, but it doesn't matter. I don't give a damn, all right? I don't care!"

Adriano kept walking, his shoulders slumped.

"Di Tadzio!" Rafe kept looking from him to Orlando. "Get back here! Where are you going?"

Orlando was staring at Rafe now, looking fascinated.

"I'm just going to check on Nic and Elan," Adriano said dully without looking back. He disappeared into the leafy shadows.

"All right, I'll be right there," Rafe called sternly. With a prickle of foreboding raising the hairs on his nape, Rafe looked at Orlando. "Come on, you heartless son of a bitch," he muttered. "Turn around and walk with your hands up."

Orlando sneered at him but obeyed. Just as they began trudging in the same direction where Adriano had gone, the single shot sounded in the woods.

No. The air left Rafe's lungs, flooding the sudden vacuum with horror. He couldn't even gasp.

No.

He began to run, shoving Orlando aside, tearing into the darkness, his heart pumping wildly.

"Noooo!"

He found Adriano slumped on his side near the mossy stream. He dropped to his knees, gathered his fallen friend into his arms, and wept, screamed with grief to the dark skies. Eventually Elan brought the horses.

Orlando had escaped.

ᵌᴵ CHAPTER ᴵᵌ
SEVENTEEN

Dani had dozed off waiting up for him, but her maid woke her near three, saying that His Highness had come home. Shaking off sleep and hurrying to him to see how the hunt for his kinsman had gone, she crossed paths in the hall with Elan.

One glance at his stooped shoulders, pale, drawn face, and red-rimmed eyes filled her with certainty that something terrible had happened. To spare Rafe the telling, Elan forced himself to take her aside and recount the awful news.

Dani covered her mouth with her hand in shock to hear that Nic and Adriano both had died. Immediately she went in search of Rafael, a pall hanging over her heart.

She asked the servants where he had gone, fearful of the shattered state in which she'd find him. At last, one of the footman told her he had seen the prince go outside.

Dani rushed down the marble hall and plunged out the back door into the chilly predawn darkness.

He was sitting on the steps that led down from the edge of the veranda to the sunken formal garden. His broad back was to her and he didn't move, as though he hadn't even heard the door bang closed behind her.

She paused as a tremor moved through her, then forced herself forward.

"Rafael?" she asked very softly a few feet behind him.

No response.

Her heart aching for him, she advanced to the top of the steps where he sat with his folded arms resting atop his bent knees, his face buried in the crook of his arm.

Oh, my poor prince, she thought as she sank down beside him.

Lifting her hand uncertainly, she touched his shoulder. When he did not protest, she ran her hand down the broad curve of his back and began stroking him gently, offering silent, probably futile comfort.

After a few moments, he lifted his face from his arm and held his head in his hands. He gave a long, unsteady sigh and stayed like that.

Dani was afraid to breathe. "My darling, I am so very sorry," she whispered.

"I have made a mess of my life," he said in a hollow voice after a long time.

"No, sweetheart."

"I failed. I can't do this. I'm in so far over my head. I just . . . don't know."

She moved closer and draped her arms tenderly around his shoulders. "Don't do this to yourself."

"He killed my friends."

"I know, honey."

He shrugged off her embrace. "He shot Nic point-blank in the chest. And Adriano . . ." He shuddered and rubbed his forehead with his fingertips, his eyes closed. He looked shaken to the core. "He killed him, too. For sheer meanness. He didn't have to do that to him." His voice dropped to a low, savage whisper, his body utterly tensed and still. "I'm going to get him, Dani. So help me, God, I'm going to find him and send him back to hell."

Carefully, tentatively, she laid her hand on his shoulder. He made a strangled sound of anguish and abruptly reached for her, startling her. She caught only a glimpse of his stark, haunted face before he embraced her almost with a violence, crushing her to him. She held him tightly, but there were no words for a moment like this.

She could feel his large, powerful body trembling in the night's chill.

Abruptly, without a word, he moved down and laid his head in her lap, holding hard around her waist.

In pained silence, she wrapped her arms around him, caressed his hair, and bent over him with fierce, protective love. She existed in that moment solely for Rafael. With tears in her eyes, she poured her strength out for him along with all the sweetness that she had to give. She knew he was devastated.

She could feel his effort to keep his grief in check as he clutched her skirts in his big, hardened fists, shuddering. She held him more tightly, gently stroked his hair, and whispered, *"Shhh."*

She did not know how long they stayed like that, until the sorrow that had risen to choke him eased its grip and his body's trembling quieted under her long, soft caresses down his back.

Dawn was still hours away, but they sat listening to the lulling sough of the distant sea.

She kissed his shoulder at length, then rested her cheek on it and closed her eyes.

She recalled the hours of waiting for word of him, dreading that he had come to harm. She leaned over him and kissed his cheek. "Come to bed, husband. You are exhausted."

He gave a huge sigh. "Yes."

Obediently, he dragged himself up from her lap and climbed to his feet, offering her his hand to help her up, in turn. She stayed close to him, slipping her arm around his waist as they made their way through the silken dark toward the door. He hooked his arm around her shoulders, almost leaning on her in his bone-deep fatigue.

They crossed the darkened, empty ballroom under the soaring dome. Wearily, they climbed the marble stairs with matched strides.

"Do you want anything to eat?" she murmured, glancing up at him in concern.

He shook his head.

"A drink of warm milk? Tea?"

"Nothing," he whispered, pressing a kiss to her hair. He led her to the room where Adriano and Tomas had brought her on the night of his birthday ball. Without ceremony, they went in and crossed the little sitting room to the chamber with the mirrored bed.

Both too tired to undress, they crawled into the huge bed and curled up in each other's arms. They lay in silence, facing each other. Rafael loosed his hair from its queue, then laid his head on his pillow again and closed his eyes.

"It's too hot to sleep," he said in a sullen tone after several long minutes.

"Try, my darling. You're tired."

He sighed.

For a long time, Dani stared at him, gently petting his head.

"I keep seeing them," he murmured with his eyes closed.

"Then look at me."

He dragged his eyes open, eyes that were glazed with suffering and exhaustion. He gazed at her. She leaned over to press a kiss to his forehead, then decided he might be more comfortable if she undressed him a bit.

Approaching the task shyly at first, she untied his cravat and slid it from his neck, then unbuttoned his waistcoat. She sat up. He said nothing, staring at her while she pulled his hands into her lap and unbuttoned his cuff links one by one. She blushed, unbuttoning his shirt down his chest, but did not falter, murmuring to him to sit up so she could pull his unfastened waistcoat and shirt off his shoulders.

He gave her no argument as she peeled them off him. She grimaced faintly at the blood on his clothes but thanked God it wasn't his. He was covered in the grimy dust from the road. He smelled of horse and earth and sweat.

He smiled wanly at her as she wrinkled her nose, carrying the sodden clothes away. She returned with the water jar, a basin, and a cloth, and sat down on the edge of the bed.

While he lay back against the headboard, she sponged him down with the cool water and the cloth, slowly wiping the caked dust and sweat from his face and throat and chest. He watched her every move, light from the single candle she had lit playing over his haggard face. Carefully, she washed his sculpted stomach and his lean sides, admiring him with loving wistfulness. His skin gleamed a ruddy, bronze hue in the candlelight. Even at a time like this, his noble beauty had the power to move her.

"Turn over and I'll wash your back," she murmured.

Willingly, he obeyed, lying down on his stomach. He folded his arms across his pillow and rested his cheek on the broad muscles of his arm. His gold-tipped lashes drifted closed while she wrung out the cloth.

She continued bathing him, running the cloth in long gentle strokes along the supple, flowing lines of his strong back. After a while, a look of restfulness stole over his angular features.

Staring at him in a sudden wave of fright to ponder the danger he had been in, she leaned down and kissed his cheek lingeringly. His jaw was golden and sandy, in need of a fresh shave.

He sighed sweetly at her kiss, long and deep. "You're a good wife," he said in a drowsy murmur.

"Oh, Rafael," she breathed, nestling her nose against his cheek, her heart beating faster.

He rolled over onto his back, drawing her down to kiss him. A moment later, he pulled her more snugly atop him, hungry for her comfort, caressing her hair and her back as he parted his lips for her kiss. She ran her hands ceaselessly over his chest and shoulders and arms, thanking God he was safe.

"Daniela," he groaned softly, closing his eyes. "I need you tonight. Heal me."

"Come to me," she whispered, sliding off him.

He wrapped his arms around her and eased her slowly onto her back. She stroked his cheek as she gazed up at him in adoration. He undressed her quickly in the dark with shaking hands, feverish on her skin. She helped him shed the rest of both their clothing. Then he moved atop her, kissing her urgently. She wrapped her arms around his wide shoulders and enfolded his lean hips between her legs in sensual, wifely welcome, giving everything until he found peace and stillness in her love.

He awoke holding Daniela, spoon-fashion. Slim and lithe, she curled snugly in the protective curve of his body as he lay on his side. His first thought on waking was that her hair, tickling under his nose, was the most wonderful cinnamon-chestnut shade.

Then loss filtered back to him through the milky dawn light and he knew it wouldn't leave him anytime soon. He closed his eyes, aching with the gaping void the previous day's bloodshed had left in his life.

Gone. As though they had been no more than a puff of breeze, vanished. It was astounding, the fragility of life . . . so many lives on his shoulders. A tremor of sheer terror moved through him to think of his kingly destiny, and he pulled Daniela closer, vowing that no matter what happened, at least no harm would befall her. He swore it to himself.

Lying with his love, he felt a fraction of serenity and it gave him power—strength enough, at any rate, to face his blistering disillusionment about his father.

There was no longer any doubt in his mind that Orlando was his half-brother. Father had mentioned sowing his wild oats as a young man. Rafe's stomach clenched with anger to wonder if the so-called Rock of Ascencion had cheated on Mother.

The very thought of it made him want to strike his father. For his sanity's sake, he decided to withhold judgment until he learned more. He could scarcely imagine how hurt his mother was going to be to learn that Orlando was the king's bastard son, for she loved her husband with selfless devotion. Maybe Father didn't know Orlando was his offspring, or perhaps fear of hurting Allegra had stopped Lazar from dealing with the matter in his usual head-on style.

The whole matter made Rafe all the more glad he had decided to swear off extramarital affairs.

Gazing at Daniela as he raised himself up on his elbow and gently petted her hair, he realized she was the only one he could really trust, besides Elan. If Orlando had gotten to Adriano, he might have gotten to anyone.

Even the ultra-loyal Prime Minister Sansevero.

Rafe realized he was going to have to find some way of detaining Don Arturo without causing a riot among the nobility. Lord, it seemed as though everything was swiftly coming to a head.

Just then, Daniela stirred, arching her soft backside against his groin as she stretched herself awake. His body responded at once, heatedly.

"Good morning, ginger cat," he murmured with a doting smile, nuzzling her ear.

"Hmmm, purr," she replied.

She lifted her lashes and he stared down into her eyes. The color of them stole his breath.

"Waterfall pools in a tropical Eden," he whispered, caressing her gently but with intense feeling.

She wrinkled her nose. "What?"

"Your eyes. You're so beautiful. I'm so in love with you."

"Silver-tongued charmer," she scoffed as she turned over onto her stomach, trying to stifle her giggle.

"That wasn't wise, if you'd hoped to escape me," he murmured, smiling as he ran his open hand down her back. His fingertips trailed over the pert curve of her backside and down the back of her thigh, lightly, tickling her legs until they parted slightly. "See? A sinner like me can always find an alternate route into heaven."

"Pagan." She giggled again and shivered slightly under his touch, then turned her face to him, her hand tucked under her cheek. "Uh-oh," she whispered, smiling with kittenish flirtation as his hungry sex nudged her bare flesh beneath the white sheet draped over their waists. She laughed drowsily as he kissed her cheek, then her shoulder. His joy bittersweet, he moved lower, leaving a soft trail of kisses down her spine and sprinkling light, nibbling kisses along the curve of her backside.

"You're a wicked rake," she chided in breathless, dreamy delight, arching her back deliciously under his lips.

"You could reform me," he suggested as he moved atop her, covering her smoothly with his body.

"I wouldn't dream of it," she purred.

He released a soft, husky laugh into the chestnut silk of her hair and applied himself to fulfilling his husbandly duties, healed somehow by her blissful surrender, and grateful from the far reaches of his spirit for the love she had brought into his life, just when he needed it most.

The state funeral for the three Royal Guardsmen was held the next day, but the greater trial of Nic's and Adriano's funeral came on the day following that: a hot, muggy afternoon with a white glare from the overcast skies. As the funeral procession made its way through the crowded but strangely still streets of Belfort, Dani saw people glancing upward frequently at the clouds, but there was still no rain.

They arrived at the cathedral where they had celebrated the royal wedding. It was filled this day with the shaken aristocracy in mourner's black.

At the front of the church, Dani stood close to Rafael, her hand linked through his.

Ascencion saw its crown prince transformed that day, she thought as the trying rite dragged on. His angular face was austere and drawn, slightly pale, as though he had been chiseled from marble. His bearing was quiet, stern, and controlled, full of dignity in grief. His chin was high, his black suit cut in smooth, clean lines.

The thousands who looked on did not know the half of what it took for him to stand here with such solid composure, she thought. Truly, she was in awe of him, knowing the full extent of his worries and seeing him so self-possessed, but she supposed all his training had been for moments of crisis like this.

The manhunt for Orlando was on, though Rafael was still keeping the matter as quiet as possible to avoid embarrassment to the royal family. He wanted Orlando to be taken alive, if possible, so that King Lazar could confront him when he returned. He had ordered the prime minister placed under house arrest until his role in the suspected conspiracy became clear.

The arrest of Don Arturo had complicated matters anew with the powerful Bishop Justinian, for the prime minister and the bishop had been great friends for years. Once more, the bishop had opposed Rafael, this time trying to forbid him from giving Adriano a proper Catholic burial. The death wound, the bishop proclaimed, was clearly self-inflicted.

Rafael swore on the sword of his ancestors that Adriano was no suicide but had been murdered. Dani asked him gently about it and he admitted to her that it was, of course, a bold-faced lie, but the sin was one he was willing to take upon his own soul. Adriano had known no peace in life; Rafael was determined that at least in death his friend's spirit should find rest.

Word of the dispute between the revered bishop and the rake prince spread. In the end, Rafael had thrust Bishop Justinian aside again and imported for the day the same amiable cardinal who had married them. Dani suspected the easygoing Roman was so obliging because he was eager to have a future king in his debt. Dani knew Rafael's unwillingness to budge before the bishop's wrath surely worried many of his ardently Catholic subjects, but whatever the cost, the prince saw his friend buried in hallowed ground.

She felt sad for Adriano and for Nic, though she had found both of them a bit difficult to get along with. Standing by the gaping grave with Rafael as the final prayers were said, her real sorrow was for her husband and Elan.

Holding Rafael's arm as the huge throng of mourners began filing out of the crowded but quiet cemetery, Dani tensed as Chloe Sinclair came walking toward them, her lovely face mottled red with pain and tears behind her black net veil.

Chloe said not a word but walked right up to Rafael and

flew at him with her fists. "How could you let this happen to him? He loved you even more than I did, you bastard, and you let him die! It's your fault!" she shrieked.

The Royal Guardsmen quickly closed in on her before she could prolong the hysterical scene she was making.

When Rafael and Dani were sitting across from each other in the state coach a few moments later, she reached over and touched his knee softly. He looked over, haggard and weary.

"Don't listen to her, love. It was not your fault," she said softly.

He nodded, but he didn't looked convinced. He wrapped his hand around hers and sat staring out the window, brooding and remote.

Shadows hugged his body as Orlando slid through the inky night, seizing his opportunity while the Royal Guardsmen around the prime minister's palazzo rushed to investigate the simple distraction he'd created. He used the fleeting interlude to vault the wrought-iron fence along the sides of the property, its spikes gleaming in the moonlight, then he climbed, quick as a spider, up the rose trellis to the second floor, where he dove in through an open window.

He cursed as he landed with a thud on his shoulder where Rafe had stabbed him, but he was in. Climbing stealthily to his feet, Orlando stole through the darkened house, past the study where the haunting portrait of Don Arturo's dead nephew hung like a shrine over the mantel. He glided silently up the curving white staircase until at last he stood looming over Don Arturo, who was snoring softly in his bed, his nightcap skewed.

Orlando sneered faintly in the dark, resenting the fact that he still needed the physically weak but politically powerful little man to achieve his ends.

Now that he had been charged with the murders of Nic,

Adriano, and the three Royal Guards, he knew his "mentor," the preening fool, was probably having doubts about his protégé. Orlando was yet in the subtle process of laying his final, greatest trap for his golden brother, but when the jaws of fate had snapped on Rafe, then, more than ever, he would need Don Arturo to bulwark his credibility. At great risk to himself, he had come to ensure that the prime minister was still his ally and the prince's enemy.

He had to play his hand with exceeding care, he knew, for only Don Arturo had the power to sway the succession of the throne in his favor when the direct male line had perished. Otherwise, the crown might go to one of the king's Spanish grandchildren.

With that thought, he donned a mask of loyal anxiety. "Don Arturo! My lord! Wake up!" he whispered.

When he touched the man's shoulder, he startled awake. "Who's there?"

"Shhh! It is I. We must talk. I don't have long."

The dignified old man rubbed his eyes. "Orlando! How on earth did you get in here? Oh, never mind—give me a moment. Got to take a piss," he grumbled.

Orlando paced, rubbing his hurt shoulder a bit as Don Arturo stomped out of bed, went behind the Oriental screen in one corner of the room, and relieved himself in the chamber pot. When the diminutive man stomped back out again, he was wearing a banyan robe over his long nightshirt, but he had removed his dangling nightcap.

"I'm sorry to interrupt your sleep, my lord."

"It's all right, lad," he muttered. "I've bloody little else to do, locked up in here."

"It is shameful what my cousin has done to you—as though you had done something wrong! How are you faring?"

"I'm fine. You're the one I'm worried about. I know they

are hunting you. I imagine you've been on the run. Have you eaten? Something to drink?"

"No, sir."

"Do you need money?"

Orlando looked at him sharply, taken aback by his solicitude. Then he looked away. "No, sir. You are . . . kind. I only came here to explain and to tell you I will get you out of this shameful confinement when the time is ripe."

Don Arturo pursed his shrewd mouth and rested his hands on his waist. "Orlando, you are wanted for murder. First that chef dies and now they say you murdered two of the prince's friends and three Royal Guardsmen—"

"The only one I killed was Nic, and it was in self-defense!" he interrupted impatiently. "Di Tadzio blew his own head off and the guards met their fates in a medieval spike pit which they could have easily avoided if they had been watching where they were going. Instead, they were out for my blood and they got careless. It wasn't my fault."

"Their deaths were an accident?"

"Yes," he said firmly. "Sir, Rafe is setting me up, don't you see? He's trying to make me out as the villain and appear innocent himself! I think he is even going to try to pin the king's poisoning on me!"

"Calm down, boy—"

"You know he is not to be trusted! Everything has turned in his favor. You and I are the only ones left who can stop him! If he turns you against me, too, I tell you, sir," he said with a show of anguish that would have fooled even Chloe, "I am a dead man!"

"There, now, settle yourself, lad. No one's turning me against you."

Orlando suddenly stepped toward him and clasped the older man hard in a filial embrace for a moment, then released him, hung his head, and pinched the bridge of his nose. "Forgive me, sir. I beg your pardon for this display," he murmured. "I'm injured, I'm alone, they are hunting me like hounds on a fox, and I . . . I must go to ground for a while to survive." He took a deep breath and met the don's startled gaze. "But I have devised a plan to rescue you from this shameful confinement when the moment is right."

"You have? How?"

"I have sent for men who work for me at my warehouses in Pisa. Rather rough types, I admit. At the appropriate time, I will order a sneak attack on the Royal Guards ringing your house. My men should be able to put them down without much noise, then they'll don the Royal Guards' uniforms. That way, when my men conduct you out of here it will appear that all is normal."

" 'Put them down?' " Don Arturo shuddered. "You don't mean murder them, I hope."

"It can be done without killing, I suppose."

"Your men will face steep charges if your plan fails. It is a crime to impersonate the Royal Guardsmen. Yet . . ." he paused. "If you bring me together with the rest of the cabinet, we can surely take power back from Rafael until the king returns from Spain."

"Precisely," Orlando said, though of course, by his design, King Lazar would never return alive.

"All right." The man clapped his arm soundly. "Good work, Orlando."

He nodded curtly. "I must go." As he stalked across the room, mentally rehearsing his escape, Don Arturo spoke abruptly behind him.

"You . . . remind me of my nephew if he'd lived to be your age."

Orlando paused and looked over his shoulder. The don's lined face was wistful, his expression faraway.

It was the closest thing to an open declaration of affection that anyone had ever given Orlando. He stared blankly at the old man with an odd, twisting pain coming up in him from his belly. Stiffening, he tamped it down under the shield of ice he had formed in himself at an early age. Without answering, he turned away and left.

For the next two weeks, they followed the plan Dani had suggested. Rafe knew that her purpose in undertaking a tour of Ascencion was to win Their Majesties' blessing in spite of her notorious background as the Masked Rider, but for him, staying constantly on the move was a deliberate tactic for ensuring her security.

He knew he was the ultimate target of Orlando's malice, but he would not put it past his half-brother to attack Dani as well, especially now that Rafe knew she had rejected Orlando's advances. He kept her constantly in his presence, both of them ringed at all times by a contingent of twenty of the fiercest Royal Guards. With but a few servants and their small but heavily armed escort, they traveled light, meeting the common people and surveying the current state of affairs in all the diverse regions of Ascencion, from the wooded mountainous interior, to the fertile farm plateaus, to the quaint fishing villages that dotted the coast.

When they met with the crowds of loyal subjects who came to greet them and to hear his brief, cheerful speeches, the uniformed guards maintained a secure barrier around them.

Wherever they went, the guards' hard-eyed gazes scanned the mobs constantly for Orlando. Rafe knew they thirsted to avenge their fallen mates who had died so hideously.

He, too, thirsted for vengeance for Nic and Adriano, and for his father's suffering.

Anger waited in him like a crouched lion.

Thoughts of Orlando gnawed constantly at him. The

manhunt continued, but the so-called duke eluded all attempts to capture him.

Sometimes Rafe trembled with an odd, sudden chill in the crushing heat, fearing that somehow Orlando might slip past all his protective measures and snuff out Dani's life as casually as he had Adriano's and Nic's. That terror shadowed him, but he hid it from her, ashamed to face the knowledge that by forcing her—blackmailing her—into marrying him, he had tumbled her headlong into danger.

As the weeks passed, the siroccos rolled over the island, a tyranny of humid, suffocating heat. The distended underbellies of the heavy clouds swelled with the pent-up moisture of the winds' journey over the Mediterranean, but still the skies refused to relent and give forth rain.

The heat and the mounting barometric pressure affected man and beast. Tempers ran short among the disciplined Royal Guards. Their fretful horses balked and nipped spitefully at each other, beset with fat stinging flies, the only creatures that could thrive in the oppressive heat. As the royal party traveled from town to town, the land under the horses' hooves languished in dust.

Rafe knew he was drifting deeper into himself: Fear for Dani's safety was not the only cause of his increasing uneasiness. Rationally, he knew that Dani was loyal to him. He knew that she was in love with him, and yet the small, niggling weed of mistrust that Julia had sown in his breast so many years ago clung stubbornly, refusing to be uprooted. He did not realize how deeply his heart had been scarred.

The more he loved Dani, the greater grew his sense of risk. Was it wise to let himself care so very deeply for a woman? How could he trust his own judgment?

But these fears he kept to himself, ashamed and confused by them, when her every glance was filled with devotion. He knew it was ridiculous to fear betrayal from so steady an ally.

He was determined to overcome this weakness. Besides, her clear, guileless smile had the power to chase his fears off utterly—and yet, they always had a way of creeping back, where they would lurk just under the surface of the happiness he shared with her.

Fear, however, was nowhere near his mind that evening at dusk as the cicadas screamed gleefully in the heat and fireflies drifted. Thunder rumbled miles away over the eastern horizon and a feeble breeze limply stirred the leaves of the oak under which he sat.

There was a smell of an impending summer storm in the air. He thought he'd felt a raindrop twenty minutes ago—but nothing.

It had been another long day of traveling, touring another little town in the drought-stricken midlands, addressing the common folk, and being feted at lunchtime by the local gentry and the town mayor. The royal party had taken over a comfortable travelers' inn for their short stay. The guardsmen discreetly ringed the property.

Rafe sat under a large tree in the field behind the inn, dozing after he'd finished reading Elan's update from the Palazzo Reale. Elan suggested cutting back water rations again.

Please, God, You've got to give my people rain, he thought as he dragged his burning eyes open and watched Dani exercise the white mare he had given her as a wedding present.

As she cantered the dainty Arabian in a figure eight, he mused with a private smile that riding was her second favorite way of releasing tension.

She glanced at him as she swept by on her horse. He smiled faintly as she passed, the mare's creamy tail floating out behind them.

Then he furrowed his brow as he saw Dani begin to change positions on the horse's back. He held his breath as she stood in the saddle, her arms outstretched, the mare's smooth canter never faltering. Rafe stared, unsure if he was delighted by his wife's audacity or terrified that she would fall and break her neck.

Horse and rider zoomed past him, and the irrepressible redhead tossed him a cocksure grin.

Love surged in a tangled wave right up to his throat, made a lump there as desperate, almost frantic emotion quickened his heartbeat. She was absurd and unconquerably free and so beautiful, graceful as a swan.

One more sweeping circle around the field, and to his relief, she lowered herself carefully to sit sidesaddle again and brought her horse to a walk, halting before him under the tree.

She reached forward and patted her mare's neck with one gloved hand, then smiled at Rafe. Her cheeks were flushed, her aquamarine eyes shining.

He thrust the report he'd been reading aside and sprang to his feet, walking over to her. He plucked her down from the saddle and carried her under the tree.

The mare walked away and began grazing on the tall grasses in the field.

"A most impressive display," he said as she laughed and whipped off her hat, tossing it with a carefree air.

"Wasn't it, though?" Her booted feet paddled cheerfully in midair as he carried her toward the tree. "What do you think of your wife now?"

"I think I should show her my talent, so as not to be upstaged," he murmured, stunned anew by his insatiable passion for her.

"I already know what your talent is, Rafael," she whispered with a fetching smile.

"Perhaps you've forgotten."

"Since this morning? I have a good memory."

"Let me give you more . . . good memories." He laid her

down in the tall grasses and smothered her under his body, loosing her chestnut tresses from her neat chignon as he plied her mouth with kiss after kiss.

Her gloved fingers raked down his back as he worked her high-necked riding habit free. "Mmm, someone's been eating peppermints. My favorite." She licked his lips.

"Perhaps we can combine our talents. Ride me," he whispered, giving her a quick, mischievous flare of one brow. He sat up and leaned back against the tree, pulling her to him. He was panting and hot for her, ready to go.

With vivid blue heat in her eyes, she straddled him. Under her maroon-colored skirts, he freed himself, parted her demure pantalettes, and slipped urgently into her tight passage, for she was already moist with excitement.

Closing her eyes, she made a sound of rapture and rode him gracefully. He held her by her waist and moved with her, his heart pounding. Lifting his hips rhythmically, he rocked her on his lap. She was liquid poetry, sweet, ambrosial fire enveloping him: a goddess of lush, exuberant sexuality.

She dragged her eyes open and reached up to pull at the ends of his cravat, leaving it hanging untied off his shoulders. Then she plucked the buttons of his waistcoat and shirt free, baring his chest.

Her gloved hands caressed him, then she gripped the open ends of his clothes in both of her dainty fists, clenched her jaw, and sank deeper on his shaft, taking him to the hilt. They both gasped with pleasure, savoring their joining in heated stillness.

She slipped her hands inside his open shirt and stroked his sides. "I love you so much, Rafael. You have me completely, everything I am inside, everything I have."

He curled his hand around her nape and drew her mouth to his. He squeezed his eyes shut tightly, willing himself to master his fears at last. He ended the kiss but did not release her, pulling the words from the most profound depths of himself. "I love you."

She moaned softly, holding him tighter.

"I love you," he whispered again and again.

"Rafael."

Suddenly the leaves above them rattled in a gust of breeze and a spattering of fat raindrops plunked onto the grasses around them.

Dani's eyes widened as she stared at him.

He looked up at the sky and laughed, thanking God, tears rising in his eyes. She pulled him into a joyful embrace. He inhaled the smell of the rain in sheer swelling gladness. He tasted it on her skin.

He wrapped his arms around her waist and laid her back in the soft grasses of the field, and he made love to her as the warm, heavy rain soaked them both, pouring in glorious rivulets from his shoulders and hair and coursing down her porcelain face. For miles around them, life-giving water penetrated deep into the dusty fields, and the parched land thirstily drank, and as the thunder rumbled distantly, he brought on the flood of her love and emptied himself like the swollen skies into the secret reservoir of creation, planting new life in her womb.

⇥ CHAPTER ⇤
EIGHTEEN

Holding her breath, her eyes wide, Dani stared at the old royal physician as he discreetly palpated her taut, almost imperceptibly changed abdomen. A moment later, he removed his hand, pulling the sheet back up over her.

"Yes, it is as you suspected, Your Highness," he said in a kindly tone, turning to her. "God has blessed Ascencion and your marriage. You are with child."

She remembered abruptly to exhale, but her heart was pounding and her face was rather drained of color. "What do I do now?"

He chuckled at her scared look. "First, stop imagining terrible things. Several ladies who have been my patients for many years have confided in me that the pains of labor are forgotten, you know, the moment a woman holds her newborn babe in her arms."

She smiled in spite of herself. "Fine words, from a man."

"All will be well. It will be months before you must restrain your usual activities. Just use your head, eat well, and get all the rest you need, but don't be frightened, my child. Do you really think that doting husband of yours would let anything happen to you?"

The old doctor knew how to deal with a difficult patient, she thought, as a broad smile broke out over her face. He gave her a grandfatherly wink and left her in the care of her maids.

Slowly, she crossed her arms over her abdomen, hugging herself thoughtfully, still amazed. She could not believe the reckless, tomboyish girl she had always been was going to become a mother.

Her thoughts drifted back to the day a few weeks ago when it had finally rained, ending the drought and bringing hope back to Ascencion. Though Rafael and she had behaved more like scandalous lovers than the stately royal figureheads they were supposed to be, somehow she knew that in spite of their many couplings, she had conceived on that miraculous day. They had ended their tour and come home to the palace when her morning nausea began. She had only told her husband she was sick of traveling and needed a rest for a while.

Her first thought as she dressed was to pull him out of his meeting and tell him her tidings at once. She knew he was going to be elated, but she decided to wait until the meeting was over and then tell him, for she needed a little time to come to terms with her own mixed emotions at the news. She was happy that their love had borne fruit, but she was still afraid of her ordeal eight months in the future, and shaken to think that with the arrival of her child, her life would be changed irrevocably.

She took a stroll in the royal gardens to collect her thoughts before speaking with him. She was inspecting some roses in a corner of the statuary garden when a footman came walking out briskly to her and offered her a folded letter on a silver tray.

"Your Highness," the man said with a bow.

Curiously, she took the letter, dismissing the servant with a nod. Was it another plea for the Masked Rider's help? she wondered. Now she had too important a reason to decline any further adventures. The doctor's attitude had been very casual about what she must and mustn't do, but she wasn't taking any chances with her own health or her unborn child's. Sometimes it shocked her to think back on how reckless she had been, robbing coaches in the dead of night. She had so much to live for now.

Unfolding the short note, she drew in her breath as she read it.

"Oh, you fool," she breathed, scanning the two short lines.

Heedless of the fact that he could be hanged for showing his face on Ascencion, Mateo was waiting at the Chiaramonte villa and asked to talk to her immediately.

Finishing up his morning meetings ahead of schedule, free for the next three hours, Rafe strode off to find Dani, whistling one of his old favorite songs, *"La ci darem la mano."* He looked in the usual places where he might find her, but seeing her nowhere, it dawned on him to ask her maid where she could be found.

"Why, my lady went out, Your Highness."

"Out?" he said, frowning.

"Yes, sir. She left twenty minutes ago."

"Where did she go? Did she take her guards?"

"Yes, sir. They accompanied Her Highness. She mentioned that she had to leave at once to see her grandfather."

"Oh, no," Rafe said, furrowing his brow in concern. "I hope the old colonel's all right."

"My lady did not stop to say, Your Highness, but if I may add, she did seem distressed."

"Perhaps I can catch up to her," he murmured, pivoting on his heel and launching into a brisk march toward the royal stables. Her grandfather was a frail old man who could easily have wandered into some kind of dangerous mishap. If something had befallen him, Rafe wanted to be there to help Dani.

Soon he was astride his white stallion, galloping down the King's Road with his usual half-dozen bodyguards, since Orlando had not yet been caught.

The ride to the Chiaramonte villa was not long, and he knew the way by heart. The villa was tucked under scaffolding from the restoration Rafe had set in progress. Crews of stonemasons and roofers were noisily at work. Their wagons, loaded with supplies, were parked alongside the overgrown drive. He noted with relief that Dani's bodyguards were posted outside the house.

"What's happened?" he asked the chief of her men as he drew his powerful white stallion to a halt.

"Her Highness wished to visit His Grace, sire," the man replied, squinting against the sun as he met Rafe with a salute.

"Is His Grace well?"

"Yes, Your Highness, to the best of my knowledge."

Rafe swung down from the saddle and strode to the front door. He let himself inside and looked around the foyer, seeing no one. Remembering the threadbare salon where he had sat with the old man that first night, he strode down the hall toward it.

"Dani!" he began calling, but upon opening the salon door, he discovered his wife in the arms of another man.

Thunderstruck, Rafe stood in the doorway and stared.

All three of them were motionless with shock, like carved figures in a frieze. The mantel clock's tick sounded like a gong in the silence. Then, all the air left Rafe's lungs in a *whoosh*.

Dani pulled away from Mateo and stepped toward Rafe. "My love—"

He threw up his hand to ward her off, as one tight, helpless syllable wrenched from his lips, "No."

Her face drained—suddenly it was the face of a stranger to him.

"Rafael—"

The first word that turned over in his mind was *betrayal*.

The first thought that materialized was that she had been planning this all along.

And he went cold inside.

He stepped back out into the hall, pulling the door shut. Stiffly, he pivoted and marched away as she came out after him. Holding himself tall and erect, while inwardly reeling, he made himself deaf to her pleas and stalked toward the Royal Guardsmen.

He did not look back.

"Don't walk away. Don't do this to me, Rafael. I can explain—"

"There is a fugitive in the house," he said calmly to the men. "Arrest him."

"Rafael!" she cried, taking his arm. "It's not what you think. I love you! Look at me!"

He shook her off harshly, rage locked in his throat, and walked away. He wanted to ask her why but could not. His hands were shaking, his movements jerky as he gathered the reins and swung back up onto his white horse.

He could barely see, let alone think, for the wrath that swam before his eyes.

"Rafael!" she screamed after him as he urged his horse into motion, riding away down the overgrown drive.

His heart still pounded in his throat.

As he turned onto the road, he saw three riders galloping toward him. He only forced himself to stop because they were waving their arms at him. When they pulled up before him, he saw they were royal couriers.

"Your Highness! Viscount Berelli sent us to find you, Your Highness!"

"What news?" he ground out. Apparently Elan was the only loyal soul left in the world.

"He implores you to go at once to the palazzo of the

bishop! Prince Leo has come back from Spain. The bishop has fetched the boy, exercising his claim as the prince's legal guardian. His Excellency says—forgive me, Your Highness—he says he does not trust you and cannot leave the boy in your care."

"How on earth did my brother come back to Ascencion by himself?" he demanded angrily, nudging his horse past theirs, already in motion. "He's ten years old, for God's sake! My parents wouldn't send him on alone."

The couriers urged their horses alongside his, flanking him. "It seems Prince Leo was squabbling quite a bit with the other children in Spain and decided he'd had enough. He stowed away on the ship returning. Had himself a grand adventure, the captain said."

"The rascal, I'll bet he did," Rafe muttered. "I'll go at once."

"Yes, Sire. The bishop refused to him to the viscount or anyone else."

"That old man is a thorn in my side," he muttered.

With Orlando still at large, he knew the bishop was not equipped to protect Leo.

With his contingent of bodyguards only now catching up, Rafe galloped back in the direction of Belfort, trying to focus his mind on getting his little brother to safety, but his heart still reeled from the blow of Dani's betrayal.

He shoved the awful image of her in the other man's arms out of his mind and urged his horse faster.

They were delayed by crowds in the street because it was market day, and all the world had something to sell for the suckers who were willing to buy, Rafe thought bitterly. The bishop's palazzo was situated not far from the cathedral. The Royal Guards yelled at the people to clear a path for him as they forged through the mobbed, hot streets under the beating sun.

Rafe had a sick feeling in the pit of his stomach every

time he thought of Dani. Over and over again, he kept feeling his astonishment anew like a mighty blow to the face.

He had banished Mateo Gabbiano. No matter what excuses she had to offer, there was no getting around that fact, just as there was no getting around the fact that the two had been clutched in a tight embrace when he had walked unexpectedly into the room. What more would have happened if he hadn't walked in?

For the fiftieth time, he thrust the thoughts from him and reeled his horse to a halt in front of the bishop's huge ornate home with its carefully tended grounds.

He and his men dismounted. Rafe strode ahead of the pack up the front steps. He pounded squarely on the door, then froze as it creaked open under his heavy knock.

He shot his men a warning look over his shoulder. Splaying his hand on the door, he reached for his sword, unsheathed it, and pushed the door open.

No servants came to greet them. He heard no mischievous boy's laughter.

He crept cautiously into the shining marble foyer. He looked to the right and left, cast a glance up the polished curving staircase, seeing no one. He walked in.

"Your Excellency?" he called. He nodded to his men and they rushed in, fanning out to search the rooms. "Leo? It's Rafe! Are you here?"

"Your Highness!" one of the men suddenly called from a distant room. "Here!"

Rafe followed the shout. He wove his way through the lavish rooms.

"Here, sir!" another of his men said, indicating a chamber to the left of the main hall.

Striding into the dining room, Rafe saw his men gathered in the middle of the room.

"Sir! It's His Excellency!"

Rafe cursed, chills of dread plunging down his spine.

Shoving into their midst, he bent down beside the bishop on the floor in a pool of blood. "Don't just stand around, find Leo!" he yelled. "You!" he ordered one. "Ride to the Palazzo Reale for reinforcements. Now!"

"Yes, sir!"

Rafe turned the old man over and grimaced at the stab wound in the middle of Bishop Justinian's barrel chest. It had seeped through his robes and Rafe got a smear of blood on his hand as he felt the man's throat for a pulse. Finding none, he laid the bishop's balding head gently on the floor. A cursory glance revealed cuts on his hands and forearms consistent with a futile self-defense.

Orlando had done this. Rafe felt it in his bones. The duke had broken in, attacked the bishop, then kidnapped Leo.

Staring down at the murdered bishop, Rafe rose in wrath just as a deep voice with an unfamiliar accent reached him.

"Your Highness, don't move."

He looked up in regal affront to see who dared address him so impudently.

There was an unfamiliar contingent of uniformed Royal Guardsmen moving cautiously into the room and slowly surrounding him, all of them with weapons drawn.

"Your Highness, lower your weapon."

"What are you talking about? What is the meaning of this?" he demanded. "Get back to your posts." He looked at them, not recognizing any of their faces.

One who appeared their leader took a couple of steps closer, holding him at gunpoint.

"What in hell, sir, do you think you're doing?" Rafe asked crisply, not lowering his sword.

"Exactly what I told him to do," drawled a familiar voice. Orlando sauntered into the doorway. "Appearances can be deceiving, can they not?"

Rafe lunged toward him. *"What have you done with my brother?"*

"Halt!" the man roared at him as the others ringed him in.

Orlando folded his arms over his chest and smirked at Rafe.

Rafe cursed and tried to get at him, but the thugs wearing the uniforms of the Royal Guard blocked his path. He swung his sword, bellowing for his bodyguards, who came running to join the exploding fray, but they were badly outnumbered. A few were cut down. Fight as he may, they fell on Rafe like dogs on a wounded bull, and when they had disarmed him and thrust him down on one knee, they wrenched his arms behind his back and clapped him in irons.

Orlando loomed over him, reciting calmly, "In the name of the king and by the authority of office of the prime minister—Prince Rafael di Fiore, you are hereby placed under arrest for the murder of the Bishop Justinian Vasari and for crimes of high treason."

"Where is my brother?"

But Orlando merely smiled, his ice-green eyes glowing with malice. When he jerked a curt nod at his men, they dragged Rafe past him out the door. They shoved him into a waiting coach and brought him before the council of his enemies.

Dani was powerless to stop them as the Royal Guardsmen seized Mateo, following Rafael's orders.

Before they took him into custody, Mateo handed off to Dani the evidence damning Orlando, which he had risked hanging to bring to her.

She had to catch up with Rafael and explain.

As her carriage rolled swiftly toward the city, she hardly dared think what conclusions he had drawn upon walking in and seeing her embracing Mateo. He had not stayed to hear her out, so how could he know that the reason Mateo had been hugging her was because she had just told him she would soon be a mother to her beloved prince's child? Mateo had been merely congratulating her with a brotherly embrace.

Judging by Rafael's coldly furious reaction, she realized that the sight had triggered all his underlying fears of being betrayed in love. She was crushed to know she had inadvertently hurt him and felt bruised herself by the frigid way he had shut her out.

His defensiveness was enough nearly to make her despair. Would he never trust her? Didn't he know she was hopelessly in love with him? When would he ever believe?

Now that almost half an hour had passed, maybe his anger had begun to clear to a more reasonable state, she hoped anxiously. If nothing else, her happy news would surely cause him to soften toward her.

At length, she arrived at the Palazzo Reale. Just as she was walking in, drawing off her gloves, Elan came running toward the front entrance.

"Principessa!"

"Where are you going in such a hurry?"

Elan seized her elbow. His face was ghastly pale.

"What's wrong?"

"Stay with your guards, Your Highness. Orlando has made his move."

"Where is my husband?"

"Don Arturo has played right into Orlando's hands. They have—oh, God, they have arrested Rafe for the murder of Bishop Justinian and Prince Leo is missing—oh, there's no time to explain! I have to go."

"What? The bishop is dead? Rafael's . . . arrested?" She stared at him in horror. "How is that possible? He's the crown prince!"

"It's all Orlando's scheming and the prime minister's old grudge!"

"I'm coming with you! Let's go!"

"No, Your Highness, you must stay here where you'll be safe!"

"Rafael needs me. Besides, I've got these!" she said, holding up the pair of folded documents.

"What are they?"

"I'll explain in the coach—"

"Tell me now or Rafe will throttle me for bringing you into this!"

"Orlando is not the heir to the di Cambio branch of the royal family, Elan," she said rapidly, lowering her voice. "He merely assumed that identity in order to explain his resemblance to the king! His real father is King Lazar! He is the product of a brief—very brief—liaison between the king and a Florentine baroness."

"Oh, my Lord," he said, eyes wide.

"This baroness—Baroness Raimondi—tried to pass Orlando off as her husband's child, but the baron never quite believed it. Orlando looked nothing like him. This is the sworn statement of Baroness Raimondi's faithful old maidservant, called Nunzia, who was also Orlando's nurse."

"But—a servant's testament, Your Highness? What weight will it carry?"

"Along with this, enough to prove that Orlando is a liar." She held up the second document. "Orlando's birth certificate, registered under the name Raimondi. If we give Don Arturo reason to at least doubt Orlando and question him, we may be able to find a chink in that demon's armor."

"All right, but I still say Rafe's going to throttle me," he muttered, wasting no more time trying to dissuade her.

Dani paused only to whisper an order in her stout, matronly maid's ear.

"Right away, Your Highness!" the woman called after her, but Dani was already marching out with Elan.

As their carriage raced through the streets to the Rotunda, the main parliamentary building, Elan told Dani of Prince Leo's arrival and almost as sudden disappearance from the bishop's custody. She mused with creeping dread on the realization that Orlando had all of the ruthless intelligence, strength, and magnetism of the Fiore men, but none of their goodness.

Drawing up to the Rotunda, their coachman had to fight his way through the huge crowd that had gathered outside as word of the shocking scandal of the bishop's murder and the prince's arrest spread. Everyone knew of the antagonism that had existed between the two.

Springing down from the coach, brushing off servants and guards, Dani and Elan ran up the front steps. The inside of the Rotunda was almost as thronged as the piazza just outside, but as royal princess, Dani was allowed through the male crowd, and Elan followed her closely.

Angry voices rang out from the floor of the Roman-style senate.

"This is a travesty! How dare you place the crown prince in chains?" demanded the navy admiral, who had always liked Rafe.

"He was caught red-handed at the scene of the murder!"

When she came to the top of the stairs that led down into the argument area called the well, Dani froze in horror at what she saw.

Below her, the floor of the senate had erupted into a violent spectacle.

Don Arturo presided, standing at the rostrum, denouncing Rafael in a state of flushed excitement. Other cabinet ministers lined the side tables, all shouting, arguing, and waving their hands. Some had risen out of theirs seats. Orlando was there, in black as usual, swaggering arrogantly back and forth across the senate floor with a slow, pacing stride, his arms crossed over his chest, glancing frequently at his younger half-brother with a mocking smile.

Rafael, crown prince, future king of Ascencion, had been forced to stand like a common criminal at the spindled, crescent-shaped wooden podium adjacent to the rostrum.

Dani could not believe her eyes. Her love, her prince—in chains, as though this were France twenty years ago, choked with its red rage, and not placid, prosperous Ascencion. His always-impeccable clothes were torn, his mouth was grim, there was murder in his eyes, and his dark gold hair hung loose and wild. He looked barbaric, like a captured Samson.

Dani charged forward, not even knowing what she was going to do.

"The whole cabinet was present the night King Lazar warned that if you did not marry one of the five selected brides, you would be passed over for the throne, and that your brother, Prince Leo, would be named your father's successor in your place!" Don Arturo thundered at him as Dani ran down the stepped aisle. "Now that you have cast aside your father's will in the matter of your marriage, isn't it true, Your Highness, that you sought to make it impossible for the king to disinherit you by doing away with your own brother? Where have you stowed the child's body?" the man bellowed.

In answer, Rafael stared at him in utter contempt but said nothing, too proud, too soaringly arrogant, Dani realized, to speak a word in his own defense. His silence expressed more than any words his contemptuous reproach for the proceedings.

As she came closer, she thought that he would betray at least a glimmer of relief to see her, even though they had just clashed over Mateo. But instead, he stared at her, going pale, at the same moment that Orlando turned in his pacing and stopped, leering at her with a slow, evil smile that grew.

Elan tried to stop her as she shoved past the black-clad Orlando and marched straight to the rostrum with a holy rage making her tremble. Too furious to speak a word, she lifted the folded birth certificate and the nurse's testimony up to Don Arturo.

The prime minister gripped the sides of the wooden platform and peered down his nose at her like a thundering judge. "Women are not permitted in this building, Your Highness." He looked up at the senate. "Perhaps now an age of filthy decadence and vice is over, and we may return to the customs that made this country great!"

"Take these papers and read them, if you are wise," she ordered him through gritted teeth.

Something in her scathing, fiery stare made him hesitate. Reluctantly, he reached for the papers and unfolded one, peering down at its contents.

"Daniela."

She looked over at Rafael, who had spoken her name so softly. She heard him in spite of the din. She went swiftly to him while, a few feet away, Elan argued vehemently with the guards to unchain him.

When she gazed up into his dark green eyes, she saw rage and humiliation and doom. "You are not safe," he said. "I want you to walk out of this building and leave Ascencion immediately. Try to reach my father before Orlando does. Warn him."

"No, I'm not leaving you here alone to them. I love you!" Tears sprang into her eyes as she reached up and laid her hand on his cheek. "I did not betray you, Rafael, I never would—"

He pressed his face against her palm, the green-gold depths of his eyes stormy. "Dani, if you have ever loved me, leave. Don Arturo is out for my blood, and Orlando has served me up to him on a silver platter. There is nothing to stop them from coming after you next. Tell Elan to go back to the old di Cambio citadel. I believe Orlando has hidden Leo there. I have a feeling my brother is alive. I think Orlando is waiting to see if he can use Leo somehow as his trump card. Tell Elan, whatever happens, he's got to save the boy."

"I will help Elan find him—"

"No! You are not to set foot on those grounds. The whole fortress is rigged with traps."

"You forget you are talking to the Masked Rider."

"Dani . . . it has happened just as my father always said," he whispered.

"No, don't give up hope now, my darling," she ordered softly. "There is more reason now than ever before to fight for our future."

He looked questioningly at her.

Her gaze swam with tears of love, but she quickly forced a wry tone before she broke down crying. "Now, for God's sake, get off your royal high horse and use that silver tongue of yours to argue in your own defense."

"Dani, do you mean—" he began.

"What are you lovebirds chatting about?" Orlando broke in, swaggering toward them with a mocking look.

They stared at each other, both ignoring him.

Dani's steady gaze bespoke her love to him. She was aware that Orlando was trying to listen in on their conversation. "I did not betray you, and I'm going to prove it to you," she whispered, but her next words were intended for Orlando as well as him. "You see, Rafael, that day on the docks, weeks ago, when I said goodbye to the Gabbiano brothers, I asked Mateo to investigate Orlando's background for me. The reason Mateo came back today was to deliver proof that your *kinsman* is not what he claims."

Orlando's eyes narrowed. "What *proof*?"

Her fight was up as she looked over frankly at him. "You'll find out soon enough, Your Grace. I have just handed it over to Don Arturo."

"Daniela," Rafael said in a tone of utter command, "get out. Now."

At the warning in his deep voice, she looked questioningly at him.

Go Leo, Rafael's intense stare seemed to say. Reading the fierce desperation in his eyes, she had no choice but to obey. Backing away before she lost the strength to leave him there in the clutches of his foes, she grasped Elan's wrist and tugged him along with her. Rafael sent his friend a hard look, jerking a nod toward the exit.

"I'll explain when we're outside," she murmured to the viscount.

Elan did not argue. The two of them ran out, climbing the steps of the aisle, her earlier care for her delicate new condition forgotten. All that mattered was saving Rafael from this mob. She and her unborn baby were in God's hands, she thought as they shoved their way out of the Rotunda and back toward the carriage.

As they made their way toward the waiting vehicle, Dani drew in her breath with a jolt of hope to see that her maid had followed her instructions and had wasted no time bringing her everything she needed.

Behind the coach Elan and she had arrived in, her white mare was saddled and waiting. The maid handed her a small, neatly folded stack of black clothing as Dani scrambled up into the coach alone, quickly pulling the shades while Elan waited.

Scarcely a moment later, she burst out of the coach in black breeches and shirt, riding boots and black leather gauntlets. No mask covered her face, while her hair spilled in a simple ponytail down her back. The crowd saw her thus and roared. Elan was staring at her in astonishment as she leaped onto her horse, her rapier at her side.

"Show me the way to the di Cambio citadel!" she shouted, waving him onto his horse.

"Yes, Your Highness!" he jerked out, commandeering the nearest guardsman's horse.

"Get out of the way!" Dani shouted at the crowd.

People began backing out of their path while a handful of the Royal Guardsmen dutifully took to their horses and followed her, looking equally stunned by her transformation.

At the far end of the square, there was much less congestion in the streets.

"This way!" Elan shouted, pointing.

Dani gave her mare's sides a squeeze and raced at a gallop onto the King's Road.

The senate had broken out into an even greater chaos than before as Don Arturo and the other cabinet members surrounded Orlando in a low-toned but apparently furious conference behind the rostrum. Rafe watched, his heart pounding, as Don Arturo questioned Orlando.

Though he could not hear all their words clearly over the din, he saw the prime minister angrily waving under Orlando's nose the paper that Dani had brought, then Don Arturo handed it to the minister of finance, who was standing beside him.

Rafe prayed the revelation would cause them to doubt Orlando enough to unchain him and bring this farcical but potentially deadly trial to a close.

The minister of finance inspected the paper, then stared at Orlando in amazement and handed it to another of the king's advisers. Don Arturo asked him a question that Rafe could not make out.

"Is it my fault who sired me?" Orlando retorted loudly enough to be heard.

"But why would you conceal your true birth from all of us?"

"Would you wish the world to know it if you had been born an unwanted bastard?" he replied caustically.

"Does the king know you are his son?"

"You'll have to ask His Majesty," he answered with a sneer. "Why are you questioning me? That man right there is the one with the blood on his hands!" he cried, pointing at Rafe. "To hell with the lot of you! I have done nothing but my duty and I'm not going to stand around here and be insulted!" Pivoting grandly on his heel, Orlando began striding toward the exit.

"Stop him!" Rafe yelled, wrenching and clashing against his chains. The few guards standing around rushed him, trying to hold Rafe back. "Stop him, damn you! He's making his escape, you fools! Stop him, if you want to save Leo's life!"

Orlando tossed him a slight, cold smile over his shoulder as he jogged lightly up the steps of the aisle, and Rafe felt a sickening spiral of fear twisting down into his stomach, for he knew with an innate certainty that Dani had not obeyed him. She had not gone to prepare to leave Ascencion. When had he ever known her to flee a fight when her own were in danger? No, she had surely gone with Elan to find Leo. He knew it; he could feel it. And he knew the reason why she would act with such reckless courage—because of her love and her absolute loyalty to him.

He recalled the image in his mind again of finding her in the villa with Mateo, and saw it in an instant in a completely different light. He had read an illicit liaison into it, not a brotherly hug. *Good God, how could I have doubted her?* Guilt blasted him, salt in the wound of his panic. Instead of leaving Ascencion on his orders to protect herself, she had stayed to try to save him, and now death in the form of his black-clad half-brother was gusting after her like a poisonous wind on her tail.

Orlando had too many reasons to destroy Dani. She had rejected his advances; now she had brought proof against him to Don Arturo, and if Rafe had understood her properly, she was even now carrying Rafe's child, the future king, which made her an obstacle in Orlando's path to power.

He had to get out of here. He had to protect her. But he was hopelessly trapped.

"Don *Arturo!*" he bellowed in a rising crescendo.

The prime minister looked over from his harried conference with the others.

"Come here," Rafe ordered through gritted teeth, his eyes ablaze.

Warily, Don Arturo approached.

"What do you want?" Rafe growled. "Name your price." He squinted up at Rafe angrily. *"What?"*

"Do you want my life in exchange for your nephew's? Is that what will finally satisfy you? You shall have it. Hang me for treason, murder, any charges you care to contrive—"

"Contrive? Nothing is being contrived here, Your Highness. You were found at the scene of the crime, standing over His Excellency's very body—"

"He is going to kill my wife, man! Let me go and save her. That is all I ask—"

"Who?"

"Orlando!"

"What are you trying to put over on me? He's not going to kill anyone." He shook his head bitterly. "I'm going to get you this time, Prince Rafael. You killed Bishop Justinian and you have been poisoning the king!"

"Don't be absurd! Look at me! I am no murderer!"

"You're not getting out of this. Orlando brought me a

witness, you see—your creature from the royal kitchens. Only, you had your minions murder the lad before he could reveal your plot!"

"Is that so? Orlando was the one who told you I've been poisoning my father?"

"That's right. He was the one who found you out and brought the truth to me."

"But Don Arturo," Rafe said, "you and I were the only two who knew the king was ill. Don't you recall? He didn't even tell my mother—he didn't want her to worry. So how could Orlando have known? He knew Father was sick because *he* was the one administering the poison."

Don Arturo stared at him with a look that was torn between horror and disbelief. When he spoke, his voice was weak. "Orlando already warned me you would try . . . to pin your crimes on him."

"Damn you, man, I am innocent! He's the one who killed the bishop, and he's the one who will rule Ascencion if you don't let me go this instant. What will it take?"

"Do you seek to bribe me?" he hissed, shaking off his uncertainty. "There is no price high enough for my nephew's life!"

"I see. This is still all about Giorgio. Very well. Then you shall have my life in exchange, but for the love of God, don't take Leo's life or Dani's or my babe's that she is carrying. You know that, whatever my faults, I am a man of my word. Let me go after her and I swear to you I will come back and stand trial for any crimes you wish to charge me with."

Rafe growled in caged fury when Don Arturo stubbornly shook his head. The minutes were ticking by while he stood chained here knowing Orlando was inching nearer to Dani. Rafe searched the ceiling, then took a deep breath and looked at the prime minister. "I will sign a confession to all of it. Only let me go and save her."

A light of vengeful triumph sparked in Don Arturo's eyes. "You will sign a confession?"

"Yes. Give it to me and unlock these chains."

"And a writ of abdication? Will you sign Ascencion over to me until the king's return?"

Rafe stared at him, paling. "I do not know if you have been plotting with Orlando from the start."

"And I don't know if you tried to speed up your succession to the throne by poisoning your father."

"I would never do that! He is my father!" he wrenched out.

"And he is my friend." Don Arturo stared at him.

"Just let me go and save my wife," Rafe pleaded. "I will come back and you may deal with me however you see fit. She's going to die if you don't let me go! I'm begging you, Don Arturo." Rafe stared at him, trembling, distraught.

"You're begging me," he murmured. "Perhaps you and I are going to have to trust each other in this." Then he lifted his chin and stretched out his hand and snapped impatiently at his assistant, beckoning. "Bring me ink and paper." Don Arturo stepped over to the table and spent a few minutes penning a page, which he lifted, blew dry, and held up for Rafe.

With a knot in his stomach, Rafe scanned the damning words, barely absorbing them, though he knew they were designed to divest him of his crown and his very life. It didn't matter. He took the quill pen, dipped it in the ink, and signed his full name without a heartbeat's hesitation.

Next Don Arturo lifted his palm expectantly, his expression smug. "Your signet ring."

Rafe clenched his jaw and gave him a hard, scouring look as he submitted to this humiliation. He removed the ring, the symbol of his rank, and placed it in the prime minister's outstretched hand.

Don Arturo gave the guards a crisp nod. "Unchain him."

"Give me my sword."

They had taken it from him when they had clapped him in irons. Don Arturo regarded him warily as one of the guards gave him back his weapon.

Rafe's right hand closed around its jeweled hilt. Sword in hand, his eyes alight with majestic wrath, he stalked across the senate floor, feeling no pain from their beatings, nor fatigue. Filled only with a terrible, shining rage of love, he charged up the steps to the exit, officials and dignitaries flinging themselves out of his path.

⊰ CHAPTER ⊱
NINETEEN

Dani urged her white mare around the towering black citadel in a path that hugged its mossy wall.

The mare was nervous, reflecting Dani's still-shaken state after the first grisly death. One of the guards had been caught in a rusty bear trap which Orlando had concealed under the forest bed of decaying leaves and twigs. Closing on him like a shark's mouth, it had all but torn the man in half. There was no telling how many more such devices lay in wait in the woods surrounding, or what other surprises Orlando had in store for any who would dare trespass on his moldering lair.

Scanning the fort's wall and calling for the little prince as loudly as she dared, Dani was reconsidering the wisdom of taking on this rescue, especially in her delicate condition. She didn't feel delicate, but then, she wasn't feeling particulary brave since that guard's death, either.

After a hard ride of about twenty miles, Elan had led her and the handful of Royal Guardsmen down the shadowy lane at the turn to the ancient di Cambio fortress. They had given a wide berth to the deadly spiked pit, concealed by a gentle rise in the undulating green landscape, and had passed it safely. Surrounding her, the men had been grim-faced and silent, watchful. Then they had ventured into the bosky woods, fanning out as they closed in on the medieval stronghold where Rafael had said he believed his little brother had been hidden.

Suddenly Dani thought she heard a high-pitched voice shouting thinly, *"I'm heeeeere! Help!"*

"Prince Leo! Your Highness!" she called again, more loudly this time.

She listened for all she was worth.

The wind was still. Not even a bird sang in the trees.

"Help!"

The voice seemed to be coming from underneath the ground. She rode back and forth in the area where she'd heard it.

"Keep yelling, Your Highness! I'll find you!"

"Here! I'm here!"

She leaped off her horse and followed the sound of the boy's cries to the rock-strewn base of the wall, some twelve feet away. She yelled for Elan as she dropped quickly to her knees and began pulling the smaller stones away.

Elan came running through the underbrush toward her. "What is it?"

"I think he's in some kind of underground chamber here! Perhaps an annex to the old dungeon!"

"Help!"

"Leo! It's Elan! We're going to get you out of there!" he cried into the chink in the wall which she had begun to uncover. He scrambled to help her.

"Elan! Get me out!" yelled the boy-prince from the bowels of the earth.

"Are you hurt, Your Highness?" Dani shouted.

"No!"

With a few more stones removed, they could see him through a hole about seven inches in diameter. The little prince stood below, gazing up at them from the darkness.

Dani turned to Elan with a grimace. "We can't possibly

fit him through this opening. We've got to go inside and try
to make our way down there."

Elan nodded. "Right. I'll go in with you, but let's have
the men keep trying to pull these stones away, just in case
we can't find another way to get him out."

"Right." Elan explained to the child what they were
going to do while Dani called the remaining guardsmen
over and set them to the task of trying to pry the fallen
stones loose from the castle wall.

"Your Highness, don't stand underneath here where
they're working! One of the stones might fall in!" Dani
called to him.

"Yes, ma'am." Leo stepped back obediently.

Elan smiled askance at her as they marched toward the
yawning entrance of the tumbledown castle. "You're going
to make a splendid, if formidable mother, if I may say so,
Your Highness."

Her jaw dropped. "How did you know?"

He chuckled. "It's written all over your face. Felicita-
tions on the blessed event."

Pleased but blushing heatedly, she gave him a harmless
scowl, then they ran, knowing that Rafael's fate depended
on how quickly they could bring his little brother back to
Belfort to reveal the truth about the bishop's death.

The gloom was deep except where the white rays slanted
in over the broken walls. The inside of the crumbling
citadel was sketched in charcoal shadows and dusty light.
All planes and angles, halved pillars lay in the once-rich
great room, whose only fine draperies now were the thick
cobwebs that billowed silkily in the draft. A staircase led
nowhere, ending in midair.

Elan and she crept across the great room, seeking a way
down into the depths of the earth beneath the stronghold,
where Leo had been spirited away. The musty darkness

thickened as they forged on into the recesses of the old castle.

"What caused the break in the royal house that sent the di Cambio line away from Ascencion, anyway?" Dani whispered in the churchlike stillness.

"According to legend, two brothers fell in love with the same woman," the viscount replied, bravely leading the way.

Dani shivered.

All of a sudden, there was a cracking, breaking creak, and suddenly the floor gave out beneath them. With reflexes honed by her outlaw adventures, Dani leaped back just in time, but Elan lost his footing, flailing wildly. He scrabbled for purchase, then dropped, disappearing with a *whoosh* straight down through the trapdoor.

Dani screamed as Elan yelled, falling.

She flung herself down on her hands and knees at the edge of the rectangular hole. "Elan! Elan! Answer me!"

A few seconds later, she heard him stirring with a groggy groan. "I'm all right!" he called up to her. "I may have broken my ankle." She heard him add a curse under his breath. "Still, I didn't land on metal spikes, so I consider myself lucky," he added ruefully. "I think it best if you go back outside and rejoin the guards, Your Highness."

"No, I can't leave that child down there. Besides, I don't think his cell is much farther." Dani hesitated, just able to make him out in the dimness. He appeared to have fallen to a holding cell about fifteen feet below. "I'll be right back for you after I've gotten Leo out."

"Don't worry, I won't be going anywhere soon," he answered wryly. "*Please* be careful. Rafe will wring my neck if you're hurt."

"I will. I'll be back as soon as I can."

Swallowing hard, Dani gathered her courage and forged

on alone, inching across the next gaping chamber she came to. At the other end of it, a large board had been propped over what appeared to be a small doorway.

She went to it, removed the board, and peered inside. As her eyes adjusted to the dark, she saw a ladder. Steeling herself, she climbed down it.

To her surprise, it stayed intact until she stepped down onto the floor below. Turning around, she found herself in some kind of dungeon. Four doorways led away from the middle chamber. Dry-mouthed with fright, she looked from one to the other, crossing her arm over her abdomen in an instinctively protective gesture, as though to shield the growing life in her womb from the dank smell of evil that permeated the musty air.

"Leo! Where are you?"

When the child answered her call, she followed the sound of his voice as best she could, and after a few false starts, finally found him. Incredibly, the key to the gridiron door barring the dungeon's large single cell was hanging on a rusty peg driven into the rock nearby. Finally, she thought as she reached for it, one thing had gone her way.

She quickly unlocked the door and went to the child. She told him who she was and gave him a hug. Leo was a sturdy little ten year old with big brown eyes, rosy cheeks, and soft dark curls. Taking his hand, Dani led him toward the door. They ran out of the cell and wound their way back through the mazelike structure to the torture chamber where the ladder waited, their sole route to freedom.

But just when Dani knew they were in the clear, running through the awful chamber of death, she felt a draft gust through the room, looked up, and saw the board lift away.

She barely had time to gasp as Orlando dropped to the floor before her, agile and huge as a graceful black panther. They stared at each other. Dani's eyes were wide, her heartbeat frantic. She stepped in front of the little prince, putting him behind her.

Orlando's bright green eyes seemed to glow vividly, cat-like, in the dark.

He took a step toward her. She reached for her rapier. He seized her by the throat and held her up on her toes.

"No, my lady," he said gently. "Put your hands up."

Choking for air, she obeyed. He removed her weapon from her side, then set her down again.

"You know what I'm going to do to you, don't you?" he whispered.

She clenched her jaw and held his stare in defiance.

He smiled slightly, his eyes aglow. "Back to the cell. Both of you."

Dani held her ground staunchly, hiding her terror. "Let the boy go. He is just a child. For the love of God, Orlando, he is your brother."

"It's too late—thanks to you, Lady Daniela. It's all over now. That fool Don Arturo has begun to realize. You threw the future away. You see the three of us here? This is how it could have been. Leo on the throne. I ruling Ascencion through him. You in my bed."

She winced in disgust and turned her face away.

"But you had to go and ruin everything. And now I'm going to make you pay for it." He pushed her, sending her stumbling in the direction from which she'd just come.

"Hey!" the little prince yelled, stepping toward the man who towered over him.

Orlando raised his hand to strike him, but Dani quickly gathered the child against her, hushing his angry retort.

Glowering at her, Orlando slowly lowered his hand.

"Come, Leo," she murmured, her arm draped around his shoulders as they headed back toward the cell. Her heart was pounding wildly in her chest. Orlando walked behind them, so he did not see Dani glance up at the ceiling, where she had left the Royal Guardsmen struggling to remove the stones.

"Go sit down," Orlando ordered the boy as he fixed his stare on Dani and slowly drew off his black leather gloves. "You might want to turn your back while I punish your auntie, Leo. This isn't going to be pretty."

Leo looked from her to Orlando in terror.

Dani was dizzy with fear. There was no escape. She could only pray that the guards were still near enough to hear.

With that thought her only hope, she lifted her ashen face to the feeble beam of sunlight that had found its way in through the rock, drew a deep breath, and let a out long, high-pitched scream to rack the very woods beyond: *"Help!"*

Her scream faded to the low, bubbling sound of Orlando's laughter.

Shaking with icy fear, Dani lowered her chin and gazed at him. When he took a step toward her, she backed away.

"Don't do this, Orlando. I—I know things about you," she said, trying to stall him.

"You don't know anything about me," he snarled, his eyes glittering.

"I know you've suffered terribly," she forced out, giving him a pleading look. "The man I sent to investigate you told me a lot about your past. He found your old nurse, Nunzia. Do you remember her?" she asked as she swallowed hard and continued backing away.

He stalked her slowly through the cell hewn in the living rock.

"Nunzia told my friend how King Lazar met your mother two years before he ascended the throne. He was just a young man, traveling the world, and he met your mother at the opera one night, and they had an affair that lasted three days before he sailed on again. I know that your mother was married at the time to a cruel brute of a man, and when she found herself with child, she tried to pass you off as her husband's son, but the baron, the man you thought was your father, never believed the lie. And I know that he treated you accordingly, punishing you every day of your life for the crime of having been born."

"Shut up, bitch," he snarled, his voice demonic. "You never should have gotten in my way."

"I know he beat you terribly, and I know your mother fed you all the while on secret stories of your real father— a just and kind and handsome king. You became obsessed with him. But you hated him for never coming to save you."

"You are going to have a very painful death, Daniela." He lunged at her.

She whirled out of the way.

Just then, male voices sounded from the direction of the chamber where the ladder still rested by the wall. Dani paused, realizing it was a couple of the guards. They must have found their way in, coming in answer to her scream several minutes ago.

Orlando turned at the sound, then shot her a searing glare. "When I get back," he said, "you're both dead."

With that, he stalked out of the cell, pausing only to lock them in.

Above them, one of the large rocks suddenly rolled back, letting in a thin shaft of sunlight.

"Your Highness!" a male voice whispered loudly.

Blinking against the light, Dani looked up and saw the last remaining guardsman. The big, burly man kept working, rocking a stubbornly wedged boulder until the opening was large enough for the child to fit through.

Dani wasted no time. "Leo!" She laid her hand on his

small shoulder and stared gravely at him. "I'm going to lift you up. Grasp the guard's hand and he'll pull you out. Then you must ride with him to the city and tell Don Arturo exactly what happened at the bishop's. Can you do that?"

The curly-headed boy looked fearfully toward the door. "Orlando said he would cut me up in pieces if I ever told anyone what he did. I think he meant it."

"He won't do that, Leo. We're going to keep you safe. Rafe will protect you from Orlando, but first you have to go help Rafe. Tell Don Arturo everything, yes?"

He nodded bravely. "Yes, ma'am."

"All right. Now I'm going to lift you up."

Planting her feet to brace herself, Daniela gritted her teeth and hoisted the boy onto her shoulders. Carefully Prince Leo stood on her shoulders until he could reach the guardsman's hands, stretched down to grasp his smaller ones. With a mighty heave, the guard pulled Leo up.

A moment later, the guard peered down at her briefly. He threw down a rope to her. Dani paced in the cell below while he went back to work trying to roll the massive boulder out of the way, but though he put all his great weight against it, as the moments passed, he could not widen the opening enough for her to slip through, skinny as she was.

"Daniela, my love!"

She looked fearfully toward the gridiron door, hearing Orlando's voice echoing to her.

"I'm coming for you now!"

Lifting her chin, she looked up, ashen, at the panic-stricken guard.

"You can't let him get Leo. The boy's testimony is the only thing that can save Rafael. Take him back to Belfort—now. There's no time. Take him now. I don't want him to—hear."

"But—"

"Hurry!" she ordered in anguish. "Pull up the rope so Orlando doesn't see. And . . . tell my husband that I love him."

The guard's face was utterly grim. "Take my weapon." He tossed his pistol down to her. She caught it in midair, her hope soaring as it landed in her hands. Then he threw down his leather pouch of powder and bullets and sent her a grave salute. "God be with you, Principessa," he said, then he got up and led Leo away.

She prayed they would make it out safely past Orlando's hideous traps as she loaded the pistol with shaking hands. She had only one shot at Orlando. She did not expect to have time to reload and fire again. What if she missed some vital part? she thought. Orlando could be wounded, but still strong enough to destroy her. If only she had some means of instantly incapacitating him. . . .

Her heart pounded, her mind ticked, and as she cocked the gun, a diabolical idea suddenly came to her.

She stared from the pouch of ammunition to the iron door.

She could make a terrible trap of her own for Orlando. It was wildly risky, but Orlando was almost supernaturally strong. A bullet might not stop him. She had to protect her unborn child . . . Rafael's baby . . . Ascencion's future king. She had to survive this, though she knew her chances were next to nil.

It's my only hope.

Stalking toward the iron door, she dropped to one knee and poured out the gunpowder in a circle about one man-sized pace inside the cell. When Orlando unlocked the iron door and came into the cell, he would have to step directly onto the circle of black powder in order to get to her, and when he did, she would fire her single shot not at him, but at the gunpowder. Struck by the bullet, the powder would catch and make a large, dangerous flare. He would be burned, stunned, and blinded long enough for her to run past him out of the cell and lock him inside. Then Rafael or even King Lazar could decide what to do with him.

What if the shot doesn't make enough of a spark to catch?

It has to.

Sweat ran down her cheek to think that her life depended on a single bullet.

She could hear him marching toward the cell now. She arranged herself in the far corner of the cavelike cell behind a small outcropping of rock. She rested the muzzle of the pistol on the rock and waited, her heart in her throat, prayers streaming, one after the other, through her mind.

He appeared in the doorway, his eyes glowing with his victory over those two poor guards, and for a moment, his smile was so buoyant and charming, so much like Rafael's, that she hesitated to pull the trigger, knowing that he could be burned horribly.

Her heart pounding, she watched him reach for the key and unlock the iron door.

As he pulled it open, she took a deep breath. And as he stepped into the cell, she fired at the circle of black powder.

Too late!

He was already stepping past the gunpowder when the flare rose behind him. He let out a bellow of pain and surprise as it threw him forward at the same instant Dani darted for the door, but with a guttural sound of fury, Orlando, on the ground, snaked his arms around her legs and toppled her. She screamed as she went down, fighting him in panic, with the aftermath of acrid smoke choking her throat.

He rose over her in the foggy haze that hung on the air. His granite-carved face was cut and bleeding from his fall. His raven hair and clothes were singed, but on the whole he was unscathed.

Merely enraged.

He called her the foulest possible name.

Thick sulfuric smoke, the aftermath of the flare, rolled through the cell, but above her, through the black cloud, glowed bright, eerie, ice-green eyes. Dani stared up into them, realizing she would never hear her baby's first cry nor taste Rafael's kiss again.

Orlando drew back his hand and struck her with all his might.

Dani went sprawling, flattened to the ground.

He picked her up to hit her again.

It was as though explosions were going off inside her head. There were three, four, perhaps five more shattering blows to her head and body. She was too stunned to react, fight, even to cry, limp as a rag doll in his vicious grip.

He is going to kill my baby, she thought, trying to rally herself to fight as his fist plunged again into her middle. But she saw double from the blows to the head and could not clear her vision, and she just wanted it all to stop, the roaring, ringing noise in her eardrums and the explosions in her head. She could taste her lip bleeding and she knew a tooth on the side was loose. She was semiconscious when he straddled her on the stone ground and seized the collar of her shirt, ripping it open partway down her chest. Orlando was muttering furiously at her, cruel, hateful things.

Then suddenly, distantly, in the dusty single column of sunlight which the Royal Guardsman had widened, she saw the apparition of an angel.

Golden and huge, he stepped closer, looming in silent gliding power behind Orlando. Her spirit breathed a sigh of relief. She was so glad to see him. She knew he had come to bear her soul away in his arms to heaven.

But as the white light bathed his hair of gold, she caught a glimpse of his hard, angular face, and it was not the countenance of a tender angel of mercy. Beautiful beyond dreams he was, but with earth-green eyes full of celestial wrath, she knew he was an angel of death, sunlight glittering on the jeweled hilt of his raised sword.

Rafael, she realized just as the thin thread of her awareness clipped gently and sent her floating out into black silence.

With a roar, Rafael drove Orlando back against the stone wall. They sliced at each other with wide, pitiless arcs of their swords.

"I am your brother, Rafe. You can't kill me," Orlando panted, parrying his relentless blows.

Remorseless, Rafe's only reaction was to press him farther back across the cell.

Dani's scream had drawn Rafe as he had searched the ruined citadel. He'd come across Elan stranded in the pit, and the viscount had sent him in the right direction.

Their fight raged around the stone. Every time Orlando tried to rush toward Dani's prostrate body to use her as his human shield, Rafe drove him back. With every passing moment, as Orlando's desperation grew, his face twisted into a more demonic rictus of rage and hatred and pain. He was bleeding and winded, imbued with the strength that came of fighting for one's life, but Rafael warred on him, his teeth bared, his hair flying over his shoulders. He spun, lunged, and suddenly thrust his sword into Orlando's black heart, the tip of it biting all the way into the stone behind his bastard brother.

He did not flinch as Orlando died, impaled on his weapon.

For Rafe, the real terror lay nearby in the chillingly still form of his beautiful, gallant, unmoving young wife. Sliding his weapon out of Orlando's breast with a final snarl, he dropped his sword across his half-brother's lifeless body.

Crossing the dim, rock-strewn chamber to Dani, he knelt down beside her, a cold knot in his stomach, his heart pounding like it would break.

Gently, he touched her face. He could barely make his voice work. "My love."

She did not stir.

Steeling himself, he swallowed hard and touched her throat, then closed his eyes. Tears rose behind his eyelids to feel her weak but steady pulse.

He bent lower and scooped her carefully into his arms. He pressed a desperate, lingering kiss to her brow. *Come on, little fighter, you've got to fight for me now. Don't leave me, Dani. Don't leave me.* He rose with her slight, delicate, bruised body draped limply in his arms, her head resting on his chest. He carried her from that place like the most precious treasure in the world, which was exactly what she was to him. He kissed her cool, smooth forehead and whispered her name, urging her to come back to him, telling her he could not possibly live without her.

Still, she didn't stir.

≈ CHAPTER ≈
TWENTY

"Mama, she is awake."

Dani heard the soft, slightly scratchy, feminine voice coming from somewhere very nearby, then a businesslike rustling of skirts.

"Don't pester her, Serafina. Let her come around slowly," chided a second woman's voice.

The first voice had a sparkling quality, like a cheerful bubbling brook, but the second was of a mellower timbre, like autumn sunlight shining through a jar of honey.

"Oh, Mama, isn't she adorable? No wonder Rafe is so mad for her. She's like a little porcelain doll lying there. She's so tiny!" A wistful sigh. "I always wanted a sister."

"I think she is very young," said the older woman, her voice tinged with the note of a motherly-sounding frown. Dani felt a soft hand alight on her forearm where it lay limply atop the coverlet.

"I wish she would wake up."

The hand stroked her arm comfortingly. "Well, she has been through a terrible ordeal, poor, brave little thing."

There was such rich tenderness in the words that Dani found the strength to open her eyes. The world was fuzzy and distorted, but she could make out two ovals above her which began to clear into faces.

The first distinct feature she made out was a pair of otherworldly violet eyes peering eagerly down at her. She had never seen eyes that color before. She closed her own tightly, ordering them to do their job properly, then flicked her eyes open and found herself staring up at the laughing goddess from the portrait.

With her breathlessly waiting expression, rose-tinged cheeks, and cascade of raven spiral curls, Princess Serafina was even more splendid in real life. Her wide, breaking smile as Dani awoke was like a gust of fresh springtime breezes.

Staring blankly, Dani turned her head slightly and saw that the older woman was gazing down at her patiently with wise, amber-brown eyes under gold-tipped lashes, and a sprinkling of buttery freckles on her mildly lined face. She appeared not quite fifty, with light golden-brown hair arranged in a loose chignon.

Queen Allegra!

In a flash of recognition, Dani was horrified at herself for lying there like a slugabed with the queen and royal princess of Ascencion staring down at her.

"Majesty," she croaked out, scrambling all of a sudden to sit up. She could not remember why she was in bed or how long she had been there. She only knew the queen was in her presence and there were protocols to be observed. Rafael's experts had drilled her in this.

"Lie still," Her Majesty commanded, laying her hand on Dani's shoulder.

Dani stared pleadingly at her for forgiveness at this awful breach of etiquette. She had never been very good at that sort of thing, but she obeyed, for her head was pounding terribly.

"Serafina, get her some water."

As Dani sank back against her pillow, closing her eyes again into the blessed darkness, she remembered everything in a flood. The ruined citadel—Orlando—Rafael saving her—and the small amount of blood that she had felt run down between her thighs after Orlando had beaten her.

"My baby!" she choked out, forcing herself up in a start.

"You did not lose it," Queen Allegra said in a firm, gentle tone.

Dani stared at her, panting with fright.

"It's all right. The doctor said you had a little hemorrhaging, but with a week or two of bed rest, he says you will both be fine."

Her whole body was shaking with the memory of what she had experienced.

Princess Serafina crossed the room to them, carrying a glass of water to Dani. She sat on the edge of the bed and offered it to her.

"Thank you, Your Highness," she said faintly as she accepted it, amazed by their kindness toward her.

As a known criminal who had married the golden boy of their family, she had expected a cool and distant reception from the royal family. In fact, she had rather been dreading their return, sure that they were going to despise her. Her head throbbed as she thought of the five princesses they had selected for Rafael and the old looming threat of Their Majesties making him choose between her or the crown. She felt as though she ought to apologize and try to explain that he had been simply too hard to resist.

Mother and daughter watched her intently.

Dani drank some of the water, then looked from one to the other, trying to gather her scrambled thoughts. "Forgive me, I am not myself yet. I can't believe I am meeting you both in this condition." She dragged a hand through her mussed hair.

Serafina let out a musical trill of sparkling laughter. "It's a better condition than you've been in the last two days. You gave us all a fright. I'm so glad you're awake—I finally get to have a sister. Well, we had better get Rafe. He's been here nearly every moment of every hour. Mama finally had to send him off to take a walk with Papa before he drove himself mad."

"Is he all right?" she asked anxiously.

"He'll be better now that you're up."

"Come, Serafina," said the queen, going toward the door. "We mustn't tax her. There will be plenty of time for us to spend together when she is feeling better." One hand on the doorknob, Queen Allegra paused and glanced over her shoulder at Dani. "You, young lady, are to get more sleep."

"Yes, Your Majesty," Dani answered as she rested back obediently against the pillows.

The queen paused, regarding her with a fond, slight smile. "You don't have to be afraid of me, Daniela. I admit I was angry when I first heard that my Rafael had ignored our wishes, but the moment I heard how you saved Leo—and when I spoke with Rafael and saw how much he loves you and how you've changed him into the man I always knew he could be—I knew you were all I could have wanted for my son . . . and my people."

Moved almost beyond speech, she blushed with embarrassment and lowered her head. "Thank you, Your Majesty."

"You don't have to call me 'Your Majesty,' Daniela."

She looked up with a quick, nervous glance. "W-what should I call you, then, please, ma'am?"

From across the room, Allegra gazed gently at her. "You could call me 'Mother' if you like."

Staring at her, tears rushed into Dani's eyes.

"Why, what is it, Daniela?" Serafina asked softly, reaching up to tuck a lock of Dani's hair behind her ear.

For a moment, Dani was almost too overwhelmed to speak, her tears brimming. "I never had a mother."

"Oh, dear little creature," Serafina exclaimed in a whisper, embracing her.

Then the queen came back, went around the other side of the bed, and hugged them both. "You do now, darling," she whispered as she pressed Dani's head onto her soft, ineffably comforting shoulder. Dani closed her eyes and sobbed with mixed joy and relief in their embrace. "You do now."

In the gardens of the Palazzo Reale, Prince Leo was running around with his Spanish nieces and nephews, who were barely younger than he. Though their laughter filled the royal park and all the nurses and governesses looked harried, the king's grandchildren did not dare misbehave too badly under the stern and masterful eye of their father.

Count Darius Santiago was standing nearby, eternally vigilant over his brood, his arms folded over his chest. Occasionally, he glanced with equal concern at the king and the crown prince, who were sitting on a stone bench under a large tree.

Poor Rafe was a wreck. Darius had never seen his carefree, roguish brother-in-law in such a grim, changed state. Lazar wasn't faring much better, he thought.

Though King Lazar's health had improved drastically, restoring him to his hearty and hale constitution, he had been shaken by the news, upon returning to Ascencion, that Orlando had been his son. He had not known.

Squinting against the bright afternoon sun, Darius looked at his six children again, who were tumbling all over the lawn, to the delight of the gaunt and elderly Duke of Chiaramonte, who was walking about with his cane in their midst, cheering on their antics.

The habitually hard, fierce expression on Darius's finely chiseled, aquiline face softened utterly when his youngest, the two-year-old Lady Anita, sought to hide behind him from her bossy older sister, Lady Elisabeta, age four. He couldn't help but smile.

Anita came running to him with a protracted wail and threw her arms around his leg as though it were a column of stone. Then the two little girls in frilled petticoats, both with mops of silky black curls, darted and circled around their papa's legs until Darius was forced to scoop them up in his arms and administer a sternly disapproving frown to each.

It was difficult to hold the disciplinarian's glower when they could see right through him, he thought with an inward sigh of defeat. Their answer to his stern look was one they had learned from their mother—laughter and kisses.

He was hopelessly outnumbered. His daughters covered his cheeks in sticky caramel kisses, giggling as they mussed his starchy white shirt with chocolate fingerprints.

He attempted to scowl. "Where did you get the candy?"

"Uncle Wafie gave it to us!" Anita said cheerfully. The two-year-old had been following Rafe around like his shadow ever since they had arrived yesterday. Darius knew it was the last thing Rafe needed, but he had not seemed to mind too much.

"Well, no more till after you've had your lunch. Don't bother your Uncle Rafe, yes?" he murmured. "He's very worried about Princess Daniela. Try and be quiet around him."

"Yes, Papa," the four-year-old said eagerly, with a show of obedience that Darius knew was designed to twist him around her little finger, another trick she had learned from their beautiful mama.

"You rascals," he muttered, giving them each a kiss on the forehead. They squirmed and kicked and giggled until he set them down again, then they tore off after their brothers.

Rafe had been watching Darius with his little girls, wondering in pain if he would ever know the fulfillment his brother-in-law had so plainly found in his role as a family man.

The doctor had told Rafe that Daniela would recover and that their babe had survived the attack, but it was hard to believe the reassurances when she continued to lie so still and unresponsive in her bed, drifting in and out of consciousness.

She had not eaten in two days and she was already too thin to begin with, he thought, worry gnawing him ceaselessly. He hadn't eaten or slept, either. He was exhausted, frayed, choked with constant dread, and quite at the end of what he could bear.

He did have a few things to be grateful for, of course. The murder charges against him had been dropped in spite of his forced confession. Leo had testified that it was Orlando, not Rafe, who had stabbed Bishop Justinian; the king had dealt the senate a blistering address for their behavior toward Rafe.

The whole senate had been sending Rafe groveling apologies and excuses and it was clear that no one took him as a joke anymore, but until Dani was out of the woods, he did not want to hear from any of them. If they had not detained him, he could have saved her more quickly and spared her the awful beating she had endured at the hands of Orlando. He was not about to forgive them anytime soon for how his wife had suffered.

As for the prime minister, Don Arturo was so ashamed of how he had allowed his spite to mar his judgment that he had handed in his resignation.

The king was obviously recovered to his former robust health now that he was no longer unwittingly ingesting daily doses of the mysterious, slow-acting poison, *cantarelle*. Rafe was grateful from the bottom of his soul for his father's recovery, for he had been humbled by his interlude as Ascencion's supreme master. He was no longer in the slightest hurry to be king. He saw that he still had a great deal to learn from his father about managing Ascencion's affairs. At last, he had the humility to seek whatever wisdom his father had to impart.

Hearing the tale of what Dani had suffered to save Leo, and how hard Rafe and Dani had worked to reach out to the people together, neither the king nor the queen could find it within themselves to disapprove of their unauthorized marriage.

Rafe was also grateful for the fact that his little brother Leo had escaped harm and that Elan had come away with nothing more serious than a broken ankle. His final reason to be glad was that Darius and Serafina had decided to move back permanently to Ascencion, and Lord knew the king and queen were overjoyed to have their grandchildren on hand to spoil.

The future looked bright for everyone. But if Dani did not recover, Rafe knew his own future would be naught but a curse to him.

He could not imagine that he had ever found another woman beautiful. She was everything to him. With every moment that she lay still and silent in that bed, he felt more hollow and lost. Everyone knew he was suffering, but he was doing his best to mask his raw emotions. His adorable little nieces and nephews cheered him somewhat, even as they broke his heart for fear over the welfare of his own child.

"Son," his father murmured, looking over at him as they sat on a bench under a tree.

Rafe glanced questioningly at him, his throat dry, his eyes red and raw.

"I have something to say to you."

"Yes, sir?"

"I've been doing some thinking. With all of the spite and hatred from Orlando, I think it's important that I tell you so you know . . ." His voice trailed off. A troubled frown lined his weathered brow as the king stared forward, then tentatively began, "I want to say that maybe I was too hard on you all these years. You were a good lad and you're a good man. I want to tell you I'm . . . proud of you. I . . . really do . . . love you, son. That's all," he mumbled.

Rafe stared at the ground with stinging eyes.

His father laid a firm hand on his shoulder.

He swallowed hard and furrowed his brow. "Thank you, sir."

When the king furrowed his brow and lowered his head in a pose just like Rafe's, he was struck by how much alike they truly were.

"She's going to be all right, Rafe."

For a moment, he thought he was going to completely fall apart. "Yes, sir." He lifted his chin, his mouth pursed.

Just then, his sister came out onto the veranda and waved hurriedly at them from across the grass. "Rafe! You'd better come quick!"

He leaped to his feet and started forward in pure dread, his heart instantly racing. "What's wrong?"

Serafina beamed a radiant smile at him. "She's awake!"

His eyes widened.

His fatigue falling away like a cloak from his shoulders, he ran toward the house. He raced inside and bounded up the stairs, taking them two at a time.

Dani was sitting up in bed when the door burst open and Rafael stood framed in the doorway, his face flushed, his golden hair tousled. He stared at her for a heartbeat.

Love filled her gaze at the sight of him.

Suddenly in motion, he strode across the bedroom to her and for a moment just stood beside her bed, gazing at her with welling green-gold eyes. He reached down and took her hand in his.

Slowly, he sank to his knees beside her bed, holding her hand fervently to his lips. His long-lashed eyes closed.

"Rafael," she whispered.

He pressed her palm to his cheek and lifted his gold-tipped lashes, tears on the ends of them. "God, I missed you," he said in a shaky voice.

She held out her arms to him. He embraced her carefully around her waist, laying his golden head on her chest. She hugged him around his neck and rested her cheek atop his hair. They held each other in trembling silence, flooded with gratitude and pain and joy at their reunion.

"I thought I'd lost you, Dani," he choked out abruptly.

"You didn't," she whispered, pouring her love out on him in every caress. "You didn't lose either of us."

His big, hard body shaking, he bent his head and kissed her belly through the white muslin of her night rail. Then he closed his eyes and laid his head on her lap.

She petted his hair back from his feverish skin, loving every line of his tanned, angular face. After a few moments, he lifted his head and stared at her, his soul bared in his eyes.

For a silver-tongued charmer, he was mute with emotion, but his tempestuous eyes said it all.

"I know, sweet. I love you, too," she whispered.

He closed his eyes with a look of pain and lowered his chin, moving his head against her caress. "You must never, ever leave me, Daniela," he said in a taut, constricted voice. "I can't live without you. You are my heart."

"I never will. Come to me, beloved," she murmured, drawing him to her.

He climbed up off his knees and lay down on the bed beside her, gathering her protectively in his arms.

They lay there, staring at each other and caressing. He kissed her occasionally on her forehead, her eyelids, her hair.

She nestled down against his chest with a sigh, feeling

wonderfully safe and cherished, knowing at last she was exactly where she belonged. He sought her hand and linked his fingers through hers, and as she listened to the slow, powerful song of his heart, like the sea's rhythmic tide laving Ascencion's shores, the vibrant afternoon light caught the golden glory of his royal signet ring and made it shine like the blaze of a thousand suns.

⊰ EPILOGUE ⊱

April 1815

Church bells clanged and bonged and pealed wildly throughout Ascencion on the day the newborn prince was christened. In the city and the newly planted fields and all across the land, no work was to be done, for King Lazar had declared it a day for feasting and song.

The Gabbiano brothers stood together in the cheering mob, staring up in still rather amazed silence at the ornate balcony off the palace where the entire royal clan was positioned behind Dani and Prince Rafael. The proud new parents stood together with beaming smiles, letting the world have a look at the tiny future king.

His Royal Highness, Prince Amador di Fiore, was a little over two weeks old. It was impossible to make out his tiny face from such a distance, but Alvi had read to them earlier from the gazettes that the babe had his mother's aqua eyes and a little downy tuft of his father's golden hair.

The former gang of gallant highwaymen stood around with a collective sigh. They had been pardoned by the queen and welcomed back to the land of their birth.

Brava, bella, Mateo thought, gazing at his childhood friend with a slight smile on his tanned face. Dani looked poised, regal, and beautiful holding her son, and it was obvious that the big, elegant man by her side adored her.

"Look, there's Gianni!" Rocco said suddenly, pointing toward the balcony where their youngest, freckled brother could be seen with Prince Leo, both boys grinning, their arms slung waggishly around each other's shoulders.

Dani had arranged for the roguish little peasant boy to be educated with Prince Leo and had him moved into the palace as Leo's companion. Prince and pauper had become instantly inseparable.

Mateo laughed at his brother's antics, then felt a soft hip bump his own. He glanced down at his new bride and his heart clenched, as usual, to see her shy smile and the slowly growing trust behind her wary dark eyes.

"Do you think they're really as happy as they look?" Carmen asked skeptically, folding her arms over her chest.

Mateo slipped his arm around her shoulders in habitual protectiveness and pulled her close gently, gently. She was so tough and yet so fragile, so young for the harsh life she had known. Fate had put him in her path so he could rescue her, he knew. He had always wanted to be someone's knight in shining armor.

"Yes, my love," he murmured as she began blushing at his slight doting smile, "but not half so happy as we."

She scoffed, but joy sparkled in her dark eyes. She took his hand and began tugging him toward the square, where countless food stalls filled the springtime air with the cooking aromas of good things to eat. "Come on, I'm hungry."

"Me, too," said his large brother, Rocco.

Mateo stole a final glance over his shoulder toward the balcony at the three generations of kings—the Rock of Ascencion, the newborn child, and the crown prince in the prime of his manhood. Rafael looked proud enough to burst. Dani glanced up at him with a calm, settled smile of quiet love, her babe resting snugly in her arms, then she turned and the royals began to go back inside their palace.

He supposed it took a hellion to tame a rake—and a rake to charm a hellion.

Goodbye, Dan, he thought, his eyes misting briefly with pride in the redheaded tomboy he had once known.

Then Carmen tugged him impatiently toward the square and he turned away, leaving them with a private smile to their happiness.

HISTORICAL NOTE

As a longtime fan of historical romances set in Regency England, the inspiration for this story came from my interest in the wild, pleasure-hunting life of "Prinny," England's George IV.

I have often wondered how differently history might have turned out if the Prince Regent had managed to find a wife who was able to bring out his potential, in place of what fate handed him—a dismal, scandal-ridden, forced marriage to the equally unfortunate Princess Caroline of Brunswick. The couple despised each other.

If you are interested in learning more about "the first gentleman of Europe," I would highly recommend *The Prince of Pleasure and His Regency, 1811–1820* by J. B. Priestly (Heinemann, 1969).

Dani's role in the story came from a quite different source. Would you believe that history truly tells the tale of a female stagecoach robber?

For this facet of my story I must credit and recommend the excellent *Wild Women* by Autumn Stephens (Conari Press, 1992).

In this outrageous, wallop-packing little volume, subtitled "Crusaders, Curmudgeons, and Completely Corsetless Ladies in the Otherwise Virtuous Victorian Era," Stephens tells the true story of Pearl Hart, born 1871, who donned trousers, picked up a rifle, and held up stage-coaches to pay for the medical care of her ailing mother. When the "famous lady highwayman" was caught, however, she was sentenced to five years in an all-male prison, where, according to Stephens, the warden's wife was afraid Pearl would corrupt the morals of the other prisoners!

So, now our tale has come to a close. Thanks for reading, and I hope you have enjoyed Rafe's story and the Ascencion Trilogy as much as I have loved writing it.

Best wishes,

Gaelen

If you enjoyed PRINCE CHARMING,
don't miss the first two books in Gaelen Foley's
Ascension trilogy:
THE PIRATE PRINCE
and
PRINCESS!

THE PIRATE PRINCE
by Gaelen Foley

Taken captive by a fearsome and infuriating pirate captain come to plunder her island home of Ascension, the beautiful Allegra Monteverdi struggles to deny her growing passion for her intriguing captor. Lazar di Fiore is a rogue with no honor and has nothing in common with the man of her dreams—the honorable and courageous crown prince of Ascension, who is presumed murdered with the rest of the royal family by treacherous enemies of the throne.

But Allegra has badly misjudged Lazar, a man with a tragic past and demons that give him no peace. He harbors a secret that could win him Allegra's love and restore freedom and prosperity to Ascension, if his sworn enemies do not destroy him first. And the greatest battle of all must be fought within Lazar's own heart as Allegra tries to prove that, prince or pirate, he is truly the man that she has always dreamed of.

Published by The Ballantine Publishing Group.
Available wherever books are sold.

PRINCESS

by Gaelen Foley

Darius Santiago is the king's most trusted man, a master spy and assassin. He is handsome, charming, and ruthless, and he has one weakness—the stunning Princess Serafina. Serafina has worshiped Darius from afar her whole life, knowing that deep in the reaches of her soul, she belongs to him. Unable to suppress their desire any longer, they are swept into a daring dance of passion until a deadly enemy threatens to destroy their love.

Published by The Ballantine Publishing Group.
Available at bookstores everywhere.

Lance St. Leger is defying his destiny. The eldest son and heir to Castle Leger, he has returned from the army determined to continue his role as rakehell and black sheep. He is plagued by an infernal restlessness that cannot be appeased, perhaps because the St. Leger legacy of strange powers is most pronounced in Lance's own dubious gift. He calls it night drifting—his ability to separate his body from his soul, to spirit into the night while flesh and bone remain behind. And it is on one wild night's mad search for a magnificent stolen sword—the icon of the St. Leger power—that he finds her. . . .

THE NIGHT DRIFTER

Rosalind, a young, sheltered widow with a passion for the Arthurian legend, mistakes Lance's "drifting" soul for the ghost of Sir Lancelot. Seeing that she is in need of a champion, the St. Leger rogue assumes the role of the tragic knight, not knowing that this woman is his destiny, his perfect mate.

by Susan Carroll

But deep down in her heart, Rosalind is all too aware she is a mortal woman with very real desires that only a man of flesh and blood can fulfill—a man like Lance St. Leger. As a murderous enemy challenges the St. Leger power, Rosalind must tempt magic herself to save her beloved from the cold depths of eternal damnation.

Published by The Ballantine Publishing Group.
Available in bookstores everywhere.

*"If you like to hoot with laughter and
have your heartstrings twanged, don't miss . . .
Maggie Osborne."*
—CATHERINE COULTER

SILVER LINING
by Maggie Osborne

As scruffy and rootless as the other prospectors searching for
gold in the Rockies, Low Down wanted nothing in return for
nursing a raggedy bunch through the pox. But when pressed
to reveal her heart's wish, she admits, *"I want a baby."* Not a
husband, not a forced marriage to the proud man who drew
the scratched marble and became honor bound to marry her.

To be sure, Max McCord was easy on the eyes, but he loved
another woman and dreamed of a different life. Yet they agreed
to a temporary marriage that could end only in disaster. But
can this strange twist of fate lead to the silver lining that both
have been searching for?

Ask for SILVER LINING in your local bookstore.
Published by Ivy Books.